PENGUI  P9-DXS-801

SEA LORD

Bernard Cornwell was born in London, raised in Essex, and now lives in the USA. He is the author of the Arthurian series, *The Warlord Trilogy*; *The Starbuck Chronicles* on the American Civil War; *Stonehenge*; *The Grail Quest* series, set during the Hundred Years War; over twenty Sharpe novels; and most recently, *The Saxon Stories*, set during King Alfred's defence of England against the Vikings. For more information about Bernard Cornwell and his books, visit his website – www.bernardcornwell.net.

BERNARD CORNWELL

SEA LORD

PENGUIN BOOKS

PENGUIN BOOKS

Published by the Penguin Group
Penguin Books Ltd, 80 Strand, London WC2R 0RL, England
Penguin Group (USA) Inc., 375 Hudson Street, New York, New York 10014, USA
Penguin Group (Canada), 90 Eglinton Avenue East, Suite 700, Toronto, Ontario, Canada M4P 2Y3
(a division of Pearson Penguin Canada Inc.)
Penguin Ireland, 25 St Stephen's Green, Dublin 2, Ireland (a division of Penguin Books Ltd)
Penguin Group (Australia), 250 Camberwell Road, Camberwell, Victoria 3124, Australia
(a division of Pearson Australia Group Pty Ltd)
Penguin Books India Pvt Ltd, 11 Community Centre,
Panchsheel Park, New Delhi – 110 017, India
Penguin Group (NZ), cnr Airborne and Rosedale Roads, Albany,
Auckland 1310, New Zealand (a division of Pearson New Zealand Ltd)
Penguin Books (South Africa) (Pty) Ltd, 24 Sturdee Avenue,
Rosebank, Johannesburg 2196, South Africa

Penguin Books Ltd, Registered Offices: 80 Strand, London WC2R 0RL, England

www.penguin.com

First published by Michael Joseph 1989
Published in Penguin Books 1993

22

Copyright © Rifleman Productions Ltd, 1989
All rights reserved

It is inevitable that some boat names in *Sea Lord* will coincide
with the names of real boats. Nevertheless every vessel in this book,
like every character, is entirely fictional.

The moral right of the author has been asserted

Printed in England by Clays Ltd, St Ives plc

ISBN-13: 978–0–140–17724–4

www.greenpenguin.co.uk

Penguin Books is committed to a sustainable future
for our business, our readers and our planet.
The book in your hands is made from paper
certified by the Forest Stewardship Council.

SEA LORD is dedicated to
Diedree and Oscar Morong,
Masters under God of the good vessel
Diedree-Anne.

PART ONE

Part One

I didn't want to go home. I'd once sworn I'd never go home, yet here I was, plugging across the Western Approaches on a flooding tide in a filthy night.

In seven years I had been home just once. That first return had been a family duty and had turned into a family disaster. I had endured as long as I could; then, overwhelmed by responsibilities and harried by lawyers, I had sailed away. It was then that I had sworn never to return to England.

Now, four years later, I was going home.

And again it was duty which drew me back; family duty.

It certainly wasn't homesickness, for in seven years of ocean wandering I had never missed England. I tried to persuade myself it was curiosity that took me north into the cold Channel waters, but curiosity needs the provocation of affection or hate, and I felt neither for my family. Yet now, if the message was true, my family wanted my return and so, dutifully, perhaps guiltily, I was going home.

The message had reached me in English Harbour, Antigua. It came from my family's lawyers who had left the message with my London bank. I'd telexed the bank, hoping some dividends had taken me out of the red, but instead of money the bank had sent me news that my mother was sick and wanted to see me. It was the first time in four years that my mother had noticed my existence or, to be fair, that I had remembered hers. I didn't want to go, but there was a pathetic appeal in the message and so I slipped my mooring and turned *Sunflower*'s bows to the eastern sea.

I didn't hurry home. Indeed, and it might have been my fancy, it seemed to me that *Sunflower* sailed sluggishly right across the Atlantic. We spent a week becalmed in the horse latitudes and afterwards, when we made the westerlies, she developed a weather-helm I'd never known in her before. For the first time in her life, my boat became a pig to sail and I wondered if this new stubborn waywardness was some

3

reflection of my own reluctance to reach England. Somehow we made it to the Azores, but then, a week out of Horta, a foul toothache erupted in the back of my upper right jaw, and I was tempted to believe that this new pain, like *Sunflower*'s weather-helm, was a mute protest against the voyage. The toothache got worse as I endured a long beat north before the west winds drove me hard towards the English Channel. I sailed alone.

Just *Sunflower* and me. *Sunflower* was a French-built steel-hulled cutter, thirty-eight foot long, with an angular hull that banged in a moderate sea and sounded like a demented field gun in a big one. She was twenty years old that springtime, and showed it. The mainsail on a modern yacht has about as much cloth as a bikini bottom, but *Sunflower* had a proper mainsail with some guts in it; a big bellying brute of a driver-sail. She had a proper boom too: a real skull-cracking spar instead of a stubby high-tech afterthought. She hadn't been built with the modern refinements of in-mast reefing or headsail roller reefing; instead she had old-fashioned reef points that needed to be tied down by hand. On a cold wet night that can be a murderous job, but better to have fingers scraped raw and bloody than a mainsail jammed in its slot and threatening a capsize in a rising gale. Her foresails had to be dragged on to the foredeck in their stiff bags, piston-hanked on to their stays, then hauled into the wind's face. She was never a fast boat, not compared to the gossamer-light multihulled speed-sleds that take all the ocean-sailing records these days, but *Sunflower* would have sailed you to hell and back, and that's all a proper seaman should ever want in a yacht.

It was all I ever wanted, for *Sunflower* was my home. She and I had done a lot of miles. We'd sailed the southern ocean, rounded the Horn, run the Agulhas Current, smelt the African jungle, anchored off Indian coral; and now, because of a message from my family's lawyers, we were pounding a Western Approaches sea; a short, grey, unfriendly sea that hammered the hull's angular chines and shredded white into a stinging cold shrapnel that slashed over *Sunflower*'s gunwales to spatter me in the cockpit.

It was night-time and the wind was rising. It was England's homecoming wind, a southwesterly, but there was nothing welcoming in this malevolent cold force. At dusk the wind had been force three or four, by midnight it was five and rising, by three in the morning I'd taken in the first reef, and now, an hour before dawn, *Sunflower* was riding a hard force seven. I'd dropped the main and was running on a working jib alone. That sounds cautious, but I did not shorten sail out of fear, only because I was dog tired. I dared not sleep, for we were near the shipping lanes, and you don't take risks with the one-hundred-thousand-ton tankers that slam oblivious through the darkness. I'd seen one such supertanker just after midnight, or rather I'd seen the great block of her bridge beneath her steaming lights, but I hadn't seen the tanker's hull because the wind was shredding the wavetops into a grey devil-drizzle that danced above the sea. *Sunflower* and I had been racing the whitecaps then, just spits of light in the darkness, and I'd known the tanker would be ignorant of our presence. She'd passed a half-mile to our south, heading towards Biscay.

The sight of the tanker had jarred me into a new alertness, but the wakefulness didn't last. Despite the foul pain in my tooth, I dozed. I sat on the port side of the cockpit, one knee crooked over *Sunflower*'s tiller, and leaned my head against the guardrails. The banging of the sea against the hull was hypnotic. I'd sleep for a few minutes then start awake to stare in sudden, uncomprehending alarm at the compass. Once or twice I rubbed my eyes to help my vision, but mostly succeeded only in grinding dried, accreted and stinging salt into my eyeballs. The pain in my tooth was a throbbing agony, but even that was not sufficient to keep me awake. But I knew I had to stay awake. Sometimes I would stand to let the spray hit me, hoping that its forceful discomfort would keep me alert, but as soon as I sat again the sleep would insidiously steal over me. I was in a half-gale, in short steep seas, in a small boat pitching like a demented rocking-horse, sailing into the world's most dangerous seaway, with an aching tooth and stinging eyes, and all I could do was sleep. And hallucinate.

I was used to the tired hallucinations of a night sail, yet familiarity did nothing to convince me of their falsehood. The hallucinations are half-dreams of an uncanny reality. That night I distinctly saw the loom of a lighthouse guiding me home and, later, a coastline. If the hallucinations had been of fantastic things, say of women or hot food, then my mind would have dismissed them as apparitions; yet that night's visions were of the things I most wanted to see – signs of a safe landfall – and so I saw a gentle twilit coast backed with church towers, trees and cliffs, and the coast even had half-obscured leading lights showing the way home. One part of my brain knew that I was seeing an elaborate illusion, but still I would indulge it. It was only when something shattered *Sunflower*'s rhythm that the mind would sluggishly tear itself away from the comforting fantasy to accept that we were indeed slamming through a shortening sea in a half-gale with no leading lights to guide us home. Those were the moments of wakefulness.

Eventually I stopped fighting the sleep. Somehow my wet clothes so arranged themselves that I had the illusion of comfort, and to move was to bring cold wet cloth against a sore chafed skin. So I stayed still, I dreamed, and *Sunflower* flew up-channel to where the big ships thumped and the black rocks waited.

And still I did not know why I came home, or what waited for me in England.

I'd fled England four years before. I'd gone home because my brother had died and I had become the new head of the family. They looked to me to solve their problems, but instead I had bought *Sunflower*, victualled her, then run away to sea. I'd scraped round Ushant against this very same southwesterly wind and had felt an immense liberty unfold before my bows. I had gone, I was safe and I was free. The unwanted responsibilities and my family's spitting accusations had dropped astern like sea-anchors cut adrift.

I'd never regretted that leaving. I'd stepped on far beaches, sailed into distant nights and made friends with people who knew nothing of my past. To them I was merely John

Rossendale, master under God of the good ship *Sunflower*, and a welcome mechanic, carpenter, welder and rigger. I was anonymous. I was free.

And now I was coming home. Alone.

I hadn't always sailed alone. When I'd first left England, seven years before, Charlie Barratt had sailed with me. We had three good years together, sailing the southern oceans; then, when my family demanded my return, Charlie had gone with me. We had been in Australia when the news of my brother's death arrived and we had been forced to sell our boat to raise the money for the air fares. We promised ourselves we'd buy another yacht in England and go back to the Pacific, but Charlie had married instead and that put paid to his dreams of far blue seas. I had struggled with my brother's legacy for as long as I could; then, in desperation, I bought *Sunflower* and went back to sea alone. I didn't sail alone for long. A German girl came aboard at Belize and stayed as far as the Marquesas where she abandoned *Sunflower* to join a ramshackle commune that shared a vast catamaran skippered by a moody Pole. I'd heard that the catamaran had broken up off the Trobriands, drowning everyone aboard, but the sea lanes are full of such rumours, so perhaps the German girl was still alive. In the Solomons I'd met an Australian who sailed with me one whole year, but she discovered who I was and wanted to marry me and, when I adamantly refused, she jumped ship in California. There had been others. The oceans are littered with hitch-hikers, struggling from one coast to another, bartering rides on battered yachts, and all believing that their freedom from bureaucracy will last for ever. Some of the hitch-hikers drown, some get murdered, some disappear, a lot become whores, and a few, a very few, go home.

Now I was going home, and I didn't want to. I hallucinated, I slept, and I dreamed of far southern seas.

I was woken sharply in the dawn. It was not the feral grey light that woke me, nor my toothache, but rather because the wind had shifted abruptly to the south and *Sunflower* went over. It could only have taken a few seconds, a blink of a dream, no more, but the tiller slipped under my knee's grip, and she broached. For a moment she was speeding along the hissing crest of a wave, then the sea smacked her over, the wavetop broke, and she was falling, tipping, slamming down on to her starboard side. Water poured like Niagara over the port gunwale. For two seconds I was standing in sudden amazement on the far thwart, then I was pitched forward into the maelstrom of white water. Just before my head went under I saw the mast-tip drop into the water, then I was thrashing in sudden panic until the safety line jerked me hard and fast. The wave was still seething round me and breaking high over *Sunflower*'s hull that was lying flat on the sea. I despaired for a moment, until the inexorable laws of physics began their work and the deep heavy keel began to drag *Sunflower* upright. No law of physics would save me. I would have to drag my waterlogged weight to the high gunwale and somehow climb back aboard, but then a merciful and freakish backwash of water flung me against a starboard guardrail stanchion. I felt a sharp blow against my ribs, but all I could think of was to cling like grim death to the guardrail as the boat righted. She came up sluggishly at first, then tore herself free of the sea's grip, and I rolled up with her to haul myself unceremoniously over the rails into the swamped cockpit.

That was the sea's alarm call. Good morning and welcome to the Channel. I crouched in the swirling cockpit and gasped for breath. The pain in my ribs stabbed at me, but there was no time to worry if anything was broken. The jib was flogging and another steep sea was charging at our beam. I rammed the tiller hard to port and dragged the jib sheet in to catch the wind. *Sunflower* sluggishly turned her quarter to the waves. Water was still streaming off the foredeck and coachroof, cascading green and grey into the white-flecked, heaving sea.

The drains were emptying the cockpit. I doubted any water had got into the boat. *Sunflower*'s washboards are of one inch teak and, like the companionway hatch, I keep them bolted shut in dirty weather. I had been lucky. The knockdown had been my own fault, but, thanks to the safety line, I was alive. I gingerly felt my ribs and, though the pain was sharp, nothing seemed to be broken.

I was soaked through after my ducking, but *Sunflower* was moving again in the broken seas. I lashed the tiller, then stripped myself stark shivering naked. It was springtime, but the Channel air still had a cutting edge and the sea was as cold as an opened grave. I unlocked the companionway, waited until *Sunflower* had been overtaken by a hissing sea, then clambered over the washboards to drop into the cabin.

I had very few dry clothes left, but I found two pairs of jeans, one pair of socks, and three sweaters. I pulled them all on. They felt warm, but I knew they were full of dry salt crystals which, exposed to even the smallest dampness, would attract the moisture and swell to make me chill and damp again. I scrubbed my hair half dry with a mildewed towel, then wedged myself into the galley and slid the Thermos out of its padded clips. I poured a big mug of tea and, though *Sunflower* was pitching and corkscrewing, I didn't spill a drop of the precious hot liquid. Practice in such small things makes for perfection. A tanker could have turned me into scrap steel in the time it took to drink the tea, but I needed something warm inside and I was craving for a pipeful of dry tobacco.

Those creature comforts gained, I went back to the cockpit and disentangled my oilskins from the wet mess on the bottom grating. I grimaced, knowing that the water inside the oilies would soak my new dry clothes, but there was no choice. I kitted up, pulled on drenched boots, then hauled up the mainsail that had three reefs already tied to the boom. *Sunflower* liked the extra canvas and became steadier. We were on a beam reach, and my boat was sailing the gale's wrath like a dream. I was wide awake now, my hallucinations had vanished with the dawn, and I was going home.

But why, and to what, I did not know.

I should have sought shelter in Falmouth, or at any of the Cornish ports, but I had a sudden reluctance to exchange my damp clothes for a landfall. The wind, still in the south, was gusting towards gale force and flensing the wavetops into a stinging white mist that obscured the grey sea. The waves were thundering from the southwest, but being crossed by

9

the new wind that filled their troughs with confusion. *Sunflower* did not mind. She was a tough beast and had taken far worse. She had a steel hull and, over the years, I'd doubled the strength of all her rigging. She'd ridden the edge of a typhoon once, and all that had been broken was some crockery in her galley. Now, in a filthy new day, she sailed up-channel. The daylight was grey, churned with spray, and cold. I was curbing *Sunflower*, not wanting a following sea to poop her, but, though she was pitching hard, she was in no danger. All that could have killed her now was a bigger ship or my own carelessness.

My first sight of home was a glimpse of the Eddystone lighthouse. It was then I turned for Salcombe. I suppose I'd always known I was going to Salcombe because Charlie lived there. Charlie and I had grown up together, chased our first girls together, got drunk together, were arrested together, then sailed the far seas together. Whatever else waited for me in England, Charlie was there, and his friendship alone made this voyage home worth its while; so, in the hard dawn wind, I turned for Charlie's home port: Salcombe.

On a chart Salcombe seems like one of the most sheltered havens of England's south coast, and so it is if you're safe inside its steep-sided web of flooded river valleys. Many a yacht has waited out Channel storms in Salcombe, and the very harrowing of hell would find it hard to disturb the innermost lakes, but in an onshore wind against a falling tide the entrance to Salcombe is a death-trap. Salcombe means safety, but reaching that safety in a southern gale is suicidal folly. A bar lies athwart the harbour entrance like a hidden barricade. The wind-driven waves are toppled by the sudden ridge on the sea bottom to make a churning turmoil of breaking seas that crash white and are made even steeper and more dangerous when an ebbing tide tries to challenge them. Only a fool chooses Salcombe in a southern gale. Dartmouth, which can be entered in any weather, is just a short distance to the east, and Plymouth, even safer than Dartmouth, is not so far to the west. Torbay, the classic shelter in a southern or westerly gale, is an easy sail up-channel, but I chose Salcombe.

Perhaps, I thought, if I was not meant to be coming home, then the bar at the estuary's mouth would tell me. I would tempt the devil and, if I lost, *Sunflower* and I would die on the bar, rolled and swamped and broken up within the very smell of home. That reasoning was the stupid bravado of tiredness, made worse by a lethal mix of self-pity and arrogance. The self-pity came from my reluctance to see my family again, the arrogance from a determination to show off my seamanship as I came home.

Sunflower's boom was hard out on the port side as we ran towards Bolt Head. We were crossing the seas now, sliding diagonally over their eastwards flow. One moment we would be on the crest of a wave, triumphant and flying, then we would plunge deeper and deeper into the watery darkness and I would see the next wave threatening astern, its top sleeked and whipping with the wind's force. The glassy dark heart of death would rear up *Sunflower*'s port quarter and, just as I thought she would never rise again, so we would be heaved up to the next crest from where I would stare ahead for a sight of land. The tiredness was gone, I did not even care that I was cold and wet. Now I was elated by the thrill of daring a sea to do its worst.

Yet the gale-driven sea was not our enemy. Our enemy was the steep rise of the bar, silent and hidden, beneath Salcombe's entrance. Charlie and I had once watched a yacht crash down into a wave trough on Salcombe's bar. The boat had come up again, but in the trough her keel had struck bottom and the compression of the blow had smashed every bulkhead inside her hull and fractured the skull of a man sitting at her chart table. Even a lifeboat had been lost on Salcombe's bar, and lifeboats make *Sunflower* look fragile. Scores of widows cursed Salcombe's bar, and now we were racing towards it, driven by a southern gale and madness.

There was a moment, early in the afternoon, when I knew I could turn east and still make Prawle Point to reach Dartmouth in safety. For a second I hesitated, tempted by sanity, then the greater temptation of tweaking the devil's tail took over. I was a Rossendale, the last of the line, and I would come home with all the savage flair of that unpleasant family's blood.

Bolt Head came up like a grey threat on the port bow. The land was blurred and soaking, the wind had a noise like an eldritch death shriek, and the sea was harrying me on to the lee shore. The waves were huge, steep and made tumultuous by the land's proximity. At the top of each breaking crest I stared forward and I knew what I would see and, when I saw it, the fear came. I saw whiteness. It's one thing to imagine a danger, but quite another to see its true malevolence, and to realise that the imagination does not have sufficient horror to match reality. The bar was frantic with shattering seas. I had a glimpse of breaking wavetops, spuming a mist of white, and beneath that mist the weight of water would be a churning maelstrom. Men ashore would have seen my sails by now. They would be knowledgeable men, and they would damn me for a fool and pray that my boat lived despite my foolishness. Doubtless the inshore lifeboat would already have been called, but only to pluck my corpse from the incoming waves.

I kept to the western side of the entrance. The water's deeper there, though the Bass Rock is waiting just in case the bar fails to kill. I saw an explosion of white spew up as a wave broke into fragments on the Little Mew Stone, then *Sunflower* dipped her bows as a wave lifted her stern, but this time, instead of riding up over the wave's crest, the great steel hull began to plane on the tons of rolling water. Now we were no different to the surfers of the Pacific. We were no longer a boat, but a scrap of material being carried aloft on a wave's violence to where the bar made a white turmoil of the sea. We were also just where I wanted to be: hard under the western cliffs. I was braced in the cockpit with the tiller between my thighs and with both hands on the mainsheet for I knew what was about to happen.

Sunflower's hard-reefed mainsail was still out to port. At any second the wind would bounce and curl off the cliffs and she would gybe. I should have furled the main and let the small jib and the big sea take us in, but to furl the main would have been to show cowardice. Let the bar do its worst. I'd chosen to play the sea's game, and I wouldn't give in.

The leech of the mainsail shivered. It wasn't much, just a tiny flicker of the heavy grey material, but it was the sign I had been waiting for and, before the cliff-turned wind could dismast me, I hauled the sheet in with both hands. I braced the tiller hard, knowing how *Sunflower* would be knocked to port when the gybe came.

It came.

Unless you're pointing dead into the wind and happy to go nowhere, the sails of a boat are always stretched either to port or starboard. There are two ways to bring them across from one side to the other. One, to tack, is to turn the boat into the wind, so that the wind slides decorously across the bows and the sails, like flags streaming from flagpoles, obediently change their direction. The other way, to gybe, is to turn the boat in front of the wind. Then it's as if the wind has sneaked fast round the flagpole and the flag is crushed up against the pole before it smacks out in its new flight. Gybing is dangerous and violent. Instead of a flag I was letting a gale rip round behind a heavy sail that was lashed to a skull-crushing wooden boom. The weight of all that gear hammering across the wind's eye could easily tear my shrouds free of their chain-plates and pluck the mast clean out at its root. Except that I had just enough of the mainsheet gathered in to act as a spring and, as the great sail and boom slammed across, I used the sheet to soak its force and tame its threat. I skinned my right palm bloody doing it, but it was a proper job. That's what Charlie would have called it. 'A proper job' was Charlie's biggest approbation. He offered it rarely, and only to practical achievements like a well-scarfed piece of wood or a neatly welded seam, or for a maniacal gybe off the bar at Salcombe.

Not that I had time to admire my own manoeuvre. We had survived the gybe, but as soon as the sail settled I felt *Sunflower*'s bows drop and I knew the bar was straight beneath the boat's stem. I whooped a crazy challenge. I was staring down into the trough where mud and sand discoloured the water. Scummy strings of foam whipped across that dull

13

patch. I was running into the killing trough and, for a few seconds, the howl of the wind was muted by the towering wave behind me. I could only hear the seething of the water. This sea had perhaps a hundred yards left in which to kill me, no more, but they were the worst hundred yards. If I broached now then nothing would save me because *Sunflower* would be turned over, her mast would snap, and the sea would pounce on us to tear man and hull into dented steel and bloody scraps. I was holding the tiller with both hands, muscles rigid, as the crest behind shattered to cascade like spilt ice down the wave's dark face. Christ, I thought, but why had I done this?

The jib was flogging, shielded by the main. We were veering to port, I dragged her back. The wave that was carrying us collapsed, its underpinning sheared off by the rising bar, and *Sunflower* was suddenly nothing but a scrap of steel in the heart of a broken tidal wave. Water bounced halfway up her mast. A new wave reared behind and *Sunflower*'s keel began to drop, crashing down through an incoherent sea towards the hidden land that could fracture her steel hull as though it was an egg. Down we went, and still down, and behind me the new wave curled at its top and I saw the glassy black beneath the fractured white, and still we dropped and I saw that I would be crushed between the bar and the following wave, but then *Sunflower*, good *Sunflower*, began to rise. She fought her death inch by damned inch. The peak of the reefed sail was drawing, forcing her on. She had way on her still and she was cutting her steel through the water. She would not give up, but still that toppling wave threatened to poop us and I knew it could kill with a blow as easily as it could drown us.

The wave broke. The dark black glossy heart of the wave was blown apart as if by dynamite. It turned white as it tumbled and as it broke into a million fragments. It fell, and it would have killed me, except that it fell a foot behind *Sunflower*'s transom and the force of the sea's fall was bounced up from the bar to lift and drive her on. On across the bar's broken water, on past the Wolf Rock and the Bass Rock, and then, just short of the Poundstone, I gybed her again, and I knew I was showing off to the people who were standing ashore to watch my death. I was proving that I had mastered one thing and, in demonstration of that mastery, I had come home in style. So I gybed *Sunflower* again, turned her, and suddenly we were sailing into calmer waters as Limebury Point stole the wind's brute force. I looked back. The bar was a mass of churning white, as bad as I'd ever seen it, but *Sunflower* had come through.

And I, in a proper job, had come home.

Charlie wasn't at home. His wife, who had grudgingly taken my reverse-charge call, said he was in Hertfordshire on business. I could tell she was not pleased that I had returned. She believed I was a rakehell who might yet take her husband back to the sea. "When will he be back, Yvonne?" I asked.

"I don't know." Her voice was guarded. Somewhere in the background a child whined.

"Tell him I called, and tell him I'm moored in Salcombe." Yvonne promised she would pass on the news, though I doubted if she would be in any hurry. I wondered why it was that Charlie, my best, closest, and oldest friend, should marry someone who so disliked me.

I said goodbye; then, ignoring the impatient people who waited to use the public phone, I tried to reverse the charges to my mother's house. There was no answer, so I had the operator call my twin sister in Gloucestershire. Elizabeth was not at home either, but her husband grudgingly agreed to accept the charges. He had once been a friend of mine, but he had chosen his wife's side in our family battle. "Do you think we're made of money?" was his greeting.

I didn't bother to explain that I'd only just landed in England and had no small change other than American, Antiguan and Portuguese coins. "Is Elizabeth there?" I asked instead.

"No she's not." He sounded drunk.

"I tried to reach Mother."

"She's in hospital."

I waited to see if he'd offer more information. He didn't. "Which hospital?" I asked.

"South Devon General. They took her in last week. She's in a private ward, which we're paying for."

The inference was that I should help with the cost, but I ignored the hint. "What's the ward called?" I asked instead.

"The Edith Cavell Ward. It's on the third floor."

"Do you know what the visiting hours are?"

"I am not an information service for the National Health Service," he said irritably; then, relenting, "you can go any time. They don't seem to mind. Bloody silly, I call it. If I was running a hospital I wouldn't want visitors traipsing about at all hours of the day or night, but I suppose they know their own business."

"Perhaps I'll see Elizabeth there?"

"I don't know where she is." There was a long pause as though he was about to add some comment, but then, without another word, he put down the receiver.

There was no one else to telephone. I knew I couldn't reach my younger sister, who was the only person beside Charlie who might be glad to hear I had come home, so instead I rowed myself back to *Sunflower* and dug out a tin of baked beans which I mashed with a can of stew and heated over the galley stove. The pain in my tooth had miraculously subsided, which was a blessing as I'd run out of both aspirins and Irish whiskey.

It had begun to rain hard. The water drummed on *Sunflower's* coachroof and gurgled down her scuppers. The wind howled above the moorings to slap halliards against noisy masts. I spooned down my meal and thought how I might even now be six seas away and running free.

But had come home instead.

The toothache had entirely disappeared by morning. For the first time in weeks I woke up without pain, except for the bruise on my ribs where I'd been thrown against the stanchion, but that kind of pain was an occupational hazard, and therefore to be ignored. Yet the tooth, astonishingly, felt fine. I bit down hard on it and did not even feel a twinge. The spontaneous cure and a good night's sleep combined to fill me with optimism.

The bus journey soon dissipated that happy mood.

It wasn't the Devon countryside which, though damp, looked soft and welcoming. Rather it was my fellow passengers. The bus was filled with young mothers and their squalling children. The sound of screaming babies is blessedly absent at sea and, suddenly exposed to it, I felt as if I was listening to nails scratching on slate. I stared through a misted window at the cars slopping through puddles and wondered how Charlie endured being a father.

The bus dropped me a mile from the hospital. I could have

waited for another bus which would have taken me up the hill, but the thought of more screaming infants persuaded me to walk. I was wearing my heavy oilskin jacket, so only my jeans got soaked with rain. The oily was smeared with grease and dirt, but it was the only coat or jacket I possessed so it had to serve as formal wear. I climbed through the pelting rain and cut across the hospital's waterlogged lawns. The big entrance hall was loud with more squalling children. I ignored the lifts, climbed three flights of stairs, and wondered just why I had sailed for six weeks across three and a half thousand nautical miles.

I had been half expecting and half dreading that my sister Elizabeth would be visiting the hospital. She was not. Except for the patients, the Edith Cavell ward was empty. On the wall opposite the ward's two beds a silent television was showing a frenetic children's cartoon. An elderly woman lay in the nearest bed with a pair of earphones over her grey hair. She eyed my sodden jeans and sneakers with distaste, and her face betrayed relief that I had not come to visit her. "She's asleep," she said reprovingly, at the same time jerking her head towards the second bed which was still surrounded by drawn curtains.

I crossed the rubber-tiled floor and gently pulled back the pale curtains.

My mother was sleeping.

At first I did not recognise her. In the last four years her gold hair had turned a dirty grey. Even in sleep she looked exhausted. She lay, wan and emaciated, with her grey hair straggling untidily from her pale forehead. She had always been a woman of great pride, foully excessive pride, but now she was reduced to this drawn creature. Her great beauty was gone, vanished like a dream. Her breath rasped in her throat. Every heave of her lungs was an effort. Once she had worn a king's ransom of diamonds, but now she struggled for life. She was only fifty-nine, but looked at least a decade older.

"She had a bad night," the grey-haired woman volunteered.

I said nothing.

The woman took off her earphones. "She won't have the

oxygen tent, you see. Stupid, I call it. I've told her, I have. I told her she should listen to the doctors, but she won't take a blind bit of notice. She says she's got to smoke. Smoke! That's what's killing her, but she won't listen. She says she can't smoke if she's in an oxygen tent. Stupid, I call it."

I dropped the curtain behind me which had the happy effect of shutting the woman up. The sound of my mother's breathing was horrid.

A cylinder of oxygen stood by her bed. A packet of cigarettes and her gold lighter lay close to an oxygen mask. I picked up the mask and heard the hiss of escaping gas. I turned off the tap, then lay the mask back on the thin blanket. I had moved very gently, but something must have disturbed my mother for her eyes opened and she stared up at me. At first there was no recognition in her face – the sun had bleached my pale hair almost white and turned my face the colour of old varnish – but then, with a palpable start, realisation came to her eyes. I was her living son, and I had come home.

"Hello, Mother," I said.

She said nothing. Instead she groped for her cigarettes but, before she could find them, a dreadful cough convulsed her body. It was a foul, grating and harsh cough, as rough as broken glass being crushed by stone. It came from deep in her chest and it would not stop. I turned on the oxygen and put the mask over her face. Somehow she fought the cough to draw a desperate breath and, as if she was fearful that I would take the mask away, she clamped her right hand over mine. Her crooked thin fingers were like claws. It was the first time she had touched me in fourteen years. I had been twenty that last time, and she had briefly embraced me beside the grave into which my father was being lowered. Since then we had never touched, not till now as she fought for life. She put her hand on mine and gripped so tight that it felt like a scaly bird's claw clinging to refuge. Her eyes were closed again. Her palm was warm on the back of my hand, her fingers were contracting, and her nails were digging into my skin.

Then, very slowly, her breathing became easier. I could feel the relief course through her body as her grip relaxed. She had left two flecks of blood where her nails had driven into my fingers. She opened her eyes and stared at me, then, almost irritably, she twitched her hand as if to say that I should take the mask away.

Slowly, not certain if that was what she really wanted, I lifted the oxygen mask away. The paroxysm of coughing had left flecks of blood on my mother's lips, while the plump rubber mask had printed a red mark on her white cheeks. Her eyes, against her skin's chalky paleness, seemed very dark and glinting as she stared up at me.

"Hello, Mother," I said again. She tried to say something in reply, but the effort threatened to turn into another racking cough. "It's all right," I said soothingly, "you don't have to speak." I moved the oxygen mask towards her mouth, but she shook her head, then closed her eyes as though she was concentrating on preventing another coughing fit. It took an immense effort of will, but she succeeded and, instead of coughing again, she opened her eyes and looked straight up into my face.

"You bastard," she said.

Then she began to cough again, and no amount of oxygen could help this time and, though I pressed the emergency call button, and though nurses and doctors thrust me aside to bring her relief, there was nothing anyone could do. Within twenty minutes of my arrival at her bedside, my mother was dead.

When it was all over a young doctor joined me in the corridor. He wanted to know if I was a relative and, though I said I was, I did not say I was the dead woman's son. "I'm just a distant relation," I said instead.

"She smoked too much," the doctor said hopelessly.

"I know." I guiltily fingered the pipe in my oilskin pocket. I kept meaning to give up smoking. I'd succeeded once, but only because I'd run out of tobacco a thousand miles out of Auckland. After three weeks I'd been experimenting with sun-dried seaweed which tasted foul, but was better than abstinence. I dragged my attention back to the doctor.

"She was very keen to see her son." The doctor peered

20

dubiously at my gaudy oilskin jacket. "He's supposed to be at sea, isn't he?"

"I think so," I said unhelpfully.

The doctor looked like a man who'd just sailed through a force twelve storm, but he was gallantly fighting the weariness in an effort to be kind. "She received the last rites yesterday," he told me, "and it seemed to calm her."

"I'm sure it did."

The doctor stifled a yawn. "Would you like to meet the hospital chaplain? Sometimes, after a death, it can be helpful."

"I wasn't that close a relative," I said defensively.

"So I suppose we should telephone the eldest daughter about the arrangements?"

"That would be best," I said, "much the best." Two men pushed a trolley into the ward. I didn't want to see the shrouded body wheeled away, so I walked back to the Devon rain.

You're supposed to feel something, I thought. You're not supposed to see your mother die and feel nothing. At the very least you're supposed to weep. My God, but a mother's flawed love and a son's reluctant duty should add up to one miserable tear, but I could find no appropriate response. I could feel neither joy nor sorrow nor surprise nor anything. All I felt was an irritation for a wasted trip, and an aggravation that I was forced to wait two hours in the rain for a bus back to Salcombe.

Once back at the harbour I phoned Charlie's house, but there was no answer. So I rowed myself out to *Sunflower* and spliced a new rope-tail on to the staysail's wire halliard.

I'd come home and I'd felt nothing. Not even a tear.

Five days later, at ten o'clock in the morning, the family assembled at Stowey.

Stowey was the family home. Pevsner, in one of his books, called it 'perhaps the finest late mediaeval dwelling house in England', which really meant that the family had been too poor to trick it out with eighteenth-century gallimaufry or nineteenth-century gingerbread. Yet, in all truth, Stowey is pretty. It's a low stone building, just two storeys high, with a battlemented tower at the east end. Halfway through building the house there came the happy realisation that Devon was at peace, so the western wing was left unfortified. Instead it was given cosy mullioned windows which now look out on gardens that bring hundreds of visitors each summer weekend. Today Stowey is a country house hotel, but it was part of the sale agreement that my mother's funeral party could gather in the old state rooms, and that the funeral service could be held in Stowey's chapel. The chapel was no longer consecrated, but the hotel had kept it unchanged and the local priest was happy to indulge my mother's wish. She was to be buried in the family's vault beneath the chapel, perhaps the last of the family to be so interred, for I could not imagine the hotel's owners wanting any more such macabre ceremonies. Indeed, they only endured this funeral because they had no legal alternative, but I noted the distaste with which they received the scattered and decaying remnants of the Rossendale family.

That family received me with an equal distaste. "I'm surprised to see you here, John," one of my least decrepit uncles said.

"Why?"

"Well, you know."

"No, I don't," I challenged him.

He backed down, muttering something about the weather being dreadful and how it always seemed to rain when a Rossendale was buried. "It rained on Frederick," he said, "and on poor Michael." Frederick had been my father, Michael my elder brother. He was always 'poor Michael' to the family; he'd blown his brains out with two barrels of number six shot and the Rossendales had been lumbered

22

with me instead. My brother Michael had been a dull, worried man, hiding his chronic indecisions behind a bad-tempered mask, but ever since his death he had been something of a hero to the family, perhaps because they preferred him to me. If only Michael had lived, they seemed to be saying with their reproachful glances, none of this unhappiness would have happened.

One member of the family was glad to see me. That was my younger sister who smiled with innocent joy as I walked towards her chair. "Johnny?" She held both hands towards me in delighted greeting. "Johnny!"

"Hello, my darling." I held Georgina's hands and bent to kiss her cheeks.

She smiled happily into my face. This had to be one of her good days, for she had recognised me. She had a young plump nun with her, one of the nursing sisters who looked after her in a private Catholic hospital in the Channel Islands. "How is she?" I asked the nun.

"We're all very proud of her," the sister said, which might simply have meant that my younger sister was at last toilet trained.

"And Sister Felicity?" I asked. Sister Felicity was Georgina's usual companion.

"She's not well," the nun said in a soft Irish voice, "she'd have liked to have come today, so she would, but she's not a well woman. We're all praying for her."

"Sister Felicity is going to heaven soon," Georgina said happily. She is twenty-six and has the mind of a backward two-year-old. No one knows why. Charlie put it best when he simply said that God left out the yeast when he made Georgina's loaf. She's beautiful, with an innocent face as heart-breaking as an angel's, and a head as nutty as a squirrel's larder.

"Sister Felicity's not going to die," I said, but Georgina had already forgotten the comment.

"I like it here." She was still holding my hands.

"You look well," I told her.

"I want to live here again, Johnny. With you," Georgina said with a touching and hopeless appeal.

23

"I wish you could, my darling. But you're happy at the convent, aren't you?" The convent hospital specialised in the care of the mentally subnormal. Before my father's death, and the subsequent collapse of the Rossendale estates, a trust had been established which would provide for the rest of Georgina's life. It was ironic to think that the only family member who did not have money problems was the mad one.

"I like it here," Georgina said again with a cruel lucidity. "With you."

For the first time since my mother had died, tears threatened me. We were a rotten family, but Georgina and I had always been close. When she was a little child I used to make her laugh, and I sometimes thought that it would only take a small miracle to jar the sense out of the place where it was locked so deep inside her head. That miracle had never happened. Instead my mother had found Georgina's presence oppressive, and so my younger sister had been put safely away, out of sight and out of mind, in her convent home. I crouched in front of her chair. "Are you unhappy?" I asked.

She did not answer. The bubble of sense had burst and now she just stared vacantly into my eyes. I doubted she even knew why she had been brought back to Stowey.

"People are very kind," she said dully, then looked up as someone came to stand beside me. It was my other sister, my twin Elizabeth, but there was no recognition in Georgina's eyes.

Elizabeth did not acknowledge Georgina's presence. Like my mother, she had always been offended by having a mental defective in the family. Whatever, she ignored Georgina and waited for me to disengage my hands gently and stand upright. Elizabeth carried a glass of the hotel's sherry. Her husband Peter, once my sailing companion, but now a failing Cotswold landowner, glowered at me across the room. I was the ghost at the funeral feast. They all blamed me for losing the family's money and for bringing the disgrace of poverty on a lineage that had owned this patch of England since the first Rossendale had taken it with his bloody-edged sword. That man had come to Devon in the twelfth century, while now his twentieth-century descendants shuffled with embarrassment in an hotel's drawing room. All except for Elizabeth, who had a superb if rancorous poise. She drew me away from Georgina's chair. "I don't know why she's here," Elizabeth said irritably.

"Why shouldn't she be?"

"She doesn't know what's going on." Elizabeth sipped her sherry, then gave me a long, disapproving examination. "I don't know why you're here either."

"A vestige of filial duty," I said, a little too lightly.

"You look disgustingly healthy." Her words were grudging. It was an effort to be polite, to pretend that we were not bitter enemies.

"Sun and sea." I was glib. "You look well yourself. Are you still riding?"

"Of course." Elizabeth had very nearly made Britain's Olympic team as a horsewoman. Perhaps, if that success had come to her, she would have been less bitter with life since.

A flurry at the door announced the arrival of Father Maltravers from London. Father Maltravers had been Mother's favourite confessor and would now bury her. The sight of the priest made Elizabeth drop her small pretence of politeness. "Will you be taking Mass?" she challenged me.

"I don't think so."

"Mother would have liked it if you did." She paused to look into my eyes as if she expected to read some message there. Elizabeth is very tall, just two inches beneath my own six feet. She has our family's bright gold hair and more than her fair share of the Rossendale good looks. "Of course," she went on with a very poisoned indirectness, "you'll have to make your confession first. Have you made confession in the last four years, John?"

"Have you?" I countered feebly. The Rossendales are one of the ancient Catholic families. We'd been persecuted by the Tudor fanatics, but had tenaciously clung to our land and put the five oyster shells beside Stowey's front door. That was the source of the line in the nursery song: 'Five for the symbols at your door'; the five marks being a sign that the old religion was practised inside and that a priest could therefore be found to say Mass. Today the hotel delights in showing its guests a priest hole where the illicit clergymen had hidden from Elizabeth I's searchers. The hotel's priest hole was in what had been my father's bedroom, and the guests were told that a Jesuit had starved to death in the hole in the 1580s, but that was a nonsense. The real priest hole was in Stowey's stables, because a Rossendale would never have let a priest into the private rooms. The so-called priest hole was actually the low cupboard in which my grandfather had kept his riding boots, but the invention keeps the tourists happy.

"Did you see Mother before she died?" Elizabeth now asked.

"Yes."

"And?" she prompted me.

I shrugged and decided the truth of Mother's last words had better stay my secret. "She wasn't in a fit state to talk."

Elizabeth paused, evidently suspecting an evasion. "But you know why she wanted to see you?" she asked after a few seconds.

"I can guess."

Elizabeth did not pursue the topic. I noticed how the other family members kept deliberately clear of us, as though making an arena for a fight. They must have guessed that Elizabeth would tackle me and consequently there was a sense of expectancy in the panelled room. They pretended to ignore us, fussing around Father Maltravers, but I knew they were all keenly alert to my confrontation with Elizabeth.

"Have you seen Mother's will?" The question, like her earlier questions, was yet another probing attack.

"No."

"There's nothing in it for you."

"I didn't expect anything." I spoke gently because I could sense the danger in Elizabeth's mood. She had the Rossendale temper. I had it too, but I think the sea had taught me to control mine. Yet now, in Elizabeth's bright eyes, I could see the anger brimming.

"She left you nothing, because you betrayed her." My sister's voice was loud enough to make the nearest relatives turn to watch us. All but Georgina who was solemnly counting her fingers. "She hated you," Elizabeth went on, "which is why she left me the painting."

The statement showed that Elizabeth had been unable to resist a full-scale assault. "Good," I said carelessly, which only annoyed her more.

"So where is it?" she asked with a savage bitterness.

We're twins, born eight minutes apart, and we hate each other. I can't explain that. Charlie often said we were too much alike, as if that was the answer, but I can't find the venom in my own soul to explain Elizabeth's obsessive dislike of me. Nor do I think we are so much alike; I lack Elizabeth's driving ambition. It was an astonishing ambition; so nakedly obvious as to be almost pitiful. She craved after a status in life which would reflect the past glories of our family; she wanted wealth, admiration and success, yet, like me, she had a knack of failure. I had accepted my lack of ambition, turning it into a wanderer's life at sea, while Elizabeth just grew more bitter with every twist of malevolent fate. She had married well, and the marriage had soured. She had been born wealthy, and now she was poor, and that failure seemed to hurt her most of all.

"Where's the painting?" she asked me again, and this time so loudly that everyone else in the room, even the uncomprehending Georgina, turned to watch us. Elizabeth's husband, leaning against the far wall, seemed to sneer at me. Father Maltravers took a step forward, as though tempted to be a peacemaker, but the intensity in Elizabeth's voice checked him. "Where's the painting?" she asked me again.

"I'll tell you once more," I said, "and for the very last time, I do not know."

"You're a liar, John. You're a snivelling little liar. You always were." Elizabeth's anger had snapped, torn from its mooring by my presence. She would be hating herself for thus losing her temper in public, but she was quite unable to control it. My silence in the face of her attack only made her anger more fierce. "I know you're lying, John. I have proof."

I still kept silent. So did the rest of the family. I doubt if any of them had expected to see me at the funeral and, when they did, they had doubtless half feared and half relished that this skeleton from the family's crowded bone cupboard would make its ghoulish appearance. Now it had, and none of them wanted to stop its display. Elizabeth, sensing their support and my discomfiture, attacked once more. "You'd better run away again, John, before the police discover you're back."

"You're hysterical." My anger was like a gnawing bitch in my belly, but I was determined not to show it; yet, try as I might, I could not keep its venom from my voice. "Why don't you go and lie down, or take a pill?"

"Damn you." She twitched her wrist and the sticky sherry splashed up on to my face and on to the cheap black suit I'd bought in honour of the occasion. "Damn you," she said again. "Damn you, damn you, damn you."

Sherry dripped from my chin on to my black tie. None of the relatives moved. They all agreed with Elizabeth. They thought I was the bastard who had made them poor. If it wasn't for me then Stowey would still be in the family, the port would flow at Christmas, and there would be no importunate bank managers and no genteel shame of an old family driven into penury. I had not played their game, I wasn't one of them, and so they all hated me.

So I didn't stay for the funeral. I glanced at Georgina, but she was in a world of her own. Father Maltravers tried to detain me, but I brushed him aside and walked out, leaving the family in an embittered silence. I washed the sherry from my face in the hotel's loo, collected my filthy oilskin jacket from its peg, then walked through the Devon rain to the village street. I dialled Charlie's number on the public phone outside the Rossendale Arms, but there was no reply. I threw my sticky black tie into the gutter, then lit a pipe as I waited for the bus. The tooth suddenly began to ache again. I explored the pain with my tongue, wondering whether it truly was psychosomatic, but decided that no such sharp agony could be purely mental, not even if it was provoked by a lacerating homecoming.

Damn the family. I'd come home, and they did not want me. Above the thatched roofs of the village the green pastures curled up to the thick woods where, as a child, I'd learned the skills of stalking and killing. Charlie had taught me those skills. He'd grown up in one of my family's tied cottages, but we had still become friends. We had become the best of friends. My mother, of course, had hated Charlie. She had called him a piece of village muck, a dirty little boy from an infamous family, but he had still become my best friend. He was still my closest friend; four years away had not changed that. I wanted to see him, but I wouldn't wait for him. I wanted to be back at sea, riding the long winds in *Sunflower*. My family would accuse me of running away again, and in a sense they were right, but I wasn't running from fear, just from them; my family.

And all because of a bloody painting.

It was a good painting, a very good painting. So good that it could have saved the family fortune.

My father's death had been a financial disaster to the family, but my mother, with a single-minded fury, had fought to save Stowey and its estates. Her legal battles had been waged for ten years, and at the end she had won her campaign and the key to it was the painting.

The house had once been filled with fine pictures. The National Gallery in Washington DC has a slew of our Gainsboroughs and Reynoldses, while a gallery in California has the pick of our Dutch interiors and the two good Constables that London's National Gallery had been desperate to acquire, but too poor to pay for. One by one the walls of Stowey had been stripped to pay gambling debts or death duties, but on my father's death there had been nothing of any value left.

Or hardly anything of value. There was a canvas which my mother swore was a Stubbs, but which Sothebys could not bring to auction as such. There was a Poussin, which probably wasn't, but if it was then the old master had been having a bad day. There was a Constable drawing, which was undoubtedly genuine, but a Constable drawing doesn't pay the revenue. The only recourse was to sell Stowey and its lands, but that was something my mother would not contemplate. Stowey had been in our family since the twelfth century.

But there was one undoubted treasure. An odd treasure for a house like Stowey, and a treasure which, strictly speaking, did not belong to the family, but rather to my mother. It was a Van Gogh.

The painting should have looked all wrong in the old house, as out of place as a drunken punk ensconced in a library, yet somehow it seemed perfect. It was a glorious, superb, demented canvas; one of the early sunflower paintings. It showed eight blossoms topping a half-glazed jar; an explosion of yellow paint touched by blue with poor Vincent's childlike signature painted on the vase itself. On a summer's day, when the sun blazoned Stowey's mediaeval gardens with light, the painting seemed like a fragment of that brightness trapped and caught inside the house.

The painting had been brought to the family by my mother. She had been left it by her father. She had hung the Van Gogh on the linenfold panelling of her bedroom at Stowey. My mother refused to lend the picture to any exhibition, though once in a while an art historian or a reputable painter would seek permission to visit Stowey, and I remember the awe with which they gazed at the lovely canvas.

It was well protected. My mother's bedroom had been in Stowey's crenellated east tower, built for defence, and the mediaeval bastion had been supplemented with the most sophisticated alarms. No one had even tried to penetrate those defences, until the end.

That end came ten years after my father's death. My mother had fought every month of those years. She had cursed and kicked and clawed at the taxmen. She had challenged their assessments and fobbed them off with small payments torn from the sale of our outlying pastures. She had fought a good fight, but then my brother had gone into the gun room and ripped her fight to shreds.

My brother's suicide gave the taxmen a new carcass of juicy death duties to chew. My mother, recognising the inevitable, knew that either Stowey or the Van Gogh had to go. Stowey won. She agreed a price of four million pounds for the Van Gogh, but on the very day before it should have left the house, it was stolen. It transpired that my brother had let the insurance lapse one month before his death. The police were certain that only a person with intimate knowledge of the alarms could have penetrated to the gun room where the crated painting had been waiting for the security van. The police were also certain that I was that person.

I had put the painting in the gun room to await collection. I had the key to the room and to the alarm systems. Only I was supposed to know where the painting was. My finger-prints were on the door's lockplates. On the day after the painting was stolen I sailed across the Channel in a friend's boat, presumably carrying my loot away. The evidence was all circumstantial, and utterly damning. I was never charged, because my guilt could not be proved, but the whole family was nevertheless certain that I was guilty. I had done it, they said, to spite my mother and because I didn't want to give the taxmen their ton of flesh. My relatives said I was a rogue, that I'd always been a rogue, and that now I'd broken the Rossendale family with my selfish greed.

The painting was never found. My mother's fight, and four million pounds, was lost, yet the taxmen and the lawyers still had to be paid, and so Stowey was sold and now caters to well-heeled tourists who gape at a boot cupboard in the belief that a priest starved to death inside. My mother moved into an old rectory on the edge of the moor, and there she slowly died. The family had made me an outcast. And I had fled to sea.

In a yacht called *Sunflower*.

There wasn't much I had to do in Salcombe because I didn't plan on a full provisioning in England. I would fill up with fresh water, put diesel in the tanks and spare cans, and stock enough food to reach Vigo or Lisbon. I wanted an estimate for a new trysail, but even if I could afford it, I would not wait for delivery, but rather have Charlie send the sail to Tenerife. There were a slew of small problems. One of the winches had worn gearing, a bow fairlead needed replacing, and *Sunflower*'s bottom was filthy with weed and barnacles.

I planned to strand her at low tide on the mud of one of Salcombe's lakes, then spend a filthy time scraping her clean before giving her a new coat of anti-fouling. She needed a good cleaning inside and out, and my clothes needed a rinse in fresh water. I would have liked to have found a fibreglass dinghy to replace the inflatable, which in turn had replaced a rigid dinghy that had been stolen in Antigua, but that could wait. I wanted a small outboard so I didn't have to row the tender. The folding bicycle needed brake pads. I needed grease for the stern-gland. There were a couple of rust spots inside the hull which needed quick attention, and there was the bloody tooth which was now flaring up again with all its old intensity.

At first I ignored the tooth on the principle that a pain ignored will go away. It didn't. Instead it got worse, so, three days after the funeral, I rowed ashore and telephoned dentists until I found one who could see me straightaway. That meant another bus ride, only to be lectured by a pompous little twerp who told me I didn't brush my gums properly. He said I'd need to make a series of visits while he first drained the abscess, then scraped out the root canal to save the tooth.

"I don't want it saved," I said irritably, "just take the damned thing out."

"But it can be saved, Mr Rossendale."

"Take it out," I insisted. Teeth are a human design fault, like appendixes, and all design faults are life-threatening at sea. This tooth wasn't one of my front ones, so the lack of it wouldn't make me ugly. Besides, it would be far cheaper for me to have the tooth drawn in England than giving me trouble across the Atlantic where you need to take out a mortgage before you dare see a dentist. The pompous little twerp was unhappy, but finally did what I demanded, grunting and heaving with his pliers. The Novocaine must have been from a weak batch because the extraction hurt like hell, but that was better than drawing the tooth myself a thousand miles to sea. A friend of mine did that once. It took him half a day and the best part of a bottle of Scotch, and when it was done he found he'd pulled the wrong one.

I consoled my pain with a large whiskey in the pub, then went down to the town pontoon where I'd left *Sunflower*'s inflatable. No one had stolen her, perhaps because I'd pasted a score of false repair patches on her faded black skin so that she looked as though she was ready to give her last gasp and sink. Her oars were underwater, weighted with a length of chain and tethered by a tatty piece of fraying rope. I retrieved them, then rowed myself slowly out through the murk. It was still raining. Grey clouds were scurrying low over Goodshelter, then depositing a misty and obscuring rain on the moorings. A crabber engine choked into life, but otherwise the estuary seemed as empty as winter. I planned to motor *Sunflower* up to the drying mud of Callapit Creek. I would spend a few days scrubbing her hull, then go back to sea. I made a mental list of things I needed to buy: galvanised shackles, valve springs, welding rods, an angle grinder, fuses. My face felt swollen, numb and tender.

I stopped rowing and turned to see if I was aiming the unwieldy dinghy in the right direction. I was a quarter-mile from *Sunflower* and way off course, blown there by the wind which was carrying the dinghy too far to the north. That's one reason I hate inflatable dinghies; they're prey to every gust of wind and current.

But if the dinghy was an unwieldy brute, *Sunflower* looked magnificent. I rested on the oars, admiring her. She looked drab and scuffed among the smart yachts on the other moorings, but her drabness was the result of long sea miles and it gave her the battered beauty of functionalism. She was weather-beaten, tough and practical. Then, as I gazed at her, a man's head appeared in her companionway. He stared around the moorings, glanced at me for a second, then ducked back into the cabin.

For a moment I was shocked into immobility. I even doubted what I'd seen. Somehow all the years of ocean travel had not diluted the prejudice that blatant thievery is more common abroad than in an English harbour; certainly not in genteel, yellow-wellied Salcombe.

And the intruder, if I had not imagined the whole thing, had to be a thief. I'd left *Sunflower*'s companionway locked tight, so he must have broken the big padlock to get inside the cabin. The intruder had not been Charlie, for the man I'd seen had black hair, and Charlie's thatch was as fair as mine. I wouldn't have cared if Charlie had broken the cabin lock, then drunk all the whiskey on board, but I was damned if some stranger would steal from me. I began rowing again. As I did so the dark head appeared again in the companionway. I rowed steadily, aiming well away from her, and the man must have decided that I posed no threat for he ducked back down into the cabin. I rowed on, keeping well to *Sunflower*'s beam. I knew the intruder might still be watching me through one of the thick cabin ports so I pretended to be going to a mooring north and east of the boat. I didn't hurry. I did nothing to make him suspicious.

I wanted to trap him. He was thieving from my boat, and I wanted to make him regret it. I knew I would have to be cunning, for he was surely alert to the possibility of the owner returning. So I kept rowing away from *Sunflower*, though now, because I was past her, I was able to watch her constantly. The man did not reappear in the companionway, so he must have felt safe.

I went a good two hundred yards past *Sunflower*'s mooring, then turned south amongst a gaggle of moored Salcombe yawls. I rowed until *Sunflower*'s bows were pointing directly towards me, then I let the ebbing tide carry me down towards her. I steered with a single oar over the dinghy's transom. I noticed there was no tender tied to *Sunflower*, which was odd, but, when I was just twenty yards away, I forgot the oddity because I heard voices. There were evidently two intruders aboard, a man and a woman. The woman's voice, sharp and penetrating, seemed to make a protest, but the man's voice overrode her.

I put out a hand and caught the rail of *Sunflower*'s pulpit. The tide was trying to take the dinghy down *Sunflower*'s starboard flank to where I would have been visible through the cabin ports, but I held the dinghy back, took a breath, then slowly hauled myself over the bows. The big hull rocked gently under my weight, but not enough to warn the intruders of my presence. I'd kept the inflatable's painter in my left hand and I quickly hitched it to the pulpit rail. The inflatable would bump softly against the steel hull, and I prayed the tiny thumping would not alert them. The man was speaking again, low and urgently, but I could not hear his exact words.

I crouched over the forehatch. I guessed that the man and woman would be in the main cabin. I could just see the twisted remains where they had forced the hasp of the main companionway. I briefly thought of making my entrance there, but my footsteps could have alerted them as I negotiated the cabin roof and I wanted to surprise them. I took the bunch of keys from my pocket and, taking exquisite care not to make them jangle, found the small key for the forehatch padlock. The dinghy, driven by the wind, thumped softly and persistently against the hull. Rain slicked *Sunflower's* teak-planked deck.

The key went unwillingly into the lock, resisted, then turned. I eased the padlock out of the steel hasp, laid it with the keys on the deck, then took hold of both latches.

Then a bellowing roar made me twist round. I should have realised that the man and woman must have used another boat to reach *Sunflower*, which boat, to prevent suspicion, had left them aboard before going a safe distance away. Their accomplice on board that other boat had belatedly seen me, and now he was accelerating towards the rescue of his companions. The rescuer was a huge man, built like a prizefighter, who conned his small boat with a noticeable clumsiness. That boat was a small aluminium dory, flat bottomed and driven by a big outboard which was flinging water white to either side. The noise must have alerted the intruders, for the man's head reappeared in the companionway. I saw sleek black hair lying close to a narrow skull, then the man turned and stared in astonishment at me.

I had snatched a boathook from its rack on the cabin roof. I kept two boathooks there. One was for hooking boats or moorings, but the other, the one I seized, had a more specialised purpose. I had sharpened its spike to sail-needle sharpness, then ground a blade edge down the outer curve of the hook. That done I had hollowed out the head of the shaft

35

and weighted the weapon with lead. In effect I had made myself a miniature boarding pike that had proved its worth more than once. Any yacht in far waters is fair game for a thief, and a lone sailor had better take precautions or else he or she will end up as crabmeat. Now, in Salcombe's supposedly peaceful harbour, I swung the weighted blade, blunt side forward, at the black-haired man. He turned away from the blow, which nevertheless caught him on the back of his neck. It half felled him, or else he was already falling, for he disappeared down the companionway.

I was shouting, part in rage that the intruders had dared to break into *Sunflower*, and in part to scare the man. I scrambled over the liferaft and coachroof, then jumped down into the cockpit where I turned and held the boathook like a poised harpoon. The dory was slewing round, spraying water in a great curved sheet. The big man at its controls shouted incoherently at his companions on *Sunflower*. I could see the woman's legs in my cabin. She was sitting on the starboard bunk, but I could not see her male companion. "Stay there, you bastards!" I shouted. I planned to trap my intruders inside *Sunflower*, cow them into docility, then use the VHF to call the police. The man in the dory was having trouble controlling his boat, which was a blessing because I didn't fancy fighting a man of his height and weight.

I was about to go down into the cabin when the unlocked forehatch swung open and the black-haired man pulled himself lithely up on to the foredeck. He was thin. He had a suntanned countryman's face and was wearing a check shirt beneath a waxed cotton coat. He had a yellow waistcoat, brogues, and cavalry twill trousers. He was dressed for the racecourse rather than the water. The dory thumped alongside, ringing like a cracked bell on *Sunflower*'s steel hull. "Come on!" the helmsman shouted at his companion, "jump!"

I ran forward. The thin black-haired man did not jump into the dory, but turned to face me instead. He brushed at his tweed jacket, and somehow the commonplace gesture slowed my attack. Then he looked up at me. He had very confident eyes. He was a handsome man, perhaps in his late thirties, with a sardonic, knowing look about his narrow features. It was a face which suggested a long acquaintance-ship with human fallibilities, but it was also a face with an intrinsic air of command. "There's really no need to get excited," he said to me in a very condescending voice.

"What the hell are you doing on my boat?" I still advanced on him, but slowly now and with the boathook held out like a pike.

"I want to talk to you, of course." He had a very crisp voice; an unashamedly upper-class voice honed by public school and effortless confidence. "Shall we go below?"

"Only after you've paid for the damage you've done."

He smiled wearily. "We're going to be tedious, are we? And for God's sake stop pointing that hook at me."

The dory's helmsman, a much coarser creature than the thin man, still held on to *Sunflower*'s guardrails. He was bald, big, and was staring with concern at the threatening boathook, but the other had already dismissed the weapon's menace. He reached out with his right hand to fend off the hook. I resisted his gesture and, in sudden anger, he gripped the boathook's head to wrest it out of my hand.

He was surprisingly strong for such a thin man, but, a second after he had seized the hook, and while he was still pulling, his brain registered a stinging pain where he had expected none. I added to the pain by twisting the haft. Blood was spilling out of his hand now, dripping on to *Sunflower*'s deck. I saw the sudden agony on his face. He snatched his right hand away, dripping blood, then groped his left hand beneath his jacket to find a slim, long-bladed knife that had been sheathed at his belt. His larger companion was evidently uncertain whether to come to the thin man's aid or keep the dory alongside, so did nothing. I lunged, skewering the boathook's sharpened point into the thin man's upper arm. He swore, tried to fend the hook away with his knife, but I had swung it away and now hefted it hard back.

He had taken enough and scrambled desperately over the guardrails. He was too slow to escape my swing and the weighted boathook caught him on the back of his head as he jumped. Blood was bright in his black sleek hair. He fell

37

against the big man who let go of *Sunflower*. The dory rocked alarmingly. I ran forward, raised the hook, and slammed it down, hoping to ram it clean through the aluminium hull. Instead I punctured a spare petrol can which began adding its fuel to the blood in the dory's scuppers.

The thin man, whom I'd wounded, was much more alert than his big companion. He threw himself at the dory's controls and rammed the throttle into reverse. The engine roared, the boat scuttled backwards like a frightened crab, and the big man nearly fell overboard.

"Bastards!" I shouted. The thin man just stared at me. Blood glistened on his waxed coat. I had hurt him, and his eyes told me that he was not a man to forget or forgive a defeat. But let him hate, I thought, because in a week's time I'd be sailing south and he could whistle his enmity at the waning moon. I watched as he pushed the dory's motor into forward gear. He was a better helmsman than his companion, and I suspected that the thin man was capable at most things he turned his hands to. He had that kind of confidence about him, but he had failed with me. I raised two fingers at him as the small boat accelerated away between the moored yachts, then the two men vanished among the moorings, leaving behind only a haze of blue exhaust smoke and a smear of bright blood on a boathook's head.

And a woman. They had left the woman behind.

So now I went to find her.

"Bloody hell." For a second I was too shocked to move, then I swung myself down the companionway.

The girl lay on my starboard bunk where the thin man had evidently gone to work on her. There was blood on her face, chest, and hands. She was wearing a woollen skirt, a blouse, and a sweater. The sweater was in remnants and the blouse bloodstained and torn. On the companionway were the tattered fragments of her raincoat which looked as if it had been torn apart by dogs. She stared at me with whimpering, scared eyes.

The bastard had also gone to work on *Sunflower*. He'd ripped her cabin to shreds, but that could wait.

"Who are you?" I was pumping water from the freshwater tank into an unbroken cup.

The girl did not answer. Her hands tried to pull the scraps of her torn sweater together.

I knelt beside her and she flinched away.

"For God's sake," I said, "I'm trying to help you. Now stay still."

I don't think I reassured her, instead I think the abruptness of my tone merely scared her into compliance. Whatever, she did not move as I used a cleanish scrap of rag to wipe the blood from her face. She shuddered when the rag first touched her skin, then seemed to accept that I was helping her.

"Nothing's broken," I said, which meant that her nose was still in one piece. The blood had come from a nosebleed, but that had stopped. One of her cheekbones was badly grazed, but the damage was really very slight, except to her nerves. I did not know about her ribs, nor was I about to investigate. The thin man had half stripped her to the waist, but I was not going to inflict a similar indignity on her. "What did he do to you?" I asked.

"He threatened me with a knife," she managed to say, "then hit me." Her voice was wavering and scared, and no wonder for she was still rigid with shock.

"Only hit you?" I asked. "Nothing else?"

She nodded firmly. "Nothing else." Meaning she hadn't been sexually assaulted. "He said I'd come to make an arrangement with you, and when I wouldn't tell him more, he tore my clothes." She had barely been able to articulate the last words, which came out as sobs. "There was nothing to tell!" she protested to me, to the whole boat, then began to shiver violently. I pulled a sleeping bag from the mess on the cabin floor and draped it round her shoulders. She shrank away from my touch. I was almost as shocked as the girl. The violence of the thin man was so gratuitous and unexpected, but any explanations would have to wait till the girl had recovered some of her composure.

"Go into the forward cabin," I said firmly, "and clean yourself up. You'll find some sweaters in the drawers.

39

They're not very clean, they're a bit damp, but they're better than nothing."

She nodded again, but did not move. She was clutching the sleeping bag round her body with her bloodstained left hand. She was still sobbing, each exhalation a tiny whimper of pain.

"It's all right," I said, "I'm not going to hurt you." I deliberately backed away and sat on what was left of my portside bunk.

Still she did not move. She was struggling to subdue the sobs which slowly died away. She took some deep breaths and finally, when she felt she was once again in control of her voice, she asked if I was the Earl of Stowey.

The question was so unexpected, and so out of place, that I just gaped at her. She frowned at me. "Are you the Earl?" she asked me again, but this time with a tone of desperation as if her recovery from the ordeal depended on my answer.

"Yes, I am." Since my brother died I've been the twenty-eighth Earl of Stowey, but I prefer the anonymity of plain John Rossendale because a title isn't any damn use at sea. "But I don't use the title," I explained to her, "so just call me John, OK?" I rummaged through the mess on the cabin sole and found a bottle of antiseptic and a half-clean towel which I held out to her. "Why don't you go forward and clean yourself up? I'll make some tea." She went on staring at me. "Go on," I encouraged her.

She took the bottle and towel, but still did not move, so I climbed up the companionway steps into the cockpit as though I was making sure that the two men had gone. Nothing stirred in the harbour except the rain slithering across the grey water. Smoke rose from chimneys in the town. I heard the girl moving in the cabin below, then the click as she locked herself into the forecabin. I took my binoculars from their clip in the cockpit cave-locker and stared towards the town, but I could see no sign of the small aluminium dory. My intruder had disappeared.

I went below again and swore under my breath. The thin man had turned *Sunflower* inside out. He had forced locked doors open, then spilt the locker contents on to the sole. He'd torn up the sole and rummaged through the bilges. He'd broken the VHF. The radio's case looked as if it had been prised apart with a jemmy. I switched the set on, but nothing happened. The damage to the boat was not immense, but the cost of making the repairs would be painful. I cursed the bastard again; then, because I could not contemplate starting to clean up, I went topsides once more, turned on the gas at the aft locker, then went below and lit the gas hob. The small galley was about the only place on the boat which had escaped the thin man's attention, presumably because I had disturbed him before he could start its destruction. The chart table had been wrenched off its piano hinge and all my precious, rare charts were torn and crumpled. The sextant was safe, which was a blessing. It didn't seem as if anything had been stolen, but I could not be certain till I had searched the boat properly.

I made a strong pot of tea, mixed some powdered milk, and jammed up a leaf of the cabin table. I packed a pipe, lit it, then waited.

It was ten minutes before the girl came nervously out of the forecabin. She was wearing one of my Aran sweaters, which suited her. She had short black hair, dark eyes, and honey-brown skin. She had also, so far as I could tell, recovered her composure, though there was still a wariness in her expression.

"Tea," I greeted her. "The milk's reconstituted. Sugar?"

"No sugar." She picked her way across the wreckage of the cabin and nervously sat opposite me. "No milk either, please."

"Rum instead of milk?"

She shook her head, then brushed her fingers through her hair. I saw that she was pretty. Even with a cut face, frightened eyes, and a mucky damp sweater she was pretty.

"Did that bastard take the forecabin apart?" I asked.

"Not as badly as this cabin." She shuddered suddenly. "I was waiting for you in the cockpit when they arrived. There were two of them, but only one came aboard. I thought he was a friend of yours." She shivered again and momentarily closed her eyes. "Thank you for frightening him away."

"My pleasure." I put a mug of tea in front of her. "Sorry there's no lemon. Does the pipe smoke bother you?"

"No." She cradled the tin mug in both hands, found it too

41

hot, and quickly put it down. She glanced around the ransacked cabin, and grimaced. In the cold damp air *Sunflower*'s accommodation seemed dispiriting and drab. The girl took a deep breath, then looked across the table at me. "I'm Jennifer Pallavicini."

I did not respond. I had been half expecting her to tell me more about the thin man, but instead she had offered me the formal introduction, so I just smiled an acknowledgement.

"Doesn't the name mean anything to you?" There was a trace of indignation in her voice.

"Should it?"

"We've been writing to you for three years!"

I shrugged to show that none of her letters had reached me, then sipped my tea which I'd generously laced with rum. The heat of the liquid scalded the tender patch where the tooth had been drawn, and I winced. "Your letters are probably mouldering in General Deliveries all over the world. I'm sorry."

"We wrote care of your mother."

I half smiled. "I wasn't the favourite child. She never even sent me a birthday card, let alone other people's letters."

"So then we heard you'd come home for your mother's funeral," she continued, "and because you never replied to our letters, I was sent down to find you."

To her it all made sense; to me, none. My mother had never forwarded a letter to me, I had never heard of Jennifer Pallavicini, and I wondered how she had discovered that *Sunflower* was moored in Salcombe. I had also noted that she had been sent to find me, implying that she was merely a messenger. "Who sent you?" I asked.

She gave me an almost hostile look. It was clear that Miss Jennifer Pallavicini was recovering very swiftly from her encounter with the thin man. This was a tough girl, I suspected, and that realisation made me look more closely at her. There was a lot of character in my visitor's face; a face blended of intelligence, beauty and determination. A formidable girl, I thought, and not one to take lightly. "So?" I prompted her.

"I work for Sir Leon Buzzacott."

"Ah," I said neutrally, though in truth her answer made complete sense. Buzzacott was the rich man who had almost bought Stowey's Van Gogh, then been denied it. He had never hidden his bitter disappointment. Buzzacott, one of the City's most glittering financiers, had established his own art collection, the Buzzacott Museum Gallery, at his country house. He believed that too many of Britain's art treasures were crossing the Atlantic or going to the Japanese, and he had sworn to stop the haemorrhaging flow of paint. The Van Gogh had been his proudest acquisition, filling a great gap in his collection, and it evidently still rankled that the painting did not hang on his museum's wall.

"What exactly do you do for Sir Leon?" I asked.

"I'm the curator of nineteenth-century Europe." It seemed either a large task or an excessive boast; anyway, it made me smile, which annoyed her. "Damn you," she said.

"Damn me?" I was taken aback by the sudden hostility. I'd saved her from a worse beating, lent her clothes, made her tea, and now she was treating me like a piece of scum.

She closed her eyes in exasperation. "Sir Leon has never relinquished his hopes of acquiring the painting. Naturally a new price will have to be negotiated, but Sir Leon will match any offer you may receive. Indeed, my lord . . ."

"John," I interrupted her.

"Indeed, Mr Rossendale," she continued as though I hadn't spoken, "Sir Leon will accept any reasonable valuation which, in present market terms, must make the painting worth at least twenty million pounds."

It's easy to pretend not to care about money, to say that a blue-water sailor only needs enough cash to keep the rust out of the hull and to patch up the sails and to buy a few bottles of hooch and tins of stew. That derision of money is the chorus of the sea-gypsies; how we've escaped the vulgar greed of the world, how we even feel sorry for the pin-striped business executives rushing towards their bypass surgery because of the stress of making money, and we're so proud that we've escaped the love of the filthy stuff, and we profess not to care about it and even to despise it, but then along comes a dark-haired girl who casually says her employer is willing to lay out twenty of the big ones, and so I gaped at her and wondered if she was mad, or if I was going deaf. "Twenty?" I asked weakly.

"Millions," she said firmly.

"Wow." I grinned. I told myself that I didn't care about money, but twenty million smackeroos? The art world must have gone mad in the last four years. My mother had thought she had done well to negotiate a price of four million, and she'd been assured that was at least one million above the highest auction price. But twenty? At least twenty, Jennifer Pallavicini had said. "You could buy a lot of boat for twenty big ones," I said wistfully.

"You could indeed," she said icily.

"There's just one snag," I went on, "which is that I don't have the painting."

"But you know who does." It wasn't a question, but a statement. This girl, just like my sister and the rest of my family, was convinced of my guilt.

"No," I said gently, "I don't."

Jennifer Pallavicini sighed, as though I wilfully exasperated her. "Before she died," she said flatly, "your mother found evidence of your guilt. She told us as much. One of your accomplices confessed."

"Whoopee," I said, "except it isn't true."

"Your mother wished to confront you with that evidence" – she ignored my denial – "and to make one last appeal to you."

I leaned back. The washboards were out of their slots and rain was flicking down into the cabin. I rubbed my face and winced as I put pressure on my sore gum. I looked up at the barometer, which happily wasn't broken, and saw that the air pressure was rising. Too soon for me. I needed a few days to make my repairs, but as soon as the next depression had passed up-channel I'd use the backwash of northerly winds to take me away from England.

"And that man" – Jennifer Pallavicini shivered at the memory of the thin man – "told me you'd come home to sell the painting."

That caught my attention. "He said what?"

44

"That you'd come home to sell the painting. But he said it wasn't yours to sell."

I stabbed at the faltering tobacco in my pipe with a shackle-spike. "So if his argument was with me," I asked, "why go to work on you?"

She seemed to consider whether or not to answer, then gave a small shrug. "When he first came aboard he asked me if I knew anything about the painting and I was foolish enough to say I did. When I told him I worked for Sir Leon he wanted to know how much we were paying you for the painting, and just when you were going to produce it. I said we had no agreement, and he didn't believe me."

"So he beat you up?"

She paused, then nodded stiffly. "And I think he rather enjoyed doing it."

"I'm sorry," I said, but my sympathy only irritated her.

"The important thing," she said distantly, "is that at last we've succeeded in making contact with you. All that we now ask is that you deal with us rather than with anyone else."

I shook my head. "But I can't deal with you because I didn't steal the painting, and I don't know where it is."

"So you say."

That churlish answer tempted me to anger. It would have been easy to give in to the impulse, for I was tired and irritated, but on the other hand I was beginning to see that Jennifer Pallavicini was a very beautiful girl indeed, and it's astonishing how pretty girls can make men's manners. So I hid the anger.

Jennifer Pallavicini was collecting together the contents of her handbag, which the thin man had spilt across the bunk. "You should know," she said as she restowed her bag, "that the painting is legally your possession. Your mother's will can't change that."

I shrugged. "I haven't even read the will."

"She left the painting to your twin sister, but as your mother had already transferred its ownership to the Stowey Trust before your brother's death, then the legacy is unenforceable." She looked up at me. "In effect, my lord, you stole your own property."

45

I could feel a pulse throbbing in the pulpy place where my tooth had been prised out. Jennifer Pallavicini's words were reminding me of the dull responsibilities I had fled after the disappearance of the painting. The Stowey Trust was, in effect, the wealth of the Rossendale family, but formed into a trust to minimise taxes and death duties. These days the Trust was bankrupt, made so by the loss of the painting. However, the chief beneficiary of the Trust had always been the Earl of Stowey, which meant that if I had stolen the Van Gogh then I had indeed robbed myself. No one seemed to think that was an odd thing for me to do, probably because they were all convinced I was stupid as well as guilty.

"Sir Leon is willing to overlook any complicity of yours in the painting's disappearance if you'll now assist in its recovery," Jennifer Pallavicini told me.

"How very kind of him," I said.

She heard the scorn in my voice, and shrugged. "We're only trying to help you, my lord."

"Don't call me that!" Despite her looks, anger had snapped into my voice. I heard the sudden emotion and did not like it. "Listen," I said patiently, "my mother never had any proof that I stole the painting, because I didn't. If she did have such proof, then she should have gone to the police. I assume she didn't, because no policemen have paid me a call since I returned to England, so I suspect her proof was all imaginary. So go back to Buzzacott and tell him I didn't nick the painting, that I don't know where the thing is, and that I can't help him. Tell him that four years ago the police questioned me for two days, and didn't charge me because they knew they couldn't make a charge stick. In short I know nothing about the painting, and that's the end of the matter."

Jennifer Pallavicini didn't blink an eye at my denial. "Sir Leon is offering twenty million pounds for the painting, Mr Rossendale, payable in any currency you desire and in any country you choose." She paused for a response and, when I made none, went on. "You may take that as a negotiating position rather than as a final offer, Mr Rossendale."

In other words I could name my price for returning the painting, and the price would be paid far away from the prying eyes of the taxmen. The only fly in that ointment was that I hadn't stolen the Van Gogh in the first place and didn't know where it was. I was also angry at the continued accusations. Four years had not lessened anyone's greed for the canvas, nor their conviction that I had stolen it. Doubtless my mother had thought a deathbed appeal would make me reveal its whereabouts, while now Sir Leon Buzzacott had sent this attractive messenger to try and bribe the information from me. But I did not share their obsession with the picture, and I was offended by their accusations. I was also offended by Jennifer Pallavicini's patronising assumption of my guilt and, to show my irritation, I picked up her mug of tea and poured it down the sink drain. "Goodbye, Miss Pallavicini."

If she was startled by my action, she was too proud to show it. She gathered up her handbag. "You expect me to swim ashore, my lord?"

I rowed her. There was no sign of the aluminium dory nor of the two men. Jennifer Pallavicini said nothing during the journey, but it was clear she was not enjoying the ride. She had gone out to *Sunflower* in one of Salcombe's water taxis, but, without a VHF radio, I could not summon one for her return journey. Instead we rowed through the drizzle in sullen silence. She didn't speak until I had safely delivered her to the town's pontoon where, once she had clambered safely out of the inflatable, she turned back to me. "Where shall I return your sweater?"

"Take it to an Oxfam shop. I'm going back to sea."

For a second she was tempted to take off the Aran sweater and throw it contemptuously into the dinghy, but modesty and the rain prevailed. She turned away; then, surprisingly, turned back. "One last question, Mr Rossendale?"

"Try me."

Her dark eyes challenged me. "Why is your boat called *Sunflower*?"

"I bought her from a Frenchman. He called her *Tournesol*. It's bad luck to change a boat's name, so I simply translated it. In other words, Miss Pallavicini, the name is pure coincidence."

She stared down at me, evidently unsure whether to believe my explanation; then, without another word, turned away towards the town while I rowed back to *Sunflower*.

I sat in my wrecked cabin and tried to string a few explanations together. Sir Leon Buzzacott still wanted the painting; Sir Leon was convinced I had stolen it and could, therefore, betray its present whereabouts. My family had convinced him of that error by claiming to have proof of my guilt.

Fine, except I wasn't guilty. No accomplice of mine could have confessed, because there had been no accomplices. I suspected that my mother, convinced of my guilt, had invented the tale.

Which didn't explain the two men, or why the well-spoken thin man had wrecked *Sunflower*'s cabin. From what he had told Jennifer Pallavicini he clearly believed that I had the painting and was about to sell it. Had he believed I had the thing concealed in *Sunflower*? Did he think I'd hide twenty million quid's worth of paint and canvas in a sea-locker? And who had told him I might have it? And what had he meant by saying that the painting wasn't mine to sell? Jennifer Pallavicini had said the painting was mine, but Mother's will evidently tried to deny me the ownership. The disagreement had all the makings of a fine lawyer's stew, which meant that I should get the hell out of it. I've learned a few good lessons in life: always shorten sail when the first impulse occurs, never sail upwind unless desperate, and never, never, never give a lawyer a fingerhold on your affairs.

And this wasn't my affair. I didn't have the painting, didn't want the painting, and didn't care about my mother's will. The thin man, Jennifer Pallavicini, and anyone else who believed I had the Van Gogh, was mistaken. So the best thing I could do was forget I'd ever been offered twenty million pounds and sail away to the blue waters.

But first there was work to do. I did a crude clean-up in the cabin, and began an inventory of what had been broken and what had not. Most of my tools and clothes, which had been stored with the spare sails in the forecabin, had been scattered about, though, blessedly, my visitor had not used his knives to search my sailbags. Undoubtedly he would have torn the sails to shreds, given time, but my unexpected return had frustrated him. The thin man had found no evidence of the Van Gogh, because there wasn't any to find, nor, thank God, had he found my subsistence money. The cash, in a variety of different countries' banknotes, was stored in a grease tin which, in turn, lay with other such battered and filthy tins in the tool tray next to the engine. No one would give the tin a second glance. But then, the thin man hadn't been after money, just a twenty million pound painting, and he hadn't found it.

But nor had he finished his search, and if he really did believe the Van Gogh was on board, then he might very well return to *Sunflower*. That thought gave me pause.

I decided that hunger was a great feeder of fear, so I found a tin of stew, a tin of new potatoes, and a tin of corned beef. I mashed the whole lot together, then heated the mixture over the stove. I sat in the cockpit and wolfed the meal down. It tasted wonderful. My gum was still tender, but the pain of the tooth was blessedly absent.

Yet the meal hardly diminished the scale of my problems. First, I had only a limited amount of money, and the repairs to *Sunflower* would take a great deal of that reserve. I'd be lucky to be left with fifty pounds, and that was not nearly sufficient to victual her for the long journey south. So, I needed a place where I could do most of the repairs myself and I needed a job to make some quick cash. I also wanted to hide from the two men; not because I feared them, but because I wanted no part of their hunt for the missing picture. Four years ago I had sailed away from all those complications, and I would be damned if I would let myself be sucked back into that maelstrom of greed and suspicion.

No one tried to board *Sunflower* that night. Which did not mean that either I or she was safe. I needed a hiding place, a job, and somewhere to make my repairs and, with the expedient neatness that sometimes characterises our unexpected needs, I knew just where I might find all three. I slept uneasily, woke early, and sailed in the dawn.

*   *   *

The weather had cleared overnight. The estuary, even at dawn, was filled with sails. Three Salcombe yawls, pretty little wooden boats, hissed past me as I hanked on the jib and staysail. A big French sloop, loaded to the gunwales with what seemed to be a dozen fecund families, made a noisily joyful exit. The sun was making the sails open on the water like unfolding white petals. My grey battered sails joined them.

The wind was back in the southwest. I motored *Sunflower* as far as the bar which, this morning, was a pussy cat. There was scarcely a ripple where, just a few days before, I'd plunged suicidally through the cascading white water. Once in the outer channel I turned off the motor and let *Sunflower* fall on to a starboard tack. The sea glittered under the rising sun. After the sordid events of the previous day it felt wonderful to be at sea again. A big white catamaran with a cabin the size of a townhouse passed me. A bearded man at her wheel shouted a genial "Good morning!" He had a startlingly pretty long-haired girl with him. She waved at me, and her friendly greeting suddenly curdled my high spirits like water poured into oil.

I like my life. I like the moment when, after departure, I can turn back and see nothing but the empty sea. Perhaps a ridge of cloud marks where the retreating land lies, but soon, I know, there will be nothing. From that moment on I am beholden to no one, responsible only to myself, and dependent only on my own boat and my own strength. There are no lawyers at sea; no accountants, no estate office, no family, no expectations, no tenants, no creditors, no tax assessors, no bank managers, no stockbrokers, no land agents. Those were the dark-suited creatures I had fled. After my brother's death I had been called home to become head of the family and Earl and Lord of Stowey, but instead I had found myself trapped between my mother's grinding ambitions and the dull, dull strictures of the men in suits. His lordship must sign this document, and his lordship should consider the tax advantages of deferring this dividend, and his lordship must meet urgently with the revenue or the bank manager, and on it went until his lordship told them that he didn't give a monkey's. To this day, when some petty bureaucrat gives me grief, I tell him to go to hell. The first Earl of Stowey was a Norman who took the land with the edge of his sword, and I would be damned if I would be hag-ridden to death by a pin-striped army of bores. I went back to sea to escape them.

And, till this return, I had avoided them. But there had been a price for that evasion, and the price was loneliness. I watched the pretty girl in the big catamaran and I felt a stab of self-pity. I hated that sensation. My God, but I'd chosen my path, and I had better stick to it, or else the world would mock my failure. That was pride, but I was a proud man. I might not like being called 'my lord', but the blood in my veins had been old when England was young. So damn the loneliness. It could always be assuaged. There would always be some empty-eyed girl, bag slung on her shoulder, waiting at a tropical quayside. It only took a nod, the girl would climb on board, and that was that till boredom or irritation dissolved the liaison. There were no ties in such relationships; no mortgages, no screaming children, no slow grinding tedium; just company.

I tacked. We were well off Bolt Head now. The sea was spattered with yachts; many, like me, heading westwards. I was not going far; just down the Devon coast. Nor was I hurrying. I lashed the tiller, then went below where I buttered a piece of bread and made a flask of tea. I breakfasted in the cockpit as terns dive-bombed the sea. There was a gentle swell, a small chop, and a steady wind. *Sunflower* was fairly tight on the breeze, but she held her course well. She bridled sometimes, threatening to luff, and occasionally, as a steeper chop slapped the hull, some of the wreckage would rattle down below.

Once clear of Bolt Tail I turned a few points to the north and *Sunflower* seemed to ease up. She was enjoying herself now, and I felt the urge to turn her bows towards the open ocean and let her sail far far away. But first I had to repair her, because only then could the two of us go back where we belonged.

By midday, under a brassy brilliant sun, we were sailing

into Plymouth Sound. We passed Drake's Island, heading for the Hamoaze. This was naval and commercial water, slicked with oil, as romantic as a sludge pump, yet out of here had sailed all the ships of English history; the *Victory* and the *Mayflower*, the *Revenge* and the *Golden Hind*.

Yet the place I sought had neither grandeur nor history, but only the hopelessness of decay. It was a boatyard consisting of a slip, a grubby dock, an empty grid, a filthy quay, a workshop, a warehouse, and a forlorn office. A few workboats were tied at the quay, but all looked ready for the scrapyard. No work seemed to be going on in the yard, though I saw an old green Jaguar parked by the offices which suggested that someone was minding the shop. After four years I'd half expected to find the old yard sold, but it was still here; a monument to sloth and carelessness.

I moored *Sunflower* to a decrepit fishing boat, then climbed a rusting ladder to the dock. A woman's bicycle leaned beside the office door which had a piece of hardboard nailed across the space where a pane of glass had evidently been broken. A similar repair disfigured the door at the top of the stairs. I pushed the door open, astonishing the secretary who sat behind the ancient desk. I blew her a kiss. "You're still here, Rita?"

"God love me!" Rita was a dim, good-natured girl who spent her days reading True Romance magazines. There was no other work for her to do in the yard except make the tea and answer the phone. "Johnny? Is it really you?"

"It's really me." I took her hand, made an elaborate bow, and kissed a painted fingernail. "Is the old sod in?"

"He's probably asleep." She stared at me. "You haven't half got a suntan!" Then, remembering something, she dutifully frowned. "I saw it in the papers about your mother. I am sorry, John."

I shrugged, as though I was unable to articulate my own sorrow, then pushed open the door to the inner office.

George Cullen started awake with a splutter. He tried to pretend that he had been working, and at the same time offered me a hurt look as though I'd offended him by not knocking, then, blinking fully awake, he recognised me. He smiled, decided a smile was not appropriate, and stood to offer me a hand. "My lord!"

"It's Johnny to you," I said, "and how are you, you old fraud?"

He shook my hand. "Johnny." He said it tentatively, as though trying the name out, though he'd known me as nothing else since I'd been thirteen. Still, George was one of those men who liked to know a peer. "Johnny," he said again, this time with pleasure as though he truly was glad to see me. "Quite a surprise! You'll have a glass of something with an old friend, won't you?"

He produced a bottle of Scotch which had a label I'd never seen before and hope never to see again. In Mozambique, which is a destination I would not recommend to passing yachtsmen, I had drunk from a bottle which purported to be Scotch. It was called 'Sbell', and bore a very poor copy of a Bells label. Sbell whisky was a drink for a desperate man, though it made an excellent all-purpose solvent. George's Scotch was of the same order. I took a sip, then grimaced. "Where on earth did you get this muck, George?"

"It was a business gift, Johnny. From an associate."

"Bloody hell." I drank it anyway, then held out my glass for more.

George refilled my glass. He's an affable crook. He looks as bent as any front-bench politician, what with his beer belly, jowly face, and small suspicious eyes, but he has a great taste for gossip and a healthy fear of the prison yard. He had inherited this Hamoaze boatyard from his father, but the yard didn't do real business any more. George's income came from fencing items thieved from boats. The police must have known about him, so the only explanation for his continued liberty must have been that he was grassing on someone. I'd known George for twenty-one years. I used to spend my holidays working in the yard. Back then there had still been a semblance of industry at Cullen's Boats, but that pretence seemed to have been long dropped.

He waddled to the window and stared down at *Sunflower*. "Been far in her, Johnny?"

"Round the world, George."

"Have you now?" He gazed at her as he stuffed his pipe with tobacco. "I've always fancied sailing round the world. Never had the chance, of course. Too busy."

George couldn't make it past Plymouth Breakwater in a gin palace, let alone sail round the world, but I smiled politely. He shrugged, then hospitably offered me his tobacco pouch. "Just visiting, are you, Johnny?"

I shook my head. "I want your grid for a couple of days, and what's left of your workshop."

"Of course, Johnny, of course. I'll have to check that no one's booked in, of course, but . . ."

"Shut up, George. Of course no one's booked in. And don't worry, I'll earn my keep."

"Ah." George frowned. I suppose he had been expecting me to offer him cash, while now I was suggesting that he paid me for odd jobs, but his cupidity was beaten by his snobbishness. A lord was a lord, even if he was penniless. George lit his pipe, then went back to his littered desk. "We'll work something out, Johnny."

"And I want something else, George."

He heard the wariness in my voice and matched it with his own. "Something else?"

"I don't want anyone to know I'm here."

George might be a sluggish old toad, but he has a nose for mischief. He slumped down in his padded chair. "The police again, Johnny?"

"Not the police. A couple of bastards think I've got something. They came looking for it yesterday, and they might come looking again. So I don't want them to know where I am."

"Anyone I know?"

I described the two men as I filled my pipe with George's black shag. I couldn't give much of a description of the big balding man who had helmed the dory, but I offered an excellent description of the thin man who had such a crisp public school accent.

"Garrard," George interrupted me when I mentioned the thin man's voice.

"Garrard?"

54

"Trevor Garrard. Used to be in the army. A right posh villain, he is. Was he carrying a knife?"

"Yes."

"That's Garrard, then. You don't have to worry about his mate, he's just a thick lump of muscle, nothing more, but you should watch Garrard. He's nasty." I was not in the least surprised that George knew the two men because there was very little villainy in the Southwest that George did not know about. "Garrard was cashiered out the army," George went on, "then he got snared by the Fraud Squad, so now he's a winkler. He did a bit of bookie's business at one time, but I don't suppose he dares show his face on a racecourse these days. He was too violent, you see, and the coppers got a line on him, so nowadays he's mostly a winkler."

"A Winkler?" I asked, wondering if the Winklers were a notorious family of criminals.

George poured himself more whisky. "A winkler," he said with plump dignity, "is a rent-control operative."

"Come again, George?"

He sighed. "Suppose you've got a property, Johnny, and there's a sitting tenant in it, paying you a lousy rent, and the law won't let you turf the useless bugger out. But you're losing money on the property and you want to put another tenant inside who'll pay you a proper rent. So what do you do? You can't hire another bleeding lawyer, because you'll get the same answer, so you hire yourself a winkler. Things begin to happen to your tenant. Nasty things. The water gets shut off, rats take up residence, and perhaps half the roof falls in. Their pussy cats get strangled and their car tyres get slashed. The tenant eventually gets fed up, moves out, and you pay the winkler for his services. He's winkled them out, you see." He added this last explanation helpfully.

"You know this fellow, Garrard?" I asked.

"Not personally" – George was being evasive now – "but I know he's done some jobs for local businessmen. He comes from Bristol, I think. Ronny's from London, but he's not such a bad lot."

"Ronny's the bald one?"

George nodded. "Ronny Peel. He'd beat you into pulp if

55

he was told to, but he's not an animal, know what I mean? But that Garrard" – George shook his head worriedly – "I wouldn't touch him, Johnny. He's trouble."

"I don't want to touch him. I just don't want him to know where I am."

"I'll keep quiet," he promised, and I believed the promise because George's criminality does not extend to violence; in fact he probably hates the sight of blood. Besides, George and I go back a long way. In the faraway past he'd given me a refuge from my family and, in his lackadaisical way, he had introduced me to boats. It was in this shabby yard that I'd learned to weld steel and work wood. It was here that I'd found my first proper job as a crew member on an ocean-going yacht. George had known me a long time, which by itself did not guarantee any favours, but I was also John Frederick Albert Rossendale, the twenty-eighth Earl of Stowey, and that helped. It shouldn't have helped, but it did. So now, because of George's aristocratic tastes, *Sunflower* and I were safe.

I had been wrong about needing George's grid for a couple of days. More like a couple of weeks. Once I got *Sunflower* out of the water I saw just how sorry her hull was: the poor thing looked more like a floating compost heap than a yacht. It was no wonder she'd been so sluggish crossing the Atlantic. I should have anti-fouled her in America or the Caribbean, but I'd been reluctant to pay American prices for anti-fouling paint.

But, by waiting, I had forced myself to do more than just anti-foul *Sunflower*. In places the old paint had abraded right back to its epoxy pitch base. What I really needed to do was strip the whole hull back to bright steel, then start again. I should have craned her out of the water, screened her off, and done what Charlie would have called a proper job, except I had neither the time nor the money to be so thorough.

Instead I would have to do the best I could on George's grid. A grid is simply a raised platform on which a boat can be stranded as the tide falls. At mean low tide, in George's yard, *Sunflower* would be perched about eight feet above the water and, between tides, I would have around seven hours to work on her before the rising flood forced me to stop. I'd thus be needing a whole series of low tides. She was well berthed to the quay, but to stop her toppling sideways into George's mucky dock I took a half-inch line from her upper spreaders and tied it to a ringbolt on the outside wall of his workshop. I knotted red rags round the rope and put a large sign by the ringbolt: 'Leave this rope alone!' I'd once watched a beautiful Danish ketch fall twelve feet off a grid in Brittany. It wasn't pretty.

I fired up George's ancient compressor, stripped myself to the waist, and hitched up his sand-blaster. Or rather sludge-blaster, for I couldn't afford to buy the proper sand so had to make do with a miserable pile that mouldered damply behind the warehouse. The diesel fuel which fired the compressor also came from George's stock, and was fouled. Even when I managed to make the compressor work, the damp sand clotted and jammed the hopper's throat every few minutes, so progress, at best, was fitful. I used the enforced pauses to slap a rust-preventing resin on to the newly cleaned patches of *Sunflower*'s hull. Between later tides I would strip the resin, then slap on a holding primer, four coats of epoxy tar, one coat of anti-fouling primer and two coats of the anti-fouling. It would be mind-numbing work, but if I did it well enough then the hull would be protected from rust for the next ten years. When the rising tide forced me to abandon work on the hull I went inside the cabin where I was beginning to rebuild the damaged lockers. I made good progress, but still my grease tin of money was taking a beating.

I needed cash. That was ironic, considering Jennifer Pallavicini had been dangling twenty million pounds in front of me, while now my hopes of earning a few quid from George were clearly ill-founded for his yard was utterly bare of work. "Why do you keep it on?" I asked him.

"Gives me something to do, Johnny. Gets me away from the wife," he chuckled. He was standing beside the compressor, watching me work. The hopper's throat had just choked up and, before I dug the soggy sand free, I was wiping resin on to the bright steel of *Sunflower*'s hull. "And there's the other side of it," George went on.

"I hadn't forgotten." The other side of it was the stolen merchandise that went through his warehouse. George specialised in bent chandlery; forcibly retired Decca sets or radios.

"Mind you," he said, "I've been thinking of selling out. The leisure market's on the way up, and someone could make a nice little bundle by turning the yard into a yacht-servicing business."

"Why not you, George?"

"I'm not a well man, Johnny." I'd forgotten how George was always suffering from some new and undiagnosable ailment.

"So the yard's for sale?"

He shrugged. "For the right price. It's prime riverside property, after all." He gestured about the yard as though he was selling a stretch of the St Tropez waterfront rather than a scabby junk heap mouldering around a smelly dock. "Are you interested, Johnny?"

"Me?" I laughed. "Just painting *Sunflower* will clean me out, not to mention rebuilding your equipment." I scrambled up to the dock and tried to restart the compressor, but the water in George's diesel fuel wouldn't drive the engine. I swore, knowing I would have to siphon the fuel and clean the system. It was my own fault, of course, for using George's yard. If I'd had the money I'd have paid to have *Sunflower* properly shot-blasted, but instead this old sand-blaster would have to suffice.

George watched me bleed the compressor's fuel line. "Johnny," he said after a bit.

"George?" I spat watery diesel into the dock.

"That painting . . ." He paused. He must have known that my trouble with Garrard had been caused by the Van Gogh, but this was the first time he had mentioned it. "Did they ever pin it on you?"

"If they had, George, do you think I'd be here? I'd be in the Scrubs, slopping out shit pails."

He considered that answer and evidently found it convincing. "Of course," he said, "now that your mother's dead, I suppose the painting belongs to you?"

"Not according to her will. She left it to my sister." I said it to discourage George's speculation, though I suspected that Jennifer Pallavicini was right and that the painting, if it could ever be recovered, was probably mine. Twenty million pounds, and all mine, except, of course, that if the painting ever did reappear there would be a salivating horde of lawyers and taxmen scrabbling to get their slices of the money. But even those rapacious bastards would find it hard to destroy all of twenty million.

"It must be worth a penny or two." George must have been guessing my thoughts.

"Several million pennies, George."

"How much?"

I straightened up from the engine. "Sir Leon Buzzacott offered twenty million quid the other day, which means it's probably worth a bit more."

George puffed at his pipe. He clearly wasn't certain whether to believe me. In his line of business a good night's work yielded a few thousand, not millions. "I don't like paintings," he said eventually. "I used to deal in a few. Rubbish, most of them. Seascapes, that sort of thing, but it was never worth the bother." He shrugged, evidently regretting some past escapade. "Those two fellows," George went on, "do you think they're after the painting?"

"Of course they're after the painting. So is Sir Leon Buzzacott. So is my twin sister. Half the damn world wants the thing, but all I want is some clean diesel fuel. Have you got any?"

He shook his head, dismissing the problem of the contaminated fuel. "So you could be a millionaire, Johnny?"

"I told you. It belongs to my sister. Now bugger off, George, I'm trying to work."

He buggered off and I worked on the compressor till five o'clock when I climbed to Rita's office where a cup of tea waited for me. I telephoned Charlie's house, but he still hadn't returned from Hertfordshire. "Is there a number in Hertfordshire?" I asked Yvonne. She said there was, but that Charlie was never there. She said he telephoned her when he needed to, but she gave me the number anyway. She sounded desperately tired. I asked her to tell Charlie that I was now at George Cullen's boatyard. She promised she would, but she didn't sound very friendly as she made the promise.

I tried the Hertfordshire number. It was the site office of a construction company and a gruff man said he hadn't seen Charlie Barratt for two days. I put the phone down. "What the hell's Charlie doing in Hertfordshire?" I asked Rita, more in frustration than in any hope of fetching an answer.

She blew on her newly-painted fingernails. "He's a big man now, Charlie is. He's ever so rich."

"And I'm the Pope." I knew Charlie had done well since he'd settled back home, but Rita's awed tones seemed to be over-egging the pudding.

"He is," she insisted. "Plant hire. You name it and Charlie's got it. Artics, tippers, cranes, earth-movers, bull-dozers." Rita shrugged. "He's got ever such a nice boat, too."

"A yacht?"

She shook her head. "A big cabin cruiser. It's got one of those thingummyjigs on the front."

I tried to guess what a thingummyjig was. "A radar aerial?"

"A hot tub," she remembered. "It's ever so smart. He brought it down here last year."

Charlie clearly had done well. When I'd left England he had been the owner-operator of an ancient Commer lorry; yet now, if Rita hadn't confused him with anyone else, his business had flourished. I was pleased for, if any man deserved success, it was Charlie. He had always been a hard worker, and had a slew of practical skills to work with. When we had been boys, he and I had worked together in George Cullen's yard and even at fourteen Charlie had shown the practical skills of an adult. His schoolteachers, naturally, had written him off as a dumb peasant, but Charlie had always been too smart to let any teacher meddle with his ambitions.

I finished my tea, went back downstairs, and stripped down the compressor's fuel system. By nightfall I had it working, ready for the morning. It was what Charlie would have called a proper job and, to celebrate it, I poured a glass of George's ghastly whisky, made myself a mushy stew, then slept.

I woke at one o'clock.

At first I thought it was the ebbing tide dropping *Sunflower*'s keel on to the grid that had woken me; then, in the tiny light leaking through the companionway, I saw the time and realised it was only twenty-three minutes away from low tide which meant that *Sunflower* must have been stranded on the grid for at least four hours. I listened for whatever had woken me. I could only hear the halliards slapping the mast, the wind sighing at the spreaders, and the slop of river water in George's dock. Everything seemed normal, but nevertheless something had disturbed me. In a night watch, in the middle of an ocean, the slightest change of *Sunflower*'s sound or motion would bring me to wakefulness, and something, even in the safe haven of George's dock, had just triggered that alarm system. I reached out for the light switch, then froze.

The gate to George's yard squealed. I realised that it had been that same creak of unoiled hinges that had woken me. It was a sound that always made me alert, even in daytime. I wanted to be left alone in George's yard, and whenever I heard the squeal of the hinges I would warily make sure that the visitor was not some unwelcome person from my past. Now, in the depths of the night, I had been woken by the warning sound. I left the cabin unlit, rolled out of the bunk, and pulled on a pair of jeans.

I had been sleeping with the companionway open, so I made no noise as I slipped up to the cockpit. By standing on a thwart I could just see over the sill of the quayside.

A dark-painted van, with no lights, was being driven slowly into George's yard. I did not move. It was possible, even likely, that these were some of George's friends who had permission to use his warehouse. The van was probably loaded with stolen goods. The only reason I was suspicious was that George had not given me any warning. Usually, when some mayhem was imminent, he would tell me not to worry if I heard something go bump in the night.

The van braked to a halt. Its motor was cut.

I slid my special boathook out of its brackets.

The van's front doors opened quietly. Two men climbed out. George always left a light burning outside his office door and, in its glow, I could see that one of the men was burly and bald, the other thin, commanding, and black-haired. It was Garrard and Peel, who now stood beside the van staring to where *Sunflower*'s masts reared above the grid. And how the hell, I wondered, had they found me? It had to be George. Doubtless he had done a favour to someone by betraying my whereabouts, and I promised myself that I'd kick his fat hide to kingdom come when I had the chance. I supposed it was my own fault for telling George that the painting was worth at least twenty million quid. George's cupidity must have overwhelmed his love of a lord.

The two men would have seen me if I'd tried to climb up over the quay. I did not want them to see me. They thought I

62

was fast asleep, and I wanted them to continue in that blissful ignorance. I glanced towards *Sunflower*'s dark cabin, wondering whether I had time to fetch my rigging knife, but knew I dared not waste a second.

For to hesitate would be to trap myself. The two men were already walking softly towards *Sunflower* as I slid over her stern and lowered myself to the grid. The water was black beneath me. I could hear the men's footsteps as I lowered myself again, this time into the black, filthy, and freezing water. I shivered, then pushed away from the grid's piles towards one of the decrepit fishing boats at the end of the small dock. The weighted boathook tried to drag me down, but I did not have far to go, and the impetus of my push carried me to the dock's side wall where a rusty ring gave me a handhold. I pushed on again, this time hiding in the impenetrable shadow between the fishing boat and the wall.

A torch beam slashed down into the dock, flicked across the water, then settled on *Sunflower*. The beam was dazzling for a few seconds, then was switched off. I was struggling forward, ducking under the thick tyres which George used as fenders. I needed to round the dock's corner to the river wall where an iron ladder climbed to the quayside.

I heard one of the men drop down on to *Sunflower*'s deck. The torch was switched on again. They had abandoned stealth by now, but their bird was flown, planning his own ambush. I was hurrying for I did not want to give the two men time to search *Sunflower*, and thus undo all my repair work. I cleared the fishing boat, hauled myself forward on its bow mooring rope and turned the corner into the tug of the tide's current. For a second I feared I would be swept downstream by this last feeble ebb, but I lunged the boathook forward and managed to snag one of the ladder's rungs. The hook made a dull clunking noise, but the two men were making enough noise of their own, and did not hear me. They were talking. The noise I feared was the splintering sound as they began to search *Sunflower*'s half-repaired cabin, but so far they only talked.

I climbed the ladder's rusted rungs. The torch beam slashed over my head like the loom of a lighthouse. I froze.

"The bastard's gone." That was Garrard's distinctive voice. I heard him grunt as he hauled himself back to the quay's top. "Try the office."

I heard the office door rattle, but it was locked and the big bald man made no attempt to force it. The torch beam began circling the yard again. I climbed to the top of the ladder, waited till the light was probing the rubbish tip behind the warehouse, then rolled into the shadow of one of the many junk piles which littered George's yard.

I would have preferred it if the two men had been on board *Sunflower*, for then, given the advantage of the quayside, I would have been above them. I'd contemplated trapping them there and, using the boathook as a weapon, forcing some answers from them. Instead both men were roaming the yard. I thought that if I stayed motionless they might abandon the search and leave me in peace. It wasn't that I was scared of a fight, but there's no point in fighting superior odds unless it's really necessary, and so I stayed still.

Garrard stayed by *Sunflower* and told Peel where to search. The bald man thus clambered futilely about George's yard while Garrard idled on the quay above my boat. And while he idled he discovered the rope that I'd tied from the upper spreaders to the ringbolt.

Garrard had a smaller torch and, in its light, he examined the bow and stern ropes and the spring lines, then flashed the beam up to trace the rope that was taut at the spreaders. He walked to the workshop wall and tugged on the rope and he saw how the added tension dragged the mast towards him. He tested the rope again, and I knew what was passing through his evil mind. Without that tether, *Sunflower*'s balance would be very precarious. She was resting on her long, deep keel and, though she weighed a good few tons, it would not take much effort to unbalance her. It was just about low tide and, with one good push, she would fall like a truck into the shallow waters eight feet below her. Her mast would break and God knew what other damage would be done.

Garrard plucked down my notice which warned no one to touch the rope and tore it into two. I tensed, ready to charge at him, but instead of drawing his knife and slashing the rope he lit a cigarette and leaned against the workshop wall. It seemed he had no intention of destroying *Sunflower*, just as, strangely, he showed no sign of wanting to search her. It appeared the two men had only one interest this night: finding me.

"Bugger's gone." Peel trudged disconsolately into view.

They spoke softly for a minute or two, too softly for me to hear anything they said. Both their torches raked once more round the yard, the beams scything over my head, but for some reason neither man searched the low heap of metal behind which I was hidden. They did shine their torches down into the moored boats, but it was clear they had given up any hope of finding me.

"Fetch the van," Garrard said.

Peel started the van and switched on its headlights. In the strong light I could see Garrard was dressed in his horsy cavalry twill, waistcoat and tweed jacket. I could also see that his right hand was bandaged from the savaging I'd given it with the boathook. He looked like the kind of man I used to know well: loud-voiced and confident, always to be found at a racecourse where he'd have known the stable lad of an unfancied horse in the third race which was worth a bob or two on the nose. Such men had knowing eyes and bitter resentments. They could be good companions for an afternoon, but not for longer.

Peel put the van into gear. The bandage on Garrard's right hand was not inconveniencing him for, almost casually, he drew his knife and reached up to *Sunflower's* tethering rope. The knife must have been razor sharp, for it sliced through the half-inch rope without any apparent effort.

I tensed again in sudden flaring panic.

I could see, in the van's headlights, that *Sunflower* had not moved. I had her leaning towards the dock, which offered a margin of safety, but my heart was flogging like a wet sail in a headwind all the same. Garrard watched her, half expecting to see the yacht crash down into the Stygian blackness beneath, but she stayed upright. He crushed his cigarette under his right shoe, opened the passenger door, and the van drove away.

I waited. The van disappeared behind the workshop. I heard the yard gates open, the van growl through, then the gates crash shut. I listened as the van drove up the street, paused at the main road junction, then accelerated away.

Silence.

The wind was lifting the cut rope into the night, but *Sunflower*, good *Sunflower*, was stable and solid.

I stood up slowly. I was freezing cold. I was wearing nothing but one pair of sodden jeans and my muscles were stiff as boards. I took the wet jeans off, walked to the quayside, and tossed them down into *Sunflower*'s cockpit. This was no time to be worrying about being naked, my priority was to retrieve that flying rope and rerig it, and that, I knew, would take some careful work.

The rope was cut, so I needed some more to make its length good. George had some old rope lying in the yard, but I did not trust it. Instead, and taking exquisite care not to upset *Sunflower*'s precarious balance, I lowered myself into her cockpit. I stayed on the dockside gunwales, adding my weight to her stability. In a cave-locker in the cockpit I had some spare warps. I found one and tossed it up to the quay, then, still staying hard by the dock wall, I groped with the boathook for the rope's bitter end.

The wind was carrying the cut rope away from me, out over the dark waters of the dock. I reached for the errant line with the boathook's full length, but the weighted head made the implement much too unwieldy for such a delicate job. I slotted the heavy boathook back into place and pulled out the other one. That did the job quickly, snagging the wind-whipped rope-end that I drew towards me. I held on to it as I climbed back to the quayside.

It took five minutes to disentangle the rope from where it had blown itself about the shrouds. The wind dried me as I worked, but I was still bitterly cold.

I tied the cut rope to my spare warp with a sheet bend, then made a lorryman's hitch in the warp. I threaded the loose end through the ringbolt, back through the hitch's loop, then hauled it tight. I felt *Sunflower*'s mast come towards me as the rope took her weight. I made two turns and hitches to make the whole thing fast, then let out my breath. *Sunflower* was secure again.

"Clever boy," said Trevor Garrard.

I turned.

He was no more than five paces from me. He held the knife loosely in his bandaged right hand, but it wasn't the long blade which disturbed me, rather his face, which was lit by the bulb outside George's office. He was utterly confident. Whatever happened now, and it was bound to be violent, this man had no fear.

"But you're not so clever as you think," he went on in a mocking tone, "because it was really rather obvious that you'd make your boat safe as soon as we'd gone, so all I had to do was stay in the yard." He smiled in tribute of his own cleverness, then gave me a small mocking bow. "Good evening, my lord."

I said nothing. Being naked made me feel horribly vulnerable. I had no weapon, and this man's calm assurance was very frightening. He might smile at me, but his eyes were feral, suggesting a man who knew neither pity nor remorse. A bitter man, fallen from grace and resentful. I backed away from him, but there was nowhere to flee to, except the river, and Garrard had carefully placed himself between me and that refuge.

I backed round the workshop corner in time to hear the main gate creak open again.

"That's Peel coming back," Garrard said. "You haven't met Peel properly, have you? I'll introduce you in a moment."

My right foot jarred against a loose metal stanchion. I stooped quickly and picked it up. It was a two-foot length of rusting angle-iron sharpened to a crude point. The weapon gave me some confidence, but it did not seem to worry Garrard. "Peel!" he shouted.

"I'm here, Mr Garrard."

"Find a tarpaulin, Peel." Garrard gave his orders as though he was still in the army. He looked back to me. "Peel is not the brightest luminary to emerge from the state-school system, but he has the gross virtue of huge bodily strength.

He used to be a professional wrestler. If you attack me with that crude piece of iron, my lord, I shall be forced to hurt you rather nastily."

"I don't have the painting," I said in a futile hope that the denial would give him pause.

"Of course you don't. My task is simply to make certain that you don't get it back."

He was so foully sure of himself, and he was confusing me. Why was he so confident that I didn't have the painting? He had surely suspected me when he had searched *Sunflower*, but tonight he had not even bothered to go into her cabin. I was trying to snatch answers from a fog, and the fog was shot through with rank fear. "Do you have the painting?" I asked him.

He laughed, but said nothing.

"Do you know who's got it?" I tried. I did not expect an answer now; I was merely trying to keep him talking while I looked for an opportunity to attack him. I was holding the angle-iron low, like a knife. I guessed I could get in one nasty blow before Garrard could use his blade. I was apprehensive, but it wasn't my first fight, and I knew these next few moments had to be carefully planned, then efficiently executed. It's like sailing in filthy weather; the better prepared you are, the more likely your survival is. I was outnumbered, and plainly Garrard was chillingly confident of his skills, but I still had an excellent chance. I only needed to reach the river and, because I was naked and they were fully dressed, I knew neither man could outswim me. In the meantime I must behave as they expected me to behave: timidly. "Do you know who's got the painting?" I asked again.

"Let us say, my lord, that I know you don't have it."

"Then why the hell did you search my boat?" I almost charged him then, but I saw a wariness in his eye that kept me still.

"I searched your boat," he said, "to see if I could discover any correspondence. But clearly, if you are planning to retrieve the painting, you've made the arrangements by phone."

"You're crazy! I haven't made any arrangements!"

"But you're negotiating with Buzzacott. We have to stop that, my lord."

"Got it!" Peel had found the filthy sheet of old canvas which had half protected George's pile of sand. He dragged it into the yard, then grinned when he saw I was bare-arsed naked. I had turned to face him, but kept glancing back to make sure Garrard did not move. He didn't.

"His lordship appears to be shivering with the cold," Garrard called to his partner, "so wrap him up. But don't mark him!"

Peel advanced on me. He had spread the canvas out like a matador's cloak. I was frightened, so much so that I could feel the goose-bumps on my naked flesh and I could hear the blood thumping at my ear-drums, but I was still confident that I might yet outwit these two and reach the river. I feared for what might happen to *Sunflower*, but at least I would escape a filleting. Then the import of what Garrard had just said dawned on me. He didn't want me marked. Which surely meant he wouldn't use the knife?

"Easy now, guv." Peel had a raw east London voice. He had lumbered to within a few paces of me and now spread the canvas wide to engulf me.

I turned and charged at Garrard. I shouted as I charged. The knife in his bandaged right hand was a sliver of mirror-bright light. I planned to shoulder-charge him and to drive the angle-iron like a rusting stake into his belly. He seemed frozen by astonishment at my sudden attack, and I felt the brief fierce joy of imminent victory. I drew the stake back for the single crippling blow, then struck.

And he moved. One second he was a sitting duck, and the next he had leaped aside like a hare. He merely put out a foot.

I tripped on his foot and sprawled on to the yard's cobbles. The angle-iron clattered away.

It had all been so shamefully easy for Garrard, who now stood over me with his knife. "Does your lordship wish to offer us any further amusement?"

I struck up at him with my fist, but Garrard avoided the

69

blow easily. He reached down with his left hand, I flailed at it, but he simply jabbed his fingers at my neck and a sudden, searing pain paralysed me. I gasped for breath, couldn't scream, couldn't move, and had to lie there, wide-eyed, as Peel swathed me in the canvas. He wrapped the clammy material round me with movements that were almost tender. "There," he said soothingly, "that didn't hurt, did it?"

Anger and fear and pain flared in me. I was angry at being so easily humiliated, and suddenly terrified because I was now at their mercy. The pain receded, and I found I could move again, but the canvas restricted me as tightly as a strait-jacket. "I promised not to mark you, my lord, but I said nothing about not hurting you." The sardonic Garrard stood above me. "So kindly co-operate with us."

I stared up at him, resenting and hating him, but utterly helpless. I'd been taught a lesson: that Garrard was an expert in violence and pain. The army had trained him to it, but had been unable to discipline him, so now he was a dangerous animal, loose and vicious. He sheathed his knife. "I always believe some explanation is a courtesy, so I will merely say, my lord, that your sin consisted in inheriting the paint-ing."

"I don't know what the hell you're talking about." Truth and desperation gave my words vehemence, but they left Garrard quite unmoved.

"So the time has come for you to pay for your sin. We must all do it, some of us sooner rather than later. Bring his lordship, Peel."

Peel lifted me as if I'd been a child. I was trying to free one hand to stab my fingers at his eyes, but he sensed what I was doing and just gripped my canvas-wrapped body in a crushing bear hug. He carried me across the yard, then lowered me on to the quay's parapet where he knelt beside me to stop any attempt I might make to free myself of the sodden and clinging material.

"The object of the exercise," Garrard announced confid-ently, "is to make it appear as though you drowned in your sleep." He swung himself down to *Sunflower*'s deck and, a moment later, reappeared with my sleeping bag which he brought back up to the quayside. "It has frequently occurred to me, my lord, that the well-educated should take to violent crime more often. Has it ever occurred to you that the success of the police is almost always due to the low average intelligence of the criminal? I intend your death to be entirely above suspicion, which is why I, and not Peel, am in charge of this operation. Is that not right, Peel?"

"Yes, Mr Garrard."

"I don't know what the hell you're talking about," I said. The fear was making me sob. I hadn't been over-fearful of the fight, I could even contemplate being hurt, but now I knew I was going to die and there was an implacability in these two men which told me there would be no escape. I was frightened. I was more frightened than I have ever been. "For Christ's sake . . ." I began.

"Shut the fuck up," Garrard said, and for the first time there was a real savagery in his voice. Till now he had been amusing himself by playing with me, but now the real evening's business must begin. "Hold him tight, Peel."

Peel dutifully kept the canvas gripped tight. I lurched suddenly, attempting to break free, but it was hopeless. I tried again, twisting and thrusting and straining, but the huge man held me down with a dismissive ease. He had doubtless taken on far bigger men than I in the wrestling ring.

I was going to die, but first I must watch *Sunflower*'s downfall. Garrard was carefully untying the knot which held her hard against the quay. There was to be no clean slash of the rope this time, for doubtless a cut rope would invite suspicion. Instead it would look as though the rope had undone itself, *Sunflower* had toppled, and I had been trapped in her canted and flooded hull.

"For God's sake, Garrard!" I shouted. "I don't know what the hell this is about!"

Garrard ignored me, but his bigger companion seemed genuinely concerned at my distress. "Calm down" – Peel patted my shoulder – "all this hollering won't help." He sounded like a kindly parent soothing a nervous child at a dentist's.

"For Christ's sake!" The fear was like bile in my throat. I

71

was staring down death's gullet and I was helpless. I was crying, and I was ashamed of crying, and I was trying vainly to twist my way out of the swathing canvas.

"Calm down," Peel said again. "It won't last long. Do you want me to ask Mr Garrard for a ciggy?"

Garrard had freed the rope and now walked with it up one side of the dock, out towards the river, so that when he pulled he would be dragging *Sunflower* away from the dock's end wall. "No!" I shouted.

"It's all right." Peel seemed very worried for me. "Are you sure you don't want a ciggy?"

"No!"

The cry was despairing.

Sunflower was moving.

It took all the strength in Garrard's wiry body. At first he could not move the big boat, but then he began to pull rhythmically and, inch by inch, the hull responded. I heard the fenders shifting against the dock's wall. I was trying to protest. I was half blinded by tears of rage, but I could still see the mast-tip moving against the night's clouds.

"No!" I wailed the protest.

The mast-tip moved a full foot, returned, then moved again, and this time it did not oscillate back. *Sunflower* was teetering on the knife edge of her long keel. Garrard grunted, strained, and I saw the mast move away from me.

"No!" But this time the cry was a sob. I twisted to the dock edge so I could watch my boat fall.

Sunflower fell. The springs momentarily checked her fall, but the weight of her steel hull was too great and I heard the cleats rip clean out of her deck. She gathered speed. Garrard switched on his torch.

Sunflower's chines crashed on to the edge of the grid. The whole boat bounced and shook. I saw the splash of water as her mast slashed down into the dock, then heard the grinding and splintering as the falling hull drove the tall mast down into the dock's bottom. Her keel was still lodged on the grid. For a second I thought the whole hull would turn over, but then the keel scraped free of the timbers and the steel hull crashed down into the shallow water. A small tidal wave creamed white to rock the moored fishing boats. The wave crashed against the dock's sides, then flowed back. I half expected the liferaft canister to explode its pneumatic contents, but the canister stayed shut as the water in the dock splashed, gurgled and subsided.

"Most successful," Garrard said happily as he shone his torch into the dock.

Sunflower lay on her port side, half sunk in the black disturbed water. Her mast was torn off in a tangle of shrouds and halliards. From this angle the hull looked relatively unscathed, but I knew that her portside guardrails would certainly have sheared, and that her scuttles were probably broken. As the tide rose she would fill, then be sunk.

"What we do now" – Garrard had walked back to where Peel guarded me – "is to drown you, my lord."

"Do I put him in the sleeping bag first?" Peel asked.

"He will be easier to manage when he is dead. Just like all the others. So take him down there, Peel, and give him a very good baptism. Total immersion, I think." Garrard mockingly touched his forelock to me. "Goodnight, my lord."

"For God's sake!" I had no fight left in me, nothing now but an abject, bowel-loosening terror. I really was going to die in this miserable dock, and I didn't even know why. "For God's sake! I haven't done anything!"

"You inherited, my lord, that is what you did wrong." Garrard laughed. He was pleased with himself, and well he might be. The stratagem he had devised for my death was nothing short of brilliant. I could not guess what means of my murder he had planned, but once he had discovered the condition of my boat he had improvised this apparent accident. In the morning, when Rita or George found *Sunflower*, it would be assumed that I had drowned in the night because I had not tethered my boat properly.

And I still did not know why my death was sought, except that it must be connected with the Van Gogh. "Who sent you?" I pleaded.

But Garrard was finished with me. He pushed back his cuff to look at his watch. "Let's get on with it, Peel!"

Peel hesitated. Not out of any sudden pity for me, but

because he was trying to work out how best to carry my wrapped body down the sheer dock wall to the water.

"Tie him up!" Garrard sounded exasperated. "For God's sake, Peel, use what few bloody brains you've got!"

"But I haven't got any rope."

"God spare me from employing cretins." Garrard strode away to find a length of rope.

"Who sent you?" I asked Peel.

"You know we can't tell you that. Are you sure you don't want a ciggy?"

"Who?" I pleaded.

"Jesus Christ!"

This was not the answer to my question, but rather a symptom of fear. Peel, who had been pinioning me, abruptly straightened up. "Mr Garrard! The police!" He hardly needed to shout the warning, for headlights were suddenly brilliant in the yard, throwing a bright light on to Garrard who was trying to shield his eyes. A car's engine roared loudly. Peel, when he drove the van back to the yard, must have left the gate open, for I'd heard nothing.

A single car accelerated into the yard. Garrard fled into the alley behind the warehouse. I was shouting. The driver of the car must have locked his handbrake for the back wheels skidded around to slash the headlights past me.

The car stopped. Peel had already abandoned me and was running for dear life into the shadows behind the workshop. I rolled over and over, trying to free myself of the constricting canvas. I could hear Peel scrambling away, then I saw Garrard sprinting across the yard towards the open gate. "Stop him!" I shouted.

I freed myself of the canvas and lurched to my feet. The car's lights were dazzling me now. I saw a tall man's silhouette. He was ignoring my attackers, and instead just walked slowly towards me. "You should have stopped them," I protested feebly.

"Bloody hell fire." The man stopped a few paces from me. He was still standing in the headlights' full glare, so all I could see of him was his shape. He laughed. "Just look at the state of you, boy! You're as naked as the day I found you in

Sally Salter's caravan. Except you were having a deal more fun that day."

"Oh, my God." It wasn't the police. It was Charlie Barratt. My knees began to shake. I was staggering with weakness and relief and happiness and the sheer backwash of a terrible and unnerving fear. "Oh, my God."

"Hello, Johnny." He ran forward because I was collapsing. "I'm all right," I said, but I wasn't.

"It's OK, Johnny." His arms caught me, held me, then leaned me gently against the workshop wall.

"Oh, my God." My eyes were tight closed, but I could still see the dark water into which, in another moment, I'd have been plunged head first. I imagined the filthy cold water forcing itself down my gullet and so real was the feeling that I suddenly gagged. I dropped to my knees and vomited. I didn't think I had ever been so near death. I was shaking, shivering, weeping, spewing.

Charlie fetched a rug from his car and draped it round my shoulders. I was trying to apologise. I felt ashamed. I was crying helplessly. I was shivering and crying and vomiting, yet Charlie crouched beside me and pushed a flask to my lips. "Drink up, Johnny."

It was Scotch. I gagged on it, spat, then seized the flask to drink it properly. "I'm sorry," I said. "Oh, God, I'm sorry."

"Shut up, you bloody fool. Drink."

And suddenly I knew everything would be all right, because I had found my friend. Or rather he had found me. And saved me.

PART TWO

Part Two

"The bastards." Charlie had taken a lantern from the boot of his car and, in its bright light, was staring down at the stranded *Sunflower*. His voice was full of disgust and shock; almost, it seemed to my confused mind, full of a personal revulsion at what Garrard had done to my boat. "Oh, God, the bastards," he said again, then, with all his old resilience, he plucked optimism out of disaster. "But don't worry, Johnny. We'll mend the boat! I'll have some lads and a crane here at sparrow's fart. We'll lift her out, bung her on a low-loader, and take her to my place. We'll make her good as new, eh?"

I was too weak to respond. I was still shivering, too feeble to help as Charlie swung down into the dock and fixed a line to *Sunflower*'s transom post. "At least we know she's not going anywhere," he shouted up to me; then, as he climbed nimbly back to the quay's top, "cheer up, boy, she'll mend. I've seen worse."

Charlie hadn't changed, except that he was more prosperous. He still had the quick smile, the same unruly hair and the same competent manner. He was a big man; hugely capable and scornfully dismissive of all difficulties. "It's not the end of the world, Johnny," he told me, "so get in the motor and we'll go home."

His car was a Jaguar; brand new with deep leather seats and a dashboard like a fighter plane's. I protested that I shouldn't sit on the seats in my soaking wet jeans that Charlie had fished out of the dock, but he didn't care. "Seats can be cleaned, you fool. Just get in."

He told me he had telephoned home the night before. "I've been out of touch, you see, but once Yvonne said you were here, I came like a shot."

"I'm bloody lucky you did." I was shivering, still in shock, still ashamed of being so humiliated by Garrard and Peel.

"We were always lucky, you and I." Charlie grinned at me,

then used his carphone to wake up his foreman. He said he wanted a crane and a low-loader at Cullen's Yard at dawn. The foreman evidently did not mind being woken at the dead of night, or else was used to it.

Charlie lit each of us a cigarette. My pipe was somewhere in the bottom of George Cullen's dock, along with my passport, money, everything. Damn George for betraying me, I thought.

"I suppose," Charlie said, "that you don't want to call the police?" He offered me the carphone anyway, but I shook my head. It wasn't that I had anything to hide, but after my experiences with the police four years before I didn't want anything more to do with them. I just wanted to sail away, nothing more. "Then let's get the hell out of here." Charlie slammed his door and started the motor. "So what were those bastards doing to you?"

"They were going to kill me." I began shivering again, so I drank more of his whisky and sucked on the cigarette as we bounced out of George's yard and accelerated away. There was no sign of either Garrard or Peel, nor of their dark van.

"Tell me, then," Charlie ordered.

I told him all that had happened. He grunted an ominous curse when I said that it must have been George Cullen who had betrayed me, but he said nothing else till I told him that the murder attempt was somehow connected with the theft of the Van Gogh. "That bloody picture!" he said with disgust.

"It's a good painting," I said defensively.

"Piss off, Johnny. It's a bloody daub, isn't it?" Charlie still had a Devon accent as broad as Dartmoor. "I've seen better flower pictures on birthday cards."

"But those aren't valued at a handful of millions. Twenty million, to be precise."

That checked him. "Jesus Christ. Are you serious?"

"Twenty million. That's what I've been offered."

"Who by?"

"Buzzacott."

He gave a low whistle. I understood his incredulity. Charlie could understand a piece of land being worth twenty million, for land could be turned into a profit, but a painting?

He drove in silence for a few minutes, then offered a scornful laugh. "It's a load of codswallop, Johnny. What was your mother offered? Four? Five?"

"Four."

"So it's gone up five hundred per cent in four years? Bloody hell, I should be in that business. I'll sell the trucks tomorrow and buy myself a paint box. I tell you, Johnny, there's more money than bloody sense in this world. No painting can be worth twenty million."

"Maybe, but those bastards just tried to kill me for it."

"Do they think you've got it?" he asked incredulously.

"No, but they seem frightened that I might get hold of it and sell it." I paused, thinking that nothing made sense. "They said that my sin was inheriting the painting."

"Bastards." He offered the dismissive judgment, then lit himself another cigarette. He had always smoked too much, but all Charlie's appetites were excessive. One day, I supposed, that over-indulgence would catch up with him, but now, in the dashboard's dim light, he looked incredibly fit and well.

He drove like a man bent on suicide, but he had always been touched by outrageous good luck, so I doubted he'd ever kill himself at the wheel. He turned on the car heater to warm me up, then told me about his company. "I mainly sub-contract plant for road construction, but I'll do anything with a profit. I've got a couple of caravan sites in Cornwall, and I tarted up those three scabby cottages at the bottom of the village and sold them for a wicked sum to folks from London. Of course I'm up to my eyeballs in debt, but who isn't these days?"

"I'm not."

"You always were an idiot," he said fondly. "There's no point in risking your own money when the banks want to lend it. I borrowed a clean million eighteen months after you left, and I'm still borrowing. Mind you, my profits are bigger than the bank's interest payments, so what the hell?" We had turned into the Devon lanes now, and the Jaguar was travelling between their narrow hedgerows like a bullet down a rifle barrel. Once or twice a rabbit froze in the harsh light, but Charlie just drove over them. He was country-bred and had no sentimentality about animals.

"Do you still have the dogs?" I asked him.

"Of course." Charlie had loved hunting with his terriers. That was how I'd first met Charlie; he had been eight years old, I was seven, and I had found him poaching my father's land. He had been teaching me tricks ever since.

There was a thump as another rabbit died. I winced. Charlie frowned, but not because of the rabbit. "I saw that your mother died."

"Cursing me."

He laughed. "She was a rancid bitch, eh?"

"She never liked you."

"That was mutual. How's Georgina?"

"Same as ever."

"Poor maid," he tutted. Charlie had always been kind to Georgina, though that kindness had never extended to my other sister. He used to call Elizabeth 'Lady Muck', and I noticed he did not bother to ask after her now. Instead, after a moment's silence, he laughed ruefully. "Funny when you think about it."

"What is?"

"I don't know." He was silent for a moment. The headlights were brilliant on the tall hedgerows. Sometimes, as we breasted a rise, the light would sweep across pastures. There were no lights showing in this deep countryside, though off to our west the reflection of Plymouth's street-lamps glowed against the clouds. It was only out at sea, I thought, that one found real darkness; absolute, impenetrable, black darkness. Everything was polluted ashore, even the night.

Charlie picked up his train of thought. "When I was growing up we used to look at your house and be real impressed by it. When I was just a tot I used to think God lived in Stowey, and it was damn nearly true. That was Lordy's house, we were just his farm labourers, and I don't suppose Lordy even knew we existed. But now look at us. I've got more money than all your lot put together."

"Well done, Charlie."

He smiled. "And you're Lordy now." The villagers had always called my father 'Lordy'. They had not really liked the family, there were too many memories of past injustices, some of the memories stretching back five centuries; but, in their own way, they had been proud that the Earl and Countess of Stowey lived in their community. Now 'Lordy' was a penniless yachtsman and the labourer's son drove a Jaguar.

And owned a house that was half the size of Stowey. I caught a glimpse of the big house as the Jaguar's headlights slashed across its façade. My impression was of raw brick and broad glass. Charlie touched a button in the car and the triple garage doors clanked open. A dog began yelping in the kennels and Charlie shouted at it to be silent. "It isn't a bad place," he said of the house as he parked the car. "Cost me a penny or two."

It was four o'clock in the morning, but Charlie made no effort to be silent. He crashed into the house, switching on lights and slamming doors. He went to the laundry room and fetched me a pair of dry jeans and a sweater. I changed in the kitchen where children's drawings were held by magnets on the fridge door. "How many kids have you got now?" I asked him.

"Still just the two. Johnny and Sheila." Johnny had been named after me, despite Charlie's wife who didn't like me. Sheila was named for Charlie's mother. Yvonne, I reflected, did not have much say in how this family was run.

Charlie scooped ice out of the freezer and filled two glasses. Even when we'd been teenagers he had liked to take his drinks American fashion; that, for Charlie, was the height of sophistication, and he hadn't changed. He grinned as I jettisoned the ice from my glass, then he filled it to the brim with single malt Scotch. "Cheers, Johnny."

"Cheers, Charlie."

It was good to be home. We touched glasses, then drank. Somewhere upstairs a child cried, and I heard footsteps as Yvonne went to soothe it. She must have heard Charlie's arrival, but she did not come down.

"Come on, Johnny, let's have a proper chat." Charlie led

83

me into a wide drawing room. Before he switched on the lights I saw that the windows looked across sloping pastures to one of Salcombe's lakes, then the view was obliterated by the glare of electric lights. He put the whisky bottle on the table, sat me down in a leather armchair, then insisted on hearing the whole story of my night once more. "I've told you once," I protested.

"But I want to hear it again, Johnny."

So I told him again. And still nothing made sense.

I woke at midday. The sun was streaming past yellow curtains. A Thermos of coffee, a jug of orange juice and a packet of cigarettes lay on the bedside table. My jeans, newly washed and ironed, were folded on a chair with a clean shirt. A radio was playing somewhere in the house.

I washed, shaved with a razor that had been laid out for me in the bathroom, then went down to the kitchen. Yvonne was topping and tailing a bowl of string beans. She was a tall thin woman with long dark hair and very pale skin. She had grown up in Stowey's village and had been the prettiest girl there when Charlie married her. She was still attractive, but now her frail beauty was sullied by an air of brittle nervousness. She wasn't glad to see me. "In trouble again, Johnny?" She sounded awkward calling me 'Johnny', but Charlie and I had long cured her natural urge to address me as 'my lord'.

"The trouble's not of my making, Yvonne."

"It never is, is it? You want coffee?"

"I've got some." I lifted the mug which I'd filled from the Thermos upstairs. "Nice house, Yvonne."

"He likes it. He built it." She said it dismissively.

"You don't like it?"

"I liked living in the village. I miss my friends." She tipped the vegetable scraps down the sink, then turned on the waste disposer. While the machine ground away she stared through the wide window at the far yachts on the distant water. "He likes it, though," she said when the machine had stopped its din; then, with a wry look at me, "he likes to show off his money, you see."

"Why shouldn't he?"

"It's the bank's money, not ours." She sniffed. "I suppose you'll be staying here for a few days now?"

"I hadn't thought about it."

"You will if he wants you to. What he wants, he gets. You're supposed to join him now."

"Where?"

"In the yard. It's on the Exeter road. You can't miss it, it's got his name plastered all over it. He says to take the jeep."

The jeep was a powerful Japanese four-by-four; what Charlie would call a proper piece of kit. I drove it to the Exeter road where, in Charlie's vast yard, *Sunflower* was standing on the bed of a low-loader. She'd been expertly cradled in timber. It was obvious that someone had worked very fast and very skilfully that morning.

"I couldn't get to sleep," Charlie greeted me from her cockpit. "So I went over to George's and knocked up the cradle myself. A proper job, eh?" He congratulated himself on his own carpentry, then tossed me down a lit cigarette. "You're looking better."

"I'm feeling better." I climbed the ladder propped against *Sunflower*'s starboard flank. "Jesus," I swore bitterly. *Sunflower*'s portside guardrail stanchions were stove in, the mast was nothing but a stump, and, as the mast had buckled and broken, it had lifted the coachroof out of true. The starboard cleats had ripped from the teak-planked steel deck, leaving two-foot holes edged with jagged splinters. The deck was thick with filth. The liferaft must have been triggered into action after Charlie and I had left, for it had inflated itself and now, torn and cut by the crane wires, lay bedraggled and wet over the foredeck. I stepped down into the cabin which stank of filthy river water. Everything was waterlogged. In the forepeak the tool drawers had splintered open. I found my pipe, passport and money and carried them back topsides. The boathooks were missing, the danbuoys had gone; almost anything which had not been shackled to the deck had dropped or floated away. The boat was a mess; a tragic mess.

"What damage?" Charlie asked cheerfully. "It's nothing!

I'll have the cabin dried out by tomorrow, then we'll put some chippies in to repair the joinery. I'll shot-blast your hull properly, instead of the dog's mess you were making of it, paint her up, and we'll rig a new mast in a couple of weeks. Your sails are already drying in my paint shop."

"I can't afford a new mast," I said bitterly.

"You probably can't afford to buy my dinner either, but we won't go hungry. Come on, you bastard, cheer up!"

"Charlie, I'm serious. I can't afford it."

He paused at the head of the ladder. "What's friendship for if it can't help out a mate, eh? Don't be daft, Johnny. You won't have to pay. I've already ordered your bloody mast. Now come on, I'm hungry as hell."

We drove to a pub where the barmaids greeted Charlie with a kiss. He knew everyone, and had a word for all of them. He glad-handed the bar like a politician on the make, but then took me to a secluded corner where we could talk in peace. "I told them to make us a proper steak and kidney pie," he said as he sat down. "You could do with some decent food."

"Sounds good."

"And no salad." He drank half his pint. "Yvonne eats nothing but bloody salad. She read this article about diet in one of her women's magazines. Jesus wept, I'm married to a rabbit. She told me I should give up the beer and the beef. Like hell, I said. I told her I expected a proper meal on my table, and by God she'd better provide it."

I smiled. "You've got a happy marriage, Charlie?"

"You know how it is, Johnny." He lit a cigarette. "They're never happy, are they? You can give them the world and they'll still find something to bitch about. But Yvonne's all right." He made the concession grudgingly. "She's a good mother, anyway. Not that I'm home much. Business."

"What were you doing in Hertfordshire?"

He touched a sly finger to the side of his nose. "Wasn't actually in Hertfordshire, Johnny. More like Bedfordshire." He laughed, then changed the subject. "I had a chat with George Cullen this morning."

"I hope you thumped the bastard rotten."

"He says he never told a soul where you were. I think he meant it too. He was upset about it."

I wasn't convinced. "Of course he told them! He knew who those men were, he even told me as much!"

"I know. He told me the same." Charlie thickly smeared a bread roll with butter. "But I don't think George did tell them. I think they just found you. After all, it isn't difficult to find a boat on the Devon coast. How long can it take to search Plymouth, the Yealm, Salcombe, Dartmouth, Torquay and the Exe? Not long, mate, not long at all. I think you were just unlucky."

"I want to make them unlucky," I said with impotent bitterness. "And I want to know what bastard sent them to kill me, and why."

He leaned back and frowned at me. "Do you really?" It was an odd question, asked in a strangely quizzical tone.

"They tried to kill me," I said in outraged explanation, "and I want to know who sent them." Till the day before I hadn't cared about the painting, or its fate, or about the people who pursued the canvas, but my humiliation in the night had set up an atavistic desire for revenge.

We fell silent as the steak and kidney pie arrived. Charlie fetched two more pints, then ladled pie, potatoes, peas and gravy on to my plate. "What I mean," he said, "is do you want anything more to do with that bloody painting?"

"Not with the painting, no."

"Then bugger off. Sail away." He pointed his knife at me. "Because so long as you're here, they'll chase you."

I was staring through the window. "Elizabeth," I said softly.

"What about her?"

"If I'm dead," I said, "then there'll be no legal complications about the painting's ownership. And Garrard told me my sin was inheriting the painting. That's it, Charlie! Don't you see?" Then my voice tailed away. I was suggesting that Elizabeth wanted me dead so she could inherit the painting, but even as the explanation had convinced me, so I found it impossible to believe that my twin sister would do such a thing.

"For Christ's sake!" Charlie protested in disgust. "The painting's long gone, Johnny. It's in some Texas vault or Swiss strongroom!"

"Is it?" I wondered aloud, then answered my own question. "I suppose it is, yes."

"Of course it is!" Charlie said with sturdy good sense, "so sail away and forget the bloody thing. But eat your pie first."

I leaned back. "I've just discovered something about myself."

"You don't like steak and kidney pie?"

"I get pissed off when people try to kill me."

He laid down his knife and fork. "Listen, Johnny. If it's any help, I'll put the word out on Garrard. I'll find him for you, and I'll skin him alive. But don't you hang about waiting for the chop. Go back to sea!"

It was good advice, but I was still suffering from the shameful memory of the previous night. "Garrard said he was making sure I never got possession of the painting. That suggests the thing is still around somewhere, Charlie . . ."

"Of course it isn't around. Use your loaf, Johnny. It must have been flogged off four years ago. Garrard's probably got his knickers in a twist, nothing else. But I promise you I'll find him and I'll discover who wound him up. You bugger off back to sea."

"I'll help you find him."

"No." He spoke very firmly. "You don't need the trouble, Johnny. Leave it to experts."

I smiled. "You're an expert?"

"Enough of one." He said it grimly. "You don't need the aggravation, Johnny. All you need is to go back to sea."

"I also need some transport."

"Transport?" He sounded suspicious.

"Some wheels, Charlie. For a girl."

He understood that reason well enough. He laughed. "Who is she?"

"Just a girl." I was thinking of a competent girl with dark hair and a quick temper. A girl with an Italian name. "The trouble is," I said, "that she's a good distance away."

"And you've got the itch. No problem." Charlie spread his

hands in a gesture suggesting that all my difficulties could be solved by his munificence. "Take the jeep. Go and chase her!"

"You don't mind?"

"You're my friend. What's mine is yours, and what's yours I wouldn't touch with a bloody bargepole. Now eat your pie."

I ate the pie.

Comerton Castle, Sir Leon Buzzacott's country house, was neither a castle nor a house. It was a late-eighteenth-century monstrosity; a mansion built to display wealth rather than to be a home. Pillared, porticoed, winged, domed, spired, lavish and vast, Comerton had once belonged to a ducal family, but, just as they had to my own family, the taxmen had flensed away until the house had to be sold. Buzzacott had purchased it ten years before. I wondered what he did with all the rooms, reputedly a room for every day of the year. Not that I would find out, for my business did not lie in the main house, but in the great Orangery that was built beside the garden terraces beneath the south front.

The Orangery alone was the size of Stowey. It was a long single-storeyed building, stuccoed white, that had once been a glasshouse, summer house and Arcadian retreat for the Duke and his guests. Now, at astronomical expense, Sir Leon had transformed it into an art gallery. Many people had criticised the gallery, claiming it was too far from any large city, and that it was an elitist exercise aimed solely at gaining Sir Leon the coveted peerage he desired, and maybe they were right, at least in the first criticism, for there was only a handful of cars in the huge car park.

I paid my pound at the door. A moving ramp led to the gallery floor which had been excavated twenty feet below the original ground level. The job had been done without disturbing any of the Orangery's masonry. The air below the ground was conditioned to a consistent coolness and humidity. Automatic louvres controlled the sunlight entering the glass domes and tall casements which, now that the floor had been lowered, served as clerestory windows.

I hadn't asked for Jennifer Pallavicini at the entrance desk. I first wanted to see this rich man's fantasy for myself. Sir

Leon's critics snidely called him Britain's second-rate John Paul Getty. It would have been better, they said, if he had donated his collection to one of the big London galleries. They said his museum was a white elephant, a monstrous underground irrelevance; yet, in truth, it was magnificent. I'd seen photographs of the galleries and I had read the newspaper accounts of their extraordinary construction, but I had never visited, so I had never experienced the uncanny sense of peace in the subterranean halls. That quietness had earned accusations that Sir Leon was making a shrine to art when, according to modern London thinking, art should be an integral part of everyday life. Meaning, I suppose, that if someone wanted to slash a Rubens to shreds, then the act should be seen as necessarily therapeutic as well as a valid criticism. For my money these paintings were well away from London.

The collection was not big. Sir Leon had bought selectively, but what he had bought was of the very finest. The scarcity of paintings made it possible to hang each to its best advantage. Instead of crowding jumbled swathes of pictures along a wall, each canvas was positioned within its own private area. Sometimes, when juxtaposition would help explain a painting's provenance, it would be displayed with others, but most of the paintings hung in solitary splendour. They hung on the outer walls of the gallery, protected by a dry moat. Visitors walked to a small balcony which faced each painting. There were no attendants visible in the gallery, which added to the quality of privacy and peace. The corridors leading to each balcony contained displays which explained the context and importance of the painting beyond the deep moat. The corridors led from the gallery's central spine down which an endless walkway silently moved. Everything had been done to the highest quality and with exquisite taste. It would, I thought, be a fitting home for Stowey's Van Gogh.

There was already one Van Gogh in the collection. It was a drawing done with black chalk and showed a woman digging in a bleak field. The notes in the corridor frankly said it was not the finest of Van Gogh's drawings, but that it was included in the exhibition because, for the moment, Sir Leon owned no other works by the artist.

"It's an early work." Jennifer Pallavicini's sudden voice startled me. "He did it in 1883. It's rather clumsy."

"Is it?" I turned to face her. She herself looked anything but clumsy, instead she was chillingly pretty. She was wearing a simple cream skirt and a striped silk blouse. She looked crisp, cool, competent, and distinctly unfriendly.

"It's self-conscious." She was looking at the drawing rather than at me. "When we get a suitable painting by Van Gogh we'll hang this in Sir Leon's private quarters. What are you doing here?"

"I came to see you."

The brown eyes' gaze flicked towards me. "We feared you'd come to steal another Van Gogh, Mr Rossendale."

I ignored the jibe. "How did you know I was here?"

She gestured upwards and I saw how television cameras were monitoring every balcony. "So far," she said, "we haven't had any fools trying to throw paint or worse at a canvas, but you can never tell. We keep a constant watch. Why did you want to see me?"

"Those two men," I said, then faltered, for her gaze was so disapproving and so off-putting that I felt gauche.

"I do remember them," she said icily.

"They tried to murder me two days ago."

"And evidently failed." She leaned on the balcony, her back to the drawing. "Did you come here for sympathy?"

"Do we have to talk here?" I asked. I had suddenly found the quietness oppressive. The barely audible hiss of the hidden air-conditioners seemed somehow threatening.

She shrugged; then, without saying anything, walked back through the corridor. I followed her. We crossed the slow-moving walkway to a door which she opened with a key. She led me up a white-painted stair, through another door, and so into a small formal garden. I walked silently beside her down the gravel path, round an ornately sculpted fountain, to a stone balustrade that looked out on the Wiltshire countryside. A tractor was harrowing a far field, but otherwise nothing moved. "Well?" she asked.

"I don't like people trying to murder me," I said, and immediately thought how lame it sounded.

"I imagine that's understandable. I didn't much like it when that man molested me." It was the most sympathetic thing she'd said to me so far, and it gave me encouragement.

"They attacked you," I said, "and now they've attacked me. I just thought that together we might find some reason for what they're doing."

"Isn't that a job for the police?" she challenged me.

I half smiled. "You went to the police?"

She hesitated, then shook her head. "What happened in Salcombe was trivial. It certainly wasn't attempted murder. I have to be flattered that you think I might be able to help, but I suggest you should approach the real experts: the police."

I leaned on the mossy stone balustrade. "If I went to the police, I'd have to tell them what happened in Salcombe. They'll want to talk to you."

"I have nothing to hide, Mr Rossendale."

"Nor do I." I spoke with sudden vehemence. "You don't seem to understand, no one does. I did not steal that painting, I had nothing to do with its theft, yet everyone, you included, seems convinced I did steal it. Why on earth would I want to steal it?"

"The usual theory, Mr Rossendale, is that you did it to spite your mother. You hated her, did you not?"

I hesitated. "I didn't hate her. I just disliked her."

"So the theory is partially correct. To that we add all the other evidence, and you must agree that you remain the likeliest suspect."

"For God's sake! That evidence was all circumstantial!"

She let that protest die away on the summer's air, then began a remorseless cataloguing of the evidence. "A week before the painting was to be transported, you removed it from your mother's room."

"She asked me to. She didn't want to be constantly reminded that it was leaving Stowey."

"You claim to have stored it in the gun room, to which only you had a key."

"Rubbish. There were a dozen keys. My sister had a key, half the servants had keys."

"Not according to the police. The painting was in your charge, Mr Rossendale, your fingerprints were the only ones found on the door's lockplate, and you told your mother that you had hidden the painting away and told no one its exact whereabouts." Her voice was biting with disbelief and scorn. "Yet on the morning of the removal, it wasn't there! It's a perfect mystery, isn't it? A locked room, undisturbed alarms, and a missing painting. I suppose you'll tell me that dozens of people knew how to disable the alarm system?"

"One or two knew," I said feebly.

"And where were you the next day? When everyone else was desperately trying to help the police? You were sailing across the Channel! No doubt carrying the painting with you, but of course no one suspected you that day, why should they? You were the Earl of Stowey, the apparent victim of the crime, but since then, my lord, your protestations of innocence have worn a little thin. Isn't it a fact that every guilty man protests his innocence, and does so as vehemently as you are now?"

"But why on earth would I steal from myself?" I challenged her with the obvious defence.

"Clearly from your dislike of your mother. So long as she was alive she shared control of the Stowey Trust with you, and doubtless she would have spent the proceeds of the painting in ways you did not like."

She was so damnably cool. Most of the evidence she had adduced was true, but it was still circumstantial or co-incidental. I hadn't stolen the Sunflowers. I closed my eyes, wondering how I could convince her. "Please listen," I said. I opened my eyes to see her level, judgmental gaze on me. "Those two men came to kill me. I'm trying to find out why they did it because, truly, I don't understand. They said they wanted to prevent me from getting hold of the painting, but I can't do that because I don't know where it is."

She laughed scornfully at my protestation of ignorance. "I can quite imagine why they should want you dead."

"For God's sake, why?"

She hesitated, then evidently decided to speak her brutal version of the truth. "It's obvious, isn't it? It's four years since the painting was stolen, and in those four years we've heard nothing. There hasn't been a whisper. We've been listening, Mr Rossendale, because there are art dealers who know about stolen paintings and we've been paying them to pass on any rumour they might hear, but in four years? Nothing. Now, suddenly, there's a flurry of activity. A man questions me brutally, the same man allegedly tries to kill you. And what has changed? Two things, Mr Rossendale. First your mother has died, and secondly you have come home. Doesn't that suggest something?"

"Not to me."

"Oh, come!" she protested at what she perceived as my intransigence. "If the painting had been recovered while your mother was alive, she would have shared in the proceeds of its legitimate sale. Now, under the terms of the Stowey Trust, you are the sole beneficial owner. Clearly it is now in your strong interest to retrieve the painting and place it on the open market."

"Jesus wept," I said in frustrated anger at her glib assumption of my guilt.

"It isn't my place to speculate," Jennifer said, but proceeded to do so anyway, "but I would imagine that the two men are working for whoever you sold the painting to. That person clearly does not want you to betray his possession of stolen goods, so is taking care to silence you. Doubtless you sold it four years ago for a derisory sum, or else you would not need to reclaim it now. It's a classic case of thieves falling out, and it's all rather sordid, and I find it more than a little insulting that you should see fit to involve me in your attempts to avoid trouble."

"I'm not a thief," I said in hopeless protest.

"So you say. But you should know that Sir Leon considers your guilt or innocence entirely irrelevant. If you can give us any information that will lead to the Van Gogh's recovery, then you'll be well rewarded as well as handsomely paid for the painting itself."

"I don't give a monkey's toss about Sir Leon's reward," I

said brutally, "but I do give a damn about people who try to have me killed."

"That's just masculine pride," she said scornfully. "No one ever accused you of humility."

"You know nothing about me," I said angrily.

She smiled. "I know a great deal about you, my lord." She made the honorific sound like an insult. "We've spent four years searching for that painting, and our starting point, and our ending point, is always you. So, my lord, I am somewhat of an expert on your grubby life. You were expelled from three public schools, you've been arrested four times . . ."

"Just drunk and disorderlies," I protested, "nothing else. Anyone can get pissed."

"One charge of grievous bodily harm," she insisted icily. "You served two months in a Tasmanian jail for that."

She had done her homework. No one had ever known that it had been the twenty-eighth Earl of Stowey in that jail, but she had somehow discovered it. Mind you, the bastard I had knifed had been pleading for trouble, but I didn't think Jennifer Pallavicini would be amenable to that excuse. "It was all a long time ago," I said feebly.

"You're a very destructive man." She ignored my plea of mitigation. "In previous times, my lord, you'd have been sent to a forgotten corner of the empire as a remittance man. Doubtless your family was very relieved when you and your friend decided to sail away. Oh, I know about Mr Barratt, too. What was his attraction for you? Was it simply that your family hated his influence on you, so naturally you flaunted him in front of them?"

"No," I said, "he's a friend."

"But he's settled down, which must leave you friendless, and doubtless not a little short of cash as well. Is that why you're here, my lord? Do you want some money to hire your own thugs who'll protect you while you double-cross your former accomplices?"

Her tone was deliberately offensive, but I did not answer. I had been staring at the green pastures, at the slow tractor, and at the long hedgerows which were bright with stitchwort and campion. I was suddenly assailed by the strangest notion that I didn't want to go away again. I wanted to stay. I'd had my adventures, and it was time to put down some roots. I'd seen the ending of the sea-gypsies, I'd seen them dying of fevers and the pox, I'd seen them selling their bodies in lousy little towns, I'd seen them crawling home in boats that were lashed together with fraying coir and untarred manila, and I suddenly felt lonely. I disliked the feeling. I forgot it as I made one last attempt to convince Jennifer Pallavicini of my innocence. "Do you really think," I said, "that if I'd stolen the painting, I'd rock the boat now? If I'd sold it to someone, and was now trying to get it back, I'd probably end up in jail myself! Why should I risk that?"

"Because doubtless you don't believe that you are in risk of a jail sentence." She pushed herself away from the balustrade. "Do you know where the painting is?"

"Of course I don't. I've already told you that."

"Did you steal it?"

"No!"

"Can you tell me anything that might help us to recover it?"

"Beyond what I've told you, no."

"Then I fail to see how you can help us. You'll find the car park is through that gate. Good day to you, my lord." She walked away.

"Where's my sweater?" I called after her.

She did not turn round, but just waved in negligent reply. It was just possible, I thought, that she raised two fingers as she waved. She was very beautiful, and I was very wretched.

So go back to sea, I told myself, where nothing matters except the wind and the waters and the cold high stars. Because here, on land, I was everybody's scapegoat, but there I was as good as the next man and better than most. And it was there, despite my sudden wish to stay ashore, that I belonged, so it was there that I would have to go.

Charlie was sharpening his chisels when I got back to his yard. "What's got up your nose?" he asked.

I told him about my visit to Buzzacott's gallery, and how the girl I had been chasing worked for Buzzacott. Charlie was scornful of my amateur sleuthing. "You're a berk, Johnny, a prize berk" – he stropped a blade on his palm and gave me a long-suffering smile – "you should know better than to get involved."

"I offered to help her find the painting," I explained.

"What painting? It's gone, Johnny. If you miss it, buy yourself a tin of yellow emulsion and paint another." He tested the newly sharpened chisel by slicing away a sliver of his thumbnail then, satisfied, dropped the blade into his toolbox. "I made you a new chart table. Say thank you."

"Thank you," I said. Behind us *Sunflower* was shrouded in a canvas tent ready for the professional shot-blasters who were coming the next day. I hated to think what the work was going to cost, and said as much.

"That's my problem," Charlie said. "I've told you I'll pay, and I will. You did enough for me in the old days, so you don't need to feel embarrassed now."

Yet I was embarrassed, because Charlie was clearly spending a small fortune on *Sunflower*'s repair, but as the days passed I also saw how much pleasure he was taking from the work. "I'd forgotten how much fun you can have in getting a boat ready for sea," he told me more than once. He threw himself enthusiastically at the task, so enthusiastically that it seemed at times as if *Sunflower* was his boat and not mine. Whatever she needed, he was determined to supply, but only the very best. He would leave the house at dawn, drive down to the yard, and start work. He found rust under the transducer plugs, so nothing would serve but that the fittings were drilled out of the hull and new steel fairings made for the depth-sounder and Pitot log heads. Charlie welded the new fairings into place himself and afterwards, in his old fashion, congratulated himself on a well-done piece of work. "Proper job, that."

In the next busy days there were dozens of 'proper jobs' performed on *Sunflower*. Her shot-blasted hull was anti-fouled and, above the blue bootline, painted a dazzling white. Her liferaft was sent away to be repaired and restowed in its canister. The guardrail stanchions were replaced, and new lifelines rigged from bow to stern. Her cabin joinery was repaired with a lovely pale oak, but not before Charlie had rewired the whole boat. "I needed a holiday," he told me when I wondered how his business was managing without him, though in fact *Sunflower* simply became Charlie's temporary office. He had a cordless telephone in his tool box and, if a problem would not yield to bullying on the phone, he would drop down from *Sunflower*'s gunwales and stride across to his real office. I was grateful for his continual presence; just to be with Charlie gave me a sense of being physically protected from Garrard and Peel, while working with him brought back memories of happy days.

The biggest difference between our old days and these new ones was the amount of money we now lavished on *Sunflower*. A new VHF radio was installed, one that was pre-tuned to all the American and European frequencies. Charlie wasn't content with such a lavish toy, but insisted on installing a short-wave radio as well. "So you can listen to all those posh voices on the BBC." He patted the panel which he'd made to house the twin radios. "Proper job, that."

I had to dig my heels in and refuse some of his suggestions. I was tempted by a Satnav set, which snatched position reports from passing satellites, but I have a fear of too many electronic toys on a boat, so I wouldn't let him buy one. He had a Decca set which he claimed to have taken off one of his old boats and which he insisted on installing over *Sunflower*'s chart table. I couldn't refuse the gift, but as Decca will only give positions in a limited number of waters I did not fear that I would become too used to its electronic magic and forget how to use a sextant. Charlie wanted me to have a radar set, but I adamantly refused; they drain too much electricity and their aerials look too ugly. I won that battle, but Charlie won others: he insisted that the new mast should have an electronic wind direction and speed vane which would display on twin dials in the cockpit and above the chart table. He made new chart drawers, and filled them with brand new charts. He took a small boy's pleasure in surprising me with new purchases: danbuoys for the stern; a radio direction finder; a stripper for the propeller; a sun awning for the hot latitudes; and bright red canvas dodgers with *Sunflower*'s name sewn large in brilliant yellow letters. Best of all he bought me a new fibreglass tender with a small outboard. "You can burn that scabby inflatable," he said.

It all cost money. So much money. Embarrassing amounts of money. I tackled Charlie about the cost, but he simply dismissed my embarrassment. "I'm enjoying it, Johnny. That's all that matters."

"You must let me pay you back."

"What with? Bottle tops?" He grinned. We'd been working till well past nine o'clock and had driven over to the Rossendale Arms for a good-night pint. Some hotel guests from Stowey sat at the bar and sneaked surreptitious looks at me; the landlord had probably told them they were staying in my ancestral home, but I could see from their faces that they weren't sure whether to believe that the paint-stained scruff truly was a belted earl.

"What is *Sunflower* costing you?" I pressed Charlie.

"I'm not counting." He leaned back on the settle and stretched his long arms. "I'm enjoying myself, Johnny. It's been too long since I did a proper job. I spend too much of my time on the bloody phone these days, or in the office. I like working with these." He held out his hands, big and scarred. "Besides, it's a way of making up to you."

"Making up to me?" I said with astonishment.

"Fetch me a pint, and I'll tell you."

I fetched two pints. That was something I'd miss, I thought, the good taste of proper ale instead of the gassy piss-weak lager that the Germans had persuaded the rest of the world to drink.

Charlie lit himself a cigarette. "I always felt guilty about deserting you," he said in explanation.

"Don't be ridiculous."

"It's true." He was entirely serious. "When we flew back from Australia I was really looking forward to going back to sea. We had some good times, you and I. But then I got Yvonne pregnant so, like a fool, I did the decent thing."

He was speaking of the time after my brother's suicide, four years before. It had been a bad time for me; trammelled with accountants, lawyers and bank managers. I had thought

99

then that I would be trapped by all those responsibilities and, though Charlie and I had often talked of going back to sea, I had never been certain that it would be possible. I used to escape Stowey's hopelessness by delivering yachts in the Channel, but I had doubted whether I could ever afford to sail far oceans again; Stowey's problems were too comprehensive for such luxuries. Charlie felt guilty that he had abandoned me, but he had never known that I had been considering abandoning him. I confessed as much to him now, but Charlie shook his head dismissively. "Of course you were going back to sea! I knew that. You were never going to stay with all those pin-striped wankers for longer than you had to!" He laughed. "Could you see yourself living with your mother?"

I smiled. "No."

"There you are, then. But I should have gone with you, Johnny, I really should."

"No regrets, surely?"

"I've made some money, I suppose." He sounded rueful. He looked at his watch. "We've got an early start in the morning, you and I, so drink up."

A week later *Sunflower* was taken to Kingswear where she was craned into the water. Next day Charlie and I drove to the marina where one of his mobile cranes was parked on the quay. "Lower it now!" Charlie took competent command as soon as he stepped out of the Jaguar's driving seat. He shouted up at his crane driver, "You take care, Tom! Gentle with her now!"

We were stepping *Sunflower*'s mast; a brand new foil-shaped beauty of extruded aluminium. Charlie had paid for it, of course, just as he had paid to have all the sails cleaned, and a new trysail made. He insisted on glueing a silver sixpence under the mast's foot for luck, but after that ritual he was content to let the riggers get on with their job while he and I moved to the greater comfort of *Barratry*.

Barratry was Charlie's boat. A few days earlier, in anticipation of these days on the River Dart, he had moved her to the Kingswear marina. She was a fifty-four-foot motor cruiser with a flying bridge, twin monster diesels, and the hot tub which had so impressed Rita. Her name was a pun on Charlie's surname, but the word also meant any fraudulent maritime act. To Charlie it carried overtones of piracy, which he liked. "Mind you, I'd have preferred to call her *Wet Dream*," Charlie laughed, "but none of the girls liked it."

At midday one of those girls arrived on *Barratry*'s pontoon. Charlie introduced her as a business colleague, but offered me a broad wink at the same time. Her name was Joanna and she was ordered to make lunch on board. "A proper dinner, mind you!" Charlie warned her. "No bloody salads, girl. Johnny here's going to sail to the West Indies in a few days so he needs feeding up."

Joanna was a redhead, lithe as a whippet in skin-tight jeans and an expensive shirt. She seemed not to resent Charlie's unbridled caveman chauvinism, but Charlie had always treated his women thus. It worked for him.

We ate lunch on *Barratry* while the three riggers tensioned *Sunflower*'s stays and shrouds. Joanna had carved two cold roasted chickens. One was solely for Charlie who, though he had the appetite of a horse, never seemed to put on an ounce of fat. "Are you really going to the West Indies?" Joanna had picked at a chicken wing, and now painted her fingernails while we ate.

"Probably." In truth I was too late for a good trade-wind passage, but I might yet make the crossing before the hurricane season. "I'll go south first, then make up my mind."

"When will you leave?"

"As soon as he's provisioned," Charlie answered for me. "And no difficulties there, eh, Johnny?" Charlie had opened accounts for me at a half-dozen Dartmouth stores. Whatever I or *Sunflower* needed, we were to have: food, equipment, clothing, anything.

"Where will you go in the West Indies?" Joanna persisted.

"Probably one of the French islands. The food's better."

"And the girls." Charlie was in high spirits. The sun was out, he was well fed, and Joanna had changed into a wispy bikini. "I've got half a mind to fly over there and join you," he said. "We could have some good sailing, eh?"

"Do you still remember how to sail?" I teased him. "My God, Charlie, to think you've bought a motor boat!"

"It's less trouble than rag-hanging," he shrugged. "Mind you, I miss the sailing sometimes, but there's a lot to be said for a good motor yacht."

"Tell me one thing."

"The beds are wider," he grinned. Despite his professed nostalgia for sail, he was clearly proud of *Barratry*. "She's a good sea boat," he claimed with a fervour that made me suspect it wasn't true. He gave me the guided tour, proudly showing me her radar system, the twin state rooms with their king-size beds and television sets, the immaculate engine room, and finally the famous hot tub. "I hardly ever take the damn thing's cover off," he said apologetically, "because it's a bugger to fill up, and there's hardly room for two in it, but the bloody salesman sold me on it."

After lunch we fired up the motors and took *Barratry* out into the Channel. It was a warm bright day and Charlie opened up the throttles so that the twin propellers whipped a path of cream across a sun-glittering sea. The boat banged across the small waves, jarring from crest to crest, but, despite the discomfort, it was still an impressive display of power. "What's her top speed?" I shouted.

"I've had thirty-eight knots out of her." He throttled back, letting the hull settle into the water. We were already out of sight of land, but the Decca repeater on the flying bridge offered us a course straight back to Dartmouth. Charlie let the big boat idle while he opened two bottles of beer. Joanna came out of the cabin beneath us and went to the foredeck where she casually discarded her bikini top before stretching out on deck.

"Not a bad looker, eh?" Charlie wanted my approval.

"Every boat should have one," I agreed.

"She works for a construction firm I do a fair bit of work for. She tells me how much to tender, and if her boss wonders why she's got the money to buy a BMW then he's got too much sense to ask. I might bend the rules a bit, Johnny, but I provide a damned good service. Hey! Joanna! We can't see you properly! Come closer!"

"Get lost, Charlie."

He laughed. He looked immensely happy. He sat on the helmsman's chair, stripped to the waist, and I could see that he was as muscled as ever. He had always been tough, with immense stamina, and monetary success had not softened him. His skin was flecked with welding burns and scars, making him look as strong and battered as one of his beloved hand-tools, but, in the days I'd worked with him on *Sunflower*, I'd seen a new wariness in his eyes. Some of Charlie's toughness had become mental and I guessed he was now a ruthless man to do business with, but I was an old friend, so the ruthlessness was never turned on me. "I might just do that, you know," he said suddenly.

"You might do what?"

"Fly over to the West Indies. I'll need a break soon, and I could take a week or two with you. We'll drink some whisky, find some women, sail some blue water."

"Sounds good, Charlie."

"Like old times." He had taken his eyes off Joanna and was staring moodily at the southern horizon. "My God, but things have changed. Do you remember our first boat?" It had been a fifteen-foot clinker-built wooden dinghy with a gaffed main and a pocket-sized jib. Charlie laughed suddenly. "You remember those two scrubbers we picked up in Cherbourg? Bloody hell, but I thought we'd have to push them overboard to get rid of them."

I smiled. "I remember their boyfriends chasing us."

"We saw them off, though, didn't we?" Or rather Charlie had seen them off. I'd helped, but Charlie's strength was awesome. We'd been eighteen then, cocksure and cockfree, lords of the Channel. We'd crossed in the dinghy to France on a night as cold as charity and we'd been ready for mayhem when we arrived in Cherbourg. "It was a good weekend," I said.

"We had lots of them, my friend. Lots of them." He lit a cigarette. "And we had some bad ones, too. Do you remember the food poisoning?"

Charlie had nearly died after eating some fish we'd caught off the reefs in French Polynesia. I'd nursed him back to health, but it had been a close thing. He grimaced. "I haven't eaten fish since."

"You remember the Tasman Sea?" I asked. That had been another bad time, a bitter ship-killing storm which had threatened to overwhelm us, but Charlie's extraordinary stamina had seen us through. I had been at breaking point, past it in truth, but Charlie had sung his way through.

He smiled at the memory, but didn't comment. Instead he shook his head wistfully. "I do envy you, Johnny."

"I can't think why."

"Of course you can." He lightly punched my upper arm. "Free as a bird, aren't you? No kids, no wife, no accountant. Just wall-to-wall Joannas wherever you go."

"Not always, Charlie."

"But enough, eh?" he asked seriously.

"Enough," I reassured him.

"You're a lucky bastard."

"Meaning you're not?" I gestured at the near-naked Joanna on the foredeck.

"Responsibilities," he said darkly. He tossed his empty beer bottle overboard and lit a cigarette. "I don't know, Johnny. I like making money, but the more you've got, the more the bastards try to take it away from you, so the more you have to work to hang on to it. I work bloody hard now, and it's beginning to interfere with my pleasures. But when you and I sailed together it seemed to be nothing but beer and bare bodies."

"That's because I was doing all the work."

He laughed. A mile off *Barratry*'s port beam a big ketch was close-hauled on a course for France. She looked like a proper boat, one that could take the blue water and Charlie watched her wistfully. "If I could make two million tomorrow, Johnny, I'd jack it all in. I'd follow you."

I smiled. "It doesn't take two million, Charlie."

"But it does, Johnny. It does. I have to settle with the banks, you see. And I can't just abandon Yvonne and the kids. I'll have to leave them with some money. But if I had two million now I'd pay the debts, sell the company and never work again. In five years' time I might just be ready to

do it, but now? Now I'd need two big ones to be really safe."
He opened another bottle of beer. "Those two blokes,
Johnny. They've scarpered."

The change of subject was so abrupt that for a few seconds
I couldn't think what he was talking about. In the last few
days I had become so absorbed in *Sunflower*'s repairs that I
had almost forgotten Garrard and Peel. "How do you
know?" I asked.

"Because I've been pulling in favours, Johnny. Asking
questions. But no one knows where they are. Mind you, on
the principle that most shit ends up in a cesspit, it's likely that
they've gone to London, but I've put the word around that if
they show their scabby faces in Devon again, I'll bury them."
He punched me lightly on the arm. "Forget 'em, Johnny. Just
worry about getting back to sea."

Which was all I was worrying about now. The memory of
that bad night in Cullen's yard was fading. At first I'd wanted
to find Garrard, and repay him, but I'd been humiliated
when I went to ask Jennifer Pallavicini for help, so now they
could all get on without me.

"Charlie?" Joanna sat up on the foredeck. "Put some
lotion on my back, will you?"

He winked at me, offered me the wheel, then went
forward. He stayed with Joanna, evidently lotioning more
than her back, while I climbed to the lower wheelhouse
where I hunched down so that I couldn't see what was
happening. I was suddenly jealous.

I supposed that my mistake had been to come home. Till
that moment when I had plunged through the broken water
of Salcombe's bar I had been a happy man. Now, suddenly,
inexplicably, I was frustrated. One part of me did not want
to go back to sea. It was not that I would ever abandon
sailing, so long as I lived I would need blue seas at my boat's
cutwater, but I wanted something else now. I wanted a place
to come home to. I wanted someone.

But there was no place, and no one. I was unwanted,
except by my sister Georgina, and she was mad, so I would
go back to nowhere because, for me, there was nothing else.

* * *

I sailed a week later. I'd provisioned in Dartmouth but, before leaving England, I sailed round the corner into Salcombe to say goodbye to Charlie. I moored alongside *Barratry* off Frogmore Creek and Charlie brought Yvonne and the children out to the boats. He also brought two bottles of champagne, one of which we broke over *Sunflower*'s bow fairlead, and the other we drank. Charlie insisted his children both took a glass, even the two-year-old. Yvonne seemed determined to disguise her dislike of me and to enjoy herself, or perhaps she was just glad that I was sailing out of her life again. She'd brought a picnic of cake and sandwiches and made tea in *Barratry*'s galley. Charlie filled the hot tub on the bows and let the children splash around as we talked about old times. We laughed at the memories of Charlie's poaching expeditions, and Yvonne shyly recalled how he'd once stolen my father's Bentley and parked it outside the house of a notorious local whore. It was a happy afternoon, and I was glad, for I didn't like to think of Charlie and Yvonne embittered.

They all went ashore at tea-time. I held Charlie back before he joined Yvonne and the children in his dinghy. "I want to say thank you, Charlie."

"For nothing." He was embarrassed. He glanced round to make sure Yvonne was well out of earshot. "I'll see you in the Caribbean, right?"

"Right."

"Maybe I'll bring Joanna. Unless you tell me there's a surplus of crumpet over there?"

I smiled. "There always is, Charlie."

He punched me on the arm. "See you, Johnny."

"Be good, Charlie."

He paused, then roughly embraced me. "You're a lucky bugger," he said, then he climbed over the guardrails and dropped into his dinghy's stern. His outboard coughed into life as I untied the painter. Charlie waved, then steered away. The tide was on the turn, about to ebb, and I was alone again.

I was provisioned, I had filled in the Customs' form, I was ready. I had one port to visit, then I would be free. There didn't seem any purpose to be served by waiting so I pulled my new rigid tender aboard and stowed it aft of the liferaft on the coachroof. I opened the motor's seacock, gave the stern-gland a turn of grease, then started the engine. The wind was coming dead from the harbour entrance, so I'd need to motor out to sea. Once at sea there would be no hurry, ever again, so I'd let the sails do the work. I cast off the lines which held me to *Barratry*, pulled in the fenders, then turned *Sunflower*'s bows to the wind and let the motor idle as I hoisted the big main. I let her drift on the slack water as I hoisted the foresails. The red ensign, battered from a hundred foreign gales, lifted at the stern. I turned to stare ashore, but Charlie's dinghy was already lost among a host of other little craft. There was no one to bid me farewell.

I put the throttle forward.

I'd been home just over a month. My mother had died, my sister had spurned me, two men had tried to kill me, and now I was leaving. I should have felt some regret, but I didn't. Neither regret, nor sadness, just the excitement of another voyage beginning, and when I felt that small familiar excitement I knew that the self-pitying disease that had made me want to stay ashore was gone. I was cured. My spirits rose as the boat gathered speed. The engine thudded happily. The sails, sheeted in tight, flapped desultorily and the compass shivered on its lubber line.

I turned due south at the fairway and let the wind belly the sails. I throttled back, allowing the wind to share the engine's load. There was a shudder in the sea as we crossed the bar, then the bows dipped to the first real wave and a shred of white foam spattered back on to *Sunflower*'s gunwales. The tide was beginning to help me so I leaned down and cut the motor, silencing my world to everything except the noises of water and sails and ropes. *Sunflower* heeled to the wind, and the tiller stiffened in my hand.

It was a good wind, a skirt-lifting force five or six; just enough to break some water across our bows. I could feel the raw and lovely power in *Sunflower*'s big sails now. She was hissing in the water, smashing the waves, creaming them back, driving through a five-foot swell like a thoroughbred.

The wind was more westerly than south, a perfect wind to cross the Channel. I had to keep an appointment in Jersey before I left home waters, then I would be gone to the wild seas. Just one more duty, then I'd be running alone and the bastards couldn't touch me ever again because, once more, I would be alone and lost and free.

They called it a Convent Hospital, but in truth it was just a big Victorian house that stood on the heights near La Corbiere Point. The sisters and their patients enjoyed six acres of land that fell steeply towards the sea. I left *Sunflower* in the St Helier Marina and rented a bike that I pedalled along the island's southern shore.

"She'll be glad to see you, so she will." Sister Felicity limped beside me down a path which twisted between laurels and rose bushes. I had tried to persuade her not to walk with me, for she looked desperately tired and old, but she had insisted on coming. "I'm not so old that I can't lean on an old friend's arm," she told me. "And when I heard you were coming, Johnny, I promised myself I'd have a day out of bed. And how are you?"

"I still seem to be getting into trouble, Nanny. I don't try, but it comes all the same."

"It's your Irish blood, Johnny. But I have faith in you, so I do. One day you'll take responsibility for someone, and that's the day you'll settle down." Sister Felicity was pure Irish. She had once been our family's nanny at Stowey, but after we had all left the nursery she had gone to take the veil. Her fondness for and familiarity with Georgina had made this pleasant house an obvious refuge for my younger sister. "Mind you," Sister Felicity went on, "it's past time you did settle down. You can't gallivant for ever."

"Why ever not?"

She paused to take breath. I was worried for her health, but she was more worried about me. "You should have children, Johnny. What will happen to the Earldom if you don't make an heir?"

"The Earldom's gone, Nanny," I said bleakly. "It disappeared with the house. We're nothing now. We're just a

108

tired old family that has squabbled its life away. In a few years we'll all be gone and no one will even remember us."

"You're so full of it, your eyes are brown!" She smiled at her own coarseness. As a child, as now as a man, I loved this woman far more than my real mother. Felicity had no guile, just a heart of pure affection. Now, unwell, she held my arm tightly as we began to walk again. "I'm sorry I couldn't cross to England for your mother's funeral," she told me, "it wasn't one of my well days."

I wondered if she ever had well days any more. "You should rest, Nanny."

"Ah, the Lord will give me rest in due time. But I wept for your mother, poor thing."

"I didn't," I confessed brutally. "I haven't even requested a Mass for her."

"You should, Johnny. She was never good to you, but she gave you life for all that."

"And she accused me of stealing her painting."

"Who cares about a painting?" She stopped where the steps turned towards the sea and we could see a small sun terrace where three patients and a nun sat on wrought-iron chairs. "And there the dear thing is!" Felicity said. "You go on alone, Johnny, I'm not sure I can manage the last steps."

The 'dear thing' was the Lady Georgina Rossendale, but I did not go straight down to her, preferring to stay a few more seconds with Sister Felicity. "Is everything all right here, Nanny?"

"With God's blessing it will be. The diocese is always talking about selling the house, and I could see why they'd want to because it must be worth a wee fortune, but so far, thank God, they haven't done it. But if they do, Johnny, we'll just pick up our skirts and find somewhere else. Don't you worry yourself."

"And Georgina?"

"On her good days she misses Stowey." Felicity made a small gesture of resignation. "Not that she has many good days, but when she does I sometimes think her understanding is just beneath the surface, like a bubble that only needs a little nudge if it's going to burst, but then she falls away again. Poor thing. But she's never any trouble, never at all. She'll be glad to see you."

I went down to the terrace, but it was not one of Georgina's good days. At first I was not even sure that she recognised me. She was placid, smiling softly, and gentle. I told her about *Sunflower*, and perhaps she understood some of what I said, for she pointed out to sea where a slew of yachts were catching the tide before turning north towards Guernsey. Lunch was brought to the terrace on trays and I gently fed Georgina and mopped up her spills.

I left her in mid-afternoon. I climbed the steps, and only then did I learn that Georgina had remembered me, for, just before I would have disappeared behind the screen of bushes, she called my name. "Johnny? Johnny?"

I went back to her. "My love?"

She was crying. She was crying very softly, but the tears were flowing in copious and silent misery. She reached desperately for my hand. "I want to go home."

"Are you unhappy?"

"I miss you."

"Nanny's here," I said, then, in case Georgina had forgotten the nursery at Stowey, "Sister Felicity's here."

"She'll die! She's going to die, Johnny, and I'll be alone."

"No, no, no." I held her tight, and I cried because there was sweet sod all I could do. I held her for a long time. Dear God, I thought, but what misery lay in this girl's madness? I remembered that the last time I had been with Georgina in this garden had been after our brother's death. Did she, somewhere in her tangled mind, connect me with death? John, Earl of Stowey, death's messenger? I held her tight.

When I relaxed my embrace to look into her face, I saw that she had gone back into her mysterious world of gentle nothingness. I kissed her cheeks and she smiled at me, remembering nothing of her desperate fears. She seemed happy again, but I was still crying.

I climbed the garden steps and let myself into the main house to seek out Sister Felicity, but a young nun told me Felicity had been ordered back to her bed. I thanked the girl, then pulled out all my small change which I put into the box beside the door. I wouldn't need British coins again for a long while, maybe never.

"Behold a miracle! The Earl of Stowey is giving money to charity!" I turned, astonished, to see my twin sister Elizabeth coming from the convent office. Her husband, Lord Tredgarth, was two paces behind her. He nodded at me with heavy disapproval, while Elizabeth just looked scornful. "I heard you had come to visit this morning," she said, "but I hardly expected to find you still here."

"I came to say goodbye."

"You're going somewhere?"

I shrugged. "Wherever."

"Don't let me stop you, brother."

I didn't move. The meeting was unexpected and sudden, yet, despite Elizabeth's rudeness, it seemed churlish just to walk away. I was also very curious about what had brought Elizabeth here. She looked very chic in a black summer dress and with her bright blonde hair cut expensively short. She wore a single row of pearls and had an expensive-looking handbag. Peter Tredgarth was certainly not paying for such baubles, and I wondered who was. She glared at me, expecting me to leave, but I stayed put as the silence stretched in the big cool hallway which smelt of wax polish and disinfectant. Lord Tredgarth was the first of the three of us to be embarrassed by the silence. "You found Georgina well, John?"

"No," I said, "she's frightened of the future."

"Don't be ridiculous, John," Elizabeth snapped. "She's half-witted, so how does she even know what the future is?"

"She's frightened that Nanny will die and leave her alone."

"There's certainly no point in her looking to you for any security if that happens, is there? What have you ever done for her?"

"Loved her?"

"Don't be impertinent. We've all loved Georgie. But some of us have to be practical as well." She looked at her watch, then grimaced at my dirty jeans and unironed shirt. "Are you flying back to the mainland now?"

"No."

111

"Then I needn't offer you a lift to the airport." She sounded relieved. "Come along, Peter."

I frowned. "You mean you didn't come here to visit Georgina?"

"I came here, brother, to make sure that her funds are still adequate. As I said, some of us try to be practical. There really isn't any point in wasting our time by seeing her; she doesn't know me from Catherine the Great, but that doesn't prevent me from worrying about her welfare. Now come along, Peter, we have a taxi waiting."

Her high heels cracked and snapped over the parquet floor. I moved into her path, making her stop and provoking a look of utter disdain.

An alarm bell had rung faintly in my head. I did not trust Elizabeth when she spoke of Georgina's funds. Elizabeth is constantly short of money, made so by her husband's ineptitude as a farmer and his failures as an investor. "Are Georgina's funds adequate?" I asked her now.

"Entirely. You don't have to worry. Not that you ever did. Now stand aside, please."

"Tell me something," I said on a pure impulse. "Did you send two men to kill me?"

Anger blazed in Elizabeth's eyes. "Peter. If John doesn't move out of my way, then kindly remove him for me."

Her husband loomed closer. He's a big and burly man, but everything he touches turns to disaster. "Piss off, Tredgarth," I said nastily, and he fell back, as I'd known he would. "Did you send them?" I asked Elizabeth again.

She paused, summoning her artillery. "You are a fool, John," she said eventually. "You behaved disgracefully at Mother's funeral, and now you're accusing me of planning your murder. Try not to be so utterly pathetic and ridiculous. I'm quite seriously worried about you. Clearly there's a strain of lunacy in our family. Georgina has it, and now it seems quite likely you do too. No, I did not send any men to murder you. I sometimes wish I had. Is there any other crime of which you wish to accuse me? No? Good. So kindly get the hell out of my way."

I got the hell out of her way. And I still didn't understand what had happened in England, or why, or who had set it all in motion. I only knew that I had a boat waiting at St Helier and an ocean to cross. So, with the questions still unanswered, I found my rented bike and pedalled off to find the world.

At noon the next day a good west wind whipped me through the Passage du Fromveur between Ushant and the French mainland. I should have stood much further out to sea, passing Ushant well beyond the horizon and thus avoiding the heavy merchant traffic that thrashes round Finisterre, but I had a fancy to run the headland's tides and, as my life was now once more governed by fancy, I stood inshore and let *Sunflower* have her head.

I had an ebbing spring tide in the passage so that we shot through at close to fifteen knots. The wind was brisk enough to shatter the waves on the rocks about the Kereon light. Seabirds screamed above the islands that were bright with gorse in the sunlight. Another British boat was shooting the passage with me, but, once he had cleared the Pierres Vertes cardinal buoy, he turned due south towards the Raz de Sein while I held west towards the open ocean. At dusk, looking back, I could see the brilliant sweep of Le Cre'ach Lighthouse marking my last sight of land. Lisbon next, I thought, and then I wondered why, and supposed it was because the first time I'd sailed away from Devon I'd made the Tagus my first port of call. I had no need to go there now. Instead, I decided, I would go straight for the Azores. I would sail into Horta and there, at those hospitable quays, meet the first sea-gypsies again. Such gypsies rarely ventured further north than the Azores, and few even went that far towards the cold latitudes, but I knew there would be a handful of weather-beaten boats and I'd hear the first tenuous strands of gossip from the world I'd temporarily deserted. Perhaps I'd find a crew who wanted to cross the Atlantic. Or perhaps I'd change my mind and go south, round Africa, to head up into the paradises of the Indian Ocean. Nothing mattered any more so, at a whim, I decided to skip Lisbon.

Sunflower and I fell into our old routine. I slept mostly by day when other boats might be expected to keep a better watch than at night. I had a new radar reflector at the mast-tip, but I doubted whether any night-time crew on a merchant vessel would be watching their radar; more likely they'd be watching dirty videos and they wouldn't even feel the bump as they drove *Sunflower* under. More yachtsmen die crushed under the bows of careless steamers than from their own mistakes, so at night, when the heavens were dazzling with stars, I stayed awake close to the self-steering gear. I'd doze at times. *Sunflower* was behaving beautifully, her newly cleaned hull making her sweet in the water. We were on a long windward beat, but the weather was good; lulling me to sleep and to reflection.

England already seemed like a bad and unreal dream. Had two men really tried to kill me? I knew they had, but now, where the memory had once made me wake sweating in the night, it seemed merely ridiculous. It had surely all been a mistake. The police had taken no interest in my return, and why should they? The only resentment had been from my family, and from Sir Leon's staff who felt cheated of their glorious picture. Had they sent the two men? The possibility intrigued me, but a few moments of thought convinced me that the notion of Jennifer Pallavicini ordering my death was a nonsense. She had no motive that I could see. Elizabeth was a more likely candidate, but none of it seemed to matter any more. The whole episode was scoured clean by a northwest wind and the ocean's long swell.

Charlie was right, I thought. The picture was long gone. It was in some Texan vault, or Japanese mansion, or Swiss strongroom. Whoever had bought it would take care to keep it safe, silent and hidden for generations. Perhaps, hundreds of years in the future, the picture would surface again and the art historians would recall that it had once been stolen from an obscure British family, but for now, for Elizabeth and me, the Van Gogh might just as well be on the dark side of the moon.

Not that I cared any more; I was back at sea, chopping my bows into the long ocean waves. I slept in the mornings. At noon, after the ritual sight, I made myself a meal. In the afternoons I found work to do. The new joinery in the cabin needed varnishing, and, day by day, coat by coat, the gleam deepened. I catnapped in the early evening, ate again, then read until the sun dropped. I had an old battered Shakespeare, Proust, *The Oxford Book of English Verse*, and Joshua Slocum's account of his solo voyage round the world. There was meat enough in those four volumes to last a lifetime. All had been soaked when Garrard had dropped *Sunflower* off the grid, but the pages had dried out and, though crinkled, were still readable. When the light made the pages indistinguishable I would prepare the sextant for the first star sight of the evening, then just sit and let the time drift past.

At night the phosphorescence glittered in our wake. Sometimes a large fish would come close to the hull and I'd see its rising track like a trailing coat of stars deep in the water. In seven years I'd never tired of that sight, nor thought I ever would. It became warmer as we travelled south. By day I rarely wore any clothes: why wear out things that cost money to replace? At night I pulled on jeans and a sweater and, in the early hours when sleep threatened most, I would go to the foredeck and exercise till I was sweating. There isn't much exercise to be had on a yacht; the toughest task is hoisting the mainsail, but, in a good year, it stayed up most of the time.

I took the sails down once. I was fourteen nights from Ushant and the weather turned. The dawn revealed a sullen oily swell above which my sails hung limp beneath a brassy sky. The glass dropped all morning, while heavy greasy clouds piled from the west to shroud the sky in an ominous darkness. At noon a heavy rain flayed the sea, then stopped as abruptly as it had begun. The rudder banged in its pintles.

I sensed a squall. There was none in sight, but the instinct is enough. At sea it's best to act on the first impulse, for there might not be time for second thoughts. I dropped the foresails and lashed them to the pulpit rails, then let down the main. I tied the heavy sail to its boom, then disconnected the self-steering gear. I slid the washboards into their grooves, bolted them home, and locked the companionway shut.

A minute later the squall struck. It came out of the west like an express train. The squall was an onslaught of wind and rain, stirred to fury, but so confined and travelling so fast that it had neither the time nor space to stir the sea's venom into threatening waves. The rain seemed to be flying parallel to the sea which was being whip-skimmed into a fine spray that struck *Sunflower* with the force of a sand-blaster. I crouched down from its fury and felt my naked back being stung red by the rain's lash. I could hear nothing but a maniacal hiss. I looked up once and saw the mast straining. The forestays were bar taut while the twin backstays were bellying out like bows. I dared not look again. The pressure of the wind on the bare pole was driving *Sunflower* backwards and I could feel the sea's pressure trying to slew the tiller. I had never known such fury in an Atlantic squall. I'd experienced them in the Pacific, but this was a timely reminder never to take the sea lightly. Then, as suddenly as it had come, the squall went.

The wind dropped to nothing. A gentle heavy rain pattered down. Behind me I could see the sea being scourged white, but ahead and around *Sunflower* the water was just a dappled black. The hull seemed to shiver as the cockpit drains gurgled.

Two other squalls struck, neither as fierce as the first, and an hour after the second the black clouds rent to show sunlight. By nightfall we were under full sail again, beating west and south as though there had been no interruption. I played myself tunes on my penny-whistle and opened a rare bottle of wine. Two dolphins investigated me, and stayed with the boat halfway through the night.

Next morning the first dawn rays of sun reflected pink on the undersides of the wings of two gulls. It was a sign that I was nearing the Azores and by dusk I could see the white clouds heaping above the mountains of Graciosa. Twelve hours later, after a sweet night's sail, *Sunflower* was safe alongside the painted wall in Horta. I recognised two yachts in the busy harbour. One, a graceful double-ender, belonged to an hospitable American couple whom I had last met in Tasmania, while the other, an immaculately maintained wooden yawl, was sailed by an obnoxious Swede who was the bane of every sailor on the seven seas. I asked in the Café Sport where the Americans were. "They had family trouble, Johnny, so they flew home."

"That's a mistake," I said fervently.

My own mistake was to go to the Café Sport. I was just addressing a dirty postcard to Charlie when Ulf, the loathsome Swede, slapped my back. "I saw *Sunflower* here. That's Johnny, I said to myself. How are you?"

Because I was back where I belonged and therefore feeling well-disposed to all mankind, even to the gruesome Ulf, I said I was in wonderful health, which rather disappointed him. I asked how he was.

"A redundant question, Johnny, as you well know. I do not get the illness, ever. Physical sickness is an aberration of the subconscious mind." He was off, unstoppable and unbearable. I'd once heard an Australian threaten to break Ulf's bloody legs to test his theories that all ailments were in the mind, but the trouble is that the repugnant Ulf stands nearly six feet eight inches tall and is built like an advert for steroids.

He drank lemonade while I drank beer. Once he had expounded his theory of human sickness he launched himself on *Sunflower*'s ills. "You have a new mast, yes?"

"Is that what it is, Ulf? I was trying to work out what that big stick was."

"I remember telling you to get a new mast. You were wise to take my advice, Johnny. But it should have been a wooden mast. Wooden masts are more easily repaired. Your shrouds are still too far forward."

"They're not."

"I know about these things. If you don't want to move the chain-plates I should take three feet off the mast. That will cure the weather-helm."

"Balls. She doesn't have weather-helm." Well, a touch, I confessed to myself, but nothing to worry about. "Balls," I said again.

He smiled. Ulf always smiles when he's insulted, and he's insulted often because he always knows what is wrong with everyone's boat and, quite unasked, offers his tedious advice. "I shall come and look her over for you, Johnny."

"I don't want you to."

"I will make no charge. My only concern is your safety." I ordered another beer. I was trying to think of some outrageous fault which I could assign to Ulf's yawl, but my imagination wasn't up to the task. The big bastard kept an exemplary boat.

"Someone was asking about you last week," Ulf said suddenly.

"Who?"

"I don't know. I just mentioned it."

"A man? A woman? A Swede?"

Ulf missed the feeble joke. He has no sense of humour, just a skin as thick as a shark's hide. "Just a man," he said airily. "A Portuguese man, I think. He wore a suit. He wasn't local, or at least I haven't seen him since last week."

I didn't like that the man wore a suit. To my mind that made him a suspicious character, but at least it hadn't been an Englishman which meant that it could not have been Garrard. "Did this man say why he wanted me?"

"No."

"You're a fat lot of help, Ulf."

"I try to be." He offered me his benevolent smile. "That is my purpose in life. To help people. But the man did say one thing that I found most notable."

"What?"

"That you are an earl of England. A real aristocrat."

I spluttered laughter into my beer. "Oh, come off it, Ulf! For Christ's sake! How long have you known me?"

"We first met, I remember, in the Marquesas, so it has been just over three years."

"Do you really think an earl would be a bare-arsed sailor?"

"It surprised me, I confess."

"It isn't true. So don't tell people it is. My father bred laboratory rats and my mother was a marriage guidance counsellor before she did a bunk with one of her clients."

He was sceptical. "If you say so, Johnny."

"I do say so."

"Then I must believe you." He sipped his lemonade. "And if this mistaken man returns, what do I tell him?"

"To take a flying fuck at the moon, of course."

"It has often occurred to me," he said blandly, "that in

119

Sweden we do not have such an offensive language as in England."

Poor bloody Sweden, I thought. "You haven't seen me, Ulf." I laid it on the line for him. "You understand that? I don't exist. I've vanished."

"I understand, Johnny. Trust me."

I didn't care who searched for me. I just wanted to be left alone.

Or almost alone. I lingered a few days in Horta, trying to sense a pattern in the Atlantic weather and hoping that some girl would offer herself as *Sunflower*'s crew. The delay also gave Ulf a chance to inflict himself on *Sunflower*. He told me that her cockpit drains were inadequate, her bow fairleads misplaced, and that her self-steering lacked robustness. He told me to replace the aluminium whisker-poles with carbon fibre rods and when I asked him how the hell I was supposed to find carbon fibre rods on some remote islands in the middle of the bloody Atlantic he told me to buy sailboard masts. It was actually a good idea. That's the trouble with Ulf; he's usually right, but contrariness makes most people do the very opposite of whatever he advises. He advised me to give up smoking, so I puffed pipe smoke at him till he left.

That evening I met a Dutch girl who was almost persuaded to jump her friends' yacht to cross the Atlantic with me, but next morning she thought twice about it before disappearing northwards to mother and safety. I began to think about leaving myself. It wasn't really the season for a southern run across the Atlantic, and the weather charts were not helpful, so I decided I should sail south, far south. I remembered how Joshua Slocum had set out to sail round the world from west to east, but, chased by pirates off the African shore, had abruptly decided to go east to west instead. If such whimsical decisions were good enough for Joshua and *Spray* then they were good enough for Johnny and *Sunflower*, so I dragged out the charts of the southern oceans. There was a river on the coast of Africa where I'd once made some friends and where I knew I could find provisions. *Sunflower*, despite Ulf's gloomy prognostications, was in fine fettle and ready to go.

So, next morning, I bought wine, cheese, fresh fruit and vegetables. I had decided to leave at nightfall. I finished provisioning at midday, sent Georgina and Sister Felicity a postcard, then went down to the cabin to sleep. It was hot and the smell of varnish still lingered in the close air. It was made worse by the odour of powdered boric acid which I'd scattered in the bilges as a lethal present to the Azorean cockroaches. I wore nothing but a faded pair of denim shorts, but I was still sweating. I'd closed the companionway to make a sleep-inducing darkness, but instead of sleeping I lay fretfully awake. I listened to the lap of water on the steel hull and tried to let it lull me into drowsing.

I had just succeeded in dropping into a half-doze when someone stepped from the quay ladder on to *Sunflower*'s deck. I swore at the interruption. With any luck it was only someone mooring their boat alongside, but then I heard the footsteps climb down into the cockpit followed by a tentative knock on the closed washboards. "If that's you, Ulf," I shouted, "get lost."

"Mr Rossendale?" It was a woman's voice.

I slid off the bunk and shot back the companionway. The sudden brightness of the afternoon sun made me blink at my visitor. I was so astonished that at first I thought I was sleeping and this was some dream apparition. "Good God in his merciful heaven," I said in greeting.

"Good afternoon," said Jennifer Pallavicini.

"Hello." I didn't know what else to say. Nor, evidently, did she because her customary certitude had deserted her. She was desperately ill at ease, perhaps because, instead of being in an air-conditioned art gallery, she was on a tiny island in a scruffy yacht with a man she had recently accused of being a thief. She looked cool enough, despite the wretched heat, in a loose white blouse and a pair of bleached designer jeans, but there was a timidity in her eyes that seemed unnatural to this chillingly capable girl. I rested my forearms on the washboards. "I've been wondering," I said irrelevantly, "how come an English girl has a name like Pallavicini?"

"My father was Italian, of course. My mother's English."

" 'Was'?" I asked.

"My father died ten years ago."

She said it almost defiantly, as if challenging me to find the right response. I grunted some dutiful regret, then slid the washboards out of place and dumped them on the chart table's chair. "I can offer you tea," I said hospitably, "rotgut Azorean wine, Irish whiskey, beer, orange juice, or instant coffee."

"I haven't come to be sociable, Mr Rossendale." That was said with a touch of her old asperity.

"Then stay thirsty, damn you." I poured myself a mug of the rotgut wine, took it and the bottle to the cockpit and sat down. Jennifer Pallavicini remained standing. "Sir Leon sent me," she said, as though it entirely explained her presence.

"I thought you'd come because you found me irresistible. Or was it to apologise?" I saw the flash of angered pride on her face. "Oh, for God's sake, girl, sit down and have a drink. I won't poison you."

"Tea," she said as she sat. "Please."

Neither of us spoke as I made the tea. This was evidently not to be a very jolly meeting. I remembered she drank her tea without either sugar or milk, so I served it black with a slice of lemon. She thanked me. I asked her how she had known where I was.

"Sir Leon alerted all the ports where you might be found. We had a man here some days ago, and he arranged with a Swedish yachtsman to tell us if you arrived."

Ulf, I thought, the smug, treacherous, bloody bastard. I hoped his precious yawl sank. I didn't say as much. Instead, because of the searing heat, I rigged the awning over the boom to shade the cockpit. If Jennifer Pallavicini was grateful for my solicitousness, she didn't thank me.

I sat down and sipped my warm wine. "Presumably Sir Leon is making one last desperate appeal to me?" She did not reply and I shook my head. "I didn't steal the bloody thing. I had nothing whatever to do with it."

She ignored my denial. Instead, and in a very fervent voice, she asked whether I had liked the Van Gogh.

Her question, and the sincere tone in which it was asked,

took me by surprise. "Yes, I did like it. Very much." I smiled. "It was like a splinter of sunlight hanging on the wall."

"He was good at colour," she said dispassionately, "perhaps the best of them all."

"I used to go to my mother's room to look at it," I went on. "She didn't approve of my doing that, but she didn't approve of much that I did. In the end she kept the East wing locked to stop what she called my trespassing."

"But you could pick the locks?"

"Indeed I could, Miss Pallavicini, and I frequently did. Does that make me a thief?"

She did not answer. I suddenly wondered whether she really was 'Miss' Pallavicini. She wore no rings.

She saw my glance at her hands, and seemed amused by it. In turn she examined me. I was sweaty, scarred, suntanned and filthy. I supposed she was a girl who liked her men ponced up with armpit anti-fouling and eau-de-Cologne, which rather spoilt any chance I might have with her. Sitting there I realised that I really did rather want a chance with her, but that could have been mere disappointment at being turned down by the Dutch girl.

"We checked your story about the boat's name," Jennifer said suddenly. "You were telling the truth."

"Thank you, your honour." I mocked her by tugging at a sunbleached forelock.

She stared quizzically at me. "How do you make a living?"

"With these." I held up my hands. "In a month or two I'll be in waters where there are no boatyards, no chandleries, no sail-lofts, but enough broken yachts to need a slew of skills. I'll mend engines, tension rigging and rebuild hulls. If I can't mend it, then it's probably broken for life."

"And those activities support you?" She sounded incredulous.

"I've a little money. I had an Uncle Thomas who shared my views about the rest of the family, so he left me a legacy." I poured myself another mug of the wine. It was rotgut, but I was used to rotgut. "What is this, Miss Pallavicini? A cross-examination?"

She stared at me as though she might find a truth hidden behind my eyes. "I wish I knew whether you did steal the painting," she said after a while.

"I didn't. Cross my heart and hope to die, but I didn't."

She paused, as if waiting to see whether I would be struck dead as a result of my childish words. I stayed alive. "If you didn't steal it," she asked, "why would those two men think you might know where to find it?"

"Because they've got their wires crossed." I paused. "I thought that perhaps you or Sir Leon might have sent them."

"That's ridiculous!" She was genuinely astonished at the accusation. "They attacked me too!"

"A set-up?" I suggested, but not too forcefully, "to make me think you didn't know them?"

"You're an idiot," she said in utter scorn, but not in her usual hostile manner.

I shrugged, but said nothing. A gull swooped down to *Sunflower*'s stern, hovered for a second, then glided away. A fishing boat, high prowed and brightly painted, belched its engine into life to gust a cloud of filthy smoke over the harbour.

"We need your help, Mr Rossendale," Jennifer Pallavicini said when the silence between us had stretched too long.

"I'm sailing south," I said. "I provisioned today, I've done my chart work, and I'm going south. I'll probably call in at Las Palmas in the Canary Islands, because a lot of girls hang about the yacht dock there looking for a lift to nowhere, and after that I'm sailing south to an African river I visited two years ago. The villagers there don't see yachtsmen from one year's end to the next and they're as friendly as hell. The approach to the place is a bit bloody, one rusted buoy ten miles off shore and shoals that shift around like a snake in a sleeping bag, but . . ."

"Please," Jennifer Pallavicini interrupted me.

"I rebuilt their generator when I was last there" – I ignored her appeal – "and I promised I'd go back to make sure it was still working."

Jennifer Pallavicini said nothing. I was as tempted as hell to say I'd help her, but only because she was such a beautiful girl. I applied sound feminist principles and made my decision as if she was as ugly as a baboon's behind. "The answer's no," I said. "I offered you my help last month, and you turned it down."

She opened her handbag and took out an envelope. I thought for a second that she was going to offer me Sir Leon Buzzacott's autograph on a cheque, but instead she took a photograph from the envelope. She held it out to me.

The photograph showed a pale yellow triangle on a white background. Next to the yellow triangle was a black-and-white measuring stick which told me that each side of the triangle was three inches long. "I'm not really an expert on modern art," I said, "but if I were you I wouldn't buy it."

She ignored my feeble sarcasm. "It's a corner of a painted canvas," Jennifer Pallavicini said pedantically, "and our tests confirm that it was almost certainly cut from the Stowey Sunflowers. A letter came with it, Mr Rossendale, demanding four million pounds for the rest of the painting. The letter was posted two weeks ago. The letter stated that if we don't pay the ransom by the end of August, then the painting will be burned and we will be sent the ashes."

"Then pay the four million," I said casually. "It seems a fair enough price for a twenty-million-quid painting."

"Pay four million pounds to a blackmailer? To a man who will only demand more? Who, once we pay the first monies, will cut a sunflower from the canvas and demand another four million?" She was suddenly and vehemently passionate. "For God's sake, Mr Rossendale, don't you understand? The thieves will mutilate it to make their money! They're barbarians, and they have to be stopped!"

"Hang on," I said. "A month ago you thought I was the thief. Now you've selected a group of barbarians."

"Maybe it's whoever you sold the painting to," she said angrily.

I shrugged and shook my head. "Not guilty."

"Or maybe it's you," she said. "Maybe you think we'll ransom the painting, then buy it from you."

"Give me a cheque for twenty-four million," I said flippantly, "and the painting's yours."

"Damn you," she said angrily, then pushed the photograph back into her handbag.

Behind me a French sloop was ghosting into the harbour. I turned to watch as it dropped its sails and a girl in a bikini went forward to pick up a mooring. Ulf was doing strenuous calisthenics on his foredeck and I saw him straighten up to eye the deficiencies of the newcomer's boat. There wasn't much wrong with the girl, not that I could see. I looked back to Jennifer Pallavicini and decided she too would look very good in a bikini. "Why do you need me?" I asked her. "You must have hired ransom experts? Have you told the police?"

"Of course we have. The officer who was in charge of the original theft has been assigned to us."

"Not Harry Abbott!"

"Detective Inspector Abbott," she corrected me. "Yes."

"Bloody hell!" I said in disgust. Harry Abbott is someone who lives under a stone along with all the other nasty things that crawl and creep on slimy bellies in the Stygian dark. He had been the policeman who had tried to pin the theft of the Van Gogh on to me in the first place. He had failed then, but I didn't fancy him trying again. "What does the bastard say you should do?"

"Persuade you to come home."

"I wouldn't go to Paradise on Harry's recommendation."

"Which doesn't alter the fact that you should be doing everything in your power to assist us. You are, after all, the legal owner of the painting."

"A minute ago," I pointed out, "you accused me of being the blackmailer."

"It's Inspector Abbott's belief" – her voice made it clear that she did not entirely share his certainty – "that the blackmailers waited till you sailed away before they made an approach to Sir Leon."

"Why would they do that?"

She shrugged to show that she had no answer. "What I do know," she said, "is that we need your authorisation for any attempts we may make to recover it. Otherwise Sir Leon could be accused of accepting stolen goods, so we need your permission to negotiate."

That seemed fair enough. "Does that mean," I asked her, "that if Sir Leon retrieves it, he'll have to give it back to me?"

"Of course," she said defiantly, as though, under those circumstances, she would dare me to take possession.

I smiled at her. "I wouldn't want it. Where could I hang it? There might be room on the lavatory bulkhead, but it would probably get in the way of the wet locker."

That small joke went down like a cement balloon. I sighed, went below to the cabin, and tore a page out of a notebook. I found a pencil and scribbled a quick message. 'Sir Leon Buzzacott and his wage-slaves have my full authority to do whatever they think necessary for the safe recovery of one painting by Vincent Van Gogh, commonly known as the Stowey Sunflowers. This authorisation is signed by John Rossendale, Lord Stowey, Earl of Stowey, and Master under God of the good ship *Sunflower*.' I dated it, then embellished it with an ornate rubber stamp that has *Sunflower*'s name, a quasi-Royal crown, and some nonsense numbers. I use the stamp to impress immigration officials in self-important but trivial countries. It doesn't reduce the bureaucracy, or the scale of the necessary bribes, but it sometimes makes them a trifle more respectful.

"There you go." I handed the note to Jennifer Pallavicini. "That's what you want, isn't it? Pity you flew all the way here to fetch it. You could have asked me nicely and I'd have posted it to you. Still, it's very good to see you. Would you like an early dinner before I sail? I do a very good *Corned Boeuf à la Bourguignonne*. I've even got some fresh vegetables."

She ignored my babbling. Instead she tore my note into shreds which, in defiance of Greenpeace's valiant endeavours, she scattered into the harbour water. "We need your personal help, my lord."

I leaned back on the thwart. "I'm always suspicious when you call me 'my lord'. What do you plan to do if I return to England? Torture a confession out of me?"

"If you agree to help us," she said, "we shall naturally assume your innocence."

I feigned grateful astonishment. "Oh, my God! You're so kind!"

She had the grace to blush, but continued pressing her case. "We need your knowledge. You can remember what happened four years ago. You know more than I do about those two wretched men. Someone fears what you know, but if you're lost in the oceans, then they won't show themselves again. So please come back, my lord, and help us."

She had asked very nicely, and she was so very pretty, so I very nearly agreed, but every time I went home I regretted it. I'd been back at sea just long enough to get the taste again, and I was dreaming of those palm-edged rivers and impossibly blue lagoons. "You have my verbal authority," I said wearily, "to do whatever you want, so go and do it. But leave me alone."

She nodded, almost as if she had expected the refusal. "I have some other news for you."

I waved a negligent hand as if to suggest that I did not much care whether she revealed the news or not.

"Your sister, Lady Elizabeth Tredgarth, is initiating proceedings to take your younger sister back to England."

She had spoken in a very matter-of-fact voice, a poker-player's voice. She had also appalled me, as she had doubtless hoped to do. "She's doing what?" I could not keep the anger from my voice.

Jennifer Pallavicini shrugged, as if to suggest that none of this was of much importance to her. "It seems there's a nun who is particularly fond of the Lady Georgina?"

"Sister Felicity, yes."

"The Lady Elizabeth feels that Sister Felicity is too old and too sick to look after Lady Georgina any longer. There's also a possibility that the convent hospital might be sold, so Lady Elizabeth wants her younger sister brought home."

"Home?"

"To where she lives, of course. In Gloucestershire, isn't it?"

I stared in horror at Jennifer Pallavicini. "That's ridiculous," I said. "Elizabeth can't stand the sight of Georgina!"

Jennifer Pallavicini didn't reply.

"How the hell do you know all this?" I demanded angrily.

"Because we take a great deal of interest in your family," she said equably. "It's a family that might bring our gallery a great treasure."

"You're making this up," I said. "You're telling me this nonsense in the hope that it will bring me back to England!"

"Your sister didn't want you to know," she said. "Indeed, she didn't institute proceedings until she'd heard you had sailed away. Of course, you don't have to believe me, but I thought perhaps the news might be of some slight interest to you."

The trouble was that I did believe her. Why else had Elizabeth been at the convent? "But we paid for Georgina," I protested, "for her lifetime!"

"A large sum of money was put into trust for your younger sister's care," Jennifer Pallavicini said pedantically, "but our legal informant tells us that the trustees retain the right to dictate how that money should be spent. If the Lady Elizabeth is confident that she can care for her sister, then there is no reason why the trust fund should not also be given into her care."

And how that made sense, brilliant clear lucid sense. Elizabeth, married to her impoverished and useless husband, would get her claws into Georgina's money, while Georgina could be stuck into a cottage on the Tredgarth farm with some harridan to guard her.

"The matter hasn't been decided yet," Jennifer Pallavicini went on. "The trustees need to be convinced that the Lady Elizabeth can provide a proper home for your younger sister, but there seems little doubt that she will succeed in so convincing them."

"Damn you," I said to Jennifer Pallavicini. "Damn you, damn you, damn you." The ties of duty, unavoidable duty, were wrapping about me. I could desert Stowey, I could watch my mother die and not shed a tear because of it, but Georgina was different. The only people who had ever been able to pierce that tremulous insanity had been Nanny, myself and Charlie. Now she needed me.

"Sir Leon" – Jennifer Pallavicini could not resist a small

smile as she played her ace – "is willing to guarantee a secure future for the Lady Georgina whether the painting is retrieved or not."

I said nothing. I was remembering the spitefulness with which Elizabeth had treated Georgina as a child. It wasn't a deliberate spitefulness, merely a reflection of Elizabeth's impatience. But, deliberate or not, it was unthinkable that Georgina should be put into Elizabeth's care.

Jennifer Pallavicini watched me, then opened her handbag and took out an air ticket which she laid on the thwart beside me. "If you go to your family's solicitors, my lord, you can doubtless stop this nonsense instantly."

I picked up the ticket. It was for a first-class seat, Azores to Lisbon and Lisbon to London. "When it comes to my family," I said haughtily to Jennifer Pallavicini, "I don't need your damned help." I tore the ticket into shreds, then scattered the scraps into the water. "Goodbye, Miss Pallavicini."

I had angered her, but I had also succeeded in surprising her. She took a few seconds to recover, then tried to turn the screw on my guilt. "It will be no good writing to your solicitors, my lord. Your objections to the Lady Georgina's fate won't be taken seriously unless you're in England to take some personal responsibility for her."

"I said I don't need your help to look after my family, Miss Pallavicini. So, goodbye."

"You're not going to help your younger sister?" she asked incredulously.

I smiled at her. "I'm going to sail away, Jennifer." I suddenly clicked my fingers as though I had been struck with a brilliant and timely idea. "Would you like to sail with me? You can cook, can't you?"

She stood up. "I cannot believe," she said with a frigid dignity, "that you could be so careless of your younger sister's future." She paused, evidently seeking some final and crushing farewell. "You are undoubtedly the most selfish and unfeeling man I have ever met."

"And you're cluttering up my boat. So if you don't want to come with me, go away."

130

She went away.

An hour later, as I was taking off the mainsail cover, I saw her being ferried out to Ulf's yawl. I assumed she was going to pay her informant his reward, so I wrestled my fibreglass dinghy over the guardrails, took the outboard from the stern locker, and motored over to join the happy party. I ignored Miss Pallavicini, instead I killed the small engine, drifted alongside the yawl, and told Ulf that he was a slime-bag.

"Johnny, how nice to see you! You know Miss Pallavicini, I think? You would like a drink with us?"

"I wouldn't drink your bloody prune juice if I was dying of constipation." I climbed out of the dinghy, hitched it to one of his shrouds, and walked down his scuppers. "I told you to keep your Swedish mouth shut."

Jennifer Pallavicini's eyes were wide with alarm. She clutched her handbag to her belly, but otherwise seemed unable to move. She doubtless believed that the huge Swede was about to pulverise me, and doubtless, in principle, she approved of that pulverisation, but it's one thing to want someone beaten up and quite another to see real blood on the deck. I also believed that Ulf would pulverise me, but I was fed up with the bastard and wanted to hit him.

"It was only a business arrangement," Ulf said smugly.

"And this is your profit." I jumped into his scrubbed cockpit and punched him in the belly. He gasped, but did not hit back, so I smacked him hard across the mouth. The blow jarred his head and brought a fleck of blood to his lips.

He still wouldn't fight. "Johnny!" He wiped his mouth. "This is not like you."

"That's because you don't know me. So listen. If you ever open your mouth about me again, anywhere, to anyone, I'll find your rotten carcass and I'll feed it to the bloody fish. Do you understand me?"

He had backed away. Jennifer Pallavicini's face showed utter horror. She made a small noise of protest, but I ignored her. Ulf waved a placatory hand. "I was only trying to help you, Johnny. Maybe it was important to you, yes?"

"Maybe it wasn't your business, you Swedish bastard."

His reward money, in Portuguese escudos, was strewn across the cockpit grating.

"It was just business, Johnny, just business." He sounded miserable, while I was mildly astonished to discover that he had a streak of jelly instead of a backbone. I'd expected one hell of a fight from him, but he was plainly scared. Nor was there any point in hitting him again, because he wasn't going to fight back. "You're a creep, Ulf. You're a real pain in the arse."

He nodded eager agreement with my judgment. "But you are a real English earl, Johnny, yes?" He had backed to stand beside the mizzen mast at the far end of his cockpit, from where he nodded towards Jennifer Pallavicini to prove the source of his information.

"And you're queen of the bloody fairies, Ulf. Piss off."

I had hardly acknowledged Jennifer Pallavicini's presence though, if I was honest with myself, I knew I'd been showing off to her. These days women might claim that they prefer enlightened men who can change nappies, do the ironing, and whip up tasty little soufflés, but in truth I suspect they prefer men who can beat the shit out of loathsome Swedes.

I motored back to *Sunflower*. The confrontation had made me feel much better, which was some consolation. Two hours later I cast off, hoisted my sails, and did what I had promised to Jennifer Pallavicini.

I sailed away.

PART THREE

Part Three

I sailed away, but I didn't go south. I went north. It was a bastard of a voyage into the teeth of a nasty wind, and a voyage made worse by a persistent equinoctial gale that tried to drive *Sunflower* into Biscay. Luckily we had enough westing to weather the two days and nights of wind, but it made the approach to the Channel a long fight against the northwesterlies that followed the storm. Once again I saw *Sunflower*'s reluctance to go to England: she blew out the clew of the storm jib, the topping lift broke, and a pin came out of a sheave in the self-steering gear. They were all simple enough repairs, but were best done in calmer weather. That weather came as we passed the Lizard. The wind died and there was only a long, long greasy swell from the west over which we crept on *Sunflower*'s motor.

I passed Salcombe by. I couldn't face Charlie. He had repaired my boat, provisioned me, and I knew all that generosity had been a vicarious adventure for Charlie. He could not be a sea-gypsy any more, so he had made it possible for me to go back to the deep waters in his place; but now I was crawling back with my tail between my legs. The time would come when I'd explain everything to him, but for now I could not bear to see the disappointment on his face, so I sailed up the Devon coast to the anonymity of the River Exe where I moored *Sunflower* at a vacant buoy. The sky clouded over at dusk and, by nightfall, it was raining. Welcome to England.

I was woken at three in the morning by an irate man who had just motored from Guernsey and wanted his mooring buoy back. I obliged him, anchoring *Sunflower* in what seemed like a vacant patch of the river instead. At five in the morning I was woken again as the falling tide grounded me. By seven *Sunflower* was lying canted on her starboard chine in the middle of a drying sandbank. It was still raining.

It took me the rest of the day to find a pub that could point me towards a man who might just have a spare mooring that I could possibly rent. In the end I found such a man and he didn't charge me a penny. He was a fisherman whose boat had stayed ashore since the winter. "It ain't worth the bother," he told me, "because there's nothing left out there, not even scruff. They've fished it clean! You can spend a week out there and only get a wet arse for your trouble." I consoled him with a pint, then told him I had to go to London for two days. "Your yacht'll be safe, boy, never you mind. But put your oars behind my garden shed, otherwise they'll be stolen, sure as eggs." I'd rowed the dinghy ashore, because I didn't want to risk using the outboard and it being stolen while the dinghy was marooned on the foreshore.

I caught a train next morning and, because there wasn't a spare seat, stood all the way from Devon to London. By the time the train pulled into Paddington I was in a foul temper.

London didn't help my mood. I'd just spent six weeks in the Atlantic where the greatest inconvenience had been listening to a yellow-bellied Swede, but London was nothing but inconvenience. It was crowded, stinking and self-important. The people had faces wan as curdled milk. They scurried like rats through their noisy tunnels, they littered, and all about them was noise. Noise, noise, Goddamned bloody noise. Trains clattering, taxis thumping, horns and voices and sirens and jackhammers battered the air. I had not visited London in over four years, and I hoped to God I would never have to visit the place again.

I caught a bus to the Strand, then walked to the solicitors' office. Sir Oliver Bulstrode was not in the building, but would I like to leave a message? The girl at the reception desk was plainly intimating that scruffy men walking unannounced off the pavement were not welcome as clients at Bulstrode, Finch, Finch and McElroy. "I'll wait," I said curtly.

I sat down in an ancient leather chair and picked up a copy of *The Field*.

"Are you a client, sir?" The receptionist was looking understandably alarmed. I was wearing my cleanest jeans, my least dirty shirt, and a pair of fairly new tennis shoes, but

I still didn't look much like the usual class of gold-plated shit that did business with Bulstrode.

"I'm a client," I said. "My name's Rossendale."

"Rossendale?"

"As in Stowey, Earl of," I said.

There was a pause of two heartbeats. "Would you like coffee, my lord? Or something stronger, perhaps?"

I smiled back at her. It wasn't her fault that British Rail couldn't run a railroad, or that I was pissed off with London, or that I was angry at my twin sister, or that I was dressed like a vagabond. "What I'd really like," I said, "is to take you out to lunch, but as I have to speak with Sir Oliver I'll settle for a glass of his best Scotch instead."

Sir Oliver arrived a half-hour later. He's a plump man with a kindly face, a real Santa Claus of a face, but the benign look is utterly deceptive for, like all the top lawyers, he has a heart of flint and the morals of a rabid weasel. He raised plump hands in astonishment when he saw me. "My lord! I had no idea you were coming! Have I mislaid our appointment?"

"No, Oliver, you have not. This is by nature of a surprise visit."

"And a very welcome surprise too! Upon my word, what a distinct pleasure this is. I shall cancel my luncheon engagement immediately." Which was his way of telling me that he would double his hourly fees for this unannounced visit, which did not bother me because I had no intention of paying. Sir Oliver and his partners had sent their children to the best schools and their wives to the most expensive fat farms on the proceeds of the Stowey Estate, and I considered it was high time he did something for me. "I see you've been given some whisky," he said. "Good! Good! Do come into my sanctum, John!" He always greeted me as 'my lord', and thereafter used my Christian name to show that he could assume intimate terms with the nobility. The man's a creep, but a clever one.

He fussed me into his office which was stiff with leather chairs and ancient hunting prints. At weekends he plays the country squire, plodding round six damp Essex acres with a shotgun and a mangy spaniel. "Sit down, John, do! I shall just rearrange luncheon, if you'll allow me."

Ten minutes later we were served plates of salmon salad in his office. He opened a bottle of Entre-Deux-Mers. "I was so sorry not to have attended your mother's funeral," he told me as he poured the wine. "I had an unbreakable engagement that day, which was so very sad." He lied, of course. If the Rossendale family had still had any flesh on their bones he'd have been down to the funeral like a shot, but as he thought he'd squeezed us dry then there had clearly been no profit for him in making the journey. "So sad," he murmured.

"I missed the funeral too," I said. "I walked out before it began."

He must have known that already for he showed no reaction, not even to enquire why I had abandoned the ceremony. Instead he smiled beneficently. "I must say, John, you do look very well. Sun and sea, eh? And still as thin as ever! You do put the rest of us to shame." He paused for a split second. "I thought you were even now sailing into the unknown? So very brave of you, I always think." He bestowed me an admiring look. In fact Sir Oliver dislikes me intensely. He's been our family's solicitor for almost as long as I can remember and, when I inherited the title, he had thought that I would be naïve enough to do whatever he told me. In the end I told him to get stuffed and went off to sea. He's never forgiven me and probably never will.

"I sailed back."

"Evidently." He smiled, then forked a chunk of salmon and mayonnaise into his mouth. "I assume you're worried about your mother's will?"

"I haven't even seen the will."

"Ah." He clearly wished he hadn't raised the matter, and swiftly moved the conversation on. "So to what, precisely, do I owe the pleasure of this visit?"

"I came to see you, Oliver, because of what that bitch Elizabeth is doing to Georgina."

He dabbed at his lips with a linen napkin. "Dear Lady Elizabeth."

"The answer is no."

"No?" He smiled happily. "No one appreciates the merits of brevity more than I, my dear John, but I must confess that your meaning has momentarily eluded even me."

"Georgina is not going to live with Elizabeth. That's clear enough, isn't it?"

"Eminently." He sipped his wine. Somewhere beyond the heavily curtained window a piledriver began smacking insistently.

I raised my voice over the din. "If you want me to sign something, I will. As head of my benighted family, Oliver, I'm telling you that Georgina's future is not up for grabs."

"I don't think we're quite ready for signatures yet," he said ominously. He poured each of us another glass of wine. "Might I ask why you're so adamantly opposed?"

"Because Elizabeth is a money-grubbing witch who hates Georgina. She only wants her out of Jersey so she can get her hands on Georgina's trust fund. You know all that, so why ask me?"

He swivelled his chair to stare at a print of Stowey that hung above a leather sofa. "I suppose," he said airily, "that at sea you must learn to view the world in very simple terms. There's no room for doubt in the ocean, is there? Yet on shore, my dear John, things can become so deucedly complicated."

"Stop wrapping it up, Oliver. Tell me."

He swivelled his chair to face me. "It's all a question of options, John. So long as your dear mother was alive she wanted Georgina to stay in Jersey, but now things are changing. The good sisters of the convent are under a great deal of pressure to sell the property; indeed, it seems increasingly likely that the diocese will force the sale, which would mean that the sisters are most likely to retreat to their mother house at Nantes. Will the Lady Georgina be happy in France?" He spread his hands to show that he did not know the answer. "Then we must consider dear Sister Felicity. She's not well, John, not at all, and all of us fear for dear Lady Georgina when Felicity dies. Imagine it, if you can: Georgina would be alone and bereft, in a strange country, with no solace but the sacraments."

The weight of it crushed down on me. I could see what was in Sir Oliver Bulstrode's evil mind. The last vestiges of my family's cash were in Georgina's trust fund. If Elizabeth took control of that money, then Oliver would get his fee. The trustees of the fund would need to be persuaded, but there were few men better at buttering parsnips than Sir Oliver Bloody Bulstrode. In short the pigs had found a honey trough and were ready to snuffle, and none of them cared a monkey's toss for Georgina.

"She can be found a good institution in England, can't she?" I tried.

"Oh, undoubtedly!" he said with fake enthusiasm. "There must be scores of institutions which would gladly care for your sister! Yet would any court of law, I ask you, prefer such an institution to the love and care of a family member? Not, I hope, that this matter will ever reach any court," he added hastily. "I'm sure we can work it out most amicably."

"You'd call Elizabeth loving and caring?" I asked incredulously.

"The Lady Elizabeth Tredgarth," he said huffily, "has undertaken to provide the most proper care and attention for her sister. I note, with the deepest regrets, your reservations about the Lady Elizabeth's suitability, yet I must tell you frankly, my lord, that I cannot see any court refusing her a supervision order. Not when you consider the alternatives."

I had noted that he had called me 'my lord'. That was a danger signal which told me Sir Oliver was on Elizabeth's side. He was on her side because she had a prospect of scooping the cash. Sir Oliver is a venal bastard, but so are most top lawyers. That's why so many of them become politicians.

"Supposing I offered Georgina a home?" I asked.

He feigned astonished pleasure. "My dear John! What a very splendid idea! And so typical of your generosity! Can you do it? Naturally, you would have to provide constant nursing care. The premises would have to be suitable, or were you thinking of making her a shipmate?" He chuckled at his own jest. "Seriously, John, such a responsibility will involve a great deal of money!"

"There's Georgina's trust fund."

"Which would hardly be made available to someone with a police record." The steel was in his voice now. "You would be asking the trustees to grant you authority over a great deal of money. Before they would even consider doing that, they would need to be satisfied that you have demonstrated some fiscal responsibility and domestic stability. I believe, unless I am entirely out of touch with your personal affairs, that you possess neither a house nor a wife?"

I stood up. I had not touched any of the salmon salad. "Georgina can stay where she is so long as Felicity is alive and the hospital remains unsold."

I had not inflected it as a question, but Sir Oliver chose to treat it as such. "She can certainly remain where she is for a time, yes. The Lady Elizabeth has not, I understand, finished preparing her domestic arrangements." He paused to shake his head sadly, as though I was disappointing him by my wilfulness. "I really do think you may be misjudging your sister. I grant you that Elizabeth can be tiresome, but I do assure you that she is making the most thorough preparations for Georgina's welfare. Why don't you inspect those arrangements? I'm quite sure the Lady Elizabeth would welcome such an inspection."

"Have you inspected them?" I asked.

"Of course. I lunched at Perilly last week, where I found the Lady Elizabeth's proposed arrangements entirely satisfactory."

They had me boxed in. I'd just sailed twelve hundred horrid miles to find that I had been utterly outmanoeuvred. I left Sir Oliver's office, ran down the stairs, and, once on the pavement, took a deep breath to rid my lungs of the leathery stench of his hypocrisy. The street air stank of fumes and filth. And Georgina, like me, was trapped.

I walked beside the embankment. I went there because there are boats moored to the wall, but they're boats which are never again going to feel ocean waves on their cutwaters, or heel to a cold cold wind as clean as a rigging knife. The boats are trapped. They're there to serve as pubs or museum pieces.

141

London has taken their guts and their pride away from them, and reduced them to gewgaws.

And I was trapped. But, God help me, I had some guts and pride left; enough, I hoped, to fillet a twin sister and her fat lawyer.

I paced the river. It began to rain, but I was oblivious to both the rain and the passing time. Up and down I went, between Blackfriars and Westminster, thinking.

I was head of the Rossendale family, but my titular authority counted for nothing because I was poor, had a police record, and a reputation for being irresponsible.

Yet, truly, neither the police record nor the irresponsibility mattered because, when dealing with lawyers, only one thing carries real weight. It isn't justice, or probity, or any other of their fine words; it's cash. Lots of cash. Lawyers love cash. They grovel for it, swill in it, lie in it, cheat for it, flatter for it and dream of it.

So I needed cash. The trustees of Georgina's fund might never entrust the money to me, but Georgina wasn't tied to the trust. If I could replace the trust fund, then I could arrange her future, so the first question to be thrashed out along the embankment was where I could find a lot of money. There was an obvious answer, of course, but my pride wouldn't let me grovel to Jennifer Pallavicini. So I had to find another way.

I could sell the few shares left in Uncle Thomas's legacy and I could sell *Sunflower*. I'd probably raise about one hundred thousand pounds which would be enough to buy a small house in Devon. I could find a job. If no one needed a welder or carpenter, then I could sell my title to some idiot who wanted an aristocrat's name on his firm's letterhead. I could join the other clowns in the House of Lords and claim my attendance money. Perhaps I could write a book: *Belting Round the World, an Earl's Story*. Perhaps the heavens would open and rain golden sovereigns on me. Perhaps pigs would fly.

It was hopeless. A small house in Devon and a job would not solve my problem because Elizabeth would still hold all the cards; she had a large house, a husband, and no record of being drunk and disorderly. What I needed was a lot of money, very fast; enough to buy a sharper lawyer than Sir Oliver.

Charlie.

That thought stopped my walking. The lights were coming on across the river and reflecting in shaking streaks on the darkening water.

Charlie would help. Charlie would throw himself into this battle with all his huge heart and soul and strength, but Charlie would be no match for a cunning bastard like Sir Oliver Bulstrode. Charlie would give me money, but the lawyers would soon drain that away and Charlie, despite his success and despite his flashy toys, was deeply in debt. Besides, this was family. This was my responsibility, and I had already taken too much money from Charlie. What I needed now was my own money; gobs of money, a lawyer's wet dream of money. What I needed was a patch of canvas, two feet three inches wide by a shade over three feet long, on which some poor half-mad genius had once painted a vase of sunflowers.

In short I needed Sir Leon Buzzacott. He had known that, which was why he had sent Jennifer Pallavicini with the message that he would look after Georgina's future.

But to secure that future I would have to crawl abjectly to Jennifer Pallavicini. Otherwise I was trapped by the short and curlies.

Unless, of course, Sir Oliver was right and I was being unfair in my judgment of Elizabeth. That was the last straw of hope I could cling to, and if that straw failed me then I would have to eat humble pie. I turned towards Westminster for the last time. It was late, fully dark, and I was soaked to the skin, so I phoned an old girlfriend and asked if I could have a bed for the night. She agreed, though she didn't offer her own bed, but I hadn't expected her to, because nothing was going right these days. Nothing.

In the morning I went to Gloucestershire. During the night I had half persuaded myself that Elizabeth was indeed doing the decent thing, and that I had been blinded to her decency by my own unreasonable dislike of her. It was nonsense, I told myself, to think that Elizabeth could cheat the trustees. She would need to satisfy them that she could provide Georgina with proper care and living-quarters, and so, by the time I caught the train, I was more than half convinced that my troubles would soon be over. Georgina would have a safe haven, and I would be free to return to my life and *Sunflower*.

Jennifer Pallavicini had called me uncaring and selfish. She was wrong about the first. I cared for Georgina; it was simply that, when Jennifer Pallavicini confronted me in Horta, I had been unwilling to dance to her insistent tune. Selfish? I thought about that as I stood in the crowded train going from London to the Cotswolds. Yes, I thought, she was probably right. I was selfish. I had always done what I wanted. I'd worked for it, if welding steel hulls in some humid tropical hell hole was called work, but I had still pursued my own desires. Yet not, I decided, to the detriment of others. I had never betrayed anyone to get what I wanted. I'd fought a few, but it takes two to fight.

So the Pallavicini, I decided, did not understand me half as well as she believed. She had believed that I would need her assistance to settle Georgina's future, but now I was proving that I could look after my sister without Sir Leon's help. I would do it quickly, then take myself back to *Sunflower* and the open sea.

I caught a bus from the station to Elizabeth's village, then walked a lane between dry-stone walls to where the drive led to Lord Tredgarth's farm. A big sign on the gate said 'Entrance to Perilly House and Equestrian Centre Only. Private. No Trespassing', while another sign ordered trades-men to use the entrance on the Gloucester road. I decided I wasn't a tradesman and pushed open the tall wrought-iron gates. The sun was trying to break through the clouds as I walked between the stumps of trees killed by Dutch elm disease. To my right was a thistle-rich paddock where a few fat ponies grazed between low jumps made from painted oil drums and striped poles. Elizabeth's 'Equestrian Centre' was really a scabby riding-school which catered to the fat children of middle-class mothers who liked to boast they were acquainted with the Lady Elizabeth Tredgarth. It was a toss up which Elizabeth hated the most: the mothers or their children. She'd never had children herself, which I considered a blessing to the unborn.

The grandly named Perilly House was really just a large farmhouse. It was a very pleasant farmhouse built of Cotswold stone, with a big central gable and two large wings. Roses grew about the front door which had been tricked out with a white Georgian portico and an antique brass bell-pull.

A nervous cleaning woman answered the bell and told me her ladyship was not at home. Her ladyship had gone to a hospital charity committee meeting in Cirencester, which answer, despite my attempts to convince myself that Elizabeth was behaving well, triggered a rush of uncharitable thoughts. I imagined Elizabeth earning every brownie point she could so long as she saw Georgina's trust fund in her sights. I imagined she would suddenly be active on the hospital charity, and the mental health fund-raising committee and even the flower rota at the parish church. "But his lordship's at home," the cleaning lady volunteered.

"Would you tell him John Rossendale's here?"

"Is it business, sir?" She had clearly been trained to be wary of all strange visitors.

"No." I was about to say I was a friend, but decided that would stretch the truth too far. "It's a private matter."

The woman looked dubious, but seemed reassured that I was not in a suit, which meant I was probably not serving a writ or otherwise adding to Peter Tredgarth's troubles. "He's at the camp, sir."

I knew where that was. In the early days of my sister's marriage, when Peter and I had still been friends, I had been a frequent visitor to Perilly, and I remembered the old camp which had been hastily built in the war to house Italian prisoners doing farm work on the surrounding estates. By the time I first saw the camp it was already derelict. At one time Peter had thought to turn the old wooden huts into a chicken farm, but in the end he had done nothing and the timber had rotted away and the undergrowth had all but hidden the concrete foundations.

I walked down a tractor-rutted path, past a spinney of alders, then turned alongside the stream which would lead me to the low hill where the camp had been built. I saw Peter Tredgarth standing beside the stream, staring gloomily at the water. He had a shotgun under his arm, making him look uncommonly like a man contemplating the benefits of suicide. He jerked guiltily when I called his name, then stared with surprise as he recognised me. "What the hell are you doing here?" he asked. I could hardly expect him to be glad to see me after our last meeting in the Channel Islands.

"I've come to see you. And Elizabeth, of course, but I gather she's not at home?"

"She never is, these days. I sometimes forget what she looks like." He peered at me, evidently trying to decide whether to be grudgingly polite or dismissively nasty. He didn't have the guts to be nasty, so offered me a grunt of welcome instead. "D'you see any heron?"

I looked up and down the stream. "No heron, Peter."

"One of the labourers told me he saw a nesting couple up by the weir. Thought I'd shoot them."

"Aren't they a protected species?" I teased him.

"Bad for the fishing, you see. Bloody bad. Best thing to do is shoot them." He broke the gun and took out the cartridges.

"Why don't you have a water-bailiff to look after the fishing?" I asked.

"I did. Retired sergeant from my regiment. Nice chap, but I couldn't afford to pay him." He looked unhappily at his water, which was choking with weeds. "Needs a bit of work, eh?"

"A bit."

"Must get down to it one day. You can get a lot for the fishing rights these days. And it's good water, you know! No damn fish farms filling it up with trout-shit."

"Why don't you build your own fish farm," I asked him, "and pollute it yourself?"

"I tried that, John, but they wouldn't give me planning

permission. Bastards. They'll let some upstart grocer build a brick bungalow on a beauty spot, but they won't let a landowner make a decent living. I should have bribed them, of course, but I couldn't afford their fees." He frowned at me, seemingly puzzled by my unexpected visit. "If I were you I wouldn't be here when Elizabeth gets back. She had a telephone call from her lawyer chappie yesterday. The one in London? You must know who I mean. He lunched here last week and scoffed the best part of a brisket. Anyway, Elizabeth's not exactly happy with you. Livid, in fact. Shouldn't be talking to you myself, but . . ." He could not think quite why he was talking to me, so his voice tailed away.

"You don't have Elizabeth's capacity to hate?" I suggested.

"Yours is a ghastly family," he said. "Always squabbling."

"And yours isn't?"

"They're pretty ghastly too," he admitted. Peter Tredgarth is big and heavy, with a permanently worried expression. He had not always been like that. When I first introduced him to Elizabeth he had been a trim Guards officer, lively and quick, who used to sail the Channel with me. He had long since given up sailing and was now weighed down with the world's griefs. "I thought you'd gone back to sea?" he said irritably.

"I did. I came back."

"Bloody silly of you. If I was you, I'd stay out there. That's what I should have done. Gone off and stayed away." He fell silent and, for a moment, neither of us could find anything to say.

"I hear you were up at the camp?" I said to fill the silence.

He gave me a fierce look. "Did you drive here?"

"I caught a bus from the station, then walked."

"I don't think I've been on a bus since I was at prep school." He grimaced, either at the memory, or as he tried to decide what to do with my unwelcome presence. "Tell you what I'll do," he said at last, "I'll drive you to the station. That way she won't find you on the premises, and I won't tell her you've visited. We can stop for a bite of lunch on the way. I know a decent little pub which does a good midday meal. Wait here!"

He didn't let me respond, but just turned away and began

walking towards the tree-fringed hill where the camp lay. I started after him. "I'll come with you."

"Wait!" He turned on me angrily, then, as if to explain his rudeness, tossed me the gun and its two cartridges. "Keep an eye out for the heron, there's a good chap."

I waited. The two heron flew past me. I ignored them. Instead I watched Peter plod up the hill and disappear into the undergrowth beyond the trees. There was a pause, then his mud-stained Land Rover appeared and bounced down the slope towards me.

"See the heron?" he asked as he braked beside me.

"Not a sign, Peter." I climbed into the passenger seat and pushed the gun into the back.

"Steak and kidney pie and a decent pint, eh?" Peter was suddenly very jocular.

I put my hand over the gear lever to stop him driving away. "I don't want to go to the pub yet, Peter. I've come here to see what preparations you're making for Georgina. If I approve of them, then I won't oppose Elizabeth and she can get her claws on Georgina's money. So why don't I just go up to the house and wait for Elizabeth?"

He stared at me, biting a strand of his moustache. "Georgina?" he finally said.

"Georgina," I confirmed.

"You're worried about her?" He seemed astonished at the thought.

"Of course I'm worried about her."

"And you think Elizabeth's going to cheat on the trust fund?"

"It occurred to me, yes," I said bluntly.

For a few seconds I thought he was going to throw me out of the vehicle for insulting his wife, but instead he just pushed my hand away from the gear lever and crashed it into first. "Right!" He spoke angrily and decisively. "You've asked for it, so you'll damn well get it. Operation Georgina." We lurched forward, turned on to the rutted track, and accelerated up towards the farm. "Elizabeth won't take kindly to you poking about the place, but Georgina's your sister, so why the hell shouldn't you see where she's going to live?" He

148

laughed, but at what I could not tell. He drove furiously. We went past the house, past the farmyard, and up a track edged with blackberry bushes. At the end of the track, and facing on to a quiet country lane, was a pretty stone cottage. Building work was evident from the scaffolding which reached up to the chimney and from the pile of plumber's junk that lay outside the door, but no builders were actually visible.

"Primrose Cottage," Peter Tredgarth announced as he stamped on the Land Rover's brakes. "A horrible name, but it has three bedrooms, two bathrooms, a kitchen, living room, walled garden at the rear, and one garage. Central heating is being installed. A perfect residence, you will agree, for one loony sister and her live-in nurse?"

"Perfect," I agreed. I was astonished and pleased. I might have persuaded myself that Elizabeth was going to do the decent thing, but I had not really believed it. Yet Primrose Cottage was indeed perfect. It offered privacy and comfort, as well as restfulness. I felt my worries dropping away. I would be free again.

"The live-in nurse" – Peter had left the motor running – "will be hired from an agency in Cheltenham. The agency specialises in cases like Georgina's. Naturally the woman will have to be given time off, so the agency will supply weekend cover and supplementary nursing care for two nights a week as part of the contract price." His voice became heavy with sarcasm. "Does that meet with your approval?"

"I think it sounds marvellous, Peter," I said warmly.

He sneered at the humility in my voice. "Elizabeth has already shown the cottage to the trustees, and they agree with you. They've also interviewed the agency and found them entirely satisfactory."

"Elizabeth's been wonderful," I ate more humble pie, "and I apologise for doubting her."

He laughed, his victory over me complete. "You've got a nerve, John." He took a silver flask from a pocket of his tweed jacket, unscrewed its cap, and took a long pull. He suddenly looked very morose. "And why the hell would you care about Georgina?"

"I just do."

"You care about her money," he said savagely, "but you won't get it, John. You abdicated, you gave up, you bottled out, you pissed off to sea, and you probably screwed the family by nicking their bloody picture as well." He began to laugh. I'd never realised before this moment that he was an alcoholic. He'd probably been drinking before I met him, and he would probably be drinking for the rest of the day. "Did you steal that picture?" he asked me suddenly.

"No."

"She says you did. She says she's met someone who helped you do it. You're a fool, John. I suppose you threw the money away?"

"I didn't steal the picture, Peter."

He ignored that. "It was left to Elizabeth in your mother's will."

"I know."

"And it ought to go to her," he said heavily as though making a point I might not have considered before. "She's got plans for the money, you see."

"Plans?"

"Buy Stowey back. Run a proper equestrian centre." He took a pull on the flask, then chuckled. "I think she imagines the Queen coming down to admire the horses, but the point of it is, John, that Elizabeth wants to use the money. She wants to restore the family's position in society! You don't, do you? All you want to do is arse around in a boat! If you had any decency at all you'd tell her where the picture is, then disappear."

"I don't know where it is, Peter." I paused. "Who told her I'd stolen it?"

"Buggered if I know." Nor did he care; it was enough that he shared Elizabeth's belief in my guilt. He peered at his watch. "She might come home for lunch, so you'd best leave." He leaned across me to open the door. "Go to the end of the lane and you can catch a bus at the crossroads."

"No pub lunch?" I asked him.

"Out," he ordered me. It was hard to believe we had once been friends. Now, whatever his unhappiness, he was on his wife's side in our family's civil war.

I climbed out and slammed the Land Rover's door.

"And don't tell her I've spoken to you!" Lord Tredgarth shouted at me.

"I won't."

He took another pull at his flask, then viciously wrenched the steering wheel to slew the Land Rover back towards the farm. I had to jump fast to save myself from being side-swiped by the skidding vehicle. Its rear wheels spattered me with mud as he drove away.

I waited till he had disappeared then walked up the path to Primrose Cottage. The new front door had still not been fitted with a lock, so I pushed into the big living room which was littered with builders' scraps. The walls were newly painted. A wood stove had been fitted in the old hearth. It was a lovely cottage, its southern windows facing across the water meadows. I wandered into the kitchen where a new double sink had been fitted. There was a pile of builders' brochures and invoices on the draining board. I sifted idly through them. Only one of the brochures was not about building materials, but was an invitation from a firm which specialised in letting holiday cottages: 'Do you have an unused farm cottage? Let us turn your empty property into profit!'

I stared through the window. I could see the camp hill across the valley. Why had Peter not wanted me to walk to the Land-rover with him? I tried to dismiss the nagging worry. I wanted to walk away, to go to the crossroads and catch my bus, then to take *Sunflower* to the limitless freedom of the seas, but there was something wrong here. I looked down at the holiday cottage brochure. Was Elizabeth planning to renovate Primrose Cottage at the expense of Georgina's fund, then let it to summer visitors?

I leafed through the stained and crumpled paperwork on the draining board. One sheet of paper was a carbon copy of an estimate from a plumbing firm. It was a hefty estimate, covering the installation of a new hot water tank, a central heating boiler, a shower room, and, at the very bottom, for the provision of a stand-pipe and two cold water connections to caravans. The estimate had evidently been successful, for the plumbers were using it as a checklist for work completed.

I saw the stand-pipe had already been finished.

I swore very softly, not really believing what I was suspecting, but knowing that I would have to find out for myself. And knowing, too, that if I was right, then my troubles were only just beginning.

I didn't cross Peter's land. Instead I walked a mile up the lane, turned south on to the Gloucester road and crossed the stream by the new bridge. Trucks carrying chipboard and frozen chickens thundered past me. At the top of the hill there was a layby where a glum family picnicked within yards of the growling lorries. I walked past them and climbed over the gate on to Peter's property. The mud track had been newly used. I followed it a hundred yards through the screen of dark trees, then through the tangled undergrowth to where a clearing had been hacked out in the old camp.

Two caravans stood on the concrete foundation slabs of the old huts. Around the slabs the undergrowth had been cleared away with a harrow, leaving scarred raw earth in which the first nettles were already growing. The caravans were quite large, but clearly second-hand. Both were locked. The stand-pipe was between them. Their windows were obscured by net curtains.

Two caravans. One for Georgina, and the other for whom? Girls from the west of Ireland, perhaps, inveigled by an advertisement in a Catholic newspaper? Such girls came cheap. My mother had used them as servants and I imagined Elizabeth would do the same. She would pretend that Primrose Cottage was to be Georgina's home, and doubtless it would be for a few months, and doubtless the Cheltenham agency would provide the nursing care, but after a while it would all quietly change and Georgina would be shuttled up the hill to this dank tomb of a wood, and Primrose Cottage could be profitably let to appreciative holiday-makers. And all of it would be done with Georgina's money.

"Bugger!" I shouted the curse aloud and thumped an impotent fist against the metal skin of the nearest caravan.

There was to be no freedom after all, but only duty, because it was time to catch a thief.

*　　*　　*

152

I went back to Devon that night, retrieved my oars, rowed myself out to *Sunflower*, and poured myself the dregs of my last bottle of whiskey. I felt an insidious temptation to let the ebbing tide take me to sea, but instead I slept and, in the morning, went ashore and found a public phone.

The bullet had to be bitten. Charlie must know that I was back in England and that all his generosity had not bought me the freedom he so envied. I phoned his yard, but he wasn't in his office, so I called Yvonne. She sounded surprised to hear my voice, but did not ask where I was or what I wanted. She said Charlie was away from home.

"In Hertfordshire again?"

"Scotland, I think." She didn't sound as if it mattered very much. "He's sub-contracting on a road-widening scheme."

"Tell him I'm back, Yvonne. I'm moored in the Exe at the moment, but I don't know how long I'll stay here, but he can always try the Channel radio stations."

She did not sound very pleased, but promised to tell Charlie when he called home. Perhaps she thought I'd come to take more money off him. I said goodbye to her, then called Directory Enquiries to find the number of the Buzzacott Museum Gallery. This was a harder bullet to bite, but it had to be done. I asked for Jennifer Pallavicini, but the man who answered the phone in her office said she was in New York. She was expected back soon, but, in the meantime, was there any message?

"Tell her that John Rossendale called and that I'm back in England. Tell her she can probably reach me by radio." I gave him a list of coast radio stations and *Sunflower*'s call sign. The man was clearly bemused, but docilely took down the information. Then, because I had nothing better to do, I took *Sunflower* to sea.

I knocked about the Channel for a few days. I was tempted to visit Jersey, but I did not know what good it would do. Georgina might be pleased to see me, but I could offer her no reassurances, so I chickened out. I visited a friend in Lèzardrieux, and tried to persuade myself I was in love with a waitress in his riverfront cafe. Jacques drove me to the casino at Dinard where, despite my avowal that I couldn't afford to gamble, I won three thousand francs. When the francs didn't change the waitress's mind I went downstream and anchored off the Ile Bréhat, where I stayed for two days. I listened to the traffic lists on the VHF, but neither *Sunflower*'s name nor her call sign were ever mentioned. I made one link call to the Buzzacott Museum Gallery, charging the cost to Elizabeth's home number, but Jennifer Pallavicini had still not returned.

After two days I decided to sail to the Scilly Isles, which I'd never visited. The forecast had promised a southeast wind, but three hours off the Breton coast the wind veered round the compass which meant that I was faced by a devil of a windward flog. I held to it, lured by the unknown Scillies, which I reached just after dusk the next day. I anchored in Porth Cressa and spent a miserable night heaving and sheering in strong seas driven by a rising west wind. The morning was filthy with rain and blowing half a gale, so, without going ashore, I hauled up the anchor, let the foresails turn *Sunflower*, and took myself off. The wind was gusting to force eight, and the seas were heaping into thumping great monsters. White crests cascaded down the wave faces. Another yacht, a big Moody, left the Scillies at the same time, but by midday I had lost her in the misting squalls which were slithering up towards Cornwall. I was enjoying myself. *Sunflower* was running well, hard before the wind and rolling her boom under every few minutes. In the early afternoon I caught a glimpse of the Lizard, black in the grey murk, but then a rainstorm blotted it out. I heard thunder to the north, and saw one stabbing crack of lightning pierce the gloom. *Sunflower* slammed her stem into a wave, scattered white water twelve feet high, then dipped her nose as a following sea swept under her counter. This was Channel sailing at its best; hard, fast, wet and exhilarating.

Next morning, in Dartmouth, I rowed to the marina where *Sunflower* had been relaunched, but there was no sign of *Barratry*. I had not really expected to see her, so I went ashore, found a telephone, but could get no answer from Charlie's house. I tried the yard, but he wasn't there either. I called Jennifer Pallavicini, but she was evidently not back from America, for there was no answer from her office.

To hell with it, I thought. To hell with it. I walked in a gusting breeze among the tourists on the quayside and I wished I was far away. Except that two caravans in a corner of Elizabeth's farm were holding me home. I needed to solve that problem, and I was achieving nothing by knocking about the Channel and brooding. I went back to the telephone box. Jennifer Pallavicini had told me in Horta that Harry Abbott was the policeman in charge of discovering the mutilated Van Gogh. Harry was a bastard, but he was a bastard who could be reached by telephone, so I called him.

He wasn't in his Exeter office, but I held on while he was tracked down. He couldn't come to the phone, but passed on a message that I should meet him next morning in the café on Dartmouth's quay.

I spent the day drying out the boat and washing the salt out of my hair and clothes. Next morning I rowed ashore early and ordered a double helping of bacon, egg, sausages and chips. I had bought a tabloid and was amusing myself by reading about the vicar who'd run off with the organist's husband when a hand tapped my shoulder.

I turned. Harry Abbott's lugubrious and unhealthy face gazed solemnly down into mine. The face smiled, revealing long yellow teeth. "Oh, God," I said.

"I haven't been promoted that high yet. I'm only a Detective Inspector, but that is very close to being God." He reached over my shoulder and stole one of my chips. "I like chips for breakfast."

"If you want some chips, order your own."

He stole another. "I've already had a plateful. Very nice they were, too, with a spot of vinegar." He sat opposite me and sprinkled vinegar on his stolen chip. "You're looking very well, Johnny," he said. "If I'd had my way, you'd still be in prison now."

"So you failed."

"Justice is like the pox," he said, "in the end it gets everyone."

"Very funny, Harry."

He ordered himself a coffee and spooned sugar into the

cup. He then lit a cigarette and blew smoke at me. "Did you know Jimmy Nicholls?"

"No."

"He died of smoking, just like your mother. Were you upset by her death, Johnny?"

"Piss off, Harry."

Detective Inspector Harry Abbott looks like a joke. He's cadaverous, tall, grey, and apparently always at death's door, but he's a cunning sod. When he had interrogated me about the stolen Van Gogh he had come foully close to persuading me to tell him exactly what he wanted to hear. I'd been innocent, but Harry had been relentless, almost persuading me that I had to be guilty. He is not a man to underestimate.

"How do you feel about some nasty-minded bleeder taking the kitchen scissors to your mum's painting?" he asked.

"It pisses me off."

"You always did like the painting, didn't you? You pretended not to, but I knew you liked it. Me, now, I don't understand it. I like a proper painting."

"Tits and bums?"

He ignored that. "It occurred to me once that you might have nicked it because you liked it so much. Oddly enough I'm not so very sure that you did nick it now, in fact I'd even go so far as to say that I believe in your innocence, Johnny. Perhaps I'm getting soft in my old age, or perhaps I've caught a nasty case of food poisoning from the milk of human kindness, but I really do believe that I did you an injustice all those years ago."

"Then say you're sorry."

"I'm sorry, Johnny." He bared his horse's teeth at me. "So tell me, you bastard, why didn't you report an attempt on your life? I know it's a miserable life, and probably not worth preserving, but we are mildly interested in murder attempts."

I abandoned the rest of my breakfast. "Who told you about that?"

"Who the hell do you think told me?" Harry took the last sausage from my plate. "The Contessa, of course."

"The Contessa?" The only Contessa I could think of was a

make of boat. A very nice make of boat. I'd nearly bought a Contessa 32 once.

Harry shook his head in grief for my sanity. "The Contessa Pallavicini. Who else?"

"Jennifer Pallavicini?"

"Oh, of course, I keep forgetting. You're a nob as well. You probably don't use titles amongst yourselves. I suppose you call her Jenny-baby or Passion-knickers. Yes, Johnny. I mean Jennifer Pallavicini."

"Bloody hell fire," I said softly. I had thought I was the one earning pennies from heaven by not using my title, and all the time Jennifer Pallavicini was hiding her own? I felt stupid and astonished. "I didn't know she was a Contessa," I said limply.

"Her mother married the title, but she's Lady Buzzacott now, so the daughter uses the handle. Mind you, those Italians seem to give away titles with their cornflakes, so perhaps it doesn't mean anything."

I gaped at him. "She's Buzzacott's stepdaughter?"

"You didn't know that either?"

"No."

Abbott was pleased with himself. He leaned back in his chair. "Surprised you, did I?"

"As a matter of fact, yes."

"Well you can stop fancying her, you evil-minded bastard. She's engaged to some Swiss businessman."

"She doesn't wear a ring," I protested a little too hastily.

"That's the modern way, isn't it? Equality and all that rubbish. Or else she keeps the ring in a bank vault. The Swiss bloke must be a zillionaire." He looked at me closely, then gave an evil grin. "You do fancy her, don't you?"

"Who wouldn't?"

"Then it's your lucky day, Johnny, because she wants to see you."

"I thought she was in New York?"

Abbott rolled his bloodshot eyes. "Not everyone crosses the ocean by hanging rags on sticks. She flew back yesterday in Concorde. We're going to meet the family, you and I. It'll be very la-di-da. Are you sure you don't want to put on a suit?"

"I'm sure." I hated the thought of meeting the Buzzacott family, for I was in no mood for social politeness, but, by phoning Harry Abbott, I had condemned myself to whatever inconvenience followed. For Georgina's sake.

Harry swallowed the rest of his coffee and snapped his fingers for the waitress to bring the bill. "It's nice to be back on crime again," he said happily.

"They took you off it? What are you now? In charge of school crossings?"

"I'm just a dogsbody," he said mysteriously. "They just gave me this case for old times' sake, and to save some other poor sod from looking up the files. So shall we go, Johnny boy? I've got a car outside. But pay the bill first."

I paid, then joined Harry in a clapped-out Rover that he proudly claimed as his own car. We drove north and I wondered about a Contessa and whether she knew that the Swiss are rotten sailors. They're good at making cuckoo-clocks, and presumably they can ski, but they're sod all use at anything else. Except making money. And that was a depressing thought, so I tried to forget Jennifer Pallavicini. Instead, at Harry's insistence, I told him all about Garrard and Peel, and how Charlie had saved me in the nick of time, and then, when Harry had sucked all the juice out of that, he told me golf stories all the way to Wiltshire.

We parked on the airport-sized forecourt of Comerton Castle. Two footmen ran down the steps to open the car doors. Harry smirked, and said he could get used to this style of life. We were ceremoniously conducted to the entrance hall where a pin-striped butler waited to greet us. He already knew Harry, but didn't bat an eyelid at my dirty jeans and crumpled shirt. "Welcome to Comerton Castle, your lordship. If you would care to follow me?"

We did so care, following his silent footfalls through rooms big enough to hold fully rigged schooners. The ceilings were painted with riotous gods and the walls fluted with marble columns. The furniture was worth a small fortune, while the pictures on the walls would not have disgraced any gallery, though clearly Sir Leon did not consider them worthy of his own. Harry Abbott wet his fingertips and tried to smear back his thinning grey hair. "Not a bad pad, is it?" he confided in me, then jerked at his jacket and straightened his tie.

"Uncomfortable, Harry?" I asked.

"Christ, no. We coppers are always slumming with the nobs."

The nobs were waiting in a glazed terrace filled with potted palms and comfortable sofas. Sir Leon and Lady Buzzacott smiled a gracious welcome. There was no sign of Jennifer. I made polite small talk. I agreed it was a lovely day, and such a change after the recent stormy weather. Yes, I had been to Sir Leon's gallery, and had been very impressed.

"My daughter told me she'd met you at the gallery," Lady Buzzacott said very blandly, which suggested that her daughter had also told her that she had put the boot in as well. "I do wish she'd brought you to the house that day and introduced you."

"That would have been very pleasant," I said with insincere gallantry. I was being polite for Georgina's sake, but I was feeling increasingly resentful. It was not that I felt out of place, for I didn't, but I did feel patronised. Two days ago I had been racing a gale, and now I had to tiptoe through the conversational tulips.

"Jenny also told us about her visit to the Azores," Lady Buzzacott went on. "She said you hit a veritable giant?"

"Only twice, Lady Buzzacott."

"You must call me Helen, and I shall call you John. Leon, I think John could do with a drink. And I know Harry wants one. I suppose the loveliest thing about being a policeman is that you can drink and drive as much as you like?"

"Quite right, your ladyship." Harry was being very obsequious, and I realised that he probably fancied Lady Buzzacott, which wasn't surprising, for she was a beautiful woman. The beauty was genuine, not purchased in spas and health farms or on some surgeon's operating table. Her hair, like her daughter's, was dark, but just beginning to show grey, and clearly Lady Buzzacott had no intention of hiding the grey.

If she impressed me, her husband rather surprised me. Sir Leon was very small, very rotund, and seemingly rather timid. I had expected to meet a frightening tycoon, but instead he seemed very eager to please. He ordered drinks, then took Harry Abbott off to see some orchids.

"They'll talk golf," Lady Buzzacott said despairingly, and I began to like her.

"I've had little else but golf all the way from Devon."

"You poor man. No wonder you need that drink." I had just been served a very large whisky. "I must say I'm delighted to meet you," she continued, "because I've heard a great deal about you. You're probably a throwback, aren't you?"

"Am I?"

"Of course you are. I've no doubt your ancestors went swanning off across the seas to find giant Swedes they could hit, but you're not really supposed to do it nowadays. We're all meant to be dull, like Hans."

"Hans?"

"Jennifer's intended. I'm afraid he's having lunch with us. He does something in cheese, or I think he does, but he's so crushingly tedious that I've never really listened."

I was beginning to like Lady Buzzacott very much. "And you?" I asked. "How do you stave off dullness?"

"I watch Leon at work. It's fascinating."

"Is it?" I must have sounded dubious because I could not understand what the attractive Lady Buzzacott saw in the diminutive and myopic Sir Leon. Except that he was coining the loot like a bandit.

"A lot of people underestimate Leon," she said with just a touch of warning in her voice. "He's a pirate. I know he doesn't look like one, but he is. He started in property, of course, most of the new money did. He still has some property interests, but mostly he deals in companies now. That's how we met Hans. He owns some food conglomerate and Leon couldn't take it over because the Swiss government is very protective of their firms, so now we're all a big happy partnership. Hans plays golf, too." She shuddered. "Is there anything more boring than golf? Now, come and sit down, and tell me why you're so wretchedly unhelpful about recovering your own picture?"

I sat down. At the far end of the terrace Sir Leon was demonstrating a golf swing with a long-stemmed watering can.

"Well?" Lady Buzzacott prompted me.

"I'm still not at all sure it is my picture."

"There's no doubt about that!" Lady Buzzacott said dismissively, then, after a few seconds of reflection, she looked rather more sceptical. "Well, of course, there's always doubt about things once the lawyers get involved, but Leon has taken counsel's opinion, and it seems that the picture has to belong to your family's Trust, and that means you. Your mother's will shouldn't be able to change that."

I remembered how Sir Oliver had skated swiftly away from the subject of my mother's will. "I haven't seen the will," I said, hoping for enlightenment.

I wasn't disappointed. "There's nothing in it for you," Lady Buzzacott said, "apart from some bad-tempered advice which I'm sure you'd do best to ignore. Instead your mother left all her property to your sister Elizabeth, and specifically included the Van Gogh in that bequest, but it's very doubtful whether she had the power to leave the painting to anyone. She'd already given it to the family Trust, you see, in an effort to avoid tax. Doubtless, when she made her will, she was hoping that the lawyers could somehow disentangle the mess. I don't know why people believe that of lawyers. In my experience they almost always make things a great deal more complicated."

"But Elizabeth probably believes the will has greater power than the original deed of gift to the Trust," I said.

"I'm sure she does!" Lady Buzzacott said firmly; then, with a small prevaricating shrug, "or perhaps not. She and your mother did try to have the trust wound up two years ago."

"They did?" That was news to me.

"But, of course, everyone needed your signature, and you were swanning off being unpleasant to Scandinavians, so the Trust still inconveniently exists. Though, of course, if you

161

died without having any children, then Elizabeth becomes the Trust's main beneficiary."

"It's very strange," I said, "how this family knows so much more about my affairs than I do."

"That's because you don't care. You have to be very dull to wade through all those tedious documents. Ah, and speaking of dullness, here's Hans." A young, tall and sleekly handsome man had come on to the terrace. He was one of those foreigners who dress in the English manner, which meant he was wearing the most expensive brogues and a tweed suit, but all the money had only succeeded in making him look like a tailor's dummy. Hans had yet to learn that the shoes and suit should be worn by his gardener for a full year's hard labour before they would look properly English. He seemed somewhat taken aback by my wardrobe, but looked reassured when I was introduced as an earl. Perhaps he thought I was one of the eccentric English aristocrats he had heard so much about. I asked him how the cheese was going.

"Cheese?" He sounded worried.

"Helen told me you were in cheese?"

"Ah! The processed cheese!" He brightened up. "Indeed. But it is only a very small part of our overall business, my lord. We would like to expand it, especially in the American market, but the American taste for cheese is not like our own. We have to develop brands with a flavour that can endure extreme refrigeration . . ."

"Oh, look at the time!" Lady Buzzacott smiled graciously at her prospective son-in-law. "Would you very much mind telephoning Jenny and telling her that if she's lunching with us she should come soon?"

Hans, clearly confused by his reception, dutifully obeyed. Lady Buzzacott caught my eye, and I saw from her gaze that she was an altogether more formidable lady than I had at first supposed. "If you think I'm being especially nice to you, John, you are entirely right. I am trying to suborn you. I want Leon to have his Sunflowers, and I want you to have a good price for them."

"I do hate the way this family patronises me," I said, though without rancour.

She laughed delightedly, then glanced through the window. "Ah, I see that Jenny is already on her way from the gallery. We shall go through to luncheon and you can hear more about cheese. Then we shall have our council of war. But without Hans, because he isn't family. Yet." And, I suspected from her tone, she was not at all sure that she ever wanted Hans as family. I decided I liked this lady very much indeed, so I offered her my arm and took her through for luncheon.

Sir Leon and Lady Buzzacott, the Contessa Pallavicini, Inspector Harry Abbott and myself formed the council of war.

Harry did most of the talking and was actually rather impressive. Lady Buzzacott said very little, but listened acutely. Sir Leon spoke when necessary, and took notes. Jennifer Pallavicini was disdainfully cold. She had been cold throughout luncheon, almost ignoring me. I had noticed that, unlike our previous meetings, she was wearing an engagement ring; a great chunk of diamond which must have cost a lot of processed cheese.

Harry began by describing the world of stolen art. The lecture was clearly for my benefit, though it did not stop Sir Leon from making notes in a small leather-bound book. The stealing of art works, Harry said, was a most specialised occupation. Only a very few professional criminals were involved. Their qualifications were not the obvious ones of breaking and entering premises, even though those premises were usually superbly guarded with high technology alarms. The essential qualification was the knowledge of who would be willing to pay for the stolen picture. "The breaking and entering," Harry said, "can be sub-contracted to run-of-the-mill villains. Naturally those villains seek an inside accomplice, which is why, when the Stowey Sunflowers was nicked, we thought Johnny here was their inside man."

Lady Buzzacott offered me a dazzling smile, Sir Leon made a note in his tiny handwriting, while Jennifer stared at the ceiling. I stared at her. She really was very beautiful, and somehow the existence of Hans had made her even more desirable.

"Once the painting is successfully stolen," Harry went on, "the contract labour is paid off. It's a straight fee; no percentage and no contingencies. . ."

"His lordship may not know what contingencies you speak of, Inspector?" Sir Leon pointed out in his low voice.

"Like, if the painting isn't sold, no cash. The contract labour gets its money as agreed whatever happens. Got that, my lord?" Harry hated calling me 'my lord', but clearly felt it was incumbent in these palatial surroundings.

"I understand you, Inspector. Please go on."

He gave me a filthy look as a reward for my own punctiliousness, then heaped sugar into his coffee. "Once the painting's nicked," he went on, "it's taken straight to whoever has agreed to buy it. And that's the key, you see, because the buyer is usually lined up before the job's ever done. I mean, no one wants ten million quid's worth of Rembrandt hanging about their house while they try to find a bloke with a bit of unused space on his living-room wall."

"Quite," Sir Leon said in a disapproving tone.

"So the painting goes to the buyer, the final cash changes hands, and that's the end of the matter. The new owner takes care to keep the picture hidden, and it may never be found until long after he's dead."

"And the buyers?" Sir Leon asked. "Who are they?"

"Increasingly, these days, sir, the Nips."

"But why don't they just buy at auction?" I asked.

"Because the particular painting they want may not be up for sale," Harry said, "and because, if the deal's successful, it's a lot cheaper than buying at auction. You can probably get a top-flight Rembrandt for a straight million on the black market."

I still didn't understand why a man able to pay a million pounds could not satisfy himself at auctions. I said as much, prompting Sir Leon to lay down his gold pen and look at me. "You have to understand, my lord, the nature of a collector's mind. It is, and I speak with some knowledge, a single-minded passion which is entirely consuming. It might apply to postage stamps, model railways, vintage cars, porcelain, cigarette cards, or" – he paused, and I thought he was going to say 'women' – "works of art. Whatever is the object of that passion becomes nothing short of obsession, even, if I might use the words, a form of unreasonable and uncontrollable lust. A man desires, say, a particular canvas by Picasso, and he will not be happy, he will not know any satisfaction, until that painting is in his possession. This form of lust is a disease, my lord, that distorts a man's perception of reality until he believes that his happiness will be incomplete until he satisfies the desire. In all other respects he may seem a most normal man, but in that one area, so secret and deep, he is unreasonable. You will have noted, my lord, that I have constantly referred to the male gender. It seems that women are not subject to this particular affliction. Have I answered your question?"

He had, and I realised he had also been describing himself. He wanted the Van Gogh, and he would devote his life to finding it. Sir Leon was a collector, a very rich one, and though he might never stoop to criminality, he clearly understood the minds of those who did and was very sympathetic to them.

But he had no sympathy at all for men who would hold a painting to ransom by mutilating it. "And it now seems certain," Sir Leon said, "that the fragment of canvas was cut from the Stowey Van Gogh."

"How can you be sure?" I asked.

Jennifer answered, describing how she had carried the cut corner to New York where the Metropolitan Museum had subjected it to tests. "The pigment and canvas are identical to other compositions he painted in the late 1880s." Her voice sounded rather despairing, and I realised how much she must have been hoping that the mutilated corner was not genuine. It was not that the painting had been irrevocably ruined by the small excision, but she was anguished by the implicit threat that yet more of the canvas could be cut. She spilt the scrap of canvas out of its envelope on to the table. I picked it up. The paint was rough and striated, like the texture of a sea blowing up in a brisk wind.

"We don't even know," Jennifer said, "whether this was

the only corner they sent to a collector. Perhaps they're trying to ransom the painting to a dozen rich men?"

"Maybe." Harry sounded unconcerned. "But I'll bet my next month's wages that they only sent the one fragment. They know how badly Sir Leon wants the painting, which means they're confident he'll pay their ransom. Their biggest worry is exactly how to engineer that payment, because they're frightened of getting caught red-handed. That's why they've given us so much time. They know Sir Leon doesn't need till the end of August to raise the money, but they need that time to work out a foolproof handover." He plucked the scrap of precious canvas from my fingers and waved it like a small trophy. "In short," he said happily, "we're dealing with amateurs."

"Amateurs?" I asked.

"We're not dealing with professional art thieves, that's for sure, or else the painting would have disappeared long ago. And no professional would ransom a painting, it's too risky!"

"Do you mean," I asked slowly, "that these people have kept the painting hidden all this time? Why would they do that? Why wouldn't they have ransomed it four years ago?"

Harry was enjoying himself. He had his audience, and was relishing his careful reconstruction of an old crime. "Let's go back four years, to when the painting was first stolen." He thrust an accusing cigarette towards me. "I reckoned that you nicked the damn thing to stop your mother selling it."

"Why on earth would I do that?"

"Because your mother would have spent the money on preserving Stowey, which you clearly didn't want. So if you stole the painting, then hid it till she died, you could have kept all the proceeds for yourself. In other words, my lord, I believed you were defending the value of your inheritance by a nasty bit of theft. But I was wrong."

Jennifer glanced at me, and I wondered if I saw the faintest blush of shame on her face. Probably not.

"So what makes you think I didn't nick it?" I asked Harry.

"It's obvious, isn't it? The painting belongs to you now, so why should you continue to hide it? If you had it, you could pretend that it had merely been mislaid all these years, discover it, sell it to Sir Leon, then go out and buy yourself a proper suit."

Lady Buzzacott smiled. Jennifer, perhaps reluctant to discard her belief in my guilt, frowned. Sir Leon glanced from me to Harry, then asked the obvious question. "So who did steal it?"

"Johnny knows." Harry, in his happiness, easily dropped my honorific. "Don't you, Johnny?"

I think I did, but I wasn't entirely ready to believe my suspicions, so I said nothing.

"Same motive, different villain." Harry lit the cigarette he'd been holding for the last few minutes. He had clearly been nervous of offending Lady Buzzacott, but his craving for a smoke overcame his diffidence. He sucked gratefully at the smoke, then looked at me. "Who becomes the beneficiary of the family Trust if you die?"

"So long as I don't have children," I said softly, "Elizabeth."

"The Lady Elizabeth Tredgarth," Harry confirmed, "who is a bitter and disappointed lady. And a very ambitious one. And in her view you are a very unsuitable heir. You don't care about the title, you never cared about Stowey, and you don't seem to mind if the Rossendale family slides into poverty, yet those are things which your twin sister takes very seriously. It would suit her very well to inherit a Van Gogh which she could turn into ready cash. And who stood between Elizabeth and that tasty little fortune?"

"My mother and I," I answered dutifully.

"Exactly. And now there's just you. And if you died now, Johnny, your sister will simply claim to have found the painting in your baggage. That's why she's so busy telling everyone that she's met your accomplice! She has to prove your guilt to establish her innocence."

He was making Elizabeth into a very cold-blooded murderer, a West Country Lady Macbeth, and the portrait did not fit. Elizabeth was bitter, and she was proud, and she could be heartlessly ruthless, as the two caravans in a nettle patch proved, yet I could not see her as a murderess. "She's no killer," I protested to Harry.

167

"Women may not be collectors," Lady Buzzacott observed mildly, "but they are not innocent of greed, and many have conceived of murder."

"She's an opportunist." Harry took up the condemnation of my twin sister. "I don't think she's had this planned for ever. It was your mother's death that sparked her. That and your return to England." He paused to tap ash into his saucer. "And remember she has a partner, and he is a killer."

"Garrard," I said more to myself than to anyone else. I could understand Garrard being a killer, but that did not explain why he had beaten Jennifer Pallavicini on board *Sunflower*.

"That was fear!" Harry explained when I raised the objection. "I've no doubt Garrard went to Salcombe to kill you, but he discovered the Contessa instead. What was he to think?"

"That I was making a deal with her?" I ventured.

"Which implied," Harry went on, "that your sister had made a deal with you. Garrard was scared that he was being double-crossed by a brother–sister agreement! He was frightened that Elizabeth would give you the painting to sell on condition that you shared the price with her. It wasn't true, but I'll bet my last brass farthing that's what Garrard believed when he found the Contessa on your boat. Sometime in the next few days your sister must have reassured him, so he went to George's yard to finish the job properly. Would your sister have guessed you might be at Cullen's place?"

I nodded. Elizabeth would indeed have remembered my old association with Cullen's yard. The pieces were falling into place, but I did not like the picture they made. It's hard to see one's twin as a killer.

"And when your friend Charlie Barratt stopped that second murder attempt," Harry went on, "what happened?"

"I sailed away."

"Which meant she and Garrard had failed," Harry was pleased with his exposition. "You were still alive, you'd disappeared, so now Elizabeth has a problem. The painting is still not legally hers, but she's desperate for the money. So she

168

has to run the risk of a ransom. But she was a little too greedy. She tried to put the screws on to your little sister's money as well, and that brought you home. Maybe she even wanted you to come home, because my belief is that she'd still rather have you dead." He looked at Sir Leon. "The painting must be worth a great deal more than the amount demanded in the ransom note?"

Sir Leon hesitated, then nodded. "The value is around twenty million."

"So there you are," Harry looked back at me. "Your death is worth sixteen million quid to your sister. Not a bad profit."

I stood and walked to the window. "But if she's already got the painting" – I was seeking a loophole in Harry's thesis – "why doesn't she just fight me in the courts for possession? She's got my mother's will as ammunition?"

"Because she'll lose," Sir Leon said harshly.

"But she wasn't even at Stowey when the painting was stolen." I raised another objection.

"Garrard nicked it," Harry said easily. "She must have given him keys and told him how to work the alarm system."

"But Elizabeth wouldn't know where to find men like Garrard and Peel," I protested.

Harry dismissed that objection. "Horses. Garrard used to be a good amateur steeplechaser before he turned bad. And the racecourses are full of villains." He looked happily at the Buzzacott family. "If you ever need a crook, that's where to go: the racecourse."

Lady Buzzacott smiled her thanks for the advice, while Sir Leon looked pained and Jennifer just frowned.

It all worked. I could see that. Harry had presented a wonderful concoction of greed, violence and inheritance, a very upper-class concoction indeed, but I still did not want to believe that my twin sister was a killer. That was not because I loved her, but rather because, just as Elizabeth feared the genetic taint of Georgina's madness, so I feared the taint of Elizabeth's murderous nature. I shook my head. "I don't know, Harry, I just don't know."

"So let's find out!" Harry said cheerfully. "You're back

now, so let's see if she tries to knock you off again. After all, she'd much rather sell the painting legally than go through the risks of collecting a ransom. And if she and Garrard do try murder again, we'll catch them red-handed."

There was silence. So this was why they had wanted my return: to be a target? None of them looked at me, perhaps embarrassed by what they expected of me.

Sir Leon cleared his throat. "I fail to see why collecting a ransom should be riskier than committing murder?"

"Murder comes out of the dark, when you least expect it," Harry said, "but if you want a ransom you have to specify a time and a place, which gives your enemies a chance to ambush you."

Sir Leon shook his head impatiently. "For my part I find it hard to believe that the recovery of the painting is intrinsically bound up in an attempt at murder." He shrugged, as though suggesting that his qualifications for making that judgment were not as good as Harry's. "I do believe, however, in their willingness to exchange the painting for a ransom." He turned his myopic gaze to me. "They have requested that we insert a coded message in the personal column of *The Times*, which message would indicate our willingness to pay the ransom of four million pounds. On receipt of that message, they will instruct us in the method to be used for making that payment." I sensed that I was hearing the echoes of an old disagreement. Sir Leon was quite ready to pay any price for the painting, while Harry was more intent on trapping Elizabeth and Garrard. Sir Leon still looked at me. "I see no need for you to be a murder target, my lord. If you're content, then I suggest you allow me to ransom the painting, then to negotiate a fair price with you."

"No!" Harry, with a surprising asperity, slapped the suggestion down. "Once you've agreed to pay the ransom, you've no assurance they'll give up the painting. They'll just soak you for another four million." He looked back to me. "I'd rather trick the bastards into showing themselves. If you'll help."

"Oh, I'll help you," I said easily, "but there is a condition for my help."

"I do assure you" – Sir Leon, perhaps piqued by Harry's strong opposition, spoke very irritably – "that I will pay you the highest imaginable price for the painting. Indeed, I'm quite certain your eventual price will be far too high. I have, after all, conducted negotiations with your family before."

Those final words whipped at my pride like the recoiling slash of a broken wire-rope. Sir Leon's voice had been smug and scornful, implying that my family, though broken and poor, had shown nothing but greed. The words told me that Sir Leon despised me, and he was showing that derision by letting me know that my greed could never match his fortune. He had the power of new money over old families, but I would be damned before I would let him patronise me. "Bugger your price," I said. That shook all of them. "I don't give a toss about your price. And don't equate me with the rest of the family. If you negotiate with me, then you satisfy my terms, and those terms are very simple, Sir Leon. You take care of Georgina's future, all of it."

Sir Leon blinked at me. He had clearly been astonished by my vehemence, but not so astonished as to forget that he was at a negotiating table. "Your price, as I understand it, is your younger sister's security?"

"And happiness."

He gazed at me. He had very pale eyes, and I suddenly saw that he was not a timid little man at all, but a very hard one. "And your monetary price besides?" he asked in his most mocking voice.

He must have known he would get under my skin. "You can have the bloody painting!" I matched his scorn with my own. "Why the hell do you think I'm here? Because I care about being rich? For God's sake, I inherited Stowey and the painting four years ago, and I didn't want them then and I don't want them now. I came here, Sir Leon, not to save a painting, but to save my sister from a squalid caravan in a dripping wood."

Jennifer was staring at me. I knew I'd overreacted to her stepfather's patronising tone. I'd lost my temper, said far more than I had wanted to say, and now found myself on the brink of giving up a fortune just to prove to this small bastard that not everyone would lick his arse to become rich. But at least I had succeeded in astonishing Jennifer, who was now staring at me as though she had never quite seen me before.

Sir Leon smiled. "I accept your terms, my lord. One painting in return for your sister's lifelong security." He held out his hand.

"Think carefully, John," Lady Buzzacott warned me in a soft voice.

Jennifer shook her head slightly, as though disbelieving that I would take the offered hand. Sir Leon smiled at my hesitation. "So you're not as pure as you'd have us believe, my lord? You wish to amend the terms of the agreement?"

"Bugger your amendments." I shook his hand.

Which meant that to surprise a multimillionaire, and to impress his stepdaughter, who was engaged to a squillionaire and despised me anyway, I'd just given away a Van Gogh. And I knew just how my ancestor, the seventeenth Earl, must have felt when he lost all the family's Irish estates and all our rich sugar plantations in the Caribbean on the single turn of the ace of diamonds; I felt like a proper fool.

Harry was almost doubled over with laughter. We had left the family and gone into the garden where we were hidden from the house by a big yew hedge. "What a berk you are! Sweet Jesus! What a bloody berk!"

"Shut up." I was far more angry with myself than I was with Harry.

"Sweet suffering Christ!" He laughed again. "You gave it away! And you only did it to impress that bird! How much is it worth? Twenty million?" He shook his head in wonderment. "You gave away a Van Gogh worth twenty millions!"

"I don't care about the bloody money," I said bitterly.

"Of course you care, Johnny, you just don't want to admit it." Harry gave a final hoot of delighted laughter.

"I don't care about the money," I insisted, "I never have. I wouldn't be a blue-water sailor if I cared about money."

"A blue-water sailor," he mocked me with cruel mimicry. "But you care about the Contessa, don't you? And it'll take more than a shabby boat to get into her knickers. She's the kind that needs a diamond necklace before every tumble, and I reckon you've just blown away your chances, Johnny."

"You're a crude swine, Harry."

"But let's hope I'm a clever one, my son." He lit a cigarette and stared at a statue of a half-naked nymph which graced an alcove in the hedge. "Clever enough to stop Sir Leon paying the ransom. That's all he wants to do, pay up, because he thinks that's the surest way to get his picture. He can't wait. He's like a kid locked out of the toyshop, but I don't believe it's as easy as he thinks. If they can winkle four million out of him now, what's to stop them going back to the well with a bigger bucket? They can't be fools, they must know it's worth more than four million."

I didn't answer. I was still trying to accustom myself to a belief in Elizabeth's guilt. I didn't like her, I'd really never liked her, but it was hard to think of her as wanting my death. Yet Harry's arguments had been persuasive. "Why don't you just search Elizabeth's house?" I asked him. "If you find the picture, then it will all be over."

"Funnily enough my grandmother taught me to suck eggs before you were born, Johnny. Don't be a cretin. She won't have a bloody Van Gogh tucked away in the attic. It's been hidden away for four years, and we're going to have to be clever if we're to get it back."

"Then find Garrard," I suggested.

"I'm looking for Mr Garrard," Abbott said grimly, "but he's done a bunk. So we have to persuade Mr Garrard to find us." He still squinted up at the nymph's mossy breasts. "A nasty piece of work, Mr Garrard."

"You know him?"

"Of course I know him." Harry abandoned the nymph to walk slowly up the newly cut grass to where a fountain sparkled prettily in the afternoon sunshine. He sat on the wall that circled the fountain's pool and looked at me quizzically. "He got slung out of the Paras for nicking the mess funds, then, because the Fraud squad found him monkeying about with some dodgy bonds, he did a bunk and joined one of those mercenary groups in Southern Africa. About five years ago he came home on leave, and he never went back. He's been small-time ever since, bookies and winkling, which is very puzzling." Harry tapped cigarette ash into the fountain's pool. "Why does a top-drawer bastard with a good brain scratch around with lowlife villains? He was making good money in Africa."

"He must be making more here."

"Not now, he isn't." Harry frowned. "But I reckon Garrard's bought a share of that picture. He's not hired labour, Johnny, but a full partner with your sister. And he'll be coming after you with a knife because he smells several million quid at the end of the road. How do you feel about that?"

"I'm not ecstatic at the prospect."

"But at least you'd die in the knowledge that you'd helped me solve an old crime."

"Up yours, too."

"Because if I'm right," Harry went on, "they'd still rather have you out of the way. With you dead Elizabeth can sell the painting on the open market and she won't have to answer any awkward questions about where her fortune came from; she'll be free, rich, and laughing."

"And I'll be dead."

"Not with your Uncle Harry looking after you" – he gave me an evil grin with his tombstone teeth – "and if I'm clever," he went on, "I'll have your sister and Garrard behind bars, Jenny-baby will be married to that Swiss cheese, Sir Leon will have his painting, and you'll be as poor as a church mouse because you gave your family fortune away. So shall we start letting the evil ones know that you can't wait to be knifed?"

I went to a gap in the hedge to see if Jennifer had followed us out to the gardens, but the empty lawns just shimmered in the day's heat. Which meant I was alone, and poor, and about to be a target.

Five days later, on a summer's day as beautiful as any that could be wished, I sailed *Sunflower* into Dartmouth. The sun shone benevolently and the wind was a well-behaved force three, just enough to shift *Sunflower* along nicely, yet not strong enough to jar the launches which carried the television news crews.

This was Harry's malicious way of baiting his hook: publicity.

Sir Leon's publicity department had made the arrangements. John, Earl of Stowey, once suspected of stealing his family's Van Gogh, was returning to England to help the authorities find it. The press release carefully ignored the fact that I had twice visited England earlier in the year; instead it was implied that like a prodigal I had just sailed back from unknown waters. As I neared the river mouth more launches joined the procession till I began to feel like one of those record-breaking circumnavigators coming home. Questions were shouted across to my cockpit, but I waved them away. I wanted to berth safely first.

A berth had been reserved for me on the inner side of the town pontoon. I sailed *Sunflower* into the narrow space which was just, but only just, wide enough for me to turn her. I was showing off. Most people would have used the motor for the final approach and the turn into the tide, but I hoped Jennifer Pallavicini was waiting for me on the quay, so I sailed *Sunflower* into the confined water between pontoon and quay, swung her bows hard over, knew I'd misjudged the flooding tide, began to panic, and prayed desperately that *Sunflower* would keep way on her as we came up to wind and tide. She didn't, but hung up, and I realised that in twenty seconds the wind and tide would drive my new mast against the bridge which led from the town quay to the pontoon. I didn't have time to start the engine, so swore instead, but then *Sunflower* was saved by a quick-witted yachtsman who told me to heave him a line. I did, and was ignominiously hauled into the vacant berth where one of the waiting reporters sincerely congratulated me on a fine piece of seamanship.

The questions were unavoidable now. Had I heard about

the damage done to the painting? Yes. What had made me change my mind and come home to help? That damage. Where had I been? Everywhere. Would I sell the painting if it was recovered? All the time I was trying to secure *Sunflower* properly, tensioning her warps and springs and sometimes cursing at a reporter who got in my way. Two of Sir Leon's publicity men were trying to impose order on the chaos and only managed to make things worse. One photographer went down into *Sunflower*'s cabin and started taking flash photographs so I hauled him out and threw him on to the pontoon. Photographs were taken of that. Another photographer cheered me up by falling overboard.

I finally succeeded in locking the boat. The publicity men shepherded me towards a nearby hotel where a room had been reserved for a formal press conference. Jennifer Pallavicini was already there. I said good morning. She said good morning. The two of us then sat behind a table while the rabble arranged their lights and microphones. A full size reproduction of the Stowey Sunflowers was framed on the wall behind us. I noticed that Jennifer was not wearing her engagement ring, and decided that she must keep it for private occasions only. Or perhaps Harry Abbott was right, and most of the time it was kept in a bank vault.

Was it true, a woman reporter opened the proceedings, that the painting was being held to ransom?

"Yes," I said.

Could I afford the price?

"You must be joking," I said. "I'm skint."

"So how will you save the painting?"

"By co-operating with Sir Leon Buzzacott." Which was a cue for the questions to be directed to Jennifer who was present on behalf of the Buzzacott Museum Gallery. She coolly confirmed that her stepfather was taking full financial responsibility for the painting's recovery.

"But if he pays the ransom," the first woman asked, "will he then have to pay a purchase price to the Earl of Stowey?"

"That purchase price has already been agreed," Jennifer said.

"How much?" That was about fifty voices.

I waited for quiet. "I've decided to donate the painting to Sir Leon's gallery."

That reply caused pandemonium. I patiently confirmed that they had not misheard me and that I had indeed given the painting to Sir Leon, and wanted nothing for myself.

"Why?" a dozen voices wanted to know.

"Because I want the painting to stay in Britain, and because Sir Leon's gallery will provide the perfect home."

But why had I given it away? Weren't there galleries that would have paid me millions for the picture?

"I'm a philanthropist," I said. "Ask the Contessa here. She can vouch for the benevolent side of my character."

Jennifer's lips tightened slightly. Not that any of the reporters noticed. How did I feel now, they asked instead, about my arrest four years before?

"I was never charged," I said, "so I feel it was all a mistake."

But I had been the chief suspect. How did I feel about that?

"Flattered."

"Did you steal it?" one idiot asked.

"Of course I didn't bloody steal it. Don't be so bloody stupid." Sir Leon's publicity men had impressed on me that I must not be nasty to the press, but I didn't really see why. They were nasty to me.

How had I heard about the damage done to the painting?

"The Contessa flew out to the Azores and told me."

How did I think my presence in England would assist the police in finding the picture?

"I don't know," I said, "ask them."

Had the police given me any indication of who they thought might have stolen the picture?

"Yes."

That simple affirmative, as it was meant to, caused a flurry of further, eager questions and, just as Harry had instructed me, I qualified the answer. I hadn't been given any names, I lied, but I had received the strong impression that the police weren't entirely clueless. The reporters tried to suck more meat off that bone, but both Jennifer and I refused to elaborate.

Jennifer then confirmed that her stepfather was employing specialists in ransom psychology to back up the police effort. That was news to me, but I imagined it was all a part of panicking Elizabeth into rashness. Jennifer gave the impression that a vast organisation was about to descend on the thieves. She was very impressive.

After the press conference I went back to *Sunflower* and did four interviews for television reporters. They all asked the same questions and all got the same answers. I obliged the radio reporters afterwards, then posed like an idiot for some press photographers. By midday the fuss had died down, all but for one man who waited till the other reporters had gone, then told me his paper would pay me a six-figure sum if I'd dictate a candid account of how I'd nicked the painting from my mother. I told him to get lost.

"Think about it, my lord."

"I told you to get lost."

"Come up to London and chat to the editor. Why not? We're not talking peanuts here."

"Fuck you," I said, and thumped him in the belly. His photographer took a picture of that, so I thumped the photographer as well. I didn't hurt either man, which was a pity.

But at least my actions saw them off. Jennifer Pallavicini had watched the proceedings from the pontoon, and now she stepped down on to *Sunflower*'s foredeck. "You're really trying to be popular, aren't you?"

"I thought the object of the exercise was to announce my intention of retrieving the painting, not to win a beauty competition?"

She shrugged that answer off. "Do you always hit people who annoy you?" she asked.

"Only men."

"Are you ever hit back?"

"Frequently. I once had the shit knocked out of me in Australia."

She frowned. I thought she'd taken offence at my language, but it seemed there was something else on her mind. "What do you care about, Mr Rossendale?"

178

"Georgina." Whom I had carefully not mentioned to any of the press.

"Why?" Jennifer asked.

I paused, wondering whether to answer. "Because," I finally said, "she's too loopy to worry about herself."

"Does that concern apply to everyone who's too weak to look after themselves?"

"Maybe."

"Meaning it's none of my business." She looked at her watch. "I think that on the whole, and despite your hostility, that was a most successful exercise. I'll see you in the morning, Mr Rossendale." I knew she was spending the night with some relatives in Totnes, but I'd somehow hoped she might spend some small part of the day with me. Because, just as Sir Leon was obsessed with my Van Gogh, I was becoming obsessed with his stepdaughter. She was truly beautiful, but just too self-composed. She had become a challenge. Just like the bar at Salcombe.

"You wouldn't like some lunch?" I asked as she walked away.

"No, thank you," she called over her shoulder, "not today."

And up yours, too, I thought, but didn't say it.

The hook was well-baited now. Elizabeth knew where I was, and knew I was trying to retrieve the painting. Harry had warned me that from this moment on Garrard and Peel might pay me another visit.

They would be walking into an ambush. Two plain-clothes policemen were always on duty to watch me. Not quite always; Harry told me that he couldn't find the manpower or the money to have me guarded throughout England, so my guardians would only be on duty when I was in Dartmouth itself. If I went away from the river, Harry reasoned, Garrard and Peel could not possibly know where I was going, so would have no chance of finding me. "Suppose they follow me?" I had asked him.

"You'd be dead, Johnny, but don't worry. The force will send a nice wreath to your funeral." After which grim jest he told me his men would work in shifts; by day idling with the tourists on the quay above the pontoon, while the night shift would keep watch from a cabin cruiser moored astern of *Sunflower*.

I didn't entirely trust the watchfulness of Harry's men so, once the pressmen had finally abandoned me, I took my dinghy upstream and found a boatyard that could sell me a couple of pounds of lead and a scrap piece of sheet aluminium. I went back to *Sunflower*, took the head off my new boathook, and drilled a hollow into the top of the wooden shaft. I didn't have a crucible or furnace so I used an oxy-acetylene lamp to melt the lead. I dripped it piece by piece into the hollow space. I worked on *Sunflower*'s foredeck which I shielded with a sheet of scrap iron. When I'd finished melting the lead I wrapped the aluminium about the hollowed section of shaft to give it strength, then drilled a hole so that the metal hook could be bolted back into place. I used a file to sharpen the back edge of the hook and, when it was done, congratulated myself on a proper job.

Then, because I might not get a chance to use the hook, I prepared my other weapons. Some, like the rocket alarm flares, were potentially lethal, while others, like the fire-extinguishers, were merely nasty. If Garrard and Peel did appear, then at least I would have a reception for them.

And I knew I might need all the weapons. Garrard's reputation was frightening: an officer gone bad, a trained killer, and a man in desperate need of money.

He did not come that first night. I slept nervously, but undisturbed. In the morning I shaved in *Sunflower*'s cockpit and watched the yachts motoring towards the sea. It promised to be a warm day. There was no sign of any plain-clothes policemen, but Harry had warned me that they would not be highly visible. "If you can see them," he had told me, "then so can the nasties."

I slung my shaving water overboard, then went below and fried myself a big pan of eggs and bacon. I made a Thermos flask of coffee, then carried the whole breakfast up to the cockpit just in time to see Jennifer Pallavicini walking down the pontoon.

"Good morning," I said cheerfully. "Coffee?"

She ignored the offer, telling me instead that we had both been asked to appear on an early evening television programme. "I've said yes for you," she said.

"Coffee?" I asked again.

She looked at her watch. "Thank you," she said in a rather grudging voice. She stepped down into the cockpit and sat opposite me. She was carrying a heavy bag that she gratefully dropped into the cockpit sole.

"Bacon and eggs?" I offered her my own plate.

She shuddered. "No, thank you."

I fetched a mug and poured her some coffee. As she drank it she watched me wolf down the bacon and eggs. "Don't you ever put on weight?" she asked at last.

"No."

"Lucky you." She flinched as I mopped up the egg yolk and brown sauce with a piece of well-buttered white bread. "Don't you have any idea about healthy eating?" she was driven to ask.

"Well fried and lots of it," I said enthusiastically.

"You like to shock people, don't you?"

"What, me? Never. Tell me about this television programme I don't want to appear on."

"It's in London."

I groaned. "Tell me how I'm supposed to get to London for this television programme I don't want to appear on?"

"We'll arrange transport for you."

"How are you getting there?" I asked hopefully.

"My stepfather's helicopter," she answered very distantly, letting me know that, even if politeness forced her to offer me a ride, I should be well-mannered enough to refuse. "I can give you a lift if you like, but I'm leaving very soon. Hans and I have to go to a lunch reception at the Hayward Gallery."

"What are they showing this month?" I asked. "Collages of squashed cockroaches? Municipal litter baskets? Finger-painting by the Islington Lesbian Collective?"

"Late-eighteenth-century English landscapes, if you must know."

I gave her a wink. "I'll give it a miss."

181

"Philistine," she said, but not angrily. Indeed, it was said almost fondly, and the warm tone seemed to surprise her as much as it did me. We looked at each other. I think we were both taken aback by the affection she had unintentionally expressed. She half smiled, then hurried to cover that tiny moment of truth. "Well, you are!" she protested too hastily. "Only a Philistine would give away a Van Gogh!"

"I did it so you'd be hugely impressed by my generosity, not to mention my quixotic soul. I have this theory, you see, that women prefer irresponsible rogues to Swiss cheese merchants."

"Rogues with twenty million pounds," she pointed out, "are marginally more attractive than rogues without."

I laughed. It was an odd moment. At one instant we had been at each other's throats and suddenly, for no apparent reason that I could snatch from the air, we were smiling at each other.

"If you must know," she said, "I thought you were an idiot to give it away."

I nodded. "That's probably a very fair assessment."

"Do you regret doing it?" she asked in genuine interest.

I pretended to think about it. "If it didn't impress you then it was clearly a wasted gesture."

She smiled, and I thought how beautiful she was. "It impressed me," she confessed, "but if you regret it, then I promise you my stepfather won't keep you to it."

"I don't back out of contracts."

She didn't pursue the subject. "Did you see the television news last night?"

"I don't have a television."

"They gave our press conference a lot of time," she said, "and they were especially kind to you. They didn't show you hitting anyone and they didn't let anyone hear you swearing."

"Untruthful bastards, aren't they?"

"And here are the morning papers." She spilt the big bag at my feet. I picked up the papers one by one. The serious papers had given us a fair bit of space, but nothing compared to the tabloids, which had jumped all over the story. There were a lot of pictures of me, most of them in *Sunflower*, but a fair number also showed me sitting in the hotel with Jennifer Pallavicini. 'Vagabond Earl Sails Home', one caption said. "You will notice," Jennifer said, "that your presence guaranteed us a heavy coverage."

"My presence? Not yours?"

"I'm not newsworthy," she said disparagingly. "No, it's the vagabond earl who caught their fancy."

I lifted a tabloid which had printed her picture larger than mine. She looked very sexy in the picture, perhaps because the photographer had been almost under the floorboards to aim his camera up her skirt. I thought again how good she'd look in a bikini. Or out of one.

"Do you ever go sailing?" I asked her suddenly.

"Sometimes." She sounded defensive.

"With Hans?" I sounded defensive.

"Hans doesn't have time for sailing. No, a friend of Mummy's has a ketch."

A friend of Mummy's would, I thought. "A big ketch?" I asked instead.

"At least twice the size of *Sunflower*," she said airily.

"You should try small boat sailing," I said. "It's wetter, and more intimate. Why don't you come for a sail in *Sunflower*?"

I expected her usual refusal, especially after I'd used the word 'intimate', but surprisingly, and after a moment's hesitation, she gave an abrupt nod. "All right. Maybe. One day."

"Only maybe?" I asked.

She smiled. "A definite maybe."

It was worth giving up a Van Gogh for that feeling. It really was. I must have smiled, for she smiled back at me, but then I had to look away because running footsteps were suddenly loud on the pontoon bridge and a voice was shouting for me. "Johnny! You bastard! Johnny!"

I twisted round, already reaching for the weighted boathook, but my importunate visitor was neither Garrard nor Peel, but Charlie. I noticed one of the plain-clothes policemen running along the quay towards the pontoon's bridge, but when I stood with a welcoming expression on my face, my guardian angel relaxed. "Charlie!" I shouted.

"God Almighty!" He ran down the pontoon, leaped on to *Sunflower*'s counter, then jumped down on to the mass of newspapers in the cockpit. "You bastard!" He was clearly pleased to see me.

He slapped my back. I introduced him to Jennifer, who nodded very coolly. "Mr Barratt," she said in acknowledgement of the introduction.

Charlie looked from Jennifer to me, then back to Jennifer. "I'm not interrupting, am I?"

"No, Mr Barratt, you are not." All her previous coolness had returned. She retrieved her bag. "I'll see you this evening, my lord."

"Where?"

"At the studios, of course. A car will pick you up here at one o'clock. You're supposed to be in London by five-thirty, so that should give you more than enough time. It's nice to have met you, Mr Barratt."

Charlie watched her walk all the way down the pontoon, then sighed. "That is tasty, Johnny. That is very tasty."

"And engaged to a Swiss cheese zillionaire."

He snapped his fingers suddenly. "She's the one who was on the telly with you last night?"

"That's the one."

"Hell fire." He sat down heavily. "Tell me it isn't true."

"Tell you what isn't true?"

He was staring up at me with a very worried expression. "You didn't really give the picture away, did you?"

"Yes."

He closed his eyes. "Christ on the cross. I saw you on the telly last night and I couldn't believe what you were saying! He's mad, I thought, off his poor little twist! You're as bad as Georgina!"

"Come on, Charlie!" His accusation had angered me. "What the hell am I supposed to do with the bloody thing?"

"Sell it, you bloody fool," he said, just as angrily.

I laughed. I couldn't stay angry with Charlie. I sat opposite him and told him all about Georgina and Elizabeth, and how I'd visited Perilly House and seen the two caravans which I suspected were intended to be Georgina's new home. I explained how Sir Leon had promised to take care of her future for me, and how that was more important than some damned picture, however glorious that picture might be.

Charlie leaned his head against the lower guardrail. "Elizabeth was going to shove Georgina into a caravan?"

"Yes."

He uttered a crisp judgment of Elizabeth, then another, less crisp, on me. "But you still gave it away. I don't believe it!"

He seemed extraordinarily worried, and it suddenly occurred to me that perhaps he had thought that, should I succeed in finding the picture, I would pay him back for all the thousands he had spent on *Sunflower*. "If it's the money, Charlie," I said, "then don't worry. Sir Leon will give me enough to pay you. I might have given up the purchase money, but I don't mind asking for a few thousand as a reward."

"Bugger the money! I'm thinking about you!" He helped himself to the mug of coffee Jennifer had abandoned. "I suppose you realise that Elizabeth will probably take you to court and challenge your right to give it away?"

"Perhaps." But not, I thought, if she was hiding it.

Charlie sighed. "You have a rare talent, Johnny, for going up shit-filled creeks and chucking away paddles." He offered me a lit cigarette, then lit one for himself. "Who's the copper on this one?"

"Harry Abbott again."

"Jesus wept." He was truly disgusted. "You're not bunking up with bloody Harry, are you?" He frowned, evidently thinking of the press conference. "And Harry knows who's got the painting?"

I smiled, knowing my next answer would amuse Charlie. "Elizabeth."

Charlie stared at me in surprise, then scornfully rejected the idea. "Harry's off his twist! He reckons Elizabeth stole the painting?"

"Or someone did it for her."

"Bloody hell! But Elizabeth married money, didn't she?"

"They're skint."

He thought about it for a few seconds, then tacitly conceded that his initial scornful rejection might have been mistaken. "She always liked money, didn't she?" He stared at me, and I saw the penny drop. "Johnny! She tried to have you killed?"

"That's what Harry thinks."

"Which means she'll try again . . ." Charlie was smart, very smart, and he twisted on the thwart to stare at the man who had chased him down the bridge on to the pontoon. He snapped his fingers at me. "You're being guarded, Johnny!"

"You got it, Charlie. Not all the time, because Harry's a cheapskate copper, but so long as I'm on the river I've got company."

"You're daft," he said, "plain daft." He had spoken ruefully. Now he stood up. "I don't know, Johnny. I thought you'd be halfway to the West Indies by now! Hell, I was going to bring Joanna out there for a fortnight!"

"There'll be other fortnights, Charlie."

"Maybe." He looked at his watch. "I've got a meeting up on the M5 extension. It's a brand new motorway and it's already crumbling to shreds. Still, I mustn't complain. It's all money. Look after yourself, Johnny."

"I'm trying."

"But if you want my advice," he said morosely, "I'd bugger off. I wouldn't trust Harry Abbott, and I certainly wouldn't trust that Buzzacott mob. They've already conned a painting out of you, so what will they take next?" He climbed on to the pontoon. "Maybe I'll drop by on my way home."

"I won't be here this afternoon, Charlie."

"Oh, of course. You're off to London with your girlfriend." He paused on the pontoon. "You're an idiot, Johnny."

"Am I?"

"You're getting involved." He flicked his half-smoked cigarette into the river, then stared gloomily at me. "Do you know why I like you? Because from the very beginning, right from the beginning, you were always different. You never gave a damn. You didn't give a monkey's about a bloody thing. You'd do anything for a dare. But now? Now you're letting those rich buggers call your tune. You're joining them, Johnny, and they'll use you." He pointed an accusing finger at me. "Go back to sea, Johnny. You'll be happier there."

"I'll go back soon."

"Go now, before they tame you."

I smiled, then watched him walk away. Had Charlie been tamed? I didn't know. What I did know was that I had let down my friend. I had let him down by throwing in my lot with other people, and I abruptly realised that Charlie was upset because, till now, he had always seen himself as my protector. Now he felt betrayed, and I felt rotten, but I wouldn't change my course, not yet, for Georgina's future and my own stupid hopes depended on it. Not hopes of a painting, nor of a reward, but of Jennifer.

I chained the dinghy to the coachroof so that no thieving creep would steal it, locked *Sunflower*, told my police guards that I'd be going away and that I'd phone the local station before I returned, then went to London.

To my chagrin, Hans had accompanied Jennifer Pallavicini to the television studio. The happy couple were waiting for me in the hospitality room where Hans greeted me politely, then stood smiling by as Jennifer and I made small talk. Her friendliness of the morning had dissipated, though she did say that she liked Charlie.

"You did?" I sounded surprised, for she'd behaved very coolly when she met him.

"He looks a very capable sort of man."

"He's that, right enough." I told her tales of our adventures together, and recounted the time when we had nearly died in the Tasman Sea storm, and how Charlie had sung all the way through the ordeal because, he said, he'd be buggered if he went to hell crying. "He's a good man," I said warmly.

"And you define a good man," she observed icily, "as being someone who can sail small boats in big storms?"

I reflected that it was a more reliable definition than being a genius with the processed cheese, but managed to avoid saying as much. Instead I was buttonholed by the programme's presenter who told me what he wanted me to say.

It was evident that I'd been cast as the rogue aristocrat; unstable, unreliable, and somewhat mysterious; while Jennifer, I assumed, had been invited in case I proved to be tongue-tied, in which case she could be relied on to keep speaking.

We did our television programme. The interviewer treated me like a cretin, and I obliged by being suitably arrogant. When I was asked why I'd given away the Van Gogh, I simply replied that I didn't want it. The audience seemed to like the interview. Jennifer was more loquacious, explaining the importance of the missing painting, then paying a very nice tribute to my generosity. The audience applauded me. The whole thing was quite painless, and all over within twenty minutes. We were shown back to the hospitality room where we were offered warm white wine and stale sandwiches. There was no sign of Hans.

"He had to catch a flight to Geneva," Jennifer explained. She looked very excited, perhaps because she had enjoyed the interview more than she had expected. "It was fun, wasn't it?"

"Was it?"

"Of course it was! Don't be so boring. I think I'd like to be on telly more often."

"You were very good," I said loyally.

"Then we shall celebrate my success by having dinner."

She was suddenly bouncing with happiness, and my own happiness was increasing because of it. We went to a restaurant where we could eat outside and, in the lantern-light, she told me about her childhood, and about the American university where she'd majored in Fine Arts, then about her apprenticeship at a London auction house and her first proper gallery job in Florence. I tried to put a time-span on various jobs, and decided she must be twenty-seven.

"And you," she asked, "what about you?"

"I thought you'd done all that research on me?"

"Maybe it was wrong." She caught my eye, and we said nothing for a moment, and I wondered if all the former hostility between us had been merely a disguise for what we had both been feeling. I think I already knew that this was a girl worth staying ashore for, and if that was an exciting thought, it was also somewhat frightening. Maybe she felt the same fear for she suddenly looked away and posed a brutal question. "Tell me about your brother. Why did he kill himself?"

"He couldn't cope."

"With what?"

"The problems of Stowey. Mother. Life. Debts. Disappointment."

Jennifer frowned. "Disappointment?"

I lit a pipe, taking my time over the job. "It was very important to Michael that he was going to be an earl. He thought it would make him important. He couldn't wait for Father to die. He wanted to see the forelocks twitching when he walked by, and he wanted to wear the ermine, and he fancied hobnobbing in the House of Lords, and when he finally inherited he suddenly discovered that it didn't make a blind bit of difference. He was still just the same indecisive idiot that he'd always been. Mother kept pushing him to do things to the estate, which he didn't have the guts to try, and she also wanted him to marry some monstrous creature from the Fens, which he couldn't face, so in the end he just bunged a double-barrel into his mouth and put his big toe on the trigger."

For a few seconds she didn't speak, then she frowned. "You can be very flippant at times."

"Can I?"

She didn't reply, instead she just stared at me as though this was the very first time she had really taken notice of me. And I, suddenly, was frightened, because I knew I was being judged, and I wanted that judgment to be favourable.

"Listen," I said. "Life can be very shitty, it can be tough, it can be the pits. So there's only one rule, and that's never to give in. Bad luck comes to all of us, so what must you do? You fight it, you claw at it, you kick the shit out of it, but you never, ever, ever give in. You only go through this vale of tears once, so for God's sake make it a good voyage. So if I'm flippant, that's only because it's better to make light of a disaster than to cry over it."

I had spoken with more vehemence than I had intended. Jennifer had looked away from me to stare down at the table, so I could not see what she had made of my words. "What do you think about when you're out there?" she asked after a while, "on your own, at sea?"

"Survival."

"Is that all?"

"It isn't all," I started, though I couldn't explain the rest of it, so shrugged instead. "You have to be there to know."

I knew my words had been inadequate. I looked round the small courtyard where diners sat at a dozen tables. They looked content, wealthy, attractive, happy. They also looked plump, self-important, and trapped. "Once," I said awkwardly, "I watched a meteor fall past the Southern Cross. It was a big one, a great blazon of light across the darkness, and I can't explain why that's important, or what I felt, except that to see it even once, in all its glory, is worth an awful lot."

"Were you alone?"

"Yes."

"And you didn't want to share it with anyone?"

"Oh, yes."

She smiled at that answer, but kept silent.

"So tomorrow" – I took the plunge for happiness – "why don't you come to Devon with me and we'll have a day at sea?"

"To watch the stars fall?"

"Maybe."

She raised her glass, waited for me to do the same, then touched her rim against mine. "OK," she said simply.

And I was in heaven.

We stayed that night at Sir Leon's house in Mayfair. I was given a guest room, and didn't ask for more. We were up long before dawn and, while I made coffee and toast, Jennifer raided the freezers and kitchen cupboards for our lunch. We were much too early for a radio weather forecast, so I phoned the commercial service and listened to their tape recording. "What do they say?" Jennifer asked me when I put the phone down.

"Sounds good," I said absent-mindedly, "a real skirt-lifter."

"A real what?" She turned on me with mock fierceness.

"Force six, gusting seven," I said contritely, then carried the bags down to the garage where she opened the door of a battered Ford Escort. "Yours?" I asked.

She heard the surprise in my voice. "What did you expect? A Lamborghini?"

"A Porsche at least."

"I'm sorry to disappoint you." She dangled the keys above the car roof. "Do you want to drive?"

"No."

"That's good. I like driving."

She raced the car through empty dark streets. Neither of us spoke much at first, it was too early in the morning, yet there was a distinct feeling of excitement. Just days before we had been snapping at each other like strange dogs; now, suddenly, we had the comfortable intimacy of friendship. There was also the anticipation of something more than friendship. It was that anticipation which touched our commonplace with excitement. We both felt it and we were both happy.

She drove like Charlie; fast, competently, and with a blithe confidence that the police would ignore her. They did.

We sped past Heathrow and Windsor, and only then did she break our silence. She talked about the books she was reading, and scorned me with laughter when I told her I thought four books sufficient for life. She described the Buzzacott Museum Gallery, calling it her stepfather's fantasy and obsession. "That's why he pursued money so ruthlessly," she went on, "just so he could build his fantasy."

191

"And he's very rich," I commented sourly.

"Very." She ignored the jealousy in my voice. "It was the property world that started him off. It still pays well, I think, but he keeps Mummy and me a long way away from the seamier side of his activities."

"Seamy?" I asked.

"A bit, I think." She didn't elaborate. The sun rose behind us, casting long shadows and promising a fine day, though I doubted, looking at the bare sky, whether the forecast of a skirt-lifting force six would prove correct. Not that it mattered, for this day was not really about sailing, but about exploring a friendship.

And we had plenty of time for that exploration, for we were in Dartmouth long before breakfast time. I hadn't told Harry that I was returning, which meant my guardian angels were home in their own beds. Their absence made me feel oddly nervous, so I didn't waste any time getting ready for sea. I cast off *Sunflower*'s springs, led the bow warp back to the cockpit, hanked on the big genoa and took off the mainsail cover.

"Aren't you going to motor her out?" Jennifer asked me.

"I'm going to show off and sail us out."

It was a happier experiment than my arrival on the pontoon. The breeze was from the east, an errant morning wind caused by the hills about the river. The tide was ebbing. I hoisted the jib, let it flap, released the bow warp, then hauled the jib flat to starboard. The wind swung our bows fast off the pontoon, just clearing the transom of the boat ahead. I slipped the stern warp, let the jib sheet run so that the sail was reaching, then hauled in all my loose warps. *Sunflower* ghosted out of the narrow space like magic.

Jennifer applauded. "I'm impressed."

"Did you see my arrival?"

She shook her head. "Don't tell me I missed another of the master mariner's impressive displays?"

"Technically," I said, "my arrival here was what we master mariners call a cock-up. I thought you might be watching, tried to impress you by doing it the hard way, and very nearly wrapped the mast round the bridge."

She laughed. "Serves you right."

I gave her the helm while I stowed the fenders, then hauled up the big main. The wind was fitful, backing north, but at least blowing us to sea. It was obvious the weathermen had got it wrong again. The wind was force two, sometimes three, but I sensed even that gentle breeze wouldn't last. The sun was climbing to shimmer the sea and already there was a haze above the slowly receding coast. I watched the river entrance as we drew away. A gaff-rigged cutter had followed us out, but had now turned eastwards towards Torbay. A whale-decked Brixham trawler was plugging in the opposite direction, but, apart from a handful of dinghy sails in the river mouth, there was nothing else in sight. "Safe at last," I said facetiously.

Jennifer looked back towards the coast. "I'd rather forgotten about those two men."

"I hadn't."

She grimaced. "My stepfather thinks you're being very foolish. He'd prefer to pay the ransom, but I suppose he can't really argue with Inspector Abbott. He's meant to be the expert."

"Harry's no fool," I said. "I might be though, making myself a target. Still, we're safe now."

She frowned. "Suppose they saw us leaving? Suppose they're following us?"

I shook my head. "They're too late." Already the river mouth was indistinct, and the land fading like a mirage. In a few minutes we would be alone in the empty sea. "Besides," I went on to reassure her, "I've got a radio, so if we see anything suspicious I'll scream blue murder to the coast-guards." It occurred to me that Harry would be the one screaming blue murder when he discovered that I'd returned without informing him, so I punctiliously called the Brixham Coastguard and gave them a routine passage report: yacht *Sunflower* day-sailing off Dartmouth, expecting to return to port sometime that evening. I asked them to relay that information to the Dartmouth police station. They must have been mildly surprised at the request, but promised to make the call.

Jennifer had installed herself in the navigator's chair and was admiring the electronic display which Charlie had insisted on building over the chart table. "What's this?" she asked.

"A Decca set."

"What's a Decca set?"

I explained the chain of coast radio transmitters which pulsed their signals to sea, and how the little black box translated the signals into a position. This was the first time I'd used Charlie's gift, so I had to tell the machine roughly where we were, it paused, then the aerial found the signals and the display updated itself with our exact position. Jennifer was enthralled. I entered the latitude and longitude of St Helier in the Channel Islands and Jennifer read the course and distance off the display. "So all you have to do is follow that course and you'll get there?"

"Not exactly." I found a chart and showed her how the Decca course would take us straight across the islands of Guernsey and Jersey. "So what we'd have to do," I said, "is put in another waypoint here," I pointed to a patch of sea north of the Roches Douvres, "then make St Helier the second waypoint."

"Waypoint?" she asked.

"Posh name for destination. You pick the waypoint and the machine tells you how to get there."

She looked at the electronic display which was showing a small bent arrow and some apparently meaningless figures. "What's it telling us now?"

"It's assuming we're trying to sail the direct line to St Helier, so it's telling us that we're a tenth of a nautical mile off course to port, travelling at 3.2 knots, on a heading of 162 true, and that we should be heading 137 true."

She stared admiringly at the display. "I thought you master mariners did it all with sextants?"

"Most of the time we do," I said, "because you run out of Decca range as soon as you leave Europe."

So then she wanted to see the sextant. I took her up to the cockpit and showed her how to bring the sun down to the horizon. She wanted to try for herself, so I settled back and watched as she braced herself against the companionway.

She was worth watching. She was wearing a shirt and jeans, and had her short black hair tied back with a band. "It's green!" she exclaimed when she first saw the sun in the mirror, then frowned as a quiver of her right hand jarred the sun loose. A moment later she managed to hold the sun steady on the mirror, then bit her lower lip in fierce concentration as she moved the index arm. The trick of it was to move the index arm to bring the sun down, while holding the rest of the instrument absolutely steady so that the horizon stayed fixed in the sight glass. "Done it!" she said triumphantly.

"Read me the scale."

She had done it, too. I checked by taking my own sight. "Is that all there is to it?" she asked mockingly.

"That and a lot of very tedious mathematics. It's also a bit trickier to do when the boat's heaving up and down in a rough sea, or if you're trying to find one star among a million, but on the whole that's all there is to it."

The genoa slapped a protest at the fading wind. I switched off the Decca and put the sextant away. I let Jennifer steer, though there was little to do for the wind was dying on us. "Whistle," I said to her.

"Whistle?"

"It's supposed to bring the wind."

She laughed, but didn't try the old magic. I stretched myself lazily on the leeward thwart. "Shouldn't you be working?" I teased her.

"Of course I should be working."

"Why aren't you?"

"Because I'm rich and spoilt, and can take days off when I like. Isn't that what you expected me to say?"

"Is it true?"

She made a face. "Partly. Which is why I usually work very hard." She hauled in the mainsheet, but it didn't make the boat go any faster. "I also wanted to be with you," she added in a shy and surprising explanation. She had not looked at me as she spoke.

I said nothing, waiting till she caught my eye. "Mutual," I said then. Happiness sometimes comes in cloudbursts.

There was a pause as we shared that happiness, then, in friendly warning, she deliberately broke the mood. "But don't be too hopeful, John Rossendale. Hans has my heart, such as it is."

"Lucky Hans."

"Except this is work really," she said hastily, perhaps wondering whether she had said too much and was now trying to draw a little of it back. "If we're going to get the painting back, then I have to co-operate with you, don't I?"

"Absolutely."

We sailed on in companionable silence. The coast was nothing but a dark blur in the shimmering haze. A small workboat sped past a half-mile to starboard. I'd watched it approach from astern, but it had made no effort to come near us. I stared at it through the binoculars and saw that it carried a half-dozen hopeful men with sea-angling gear. I could not see Garrard on the boat, so I relaxed. It was getting warmer, so I stripped off my shirt, then lay back again and pillowed my head on the coiled genoa sheet.

"Sleepy?" Jennifer asked.

"Just lazy. I'm not used to being chauffeured."

"Don't you get bored with sailing alone?"

"I don't always sail alone."

She thought about that for a while. "Girls?"

"Thank God, yes." I told her about the hitch-hikers who wandered the trade-wind routes; how they lived from island to island, boat to boat, and one summer's day to the next.

"They make me feel very dull," she said.

"I can't think why. You seem very exotic to me."

"Exotic?"

"Rich, beautiful and engaged to the King of Swiss processed cheese."

She laughed. "I can't think why you're so nasty about Hans! You only met him twice, and he was perfectly pleasant to you."

It was my turn to betray an intimacy; to offer her some vulnerability of my own. "I dislike him because he's engaged to you. I'm jealous."

She smiled acceptance. "How nice."

It was that kind of morning. Flirtatious and happy, and the flirting sometimes veered very close to something deeper, but we both avoided it. I wasn't going to hurry her. One learns patience at sea, and I would be patient.

By late morning we had entirely lost sight of land. The wind had died to nothing and the sea was slapping petulantly at *Sunflower*'s hull. We simply wallowed in a long, lazy swell. The small fishing boat was drifting a mile away. I guessed the men had abandoned hunting inshore for bass and had come out to the deeper water to find mackerel.

Jennifer stood up and, rather decisively, peeled off her jeans and shirt. The abruptness of the gesture somehow invested it with importance, as though she had taken another deliberate step on the road to intimacy. She was wearing a yellow bikini. I had been right: she did look good in a bikini. In fact she looked wonderful, and I said as much.

"I didn't think you'd be able to resist a comment," she said tartly.

"And I very much hoped I wouldn't be able to resist one."

The hull rocked in the small waves as the sails slatted from side to side. Jennifer abandoned trying to sail *Sunflower*, and instead stretched herself out on the opposite thwart. She lay with her head towards the stern, while mine was nearer the cabin so we could look at each other across the cockpit. "Daddy didn't want me to go to the Azores," she said suddenly.

I assumed Daddy was Sir Leon. "Why not?"

"He thought Inspector Abbott should go. I persuaded him that I stood a better chance of convincing you."

"If you'd have dressed like that, you'd have succeeded."

"If we become friends," she said, "will you persist in making sexist remarks?"

"Yes."

She smiled. "You are a philistine."

"So why did you go to the Azores?" I asked.

She paused for a heartbeat, wondering whether to offer the confession, then looked across at me. "Because I wanted to see you."

"I thought that must have been it," I said complacently.

"You are a bastard!"

I grinned. "For someone who wanted to see me, you weren't very friendly."

"What was I supposed to do? Jump into your boat singing 'I'm Just a Girl Who Can't Say No'?"

"It might have broken the ice." I sat up momentarily to check that no shipping threatened to run us down. Nothing did. The only vessel in sight was the mackerel boat which had drifted slightly closer. I lay down again. "I very nearly did go back to England with you."

"Why didn't you?"

"Because you made me feel like a puppet."

"Something went right, then."

I laughed. A gull floated above us, decided we weren't a fishing boat, and slid away. *Sunflower*'s sails and her red ensign hung limp, while Charlie's wind vane at the masthead lazily boxed the compass.

"Mummy likes you," Jennifer said suddenly.

"I like Mummy."

"Do you? Yes, I'm sure you do. Men always do."

"I prefer her daughter."

Jennifer treated that compliment as merely dutiful. "Did she talk to you about Hans?"

"Yes."

"What did she say?"

"In the first place that he's dull, in the second that he's duller, and in the third that he's very dull. She added later that he's extremely dull."

She laughed, but didn't say anything.

"Is she right?" I asked.

"Mummy's usually very acute about people."

I digested that one. I'd left the VHF switched on to Channel 16 and I heard a squawk as someone called the coastguard to report their passage. I waited for the conversation to be switched to the working channel and, in the ensuing silence, looked across the cockpit. "Jennifer?"

"John?" She mocked my solemnity with her own.

Perhaps I wasn't so patient after all, for I suddenly wanted to short-circuit the morning's flirtatiousness. "I think I'm in love with you."

She looked at me for a long time in silence. I wondered if I had spoilt the mood by being too serious, but then she smiled. "How very inconvenient."

We smiled at each other. I knew then that everything was going to be all right. It really was. Hans had lost. I didn't know how it had happened so quickly, or what would happen next, but I knew everything was wonderful. Happiness filled me like a great glow.

She sat up, pulled off her headband, and ran fingers through her hair. "I'm told," she said happily, "that the way to a man's heart is through his stomach?"

"There are alternative routes."

She stood and gave my belly a reproving slap. "For now, John Rossendale, it will be the stomach. Lunch?"

"I'll get it."

"You stay there. I know what food I packed, and you don't. Besides, you doubtless believe a woman's place is in the galley, so why pretend otherwise?" She stooped and gave me a very swift kiss on the lips. I made a grab for her, but she was too fast for me. She laughed, and swung herself down the companionway steps.

I listened to her unpacking the food. I was happy, so very happy, transported to some new region of gold-touched, warm and loving contentment.

"Where's the tin-opener?" she called.

"In the cave-locker behind the sink."

"Wine glasses?"

"Hanging in a rack over your head."

"Soup plates?"

"Use the big coffee mugs."

She began singing 'I'm Just a Girl Who Can't Say No', and I wanted to laugh aloud because I knew she was as happy as I was. *Sunflower* rocked gently. Small waves slapped at her steel chines. The sky was pale blue, with just the faintest hint of high cloud wisping.

She stopped singing. "Matches?"

"In a waterproof plastic container beside the cutlery tray.

You strike the match on the inside of the container lid."

She started singing again, then stopped almost immediately. "Why won't the gas turn on?"

"Because you have to switch on the gas feed tap which you'll find by the engine bulkhead under the companionway steps, and I have to switch the main feed on back here."

"Then do it," she said.

"Aye aye, Captain." I sat up. I saw that the skipper of the mackerel boat had started his engine and was going away from us into the heat haze. I opened the transom locker where I kept the cooking gas bottles. The locker had a drain to the open air, thus, if one of the bottles leaked, the lethal gas would drain harmlessly outboard.

I heard Jennifer grunt as she turned the feed tap which was uncomfortably stiff. She started singing again as she went back to the narrow galley which was midships on the starboard side. I reached into the locker and tried to turn on the main valve. It wouldn't turn. I heard the rattle as Jennifer opened the matches, and I suddenly realised that the gas valve was already turned on and I had never, ever, left it turned on, not once in four years, which meant that someone else had been aboard *Sunflower*. I twisted desperately round.

"No!" I roared.

But she struck the match just as I shouted.

And the happiness vanished.

Ask any sailor what they fear most and they won't cite the sea, or careless merchant ships, or rocks, but fire.

And almost every yacht afloat carries a fire-bomb aboard: the bottles of liquid gas they use for cooking. The gas is heavier than air. If it leaks it settles down to the bilges where it lies, hidden and deadly, waiting for the spark. Some yachts carry a gas detector, but I'd never thought to put one on *Sunflower*. Instead I relied on the taps: one on the bottle itself, one where the gas pipe enters the main cabin, and the usual taps on the galley stove. I was punctilious about keeping all the taps closed unless I was actually cooking, for there is nothing I fear so much as a gas leak. Most days I hand pumped the bilges, not for any water, but just in case a

200

tiny amount of gas had leaked. The pump will carry it to the outside air, but it was a chore I usually performed in the evening. That day, wallowing in the swell off the hidden Devon coast, the bilge and the cabin sole were unpumped and lethal.

Because while I had been in London, and while the boat had been unguarded, someone had been aboard *Sunflower* and they had turned the taps and let the silent deadly gas seep into the cabin. The gas doesn't smell. It just waits for a spark or a flame.

Jennifer struck the match.

And screamed.

It was not an ear-splitting explosion. It was a soft roar. Red flame filled the cabin. I could hear Jennifer screaming beyond the fire's noise. Her scream seemed to go on and on and on. The fire was thickening with appalling swiftness; flame and smoke pouring out of the open companionway as if it was a chimney. The slatting mainsail was already scorched up to the third reef points.

The noise of the fire was like a seething hiss, beyond which Jennifer's scream slowly faded.

I was shouting incoherently, merely making a noise to tell her that I was there, and shouting to give myself courage. There were a dozen things I maybe should have done. I should have turned off the main gas valve. I should have dragged one of the fire extinguishers out of the starboard cockpit locker. I should have darted a hand through the fire to grab the VHF microphone and send a Mayday. I did none of them. Instead, and without really thinking, I plunged down into the flame.

I had been turning and shouting in the cockpit as the explosion erupted out of the cabin and I did not pause to think that I was throwing myself down into the fire. I simply kept moving towards the sound of Jennifer's fading scream. I put my hands on the coachroof either side of the companionway and swung myself down. I dropped into unimaginable pain. It was like falling into the jet-flame of an oxyacetylene lamp and I saw, as I dropped down, how a piercing lance of flame was seething into the cabin from the engine bulkhead. My ankle was on fire, bubbling and spitting. Even through the pain I realised that it was there, where the pipe came through the bulkhead, that the gas line had been cut. I scrambled away from the flame jet and fell against the cabin table. I had to take a breath and filled my lungs with burning gas. I was blinded by heat and smoke, choking and sobbing, and still trying to shout to Jennifer. I wanted to tell her to survive, to hold on, to live. Light flared to my right; a brilliant and searing light as the charts caught fire.

I didn't feel the pain. I lunged through the smoke to the galley compartment where I felt Jennifer rather than saw her. She was crouched down and I simply scooped her up as if she was an unwieldy sailbag and kept on moving. I hit the forecabin's door and smashed it down with our combined weight. Jennifer screamed with pain. The air was suddenly cool, then instantly heated as the fire found the new oxygen and slashed in after us. Jennifer was moaning. Black smoke writhed round us.

I dropped her against my small workbench, reached up, and undogged the forehatch. "Get out!" I was shouting at her, but at the same time pushing her upwards. Smoke poured past us. I realised she was beyond helping herself, so shoved her out. I followed her, then slammed the hatch shut.

The main cabin looked like a blast furnace as it belched a horror of flame and smoke out of the companionway. The mainsail was on fire. There was no chance of reaching the radio now. I could already feel the heat coming through the teak planks laid over the thin steel deck. I could see no other boats. I didn't want to look at Jennifer. I had caught glimpses of her burned skin, and I had heard her screams.

The dinghy was still chained to the coachroof so I yanked the liferaft's lanyard. The lanyard pulled out the split pin which held the metal container to its securing bolt. The container rolled towards me. I picked it up and hurled it over the guardrails. It splashed into the calm sea, tethered to *Sunflower* by its line and ripcord. I yanked the ripcord which was supposed to inflate the raft, but instead it just floated like a fat white keg of beer. I jerked the cord again, achieving nothing. I swore at the bloody thing. The deck was already burning the soles of my feet, and I knew the coachroof would already be red hot so I couldn't reach the chained dinghy. A scrap of burning sail material landed in my hair. Something exploded in the cabin below, and I assumed the fire had reached the emergency flares. The hull lurched and I knew the fire must have burned through the plastic lavatory pipes and that the sea was already flooding through the seacocks into *Sunflower*. She was doomed.

I had two life-jackets, but they were aft, where the fire was hottest. So was my single lifebelt which was attached to the danbuoy on the stern. I began to dance on the deck, trying to cool my feet. Jennifer was twitching and moaning. Her scalp was smoking where her hair had burned away. Her legs looked as if they'd been skinned and blackened. She was going to die because the bloody liferaft wouldn't work and because I didn't have a radio any more and because some bastard had broken into my boat and made it into a death trap.

Jennifer suddenly screamed again because of the heat in the deck. She reached towards me with fingers turned into stiff dark claws. Further aft the teak deck planks were lifting and smoking. Burning scraps of sail were falling around us to hiss on the sea or flame on the deck. There was no choice left now, none. I picked Jennifer up in my arms, making her scream, and I knew she would scream more in a moment because of the salt water, but I would give her a few more minutes of life because there's always a chance of a miracle so long as you don't give up. Never give up. Never. I carried her to the port gunwale, put one foot over the guardrail, then jumped.

The sea was blessedly cold, but the salt must have been like acid on her burned skin. I held her body above mine so that her grotesquely blackened head was out of the water. I had one arm round her neck, the other about her waist, while I kicked with my legs to force us away from the burning boat. I could smell her roasted flesh. She was babbling, moaning, screaming, choking. I was talking to her; telling her she would live, that everything would be all right, that she mustn't give in. Every few seconds the water would slop into my mouth, choking me.

I twisted my head to catch a glimpse of *Sunflower*. The fire had reached the aft locker where the spare gas bottle was kept. At first the fire merely melted the regulator valve so that a white spear of flame seared across the smoke in the cockpit, then the gas bottle exploded. The diesel fuel was making the flames deep red and the smoke even blacker. Her red ensign disappeared in a single flare of fire.

She was settling by the bows. Her mainsail was gone and her genoa was burning into ash. Somehow the mast stayed up. I could see the liferaft container bobbing merrily and uselessly alongside the blistering hull.

The bows dropped further. Everything flammable in the cabin must have been well aflame by now; lockers, foam, bedding, papers, clothes, cooking oil, table, chart table, my money, my passport, everything in the world I owned, all now an inferno that pumped flame and smoke out of the open companionway. *Sunflower* suddenly lurched sideways and I feared the mast would fall on us so I kicked with my feet again and the motion pushed my head underwater.

When I surfaced again I saw she had dipped her bows under. The sea reached the hawse-hole and filled the chain locker. She sank further. I was treading water desperately. I was tiring. I was beginning to feel the pain where my legs had been burned, and the moment I began to feel it, so the pain suddenly became excruciating and I knew that the anaesthetic effect of adrenalin was wearing off. It must have been worse for Jennifer, except she was only half conscious.

The sea reached *Sunflower*'s forehatch which, undogged, fell open and let the water surge in. The stern swung further up so that I could see her rudder and propeller. Steam was hissing and mingling with the smoke as the fire fought the sea. The sea would win, because it always does, and slowly, slowly, I saw my boat begin her long slide down to the sea bed. She'd taken me to far, far places. We'd sailed the blood-red sea off Cape Non and hove to off the cliffs at Cape Bojador, which the old navigators had thought was the place the world ended. We'd sailed the Whitsunday Islands, and dared the pirates in the Philippines. We'd anchored in mangrove swamps in Florida, and sailed the harbours of Maine. We'd rounded the Horn twice, but we'd never sail together again for now she was sinking and it seemed as if the fire was compressed, or else the steam was superheated for the jet of vapour and flames and smoke became a solid roaring plume that was being pumped three hundred feet into the summer sky. It seemed extraordinary that one small boat could make so much filth.

Then she went. The mast-tip went under, the cockpit reared up, then, with one last puff of flame and dark smoke, *Sunflower* dragged herself down. Something hissed on the sea's bubbling surface. There was a pause, then the liferaft, still tied by its rope to the sinking hull, was pulled down and out of sight. Floating burnt wreckage was all that was left; that and a dirty smear of smoke that lingered in the summer air.

Jennifer was moaning and I knew she was dying. I also knew I was tiring and that soon I would be forced to let her go and she would roll over, her mouth would fill with water and she would drown. That realisation made me angry, so I cursed her for dying. I told her she would live. I told her she would bloody well live. I told her to stop her pathetic whimpering and to start kicking with her legs. I told her she was a spoilt damned rich bloody bitch who deserved to die if she didn't wake up and swim. I cursed her in three languages and four letters, and I might as well have saved my breath for she did not recover consciousness and I was tiring and every swear word drained another scrap of precious energy.

In the end I stopped cursing her. I remember telling her that I loved her, but then I had no more energy to talk for all my strength was needed to keep us afloat. My legs were agony, and felt like lead. More and more often the water would slop into my mouth. I would choke and spit and struggle to gain an extra inch of airspace. I held Jennifer with one arm and paddled with the other.

But I was losing the battle. The hallucinations began. I saw a boat coming to pick us up: it was a great schooner, white-hulled with a reaching bowsprit. The illusion was so exact that I could see the chain bobstay beneath the bowsprit and the gilded wood carving where her figurehead might be. Men leaned over from the bows to pluck us from the water and I reached up to catch their hands and the act of reaching up plunged me underwater and the hallucination vanished in a blow of reality as sea water choked my gullet. I struggled up and pulled Jennifer's burned head from the water. For all I knew, she was already dead, but I would not let her go. I was crying, not out of pity, but frustration. There was no schooner. There was nothing but the sea and *Sunflower*'s funeral smoke and one seagull gliding past.

I saw a beach. It was very close. The beach was long and sandy, backed by low grass-covered dunes. No one was on the beach, but a shingle roof rising above the dunes promised a refuge. I swam towards the beach. The hope of safety seemed to give me a new manic energy and I muttered in Jennifer's ear that we were going to be all right now, that all we had to do was survive the surf and I'd go to the house and find help. "We've reached America," I said, because now I could see the Stars and Stripes flying from a flagpole in front of the house. The illusion was so damned real that I was even wondering how to persuade an American hospital to treat us when we didn't have any credit cards, but then a small wave splashed my face and when I opened my eyes again the beach was gone, and the flag and the house had vanished with it and there was only the empty sea and sky. Jennifer was heavy in my arm, the sea was seeping its fatal coldness into me, and the tiredness was filling me with a great weakness.

I almost let her go, but I made myself hold on to her burned flesh. I tried to keep her head above water, but my kicking was becoming more and more feeble so that more and more water broke over my face to sting my eyes and fill my throat. I told her once more that I loved her. She neither made a sound, nor moved.

A helicopter appeared in the sky. I cursed this new hallucination because now I only wanted to die in peace. The helicopter made a huge clattering noise, disturbing me, and I swam feebly away from it in the hope of finding a place of great quiet and slow gentle dying. Again the illusion was crystal clear, even to such details as the helicopter's shadow sweeping over us and the water churning beneath the blade's downdraught. I saw the winchman peering down, but I fought the illusion because I dared not cling to such imaginary hopes, yet the mind persisted, and I hallucinated the rope dropping down and touching the water to discharge the helicopter's static electricity. I cursed the dream.

A wave swamped us. I choked, but this time there was no air to breathe. I had gone underwater. I still clung to Jennifer, but now I was drowning and she was drowning with me. I opened my eyes and found peace. The water's surface was like a sheet of waving silver above me. No helicopter disturbed that pretty sight. My pain had gone, my ears were filled with the long, hollow booming of the sea, and there was peace and gentleness and a shot-silk silver sky of coalescing wonder.

Then the great shape hammered the silver black, and it seemed that a man was in the water, huge and thrashing and intrusive, and I closed my eyes to get rid of the dream and I let Jennifer go as I drifted away to nowhere and nothing, because it was all over now; it was all over and I was finished and everything was ended.

PART FOUR

Part Four

Ulf, of all people, bloody Ulf, was telling me that *Sunflower*'s mast was too high and mounted too far aft. He was saying to wake up and move the thing. I tried to tell him to shut up, but his voice droned on. You're all right, Johnny, he said, you're not going to die because death is just a mentally induced self-deception, and I told him to stuff his opinions and then I saw that Ulf was dressed all in white and had a black face, and I wondered how the hell he'd ever got into heaven to become a white-robed angel, and I felt a vague surprise that everyone in heaven was black, though it did seem a fairly heavenly solution to an earthly problem, then I wondered how I'd ever got permission to enter heaven myself. "There's been a mistake," I said.

"You're all right now," said the hallucination of Ulf which resolved itself into a black-bespectacled doctor who was bending over me. "Move your hand," he said, "that's good."

My left ankle and calf were a mass of pain, like the time I'd been stung by a jellyfish off the Malaysian coast. I hissed and jerked as the pain struck me, then tried to explain it. "Jellyfish," I said.

"My name's Mortimer," the doctor said, "Doctor Mortimer. And you're the Earl of Stowey, yes?"

"John," I said, "call me John." A siren was wailing somewhere, and the sound reminded me of Jennifer's screaming. I turned my head to see I was in a small brightly lit room and there was no sign of Jennifer. "Is she alive?"

"She's alive," the doctor said, but I was already responding to the drugs that were sparing me pain. I slept.

It had been the mackerel boat which saved our lives. They had seen the smoke churning up, turned back to investigate, and seen *Sunflower* burning. They had called the coastguard on Channel 16, who had summoned the Royal Naval Air Service. It had taken just eight minutes from the time that the skipper of the mackerel boat had made his emergency call to the arrival of the helicopter. It had seemed like an hour. Even now, looking back, and having read the coastguard's log, I cannot believe it was only eight minutes.

My legs were badly burned, I'd inhaled smoke, and my hands and forearms were scorched. It could have been much worse. For Jennifer it was, though just how bad, in those first days, I wasn't told.

Harry Abbott was my first visitor. I was barely conscious or coherent. I gathered that as soon as the police heard of the burning boat they had feared it might be *Sunflower*, and had sent a man to the hospital to identify us. I tried to tell Harry it was attempted murder, but he must already have assumed that because I later learned that a police guard stayed in the corridor outside my ward all the time I was in the hospital. I do remember that Harry brought me some grapes that he ate himself. I asked about Jennifer and he just shrugged and said she'd been flown to a big London hospital that specialised in burn victims.

Charlie came the next day. I had never seen him so troubled. I tried to tell him that I was all right, that I would walk again, but Charlie seemed to think he had let me down. "I should have found those two blokes and fucking killed them."

"You tried, Charlie."

"Bastards." He sat beside the bed. "Bastards."

"I'm going to find them," I said, "and I promise you they'll wish they'd never been born."

"Bastards." He was too restless to stay seated and began pacing the floor. "What happened?"

I told him about the severed gas pipe. "They did a proper job, Charlie," I said bitterly. "They must have cut the gas pipe in the engine compartment, then pushed the broken end into the hole in the bulkhead." They had also done it without dislodging the feed tap inside the cabin, because otherwise Jennifer would have seen the break.

"Didn't you lock the engine compartment?" Charlie asked.

"It was only a cheap padlock."

212

"There you go," he said hopelessly. It was Charlie who had first taught me how to open a locked padlock; you just brace the loop against something solid, then tap the keyhole end with a hammer. If the lock doesn't jump open first time, tap harder. There are expensive makes that won't respond to the treatment, but I'd lost my good padlock when the two men had pulled *Sunflower* off the grid and my replacement had been a run-of-the-mill lock.

"And the liferaft didn't work," I added.

"Jesus." He was horribly depressed, but he forced himself to talk optimistically about the boat which would replace *Sunflower*. He said we'd pick her out together, equip her together, and make her maiden voyage together. "But this time we'll make sure there's a gas alarm in her."

I shook my head. "There won't be another boat, Charlie."

"Of course there will!"

"I can't afford one, and I won't take your money. You've given me enough already."

"You'll take what you're given, Johnny." He stopped his pacing and stood staring out of the window. "Bastards," he said softly, then he turned ruefully towards the bed. "I told you not to get involved."

"I'm involved now. I'm going to kill those two. For Jennifer's sake."

He smiled. "Like that, is it?"

"It's like that."

He grimaced. "I often wondered when you'd fall, Johnny. I get Yvonne and you end up with a millionaire's stepdaughter."

"If she lives, and if she wants me."

"You saved her life," he said as though that gave me full rights over that life.

"No," I said disparagingly. Yet I probably had saved her. The helicopter pilot came to tell me as much, and so did Harry Abbott on his second visit. He listened glumly as I described the fire, and to my conviction that the gas pipe had been deliberately cut.

"I didn't think to guard the boat," Harry said ruefully, "only you." He seemed genuinely upset at what had happened.

"I want those two, Harry."

"We're looking for them, Johnny, we're looking for them."

"And Elizabeth, if she's behind it."

"Who else?" He lit a cigarette and stared moodily at the bandages on my ankle. "Mind you," he went on, "she's taking damned good care to keep a long way out of it."

"Out of it?"

"She's done a runner. I went to question her, see, but her husband says he thinks she's in France. Thinks!" Harry said disgustedly. "I'll not be able to nail her, Johnny, not unless I can find Garrard and persuade him to talk."

"Then find him, Harry, and give me a few minutes alone with him when you do."

"You know I can't promise you that."

I took a cigarette off him. My precious pipes were gone, as was everything else. Doctor Mortimer, my black angel, had forcibly suggested I use the opportunity to give up smoking, but I'd failed again. "How the hell does Elizabeth have the money to go to France?" I asked Harry.

"I asked her husband that. He says she sold your mother's house." Harry frowned pensively. "That Lord Tredgarth, he's a miserable sod, isn't he?"

I didn't want to talk about Peter Tredgarth. "Tell me how Jennifer is, Harry."

He didn't answer for a long time, then he shrugged. "Bad."

"How bad?"

"I don't know." He shook his head. "Don't ask me, Johnny, because I don't know."

I found out the next day when Helen, Lady Buzzacott, came to visit me. I was sitting in an armchair by the bed and tried to stand when she came into the room. She told me not to be so silly and to stay seated. She put a bunch of grapes on the bedside table. "Why do the English always take grapes to hospital patients? It's really a ridiculous habit, but quite unbreakable. I was getting quite frantic because I hadn't bought you any, so I made Higgs drive through the town centre and stop outside a fruiterer. So there they are, and you'll probably tell me you hate grapes."

"I like grapes."

She sat on the edge of my bed. "You're looking better than I expected, John."

I closed my eyes. "I'm sorry," I said.

"Whatever for?" She asked the question too lightly.

I opened my eyes. This was difficult. This was a meeting I had been dreading, but I had to say my piece and I had to let her know that I meant what I was saying. "I'm sorry for taking Jennifer out in the boat. I'm sorry that I didn't check the gas line before we sailed. I'm sorry I didn't pump the bilges. I'm just sorry about what happened." I had begun to cry, so closed my eyes again. "I'm just sorry, Lady Buzzacott. It was my fault."

"I'm sorry too," she said, "but I don't blame you."

I couldn't say anything. I was blubbing like a child. I felt entirely responsible for what had happened to Jennifer. I'd taken a lovely girl and I had turned her into burnt meat.

"It wasn't your fault," Helen Buzzacott said very clearly. "Of course you can look back and see a score of things you might have done to prevent it happening, but that isn't the point, John. The point is that you did nothing to cause the accident. All you did was go for a day's sailing, and I can't think of anything more innocent than that."

"Shit," I said, and reached for a paper handkerchief.

"And Jennifer's going to be all right," Helen said.

I looked at her through a blur of tears, but said nothing.

"Or rather we hope she'll be all right," Helen amended the statement. "The burns are really quite frightful, but I'm told they're very skilled at these things nowadays." She spoke in a very matter-of-fact voice, but it was clear that she had suffered agonies for her daughter in the last few days. "Of course it will take a lot of time, and a horrible amount of surgery, but she's got a very pompous doctor who says that in the end she'll be as good as new. Of course one can't tell if he's just telling professional lies, but he's certainly a very expensive liar if he is." Tears were glinting on her cheeks. She tried to ignore them. "They're starting the first skin grafts tomorrow, but I shouldn't be telling you all this. I should be asking about you."

215

I pushed the box of paper handkerchiefs towards her. She took one, then caught my eye. "Shit," she said through the tears. She blew her nose, sniffed, and wiped her eyes. "I don't know, John. I looked at her and I think it's impossible that she'll ever recover. She's no hair left, but her face isn't too bad. It seems she crouched down and put her face in her hands, you see. Her hands are quite shocking, and I gather they're the most difficult to repair properly, but at least she can wear gloves, can't she?" She was crying again. "Then her legs and her back are very bad. Her bottom is awful, but the pompous man says it really will be all right, and I can't do anything but believe him. Hans says she should go to Switzerland, but I can't see why."

"Nor can I," I said fervently.

"Hans says they've got very good cosmetic surgeons there, but I think he's just being xenophobic. He did go to see Jennifer, but he found it rather upsetting. She's been on one of those air beds like an upside-down hovercraft. It's too silly, really." She blew her nose again. "She's not entirely *compos mentis*, but she did ask after you."

"Tell her I'm fine, and very sorry."

"I won't tell her you're sorry. You can do that yourself. And are you fine? Doctor Mortimer says you're an appalling patient. He says you won't give up smoking."

"I can't."

"You should, but I didn't think you would so I went to Dunhills and bought you some pipes. I don't know anything about pipes so I've probably done the wrong thing, but here you are." She gave me a big bag full of the most expensive pipes. "I chose some tobacco at random," she went on, "the man in the shop said you'd probably be very particular, but I just bought what smelt the nicest."

I took the tobacco. "You're very kind."

"You did save my daughter's life."

"And risked it," I said bitterly.

"Don't start all that again. Leon spoke with the helicopter crew and heard all about what you did. You're a very brave man."

"No, I'm not."

"I won't argue." She took a deep breath. "I came here to cheer you up, and all I do is weep. Poor John."

"Poor Jennifer."

"She's a tough creature. She takes after her father, I think. She's certainly too good for that bloody Swiss man."

"I agree with that."

"But Leon doesn't. He's very keen on the marriage. He never had children of his own, you see, so he rather thinks of Jennifer as a daughter. I keep telling him that all Hans ever did was to inherit a vast business. Any fool can inherit money."

"While it takes a sensible man to make it?" I asked, and reflected that I had made none.

Helen smiled mischievously. "A sensible man marries it, John, but I think you know that already. Now I won't tire you any more. I know Leon wants to see you soon. He's made some arrangements for your younger sister and I'm sure they're perfect, but you need to take a look for yourself." She balled up the scraps of paper tissues, then collected her handbag. "If you've got nowhere to go when you leave hospital, then you'll be very welcome at Comerton."

"I shall be fine, don't worry. And give my love to Jennifer."

"I already have." She stood up. "Let us know where you are, and don't hesitate to ask if you need somewhere to stay."

I left the hospital a week later. I went with Charlie and, because I felt safe in his company, I told Harry to take away the police guard. Charlie drove me to his house where I limped upstairs and lay down on the bed. My legs still hurt like the devil, but, apart from the one ankle, the scarring would be minimal. I flinched when I thought of Jennifer, and the ordeal she faced, so that evening I phoned Comerton Castle and asked for Lady Buzzacott. Sir Leon came to the phone instead and told me his wife was with Jennifer in London. And where was I? he asked. I gave him Charlie's number, there was a pause as I imagined him writing it down in his small leather-bound book, then he said he wanted to see me.

"Of course."

"I want your approval for the arrangements I'm proposing for the Lady Georgina. Will tomorrow be convenient?"

I wasn't certain I really felt fit enough, but nor did I think I could bear a day of Yvonne's long face, so I said tomorrow would be fine.

"Shall I send a car?"

"I'm afraid you'll have to." I was not only homeless, but penniless as well.

The car came in the morning. The driver took me to the Mendip Hills where, in a sheltered south-facing village, we turned into a long driveway which led to a large white-painted Victorian house. Sir Leon himself met me at the front door and introduced me to a fresh-faced man of about my age. "This is Doctor Grove," Sir Leon said, "the medical doctor of Lovelace House."

Sir Leon was touchingly anxious that I should approve of Lovelace House. "I had my staff do a great deal of research," he told me, "and I assure you that Lovelace met our most stringent requirements."

It was, so far as I could tell, ideal. Lovelace House was privately run, outrageously expensive, and self-evidently caring. Many such places, catering to the lunatic members of rich or titled families, are scarcely more than prisons, but at Lovelace each patient had a private suite, personal nurses, and as much freedom as their condition would allow them to receive. Whenever we met a patient in one of the airy corridors I was gravely and courteously introduced. A Marchioness enquired whether I had planted the banana tree yet, I replied no, and she told me my employment was in severe jeopardy. I bowed, then limped on to see the suite that had been reserved for Georgina. Wide French windows opened on to a terraced lawn, beyond which empty paddocks stretched to the wooded hillside. The view was not unlike that from the windows of Stowey, and I said as much. "Except for the horses, of course."

"Is the Lady Georgina fond of horses?" Doctor Grove asked.

"She used to be. My sister wouldn't let her ride, but a

friend and I used to lead her round on a docile old mare. She was always very happy when we did that."

Doctor Grove made a note. "I think perhaps we should explore that avenue. Thank you, my lord."

"John," I said automatically, "call me John."

I dutifully inspected the kitchens, the drawing rooms, the communal dining room and the consultation rooms where, I was told, the best London psychiatrists came to weave their spells. If Georgina could be happy anywhere, I thought, then surely it was in this kindly place.

After the inspection, and after I had expressed my wholehearted approval to Doctor Grove, Sir Leon asked for a moment alone with me. He led me out to the southern gardens where a curious group of patients inspected his helicopter which stood with drooping rotors on the wide lawn. Sir Leon steered me away from the machine, preferring the solitude of a gravel walk. "My lawyers have already opened negotiations with the Lady Georgina's trustees," Sir Leon said in his precise and pedantic voice. "I think I can assure you that there will be no hindrance to her coming here."

"Sir Oliver Bulstrode might not agree," I suggested grimly.

"Sir Oliver, like all top London lawyers, will decide in favour of the richest party."

I smiled to hear this dry little man confirm my own opinion of lawyers. I was beginning to feel quite fond of Sir Leon, which I thought was only appropriate considering how I felt about his stepdaughter. We paced on in silence for a few yards, then he shot me a very shrewd and rather unfriendly glance. "And what of your own future, my lord?"

Something in his tone alerted me. Perhaps I'd been too quick in my warm feelings. I'd thought it slightly strange that a man of his importance should see fit to show me round a high-class lunatic asylum, but now I sensed he had quite another reason for meeting me this day. "I haven't thought much about my future," I said casually, "and please do stop calling me 'my lord'."

"If you wish." Sir Leon had noticed how walking pained me, even with the help of a walking stick that Charlie had

219

found in his junk room, so now he stopped by an ornamental urn. "Forgive me asking, but was your boat insured?"

"No."

He frowned severe disapproval. "That was imprudent, was it not?"

"Insurance companies won't touch deep-water yachts. If you stick to cruising the Channel or the North Sea they'll offer you a quotation, but if you sail beyond the sunset, and especially if you sail alone, they won't look at you."

"I see." He stared down at the urn's base, frowning slightly. "So, forgive me again, but what is the extent of your loss?"

"Ninety thousand pounds?" It was a guess.

He looked up sharply. "As much as that?"

"She was a good boat," I said defensively. "She wasn't a plastic tub tricked out with veneered chipboard. She was a deep-water steel boat with hardwood fittings. She was well equipped, Sir Leon. She was what a sailor would call a proper boat." That, I supposed, was *Sunflower*'s obituary, and a good one too. She had been a proper boat, and I mourned her, but I don't think the full extent of the loss had yet occurred to me. I might put a financial value on the hull and rigging and fittings, but there was an emotional loss that was incalculable. A boat becomes a companion, a person you talk to, a creature that shares the good times and helps you survive the bad. *Sunflower* had also been my home, and I'd lost her.

"I would take it as a great kindness if you would find yourself another yacht." Sir Leon said it so softly that at first I thought I had misheard. "At my expense, of course," he added just as softly.

"I'm sorry?" I said with incredulity. His manner in the last few minutes had been touched with a cold hostility, yet now he was offering me a boat? I warmed to him again.

"It's quite simple." He seemed irritated by my obtuseness. "I am offering to buy you another ocean-going yacht."

"But that's ridiculous!" I hoped to God he wouldn't agree with me. Pride would make me protest, but not for long. I needed another boat desperately.

He offered me the ghost of a smile. "Not so ridiculous, my lord, as giving away a Van Gogh." He was plainly determined to go on calling me 'my lord'. "Of course," he continued, "if you don't want another boat, then I shall quite understand."

"I do want one," I said fervently. His equation of my gift of the Van Gogh with his present of a replacement boat made the transaction seem less astonishing and more acceptable. I had also decided that this was a man who liked to hide his kindnesses behind a pernickety façade.

Sir Leon stirred the gravel with a well-polished shoe. "I assume, my lord, that if you have another boat you will resume your wandering way of life?"

"I really don't know."

He had asked the question casually, and my reply had been just as offhand. Yet my careless answer provoked a very cold look indeed. "Does your uncertainty have anything to do with my stepdaughter?" The abruptness of the question, and its acuity, astonished me. I said nothing, and Sir Leon frowned. "My wife seems to think that the two of you might be suited, but I must tell you that I often find Lady Buzzacott's ideas whimsical."

Now the thing lay in the open; the boat wasn't a recompense for the gift of a painting, but a bribe to take me away from Jennifer. This wasn't a man who hid his kindnesses, but simply purchased what he wanted. Now he wanted my absence. I felt foolish for liking him, for it was suddenly plain that he detested me. "You'd prefer Hans to become Jennifer's husband?" I asked forthrightly.

"Of course I would," Sir Leon said blandly, as though we merely discussed our preferences for cars or boats. "Hans is a most steady and sensible man. It might take flair to build a financial empire, my lord, but it takes steadiness to maintain it, and Hans has succeeded very well at preserving and expanding his inheritance. So, you see" – and here he offered me the smallest of smiles – "I would be very well advised to help you find a suitable boat and thus tempt you to very distant waters."

At least, I thought, the bastard was honest. He wanted me

gone because I wasn't suitable. I was a rogue and vagabond. I was a mongrel sniffing round his thoroughbred.

"And I assume," he pressed me, "that if you are equipped with a suitable boat, you will indeed resume your previous way of life?"

"Not necessarily, no." I would not give him that satisfaction, even if it meant that the bastard withdrew his offer.

"May I ask what other inducements might keep you ashore? Besides Jennifer?"

"I might go into business," I said airily, then, despite my dislike of him, found myself articulating an idea which must have been simmering in my mind ever since I had returned to England. "I sometimes think it's time to give myself a proper base. I live on a very narrow knife edge between poverty and bankruptcy, and that's fine for a time, Sir Leon, but after a while it becomes tedious. I need something to make some money, something that will let me sail away when I want to, but something that will go on earning money while I'm away."

"It sounds very desirable," he was amused, "but rather a pipe dream, surely?"

"There's a property on the Hamoaze," I heard myself saying. "It belongs to a plump old crook called George Cullen, and if I could raise the money I could make it into one of the finest yacht-repair yards on the south coast. It's no good looking to the banks, of course, so it is probably a pipe dream, but I've got a friend who might be interested. Except that he's rather over-extended financially."

"You have the necessary skills to run a yacht-repair business?"

"All of them," I said proudly.

Sir Leon looked up at me. "If you had not given me the Van Gogh, my lord, you would doubtless have received all the capital you might need. But, alas, your own generosity seems to have condemned you to the wanderer's life." He gave me one of his very small smiles, as if to show that he had proved that my only chance of financial survival lay in accepting his offer, and thus leaving his stepdaughter alone. He glanced towards his helicopter and I assumed he was about to walk away, but instead he offered me an irritated frown. "I must admit that I am sorely disappointed in Inspector Abbott. His ploy of making you a target seems to have misfired very badly."

"Indeed." I could only agree.

"It now seems clear to me that Inspector Abbott has very small chance of finding these wretched people, so it seems I have no choice but to deal with them myself."

"Pay the ransom, you mean?"

"What else?" Sir Leon did not sound dismayed at the prospect. "I have already inserted the coded advertisement in *The Times* indicating my willingness to do so. I now await their instructions which I will follow punctiliously. Inspector Abbott advises me that the criminals might renege on the arrangements, but that is a risk I must be willing to take. Following Inspector Abbott's advice has so far only succeeded in putting my stepdaughter into hospital, so you may imagine that I am not enamoured with his ideas."

He had spoken with unnatural venom when he mentioned Jennifer. I blushed. "I'm sorry —" I began.

"My wife has already assured you that there is no need for an apology," he interrupted me. "I don't entirely agree with her, but we shall nevertheless consider the matter closed. The important thing now is to provide Jennifer with the very finest medical attention. Hans has some very sound ideas, but I do assure you, my lord, that none of this any longer concerns you." He looked up at me and I saw how deceptive were those myopic pale eyes. This was a very formidable man indeed, and one who disliked me intensely. "I believe in making things very plain in negotiations," he went on, "so I am here to tell you, my lord, that your association with my affairs, and with my family, is concluded. Jennifer will be moved to a private clinic in Switzerland where, I assure you, her visitors will be strictly controlled. I hope you understand me?"

"Keep my dirty hands off her?" I said flippantly.

I annoyed him, as I'd meant to, but he controlled the annoyance. Instead he took a business card from his top pocket. "That is the name and address of my financial controller. He will henceforth make all the arrangements concerning the Lady Georgina, and he will also pay the bills contingent on your new boat. I shall instruct him that you are to be given credit of one hundred and twenty thousand pounds. Should you wish to have that money paid to you in cash, then feel free to ask, but I should advise you to arrange payment in some place where the taxman might not notice." He handed me the business card, then took a long brown envelope from his inside pocket. "At the same time, my lord, I do not wish you to think that I am ungrateful for your efforts on my behalf, so perhaps you will also accept this small token of my thanks?"

I took the envelope. I didn't open it. I was hoping he had been so generous that I would feel constrained to refuse the gift, and I knew I couldn't afford that quixotic gesture, not since my own money had sunk to the bottom of the English Channel.

Sir Leon held his hand out to me. "Should your sister challenge your right to give me the painting, then I trust you will make yourself available to my lawyers? My driver is at your disposal for the rest of the day." I shook his hand, then he turned away. I wondered how such a dry little sod had ever attracted a woman like Helen. Not a week before she had offered me a bedroom in Comerton Castle, now her husband was giving me the boot.

"Sir Leon!" I called out when he was a dozen paces away.

"My lord?" He turned back.

"I haven't given up my hopes of Jennifer."

He shrugged. "I cannot command your hopes, my lord. I can only make my own views very plain to you both. Good day to you." He nodded coldly, then walked between the lunatics to where his pilot waited.

I opened the envelope. It had a thousand pounds in it, and I knew I probably would have felt obliged to hand it back. I wondered if he would have taken it. He wanted rid of me, and would happily pay a hundred and twenty-one thousand pounds for the privilege. I watched his helicopter take off and reflected on the fact that, for the first time in my life, I'd actually been fired. And that I was in love. And that I had a new enemy.

*   *   *

I had Sir Leon's driver take me to Exeter where, in a shabby pub close to the police station, I found Harry Abbott. He watched me limp between the tables, then ordered me a pint of bitter. "I tried to telephone you today," he said grumpily, as though I'd inconvenienced him by being away from Charlie's house.

"I was with Sir Leon Buzzacott." I took a first sip of the pint, and sighed with relief at the taste. "I've just been fired, Harry. It was very nicely done, and he even gave me a golden handshake, but it was still a firing."

"Fired?" Harry asked in puzzlement.

"My services are no longer required for the retrieval of the painting." In truth I was still rather dazed by the experience. Sir Leon had spent weeks seeking my help and, at the first stiff hurdle, had brushed me away like dirt. "He gave me the heave-ho, Harry, then warned me off his stepdaughter."

"You can't blame him for that," Harry said reasonably. "Who wants a nice girl like Jennifer being mauled by some dirty-minded bastard like you?"

"I was beginning to like you in the last few days, Harry. I can see I was wrong."

He grinned. "So what's little Sir Leon going to do now? Pay the ransom?"

"Yes."

Harry grimaced. "He was bound to do it in the end. He wants to get his paws on that picture, doesn't he? God knows why. I know a fellow in Okehampton who could knock him up an identical fake in a couple of weeks. Who'd know the difference?"

"Beats me, Harry. So why were you trying to telephone me?"

"To tell you to bugger off, Johnny." He spilt a packet of pork scratchings on to the bar and generously pushed one small sliver towards me. "I've drawn a blank, you see. Garrard's gone, and so has his thick friend. I can't find hide nor hair of them. I'm sorry, Johnny, but they've disappeared."

"Just like Elizabeth," I said grimly.

"Who's probably still in France," he said, "and I can't issue a warrant for her because I've got damn-all evidence. I can't even get a search warrant for her bloody house. Of course there'd be plenty enough evidence for a warrant if she was just some housewife, but as she's the Lady la-di-da Tredgarth I can't get near her."

"I thought you said it wasn't worth searching her house?"

"I don't expect to find a Van Gogh hanging in the downstairs loo, Johnny, but I'm getting desperate now. I'll settle for her private telephone book, or her diary, or anything." He wiped beer off his lips. "You never know, we might find Garrard's phone number written down in her book, but without a search warrant?" He shrugged, then flinched as a piece of scratching irritated a loose filling in his teeth.

"What about George Cullen?" I asked.

"What about George?"

"He knows Garrard."

"Listen." Harry tapped my forearm to emphasise his next words. "George Cullen is terrified of me. He'd fly to the moon rather than hold out on his Uncle Harry. I told you, I talked to him, and George doesn't know a dicky-bird about it."

"So who does?"

"That's what I'm trying to tell you, Johnny. No one. Unless those bastards have another go at you, we're done. And frankly I can't get the manpower to look after you any more, so the best thing you can do is go. Get yourself another boat and piss off."

Sir Leon had given me the same advice, though couched in politer and more practical terms. I scooped a handful of Harry's pork scratchings off the bar. "Can you give me a lift to Charlie's house?"

"All the way to Salcombe?" He sounded outraged.

"I'll buy you a pint on the way."

"You'll buy my bloody supper, you miserable hound."

So he gave me a lift, and I wondered just what I would do now. All I knew was that I didn't want to run away to sea again, because this time I had someone worth staying for. Which meant that, despite the bastards who were trying to see me off, I would stay.

*   *   *

226

Charlie was not at home that night, which made staying at his house an awkward experience. Yvonne was watching television when I arrived, so I went straight to bed. At four in the morning I woke up in a muck sweat, panicking because I had been dreaming that I was drowning. I couldn't get back to sleep, so as soon as I heard Yvonne up and moving, I went down to the kitchen and asked if she'd mind driving me to where I could catch a bus. She grudgingly agreed. "He should be home tonight," she told me as she drew up at the bus stop in Kingsbridge, "but you can never tell."

"I might be back, I might not. I've got a lot to do today."

"You're just like him, aren't you?" She drove off before I could thank her for the lift.

I caught the first bus to Plymouth. The weather was warm and calm. The south coast seemed trapped in one of those rare bubbles of high pressure which would fill the beaches and becalm the yachts. Not that my concern this day was with the sea. Instead, and perhaps foolishly, I would retrace Harry Abbott's steps.

I reached George Cullen's yard a few minutes after nine. Rita was making the day's first cup of tea. "Look at you!" she said in shocked sympathy. I was still using Charlie's cane, for my left ankle was fearsomely painful. "You poor man. I saw it in the papers. How did it happen?"

"Like they said, an accident. Gas leak." The papers had speculated about sabotage, but someone, presumably Harry, had killed that notion. The story had run for a day or two, then disappeared.

"You should take more care of yourself, Johnny." Rita took down a third chipped mug into which she poured a dollop of milk. "He's in there," she said, "and I'll bring your tea in."

George half smiled when I limped into his office, then his face assumed a properly sympathetic look. "Johnny," he said as greeting.

I didn't say anything, but just limped over to the desk. He had a tabloid open at a page showing a naked girl with a pair of breasts like over-inflated lifebelts. Other similar pictures faded on his walls.

"Johnny," he said again. "You had a spot of bother, I hear."

I slammed the stick on to his newspaper so hard that everything on his desktop jumped a full inch into the air. "Listen, you fat swine, I'm going to ask you some questions, and your miserable life depends on the answers you give me. Do you understand that, George?"

He golloped at me like a dying fish, then nodded hastily. "Of course, my lord. Of course I do. Anything you want. Just ask."

I shoved the metal ferrule of the stick into his fat gut. "You know who Garrard and Peel are, don't you?"

"Course I do. Yes. I told you I did." He was staring bug-eyed at me.

"So did you tell them where they could find me on the night when they tipped *Sunflower* into the dock?"

"No, Johnny. No, my lord. Honest! I didn't!" I was driving the stick into his belly, making his waistcoat distend about the bulging and displaced flesh. "On my mother's grave, Johnny, I didn't!"

I believed him, because I was sure by now that it had been Elizabeth who had guessed that I'd make for George's junk yard. That wasn't the question I'd come to ask George, but it was a good way of softening him up for my real query. I released the stick and George scrabbled in a drawer for a bottle of pills and quickly swallowed two of them. "I didn't say a word, Johnny, I wouldn't. You're a friend!"

"So where do I find them, George?"

He gaped at me. "I don't know." He flinched from the raised stick. "I mean, they could be anywhere! It depends who they're working for!"

"So who do they work for, George?"

He shrugged. "Anyone, of course."

I slammed the stick down again, spilling pills across the naked girl's photograph. "Who, you bastard?"

"Anyone who's got property troubles, of course."

"Name them."

He was saved the need to answer by the arrival of Rita carrying a tray of tea and biscuits. She must have overheard

228

my angry voice and the noise of the walking stick hitting the desk, but she only beamed a happy smile and said it looked like being another fine day. I waited till she had left. "Who do they work for, George?"

He gave me the names of two men who owned discos and pubs in Union Street, but then warned me against those men. I had enough sense to heed his warning. Every maritime city has a Union Street, a place for homecoming sailors to get drunk and laid, and the men who ran such streets were harder than steel. If I limped down Union Street with naïve questions then I would be lucky to leave alive. Harry Abbott could have done it, but I guessed Harry had already exhausted the names George had just given me.

"I haven't seen hide or hair of them in weeks," George said miserably. "I'd tell you if I had, Johnny, you know that."

"They tried to kill me," I told George.

"Harry told me." George tutted disapprovingly to show that his sympathies were with me.

"Not just that night in your yard, but last week. They filled my boat with gas, and like a fool I didn't check."

"Jesus." He gaped at me.

"That's why I want to find them, George, so I can cut out their livers."

"I wish I could help you, Johnny. You know that! I'd help you if I could!"

I'd drawn a blank. I swore. I crossed to the window and stared down into the dock. It could make a very nice business, I thought, a most splendid business. I could store boats in the winter, have two covered repair shops, and a permanent berth for whatever boat I ended up buying for myself. Except to buy George's yard would take more money than I was ever likely to have.

"Have a drink," George said soothingly. "It might help."

"Not this early." I sounded annoyed.

"I'll do anything to help," George said pleadingly, "you know that, Johnny! I'll do anything."

"Then drive me to the train station."

He drove me to the station, and I'd learned nothing.

*   *   *

229

I caught a train to London. I had a piece of personal business to transact before I resumed Harry's trail. The business was with Jennifer. I wondered if I'd be refused entry into the hospital, but evidently Sir Leon's prohibition either carried no weight or had yet to be pronounced.

Jennifer had been taken off the air bed, and now lay belly down on a high, metal-sided bed. I couldn't see how badly she was burned for her body was covered with a kind of plastic tent. Tubes had been poked into her nostrils. Other tubes disappeared under the tent. Her scalp was smothered with a wig made of some pale liquid over which had been pasted small squares of cotton gauze. Lady Buzzacott had said her face had been spared, but it was patched with the same small squares of cotton. The truth was that she looked dreadful. "Hello, gorgeous," I said.

"Hello." Her voice was very hoarse.

"Where can I kiss you?"

"You can't. Mummy kisses one of the drip bottles."

I kissed one of the drip bottles.

"I hoped you'd come," she said.

"I came to apologise."

She made a tiny shaking motion with her head. "No need."

"I feel like a shit, and everyone's being so nice." I could feel the tears pricking my eyes. "It was my fault. I should have checked the gas. I'm sorry."

"But you're all right?" she asked. "You look tired."

"I've been sleeping badly. And I limp a bit, but it'll pass. They tell me you're going to be fine."

"They say that." Her voice was very laboured, the effect, I guessed, of all the fumes she'd inhaled. "But they would, wouldn't they?"

"No," I said. "They'll tell the truth."

Again there was the little shaking motion of the head. "It's going to take a long time. My front isn't too bad, but my back is pretty foul. My hands are the worst. My hair is beginning to grow again. The doctors say I was lucky, that the fire blew past me, but I don't feel very lucky." She gave another tiny shake of her head, almost in resignation. "It

230

doesn't hurt nearly as much as it did, but it's still pretty bloody."

"I'm sorry," I said helplessly.

"They tell me it will be all right," she went on, "but when it's all done I know I'll still look horrid."

"No," I said, though looking at her I could not see how they could possibly put her beauty back together. "I should have brought you some grapes."

"You'd have had to mash them up and put them in a tube."

"Actually," I said, "I brought you something else."

"What?"

"This." I could not give it to her, so I opened the box and showed it to her. It was an engagement ring. It wasn't a very fine ring, not a chunk of diamond like Hans had bought her, but it was the best I could find in the jewellery shop closest to the hospital.

"Oh, John," she said, and sounded rather sad.

"It isn't a very good ring," I confessed, "but your stepfather is trying to buy me off and gave me a chunk of cash, so I blew most of it on the ring. I didn't blow it all, because I need a bit for bus fares, but it isn't a bad little ring. It glints in all the right places. Look!"

She smiled at me under the cotton pads. "You're mad, John."

"So marry me." She didn't say anything, so I burbled on. "Your stepfather disapproves. He thinks you should marry Hans because Hans is sensible and steady, and the Buzzacott millions will need a bore to run them. So I have to tell you that you'll be upsetting your stepfather when you marry me, but I think he'll get over it. I suspect your mother will approve, and I imagine she can usually get her own way with him?"

Jennifer nodded very slightly.

"Is that acceptance?" I asked.

"No, it isn't. I can't marry you."

"Why not? I'm eligible."

"I shall be ugly."

"Good. I don't want other men lusting after you. I shall do all the lusting you'll ever need."

She watched me with her dark eyes; the only recognisable things left of her. "You're being foolish," she said.

"I love you."

"That's what I mean." She took a rasping breath. "Anyway, there's Hans."

"Bugger Hans," I said. "He'll just put you down as a bad business investment and find himself a little Swiss bird with big tits and skier's thighs."

She shook slightly, and I think she was laughing. "I can't marry you," she said after a while. "You're just making a gesture."

"Of course I'm making a gesture, you silly woman. I love you. For our honeymoon we'll sail somewhere delicious."

"John . . ." Again there was a sadness in her voice.

"Mind you," I said, "I can't marry you yet because I've got to find the two bastards who booby-trapped the boat, and when I do I'm going to kill them. I'll bet Hans wouldn't kill someone for you?"

"I don't think he would, no."

"That proves it, then. I'm a better man."

"You're a very impractical man. You're just making a gesture because you pity me."

"Balls. In fact I'm being very practical. I'm marrying an excessively rich girl, and it occurs to me that you'll probably inherit the Van Gogh if we ever get it back, so I'm not really giving it away at all." I smiled down at her. "Would you very much mind marrying me for your money?"

She paused. "You'll hate me, John. I'll be ugly."

"I will love you" – I looked into her dark eyes – "and within a year you and I will be married, and two years from now we'll have a child, and though I must confess I can't stand the sound of a baby screaming, I will love him because he's yours. So hold on, my love, because we have a lot of living to do."

"Hold on," she repeated my words. "You said that to me in the water."

"You remember?"

"You were swearing," she said, and I saw she was crying,

and I was crying too, so I bent down and kissed one of her closed eyelids. Her tears tasted salty.

"You told me I was a pathetic bloody girl," she said, "and that I was too feeble to live, and I thought I'll show you. I'll prove I'm not feeble."

"Good for you," I said. "So now prove that you can get better."

She smiled, making the little gauze squares twitch. "I will, I promise. But it's going to take a long time."

"I'll wait."

The edge of the plastic tent shifted and I saw she was putting out her hand. I thought she wanted me to hold it, then I saw that her hand was nothing but black claws inside a plastic bag. She was watching me, and I sensed this was a test. She wanted to see if I'd flinch from the sight. Instead I bent down and, very gently, kissed the plastic bag. "It's a bit difficult to put a ring on now," I said, "but I will one day."

"Maybe," she said. She sounded tired so I placed the ring on the bedside table where she could see it. "I'll come back," I said.

"Please." Her voice was a whisper.

I thought she was falling asleep so I tiptoed to the door. "John?" Her voice was very low.

I turned back. "My love?"

I waited a long time for her to speak, and when she did her voice was distorted because she was crying. "I love you," she said, "but it all seems so bloody hopeless."

"I love you too," I replied, "and everything will be fine." Then I left so she shouldn't see my own tears.

I limped through dusty London streets. I was oblivious to the traffic or to the noise, oblivious to all the horrors of the city, blind to everything except the realisation that at last I had found someone to love, to cherish, but, first and most important of all, someone to avenge.

I reached Perilly House in the early evening. I had gone by train, bus, and foot, and my left ankle felt as if a white hot steel band was being slowly contracted about the bones. I wasn't very sure how best to proceed for, despite my reputation, I was not a practised burglar, yet this evening I planned a burglary because, if Harry could not legally search Elizabeth's house, then I would do it illegally. It was clear that I had arrived at an inopportune time for Elizabeth's two stable girls were still busy giving riding lessons, and the presence of a car parked beside the Land Rover outside the front door suggested that Peter had a visitor, so I decided to wait till the house was either empty or Peter was alone and, presumably, drinking. I limped off the driveway to a copse of trees and settled down to wait.

By half past six the riding school pupils had been driven away by their mothers. Forty minutes later the stable girls locked up the yard and rode their bicycles down the tradesmen's driveway. Peter's visitor stayed another half-hour, then drove away. I stayed where I was, giving Peter time to start on his second or third bottle of the day, but it seemed my luck was in for, just a few moments after the visitor had left, Peter appeared at the front door, climbed into the Land Rover and accelerated down the drive.

I stood up, brushed the leaf mould off my jeans, and walked across the pastureland. I'd seen Peter lock the front door, so I went round the back where the house was an ugly clutter of gun room, dairy, sculleries, kitchen and coal stores. The doors were all locked, but I spotted a half-open window high up on the main scullery wall and, abandoning Charlie's walking stick, I used an empty rain-butt to climb up to the window. It was a tight squeeze, and my left ankle threatened to spill me off the wobbly barrel, but I finally wriggled through the window on to a cobwebby shelf that creaked dangerously under my weight. There was a clatter of food tins hitting the floor as I pulled my legs through the window. I was proving to be a lousy burglar, but it was evident the house was deserted for no one came to investigate the noise.

I put the tins back on the shelf, wiped the cobwebs off my face, and opened the door. I knew the house from the old days. I was in the kitchen passage that was thickly hung with reins, bridles and whips. The kitchen was to the right and the family rooms to the left. I went left, through the baize-covered door, and paused in the hallway.

234

I knew Elizabeth had a small office behind the dining room, so I decided to begin there. I first unlocked the front door so that if anyone came home I could claim to have found the door open. The décor of the house had not been changed in the years I'd been barred from Perilly House. Peter's gloomy pictures of long-forgotten battles and Elizabeth's prints of spindly-legged racehorses jostled for position on the fading wallpaper. A dish of dusty cobnuts sat on the vast sideboard in the dining room. I opened one with the silver-gilt nutcrackers and ate it as I pushed open the unlocked door of Elizabeth's office.

I knew within minutes that I would find nothing incriminating in the office. The only papers in the file drawers were records of her horses, receipts from the feed companies, vets' bills, and details of forthcoming Pony Club events. It was plain that the stable girls also used the office, for Elizabeth had left them a message pinned to the top of the rolltop desk: 'Mrs Peabody owes us £16 so her wretched child is NOT to be given any rides until the bill is paid in FULL.'

I scouted the living room, but found no place where any papers might be hidden. I went upstairs. It was obvious that Lord and Lady Tredgarth slept apart, for the large bedroom was filled with Peter's things and held nothing whatever of Elizabeth's. His clothes were strewn on the floor, suggesting that the cleaning woman never reached this dismal domain. A half-empty bottle of whisky stood on a side table with a copy of the *Farmer's Weekly*. There was a blurred photograph of his old yacht hanging on the wall. I remembered the boat well, a fine old Vertue 25 that had been his pride and joy, but marriage and financial worries had scuppered that dream. Next to it was a framed photograph of Elizabeth, taken some years earlier at an exotic tropical resort. She was in a bikini top and wrapround skirt, smiling at the camera, and the photograph reminded me of just how attractive my sister was. I wondered if Peter kept the two pictures on his wall as a reminder of old and happier days. The present days were typified by a girly magazine that lay under the unmade bed. The room's decrepitude reminded me of my brother's bedroom and also made me feel dirty. There was something very distasteful in my prying, but there was something equally distasteful in a bilge filled with lethal gas.

I closed Peter's door, then searched the four guest rooms and the two bathrooms, but they were all quite innocent. Which just left Elizabeth's room. I tried the door, but as I'd feared, it was locked.

I had a choice now. So far, if I'd been found, I could righteously claim to be Lady Tredgarth's brother who had come into an open house to wait for her, but if I broke down the door I would be committing an offence. I tested the lock by pushing on the door, but there was no play in it. It was an old-fashioned keyhole-type lock of the sort I had used to pick at Stowey, but I had no tools, nor did I know whether the skill was still with me.

I tried. I found some skewers in the kitchen, bent their tips, and tried to find the lock's levers. After fifteen minutes I had achieved nothing other than a frayed temper. It also occurred to me that Peter might have gone no further than the local pub and could be home at any moment, so I gave up being delicate and just put my shoulder to the door. It took a half-dozen huge heaves, and one painful kick with my right foot, but finally the lockplate splintered off the jamb and the door swung open.

There was a bed, a chest of drawers, a dressing table, a vast wardrobe that had once been in my father's room at Stowey and, to the left of her fireplace, a long table covered with papers. Above the table was a crucifix carved in ancient, hard wood, while beneath the table was a japanned tin trunk that was closed with a padlock.

I started with the papers on the table. There were letters from old schoolfriends, minutes of charity committee meetings, specimens of wallpaper, and overdue invoices from the builders who were renovating Primrose Cottage. I found the newspaper cuttings of the press conference I'd given with Jennifer, but that was the only matter relevant to my search and it neither confirmed Elizabeth's guilt nor added to what I already knew.

I pulled open the drawers and found nothing but a tangle of underwear and stockings. I opened the wardrobe. Nothing.

I looked under the high brass bed and found nothing but an old-fashioned chamber pot and a pair of furry slippers. I looked round the room for a hidden safe, but the lumpy plaster walls were covered with a fading wallpaper which clearly concealed nothing. I tested some of the floorboards, but they were nailed tight. There wasn't a diary or a phone book and I supposed she must have taken such personal things to France. All that was left was the japanned tin trunk.

I pulled the trunk from under the table and used the brass handle of the poker as a hammer to open its padlock. It yielded to the third smart tap. I eased the shank out of the hasp and pushed back the lid. It was getting darker outside, but I dared not switch on a light, so instead I took the bundles of papers to the window.

They were letters. Packets and packets of letters held together with elastic bands. There were scores of packets holding hundreds of letters and all of them, so far as I could see, were love letters. They were addressed to Elizabeth at the riding school, and I supposed that the school's mail came separately from that addressed to the main house. Some of the letters were ten years old, but others were very recent. I recognised none of the handwriting. Some of the packets had dried flowers trapped under their elastic bands, while others had photographs; small reminders of a stolen moment's happiness.

I don't know why I was so astonished. Elizabeth's marriage was dead, yet presumably she was trapped in it by her ancestral attachment to the faith. I looked at the crucifix hanging on her wall, then back to the bundled evidence of her carnal sins and I suddenly felt sorry for her, and even guilty at having discovered the letters. Elizabeth herself appeared in some of the photographs, smiling and happy, holding on to the arm of her lover. She seemed to like tall athletic men. They were photographed on ski slopes or mounted on powerful horses. Seeing their strong confident faces made me realise how horribly unhappy Elizabeth must be.

Even the window light had now faded to a velvety gloom, so I risked turning on the small bedside lamp to look at the

237

pictures. I was hoping to find a photograph of Garrard, but he was not there. There were only her hard-eyed, anonymous lovers. I dropped their letters back into the trunk and refastened the padlock.

I'd failed. There was nothing here for Harry Abbott, nothing at all. I sat on the bed, ran my fingers through my hair and stared up at the cold grate where spiders had made thick webs about the unburnt birch logs. Damn it, I thought. Damn it, damn it, damn it. Sir Leon would pay his ransom, he would get his picture, and I would never prove who had so nearly killed Jennifer and me.

A door creaked downstairs and, like a guilty thing, I jumped.

I should have run for it, but my ankle would not let me.

"Whoever you are," Peter's slurred voice shouted from the downstairs hallway, "stay there! I've got a gun, and I'm calling the police!"

"Don't worry about the police, Peter." I limped to the door, then out to the landing. "It's me, John."

He switched on the hall lights, then came a few suspicious feet up the stairs. He held a double-barrelled shotgun very menacingly. "It is you!" He sounded disappointed, as though he'd been looking forward to shooting an intruder. "You broke into her bedroom!"

"I'm sorry about that."

"I thought I'd found a burglar." He let the barrels drop. "I was driving back from the pub, you see, and saw a light in Liz's room. That's it, I thought, I'll have the bugger. Left the motor at the end of the driveway and walked the rest of the way."

"Very clever of you, Peter."

He gave me an unfriendly look. "So what the hell are you doing here?"

"I came to see you and Elizabeth," I said very nicely. "I thought it was time to make peace." I was winging it, hoping that he wouldn't use the shotgun. He was certainly well on his way to being drunk and I didn't trust him.

"Make peace?" I'd puzzled him.

"Silly family squabbles," I said vaguely.

238

I hobbled down the stairs. Peter let me pass, then followed me down to the hall. "So long as you're here," he said grudgingly, "you might as well have a drink." He led me into the drawing room and poured two very stiff whiskies. "She won't be back, not for a bit anyway."

"How do you know?"

"Because she phoned her bloody riding girls and told them. She wouldn't telephone me. Cheers." He drank that first glass of whisky as if he were a dying man coming out of the desert, then poured himself another, just as generous. "Funny thing, the telephone."

He was drunk, morose, and lonely. I wondered how he managed to drive, but supposed the pub was nearby, the lanes empty, and the police a long way off.

"It rings sometimes," he went on, "and I answer it, and there's no one there! No one! Does that strike you as odd, John? I mean, you're a man who's knocked about the world a bit, so doesn't that strike you as odd?"

"Very odd, Peter."

"I'll tell you something even odder! It never happens to Elizabeth." He was peering at me with the fervent intensity of a drunken man holding on to a scrap of good sense. "It never happens to her. Do you think the telephone knows when a woman's going to answer?"

"No, Peter, I don't think that."

"I don't know," he said. He had dropped the gun across an armchair. I wondered if it was loaded, and whether I should take it a safe distance away from him. He drank most of the second glass of whisky, then shuddered. "I can talk to you," he said suddenly.

"Good."

"You're one of us, you see. I mean they're a very nice set of fellows down the pub, all top drawer, but there's always a bit of you know what." I didn't, but he explained for me anyway. "They know I'm a lord, and it makes them, what do you call it? Shy?"

"Shy," I confirmed.

"You're not shy." He poured himself more whisky. "You're quite right. Silly family squabbles. They shouldn't be

239

allowed. It's her lovers, of course." He didn't sound drunk at all as he said the last words.

"Lovers?"

"Who telephone, you fool, and don't say a word when I answer. I'm not an idiot, John. People think I am, but I'm not."

"No, you're not."

"And she's a good-looking woman," he said sadly, "she's a damn good-looking woman. All your family's good-looking, blast you." He stared at me balefully. "What were you doing in her room?"

"Looking for a Van Gogh."

He stared at me for a few seconds, then guffawed. "That's rich, John! Very good!"

"Seriously, Peter."

He swallowed a gulp of whisky. "It's your own bloody fault, John. I can understand why you did it! Truly I can." He had become drunkenly earnest. "But what I don't understand is why you don't come clean! I'm sure Elizabeth doesn't want to see you in jail. Why don't you cough the damn thing up, and give Liz half the proceeds?"

"Because I don't have the painting, Peter."

He wagged a finger at me as though I was an irritating child. "Sold it, did you?"

"I never had it, Peter."

"That's where you're wrong, old boy. Liz nailed you on that one three years ago. Found one of your partners in crime, you see?"

He was being entirely serious, even though he was as drunk as a judge. I gave him a rueful smile, as though I was playing along with his ideas. "How did she find me out?"

"She hired some private detective. Some slimy type she met at Newbury. Don't know much about him, to be honest. Never met the fellow. Liz keeps herself to herself, you see." He was beginning to make less sense as the whisky fractured his memories.

"Why didn't she go to the police?"

"That's what I said! I was told it was none of my business.

240

Mind you, she went to that jumped-up little businessman, Buzzafuck or whatever he's called."

"Buzzacott?"

"He gave her money! I'm sure of it! Two of his henchmen came round with an attaché case. It's my belief" – here he slumped down on to the arm of a sofa and pointed an unsteady finger at me – "that Liz wanted to wait till your mother was dead. No need to share the loot, what?"

"So why hasn't she found the picture now?"

"Damned if I know. Perhaps you hid it too well?" He chuckled conspiratorially, and I smiled back. "So where is it, John?"

I spread innocent hands. "Beats me, Peter."

He drained the whisky. "You can tell me."

"Why did Buzzacott give her money?"

He walked unsteadily to the sideboard and poured himself another whisky. "To pay for the private detective chap, of course."

Garrard. Maybe I was jumping to a conclusion, but somehow I reckoned the private detective had to be Garrard, which meant that, quite unknowingly, Sir Leon had bankrolled the bastard who had half killed his stepdaughter.

But if Elizabeth had stolen the painting, why would she need a private detective? Or perhaps there never had been a private detective. Perhaps that was just Elizabeth's story, part of the necessary deception that I was guilty. And perhaps Buzzacott's payments were a sweetener to make sure that Elizabeth did eventually sell him the painting. Whatever, the little bastard had clearly been backing both horses, Elizabeth and me. Or perhaps Peter's drunken maunderings added up to sweet nothing.

"What I reckon" – Peter turned back to me – "is that you sold the painting to someone, Liz has found you out, and you're protecting whoever it is."

"It isn't like that, Peter."

"Then for God's sake tell me the truth!" He was angry suddenly. "No one tells me a bloody thing!"

"I'll tell you," I said, "if you tell me which of the caravans you planned to put Georgina in."

He stared at me with pretended outrage for a few seconds, then laughed. "You're a fly one, John, I'll give you that! Too fly for your own good, eh?"

I smiled, then glanced through the big window to where the bats flickered dark in the newly fallen night. "Was there a fellow named Garrard in your regiment, Peter?"

"Don't remember him. What sort of fellow was he?"

"Thin, dark. Joined the Paras."

He shook his head. "Never heard of him. Why?"

"Because he tried to kill me, that's why."

That answer was a mistake because Peter immediately thought I'd accused him of being an accomplice to attempted murder, and his face flushed with a sudden and dangerous anger. "Get the hell out of here!"

I held up a placatory hand. "Peter!" I said chidingly.

"I said get out!" He snatched up the gun. "I'll use it! I bloody well used it on some Mormons last year!"

I left him. He didn't follow me. I half expected him to fire a volley over my head, but he just stayed with his misery and the whisky decanter.

I limped to the village, but the last bus had already left. I knew I'd be lucky to reach the station in time for the last Exeter train, but I began to walk anyway. I'd left the walking stick in Peter's back yard, and my ankle was hurting. I tried to hitch a lift, but it was over an hour before anyone took pity on my hobbling. I was too late for the train so I asked the driver to drop me near the motorway. I stood on the access road for what seemed like hours and, though I left my thumb stuck out, no one stopped. I probably looked too scruffy. The headlights flicked past me and I tried to make sense of Peter's alcohol-sodden memories.

Elizabeth had probably been taking money from Buzzacott, and that money had been extracted on the promise that she had located one of my accomplices. That meant, I was certain, that Elizabeth had begun to cover her tracks very early in the game. She had spent at least three years spreading tales of my guilt so that, when she did produce the painting, no one would accuse her of stealing it. Yet, as I stood in the darkness beside the road, I realised just how little Peter had revealed. Perhaps, I hoped, one of the lovers whose letters lay hidden in the trunk was concealing the painting, and perhaps Harry could get a search warrant and go through the bundled letters, but it seemed like a very long shot. My day, I thought, had yielded nothing except an engagement ring.

I began to wonder if I should have to sleep rough, but finally a lorry driver took pity on me. He was carrying steel reinforcing rods to Plymouth, so took me all the way to Devon and dropped me off at the Kingsbridge turning.

It was two in the morning. I walked for another hour, but my ankle was making me sob with the pain. There was no traffic, thus no chance of a lift, so in the end I climbed a gate into a field, kicked a protesting sheep to its feet, then lay down on the warm dry patch of earth I'd uncovered. I slept badly for three hours, and woke shivering and wet to a limpid dawn. It occurred to me that I really was homeless; just another tramp on the southern summer roads. The first Earl of Stowey had ridden down these valleys with a retinue of steel-helmed men, and now the twenty-eighth Earl stumbled unshaven and filthy out of a sheep run.

I walked till I found a public telephone in a village. I phoned Charlie. I hesitated because it was early and I didn't want to wake Yvonne, but she had said Charlie would probably be at home so I took the risk.

Charlie answered. I had woken him up, but he didn't mind. Indeed, he seemed immensely relieved to hear my voice.

I shared his relief. "For Christ's sake come and get me, Charlie. I'm all in."

"Where the hell have you been?"

"Hitch-hiking. Sleeping rough."

"For Christ's sake, Johnny, they've been looking everywhere for you!"

"Who has? Harry Abbott?"

"Buzzacott. He started phoning yesterday afternoon. He's desperate for you!"

"Why!"

"He wouldn't tell me, mate, I'm not a bleeding earl. Christ Almighty, look at the time! Where the hell are you?"

I told him.

"Hang on there, Johnny, I'll be with you in half an hour."

So I hung on, and Charlie was as good as his word. I wondered how on earth I'd survive without a friend like him, then collapsed into his Japanese four-by-four and fell fast asleep.

Charlie woke Yvonne and demanded breakfast. She came downstairs in dressing gown and slippers, offered me one disgusted look, then banged the frying pan about the stove in noisy protest.

"I'm sorry to be a nuisance, Yvonne," I said humbly.

She didn't reply. She didn't need to. I was about as welcome as a skunk.

"He's only a bloody earl," Charlie said in an attempt to placate her with humour, "and he's been sleeping rough!"

"So have I." Yvonne slapped a packet of bacon on to the counter.

Charlie gave me a wry look, then took me out to his kennels where we fed his terriers. He kept some of his dogs for ratting, and others, trained to bite less hard, for rabbiting. "Don't get married," he told me as he tossed raw meat into the troughs. It was a comment that didn't require a response, so I made none. Charlie fondled one of his favourite dogs, then stared at the early morning mist shrouding the Salcombe lakes. "I don't know if it matters," he said casually, "but Buzzacott said you should telephone him. He doesn't care how early you call."

"Sod Buzzacott," I said.

Charlie laughed. "Fallen out, have you?"

"He doesn't want my help any more. He's paid me off. He told me to buy myself a boat, disappear, and never talk to his stepdaughter again."

"Buy yourself a boat?" Charlie was immediately interested.

I grinned. "You and I have got a hundred and twenty thousand quid to spend."

Charlie didn't believe me. "You're joking."

"I'm not. I promise you." Back indoors we found some children's crayons and drawing paper and I made Charlie a quick sketch of the hull that I was planning. "It'll have to be steel, of course. Long keeled." I drew in two masts. "I'm thinking of a ketch."

"Why?"

"More flexible sail arrangements."

"More to go wrong," he said dubiously.

"I'll double rig her." We spent a happy breakfast planning

245

the perfect ocean-going boat. Not that I intended going permanently to sea, not till I sailed with Jennifer, but planning the dream boat was a good way to start the day. Charlie and I had done almost everything to that boat except paint her name on the stern when the telephone rang.

It was Sir Leon Buzzacott, and he wanted me.

"Shall I tell the bugger you're here?" Charlie didn't bother to put a hand over the receiver as he asked me the question.

"I'll speak to him." I took the phone.

Sir Leon's message in *The Times* had been answered. The kidnappers – that's how he described them – had sent him their demands. The money was to be paid over by me. They would accept no one else; only the Earl of Stowey.

He finished speaking. I said nothing. It was so blindingly obvious why they wanted me to deliver the money; so they could kill me and thus bequeath the picture to Elizabeth. But Elizabeth, I thought, had been taking money from Sir Leon, money which had let her hire the thugs who would do her killing today. "How much did you pay my sister?" I asked Sir Leon.

There was a silence, then Sir Leon's cautious voice. "My lord?"

"How much did you pay my sister three years ago?"

"An honorarium," he said evasively, "merely an honorarium."

"You bastard. Don't you realise what she did with your damned honorarium? She hired Garrard. She hired the man who put Jennifer into hospital. You bankrolled this, Sir Leon. You gave her the money that let her wait till our mother died."

"At that time I had no reason to believe in your sister's guilt." His voice was very stiff.

And what did it matter anyway? Of course Sir Leon would back both of us, because all he had ever wanted was the painting. He did not care who had stolen it, only that it came to him.

I had said nothing for a few seconds. "My lord?" Sir Leon prompted me.

"How did these people communicate with you?" I asked.

246

He paused, evidently finding the question irrelevant. "By letter. It was delivered by messenger yesterday."

"Have you given it to the police?"

"I don't intend to involve the police."

"Damned if I'm going to be involved then. Those people have tried to kill me twice, and if you think I'll wander into their trap just to get you a pretty picture, you're wrong."

"I beg you —" Sir Leon began.

"Call Harry Abbott." I was tired, and I really didn't care any more. I hung up the phone before he could say another word.

"What was all that about?" Charlie asked.

I told him. It was all so clear to me. If Elizabeth's plans went well today she would receive a ransom of four million pounds. She would also receive the gift of my death, which would make her the beneficial owner of a Van Gogh. Sir Leon, if he wanted to hang that painting in his gallery, would be forced to negotiate a price with her, and I was damned sure the price would be greater than twenty million. Sir Leon would doubtless claim that I had given him the painting, but he had nothing on paper and Sir Oliver Bulstrode would chop him into shreds. In brief, Elizabeth was about to become a very rich woman. She could buy Stowey back and start an equestrian centre that would dazzle the world. She doubtless imagined Royalty coming to her stables and she foresaw winters in warm palaces and summers on the languorous beaches of the very rich.

And to make all that happen, to give my sister the fulfilment of all her dreams, I only had to deliver the ransom.

"Don't do it," Charlie said earnestly.

"You heard me," I said. "I told him to call Harry." Except, I thought, my one last chance of revenging Jennifer was to co-operate with Sir Leon.

But I was not the best instrument of justice. Harry Abbott was, and if Sir Leon wouldn't tell the police that the ransom was being paid, then I would. "Can I use the phone, Charlie?"

"Help yourself."

The phone rang a half-second before I picked it up. It was

Harry Abbott himself. "I was about to phone you," I said.

"Don't do a thing, Johnny." He sounded excited. "I'm coming to get you."

"What for?"

"Why do you bloody think? We're off and running, of course. Buzzacott just phoned me. I've got a police chopper . . ."

"Harry!" I almost shouted his name to calm him down. "For Christ's sake. They want to kill me!"

"Of course they want to kill you. Just stay there, Johnny, I'm coming to get you." He slammed the phone down.

"Bloody hell," I said to Charlie, "Harry's bought the idea. They want me to pay the ransom!" I felt a chill crawl up my back.

Charlie pointed at me. "Don't do it, Johnny. Don't do it! They'll push you up shit creek without a paddle!"

"I know." But I'd also made a promise to a girl I wanted to marry, so perhaps the creek had to be risked and a paddle improvised. For revenge.

Harry arrived in a police helicopter. The thing thwacked across Salcombe harbour, reared up to flatten Charlie's unmown grass, then settled down close to his kids' sandpit. Harry jumped out and ran crouching across to the house. He was full of his own importance; they'd given him a chopper all of his own, and he felt like a policeman in a TV programme. "Are you ready?" he shouted at me.

"No, I'm bloody well not ready. Come in."

He was clearly reluctant. Things were at last moving, and the villains were being forced to show their hand, and I was being obstreperous. But Harry needed me, so he had to come into Charlie's kitchen where the double glazing cut down the thumping noise of the helicopter's engine.

"So tell me what they want me to do," I said.

Harry glanced at Charlie, then realised that I would insist on Charlie listening anyway. "We don't know yet."

"Oh, terrific!" I said. "You mean we're skidding about the sky like a blue-arsed fly and we don't know why?"

"We have to go to Exeter. There's a plane waiting there to

take us to Guernsey. We meet Sir Leon at St Peter Port and wait at the outdoors café at the Victoria Marina. That's all we know."

"Don't go," Charlie said to me.

"Piss off, Charlie." Harry had known Charlie a long time.

"Who's we?" I asked.

"Just you, really," Harry admitted. "The bastards insist they'll only deal with you, but I've got a back-up team arranged." To listen to him you'd have thought the SAS were on alert, but I suspected the 'back-up team' was an overweight squad of Harry's usual dipsomaniacs.

"They've already tried to kill Johnny twice," Charlie protested.

"I know that," Harry said impatiently, "and of course it's a trap. A demented four year old would know it's a trap, but if you go slowly, Johnny, we'll be with you all the way. You don't have to go the whole way, not if you think it's dangerous. We'll be a half-step behind you, but if you lose us, then get the hell out of it. And if I think it's becoming too risky, I'll stop everything. The object of the exercise isn't to give them the money, but to spot them, and once we've done that you can leave the rest to me."

"Don't do it," Charlie said to me. "It's only a bloody picture of some rotten flowers."

The helicopter whined and pulsed beyond the window and Charlie's dogs, safely kennelled, whined back. Harry waited for my decision and, when none came, tried a last appeal. "They're showing themselves, Johnny. If we don't respond then they might not risk it again. We've got to go! For God's sake, don't you want to know who tried to kill you?"

"I know who it is," I said. "It's Garrard and Peel. And if you lot were any good, Harry, you'd have had both of them wired up to a generator and singing their hearts out by now."

"I'll never have a chance of doing that if we don't catch them."

"Don't do it," Charlie said to me.

Except I knew Harry was right. By collecting the ransom, our enemies had to show themselves, which meant we had a chance, a very narrow chance, of trapping them. And it was Garrard, I was certain, who had condemned Jennifer to months of pain, and I had promised her to pay back that pain. I sighed, then I shrugged. "OK, Harry."

Charlie's face stiffened into an expression that I knew only too well. It was Charlie's stubborn look, the face he wore when things were bad, and when the only solution lay in his own strength and abilities. He had worn that face in the Tasman Sea, and now he had it again. "If you're going," he said to me, "then I'm going too."

"Hang on . . ." Harry began to protest, then realised it was no use. "You'll be about as much use as an ashtray on a motorbike," he grumbled.

"Johnny needs someone to look after him, Harry, and that's me." Charlie grinned. His tiredness dropped away because there was a prospect of mischief and he was involved. The two of us were back in business together. He grabbed his coat, shouted to Yvonne that she shouldn't wait up for him, then followed us out.

The helicopter took us to Exeter airport where a small plane waited to fly us to the Channel Islands. Two plain-clothes policemen waited by the plane, but one of them had to stay on the ground because Charlie claimed his seat. Harry, unhappy at losing one of his men, could only agree for he knew how unstoppable a determined Charlie could be.

Both Harry and his man had guns. They showed the weapons to us as we climbed up from the Devon coast. The sight of the black-handled automatics made my blood run chill. It reminded me that this was a very deadly game, and not just another adventure with Charlie. Harry sensed my change of mood. "Remember, Johnny, you don't have to go through with it. Go as far as you can, but don't risk your life."

"I won't let him," Charlie said.

"The further you go" – Harry ignored Charlie – "the more chance you give us of spotting the bastards, but I don't want to be scraping you off the floor, Johnny, so don't push your luck."

"Do I get a gun?" I asked.

Harry shook his head. "Not from me, Johnny. These are police issue. It would be more than my job's worth to let you have one."

I shrugged off his refusal. He was probably right to turn me down. I'd never fired a handgun in anger, and would probably make a mess of it. I stared down at the sea. It looked so very calm, all its treachery smoothed out by our height. I took a cigarette from Charlie. I was nervous. I was being enticed into danger, like making a night approach to an unlit coast without any charts. I suddenly wished I had not accepted so easily, then thought of Jennifer's pain and knew I had no choice. "Why Guernsey?" I wondered aloud.

Harry could only guess at the answer. "Perhaps they think the island police are dozy? And think of all those tight little lanes. You could get lost there very easily."

"Is that what they want?"

"They want to know they're safe. The danger point of a ransom is the handover, because it's possible the police will be watching. So the usual trick is to send the bagman from public phone to public phone. The route will appear to be random, but they'll be watching somewhere and looking out for cars following you. If they see the same cars too often, then they'll pull out."

The pilot turned in his seat to interrupt Harry. "Fog," he said laconically, and I twisted round to see that a milk-white fog bank was stretching across the sea ahead. The Channel Islands were notorious for their fogs, and the recent still weather had made such fogs more likely.

"Bugger," Harry said viciously.

The pilot was radioing ahead. He listened on his earphones, then turned to give us the news. "Guernsey's still clear. That lot's over Alderney and the Casquets. But they think the larger islands may get socked in later."

"Just get us there," Harry said, "never mind what happens later."

Charlie was peering down at the thick white cloud blanketing the sea. "Remember that night off the Casquets?"

I nodded. We'd been seventeen or eighteen years old and

had made a night crossing to Cherbourg. Except that we misread the tides and had been swept much further west and south than we knew. The wind had piped up, the sea was kicking, and we were in our open dinghy. We'd turned east on to a broad reach, expecting to see the lights on the Cap de la Hague, and instead we'd found ourselves being driven on to the rocks about the Casquets' light. It was one of our earlier lessons in seamanship. A tough lesson, too, for we damn nearly died on the vicious Casquets' bank, but somehow we'd scraped round to the west and had run down to Guernsey where we'd gone ashore like half-drowned rats. It seemed funny now, but at the time we'd both been scared rigid.

The fog bank slipped away behind, revealing a calm sea, though more fog lingered towards the French coast. "The forecast says there could be wind later," the pilot volunteered.

"That'll get rid of the fog," the plain-clothes policeman said.

"Not round here," Charlie said with the satisfaction of superior knowledge. "I've seen these waters blowing a full gale and still shrouded in a fog as dense as a Frenchman's armpit. Bloody dangerous place, this."

"Cheer me up," Harry said gloomily, then settled back to watch as we descended towards Guernsey. The island came nearer, a labyrinth of narrow roads, ugly bungalows, greenhouses and cars, then our wheels thumped on the tarmac, the smoke spurted from the protesting rubber, and we had arrived.

The local police met us and drove us to St Peter Port where Sir Leon Buzzacott waited at an outdoors table by the marina café. An untouched cup of coffee stood beside a very slim leather attaché case on the table. Two very large and taciturn men flanked and dwarfed Sir Leon. If we were trying to be inconspicuous then we were failing hopelessly for, with Harry's local reinforcements, we now numbered ten men, and all but Charlie and myself were dressed in heavy suits, while around us the holiday-makers and yacht crews lounged in shorts or jeans.

"I've got other chaps located round the marina," the local policeman said. "They're disguised, of course."

Sir Leon greeted me. Considering that I was about to risk my life to get him a picture that I'd already given to him, I thought his greeting lacked warmth, but then my last conversation with him had not exactly been amicable. We didn't mention Elizabeth, nor his dealings with her. I introduced Charlie. Sir Leon gave him a cold look and a bare acknowledgement. Charlie nodded happily back. "Nice morning for a bit of nonsense," he said cheerfully.

Sir Leon ignored the remark. "The money," he said, and nudged the thin leather case towards me.

"Four million?" I said disbelievingly. I've seen enough movies and television films to know that four million pounds would need a fair-sized suitcase rather than this slender and expensive case. For a second I even wondered whether Sir Leon had simply written them a cheque.

Sir Leon unzipped the bag and showed me its contents. "These are unregistered Municipal Bearer Bonds, my lord, from the United States. Safer than cash, just as anonymous, and negotiable anywhere in the world."

"But traceable?" Harry Abbott asked hopefully.

"If you can persuade the authorities in various tropical tax havens to co-operate with you, yes," Sir Leon said disparagingly, "but I wouldn't pin your hopes on that co-operation. I assure you that our enemies won't be using the bond coupons to claim their interest payments, which would betray them, but will simply sell the bonds themselves. Nor will they have any shortage of buyers. Unregistered bonds are becoming a rare and precious commodity."

"So are Van Goghs," I said helpfully.

Sir Leon ignored that. Harry zipped up the case and pushed it towards me. "Let's hope we get the blackmailers before Johnny has to hand the stuff over." Harry was in a fine mood again, relishing the chase. He looked round the marina as if he expected to see men with stocking masks over their faces.

I looked at Sir Leon. "You know they want to kill me?"

He nodded primly. "It had occurred to me, my lord."

"And you set this up. You encouraged my sister. You gave her the money to hire the killers."

The pale eyes didn't blink. "I shall assume," he said, "that the day's events are making you overwrought. I trust that when the moment of crisis comes you will not allow that stress to affect your judgment."

"And fuck you, too." I doubted whether anyone had ever said that to Sir Leon Buzzacott, and he looked gratifyingly startled. I leaned over the table. "Tell me something. What will you put on my gravestone? That I wasn't good enough to marry your stepdaughter, but I graciously died for your gallery?" He said nothing. One of the security guards moved closer to me, perhaps fearing that I would hit Buzzacott, but I ignored the man. "Do you know why I'm doing this, Sir Leon? I'm doing it for Jennifer. I don't give a tinker's cuss for your painting. But I'm going to find the man who burned Jennifer and I'm going to pull his guts out and shove them down his throat. And when I've done that, Sir Leon, I'm going back to Jennifer and I'll marry her. And if you try to stop me, I'll have your guts for dinner too."

Charlie laughed. Sir Leon just blinked.

I turned away from him. My anger had cowed Sir Leon, but it had been nothing but bravado. My chances of taking revenge this day were very slight; the best I could hope for was that Harry would succeed in making an arrest. I looked around the marina complex, but I could see nothing untoward. The huge car park which served the town centre was full. If Harry was right then one of the parked cars would probably be the one in which I would spend the next few hours criss-crossing the island's leafy and twisting lanes. The thought made me nervous.

I distracted myself by watching the boats. The Victoria Marina at St Peter Port is a stone-walled harbour filled with pontoons. The entrance has a raised sill to trap the falling tide, but we had arrived just after high tide, so the sill was invisible and the passage was still clear for yachts to leave or enter. I guessed there were a hundred yachts berthed at the pontoons. Most were French. The Channel Islands are a wonderful playground for French yachtsmen. Two girls in tiny shorts climbed one of the pontoon bridges and walked towards us. All of us, except Sir Leon, watched them. They put on a wiggle for our benefit, called *bonjour*, and strolled past us into the café.

"If we weren't here on business," Charlie said wistfully, "I'd be doing a spot of parley-voo by now."

"Like old times, Charlie."

Then the girls had to be forgotten because an ancient taxi, blue smoke pouring from its exhaust, braked close to the café tables. The driver, clearly puzzled by his errand, leaned out of his window. "Is one of you the Earl of Stowey?"

For a second none of us moved, then, plunged into unreality, I nodded. "I am."

"I don't know what this is about, but this is for you." The driver held out a brown business envelope, then gasped as four policemen closed in on his car. "Hang on!" he protested, but the police had their first link with the villains, and the driver was hauled away to be questioned. "Not that we'll learn anything," Harry said complacently. "These people aren't fools, but we have to go through the motions."

Sir Leon wanted to open the envelope, as did Harry, but I was the addressee, and I insisted on the privilege. One of the local policemen had a pair of plastic tweezers which I used to extract the single page. After I had read the page it would be taken away to be finger-printed, though none of us really believed the senders would be so foolish as to leave such marks. I clumsily unfolded the sheet and read aloud its typed instructions. The instructions were very simple and very clear. I was to strip down to shorts, pick up the money, and go to the pontoon nearest to the marina café. I was to carry nothing except the money, and should I feel like disobeying that order, I should know that I would be watched all the way. At the end of the pontoon I would find a yacht named *Marianne*. I was to get on board alone. No one was even to walk down the pontoon with me. Once on board I should take *Marianne* to sea where further instructions would be provided. No boat should follow me, and if such a boat was detected the Van Gogh would be destroyed. But if the instructions were followed faithfully, and the money was safely handed over, a telephone call to Sir Leon's gallery would reveal where the Van Gogh could be found.

"Damn it," Harry said softly. Till that moment I don't think any of us had imagined that the money might be handed over at sea, yet the insistence on me, because I was a sailor, and the choice of Guernsey, a yachtsmen's paradise, should have told us that the handover might be made afloat.

"Right!" Harry was trying to regain the initiative. "*Marianne*! There must be a record of her. I want her photographed, and I want the registers searched. Who owns her? Who sold her? Where's she normally berthed? Talk to the Frogs, the name sounds French. Go on! Move!"

"I'm coming with you," Charlie said to me.

"No!" Sir Leon snapped.

Charlie leaned on the table so that his big shaggy head was very close to Sir Leon's face. "He's my friend, and if he's going to risk his life, I'm going with him."

Sir Leon was quite unmoved by Charlie's physical proximity. "We are going to follow the instructions very precisely. I assume" – he turned to one of the Guernsey policemen – "that this boat can be followed with an aircraft?"

"Indeed, sir."

"Then be so good as to arrange it, but tell your people not to make the coverage obvious." He looked down at the notes he had made. "Are there any naval forces on the island?"

One of the local policemen thought that a fisheries protection vessel was in the outer harbour. Sir Leon looked up at Harry. "I imagine a telephone call to London will secure their co-operation, but tell them they're to stay out of sight of the yacht. They will have to follow directions from the covering aircraft."

Harry pushed buttons on his mobile phone, while Sir Leon glanced down at his notebook. Sir Leon had taken over. He was showing an impressive, natural authority, but expressing it so calmly that he radiated an air of confidence. He ticked two items off his list of notes, then offered me a cold look. "I trust, my lord, that these precautions will convince you that I am not attempting your murder?" He didn't wait for an answer, but just glanced at his notes again. "I imagine their insistence on your wearing nothing but shorts is to make certain that you carry no weapons on board."

"Or a radio," I said.

"I hadn't thought of that." He sounded surprised that I might have had a notion denied to him, and even made a small note to that effect. "Quite. Well, my lord, are you willing to follow these instructions?"

I supposed I was. I certainly hadn't come this far to back down. The only immediate difficulty I could see was that we had four million pounds in funny money but not a single pair of shorts between us. "Give us your knife, Charlie."

He gave me his pen-knife and I slashed at the legs of my jeans. Once the denim was cut, they tore easily. I ripped the legs off, stepped out of them, then pulled off my shirt and deck shoes. I saw Sir Leon look at the fresh scars on my legs and give a small grimace of distaste.

"I'm coming with you," Charlie said stubbornly.

He couldn't win that argument. Both Sir Leon and Harry Abbott were against it. If we broke the rules, both men insisted, then all might be lost, so our best hope was to follow the instructions exactly. "But remember" – Harry was trying to demonstrate his own authority in the face of Sir Leon's formidable competition – "I'll pull you out if it looks dangerous, Johnny."

"I'm going to be OK, Harry." I sounded a great deal more confident than I felt. All around me men were talking urgently into police radios, but I was the one who had to walk almost naked down the pontoon, which, I was sure, would lead me to two killers.

"I want everyone watching!" Harry said loudly. "They've got a lookout here, and I want him spotted!" He turned back to me, shrugged, and pushed the attaché case towards me. "We might as well do it, Johnny."

I pushed my pipe, my pouch of tobacco and some matches into the seat of my sawn-off jeans, then picked up the attaché case of money. It was feather-light. "See you, Harry."

"One minute!" Sir Leon frowned. "These people were

particular that you carried nothing but the case. Leave your pipe here, my lord."

I smiled very sweetly at him. "I might risk my life for your painting, Sir Leon, but I'm damned if I'll do it without a smoke."

He looked into my eyes, saw he would lose, so gave a cold nod of reluctant acceptance. Harry and his men wished me luck, then Charlie walked with me across the car park to the head of the pontoon. "Are you sure about this, Johnny?"

"Of course I'm not sure, Charlie, but what the hell else can I do?"

"Bugger off. Leave them. It's only a rich man and his painting. It isn't life or death!"

"But it is, Charlie. They tried to kill me and they damn nearly killed Jennifer. So it's personal."

"You're a fool." His solemnity surprised me, but then he shrugged away his unnatural gloom and forced a grin on to his broad face. "We could make a run with the money?"

"Why not?" I'd been waiting for him to make that suggestion. We both laughed, but there was suddenly nothing else to say, so I punched him on the shoulder. "Have a pint waiting for me, OK?"

"How about one of those French birds as well?" He slapped my bare arm in friendly farewell, then stepped back.

I knew he was watching me all the way down the pontoon, and I was touched by the worry I'd detected in him, but it was too late to turn back now. So I went on. Alone.

PART FIVE

Part Five

I think I'd known from the very start that I wouldn't follow Harry's advice. Once I had committed myself I would not pull back at the end. I wanted to go through with it. Just like that day when I'd plunged into the heart of a gale-broken sea above the bar at Salcombe, I would risk death because, if I did not, I would prove myself a coward. I didn't want to do this thing, but once committed, I would go as far as I could. And not just to prove that I was brave, but because of a girl who lay in foul pain on a hospital bed. I wanted to find the bastards who had done that to her, and I wanted them to regret what they had done.

An ignoble motive, I know. These days a man is supposed to be above such stupidity. Today we're supposed to exemplify the virtues of sympathetic understanding. We're supposed to feel sorry for the criminal because it's clearly his education, or his broken home, or just society itself that has driven him to crime. In short we're supposed to eat lettuce instead of raw meat, but I'm a throwback. I'm the twenty-eighth Earl of nothing very much, but there's still enough pride left in the nothingness to want to see my enemies wishing they hadn't been born, and enough pride to want to tell my woman that I'd revenged her, and enough pride to go to the bitter end of a nasty little game in which I was naked and my enemies held all the cards.

I felt truly naked as I walked barefoot down that pontoon. I knew I was being watched, not just by the police, but by one of Elizabeth's people. That person could have been any one of the loungers on the big moored yachts, or any of the idling holiday-makers who leaned on the railings to stare down into the marina's pool. Who were these people whom Elizabeth had found? I'd met two of them, Garrard and Peel, but who else?

Then I saw *Marianne*.

She was a filthy little boat; a home-made French job glued

261

together out of marine ply then painted ox-blood red. You see hundreds of boats like her throughout Europe; I'd even seen a couple in the Pacific, sailed there by French youngsters who couldn't afford anything sturdier. This boat was about eighteen feet long with a small cabin, a single mast, and an outboard motor mounted in a stern well. There was a compass mounted on her cabin roof, a grubby mainsail was roughly lashed to her boom, and a single jib was hanked to her forestay. I looked at her masthead and saw neither a radar reflector nor a VHF aerial, but, oddly, a Decca aerial was bolted just behind the outboard well. Except for the Decca, the villains had clearly found the cheapest boat they could.

I stepped down into her cockpit. She might have been a scabby little boat, hardly fit to cross a park pond, but she was still a yacht and it felt good to be afloat again. I tried the companionway and found it unlocked. The interior of the boat had been stripped bare; there were no bunks, no galley, not even a cockpit sole. The bilges were exposed and, I noted, dry. They had been swept bare and clean; evidence that whoever had provided this boat had been intent on leaving no traces.

Yet, strangely out of place in such a bare boat, some high-tech aids had been put aboard. A Decca set was screwed to the after bulkhead and, to power it, a twelve-volt car battery rested on the ribs beside the centreboard case. There was also a hand-held VHF radio, and the existence of that radio cheered me up for it seemed to be the first mistake my enemies had made. Doubtless they had provided the radio so they could communicate with me, but it also meant that I could talk to Harry.

I crouched inside the empty cabin and stowed the thin case of bearer bonds beside the battery, then lowered the centreboard. I noticed the Decca was already switched on, registering the latitude and longitude of St Peter Port. I left it on and picked up the radio. It was the size of a telephone handset with a short rubber-sheathed aerial and powered by internal batteries. I carried the radio up to the cockpit and ostentatiously waved it so Harry could see it. I turned it on,

262

tuned it to Channel 16, and laid it on the back cockpit thwart.

I opened the petrol tank of the outboard and saw I had a full tank. It was only a three-and-a-half horsepower engine, so it wouldn't drive me more than six knots, but I guessed it would run for a long time on a full tank. The engine started on the first pull of the rope. I left it in neutral while I went forward to cast off the bow line. *Marianne* had not been given any springs, nor any fenders, just two warps. I cast off aft. We drifted backwards till I put the engine into gear.

Marianne and I puttered out of the marina into the harbour. I followed the buoys round the outer perimeter, past the fuel stage, and out to the lighthouse which marks the harbour entrance. A fast patrol boat of the Navy's Fisheries Protection Squadron was moored close to the harbour entrance. An officer stared down from the grey-painted bridge with more than usual interest as *Marianne* passed, and I wondered whether Harry had succeeded in co-opting the patrol boat. It had huge speed, a splendid radar and a wicked-looking gun. It would be nice to have such a vessel on my side, but its presence would clearly upset the careful ransom arrangements, so I didn't expect to see it again.

I gave the officer a wave, then *Marianne* was out of the harbour and in the Little Russel. We had no choice of which way to turn. The tide goes through the Little Russel with the force of a steam train so *Marianne* and I would go north, for we didn't have the power to fight our way southwards.

I turned north, slowed the engine, and went forward to hoist the jib. It was a rough piece of sailcloth, but I guessed it had some life left in it. I pulled up the main. Even *Sunflower*, after crossing the Pacific and rounding the Horn, had not had a sail so dirty, but this one drew well enough, so I went back aft and switched off the motor to save fuel. I tilted the motor up so the propeller wouldn't drag, then sat at the tiller. The wind was a light southwesterly. It wouldn't have moved *Sunflower* very far, but the small light *Marianne* seemed to like it. She didn't sail badly. She chopped a bit, and she could fall off the wind very fast, but her helm eased when I trimmed her sails. I opened the cockpit lockers to find them empty. There was nothing on board except the Decca, its battery, me, a compass, a radio and four million pounds. And, I remembered, the two mooring warps. I used one to lash the tiller and coiled the other on the cockpit sole. My enemies had taken care to leave me without weapons, but I had the two ropes and perhaps they would be useful.

A small plane was flying above St Peter Port towards Herm. It banked halfway across the Little Russel and swooped down low. The sun flashed harsh off its windscreen, then the plane was past me and climbing away. It seemed I had friends. I glanced at the radio, half expecting Harry to make contact, but it was silent. A fishing boat thumped past me. There were at least a dozen yachts in sight, one of the big hydroplane ferries was coming up from the south and a small coaster was moored off St Sampson's. The coaster had just fired her boilers and I saw how the smoke from her funnel drooped in a sagging plume to drift low above the water. I wondered who watched me. I wondered what they had in store for me.

Then the radio startled me. It hissed suddenly, then a woman's stilted voice sounded loud. "Fourteen," the voice said.

I didn't respond. I was tuned to Channel 16, the emergency and contact channel, so I could expect to hear a lot of stray traffic. The single word I'd heard seemed to have been broken from a longer transmission and I wondered if the radio was working properly. Then, perhaps a minute later, the voice sounded again. "Fourteen."

Still I didn't react. Another minute or so passed, then the single word was patiently transmitted again. "Fourteen." The intonation was bland, not at all insistent, almost robotic.

It occurred to me that I'd heard no other traffic, and clearly the word meant something, so I picked up the radio and pressed the transmit button. "Station calling *Marianne*, station calling *Marianne*, identify yourself and say again. Over." I suspected Harry would already have arranged for direction-finding gear to track down the source of any mysterious transmissions, and I wanted to make the caller speak longer to give that gear a chance. At least, I thought, the woman had used Channel 16, the emergency and calling channel, and the obvious wavelength for Harry to monitor, so all I had to do now was persuade the woman to speak for the two or three seconds it would need for the DF to spot her. "Station calling *Marianne*," I transmitted again, "identify yourself and say again your message, over."

The radio was silent, and I began to suspect that my enemies were not so foolish as I'd thought. I tested that assumption by pressing the transmitter button again. "St Peter Port Radio, St Peter Port Radio, this is yacht *Marianne*, yacht *Marianne*. Radio check please. Over."

There was no answer. I switched to Channel 62, St Peter Port Radio's working channel, and asked for a radio check again.

Nothing. Which meant the radio wasn't transmitting. It could receive, but it wouldn't transmit. The clever bastards, I thought, the clever, clever bastards, and I began to turn the dial back to Channel 16 when the radio, ignoring the fact that I was flicking the tuner across the channels, sounded once more. "Fourteen," said the toneless voice.

So not only had the enemy made sure that I couldn't transmit, but they had by-passed the tuner so that the radio was permanently fixed on an unidentifiable channel. It could have been any one of the fifty-five public channels, or one of a dozen private channels, or they might even have installed an American channel into the radio. Doubtless Harry was combing the VHF bands to find any transmissions that sounded suspect, but I was beginning to have a great respect for the people who had designed this voyage and I did not see Harry succeeding quickly.

"Fourteen," the woman's voice said a moment later.

So what the hell did that mean? It clearly wasn't a course. A buoy perhaps? I looked around to see if there were any numbered buoys in sight, and then the solution struck me. *Marianne* had been stripped to functional bareness, yet someone had thought fit to install a very expensive Decca set. That wasn't there for decoration. Whoever was transmitting to me was providing me with a waypoint. These people were not just clever; they were very clever. They had doubtless programmed the Decca with ninety-nine waypoints scattered randomly throughout the Channel Islands and they could use the waypoints to send me skittering about the sea while they made sure I was not being followed. Finally, when they were certain that I was alone, they would use the Decca to point me towards the rendezvous. Instead of public telephones, they were using invisible points in a vast sea.

I crouched in the low cabin. The instruction book for the Decca was jammed behind the power-lead, but it was the same brand of set as the one I'd possessed for such a brief time on *Sunflower*, and that made me remember Jennifer's childish delight in the machine. I said a brief prayer that I would one day share that childish delight with her again, then punched the buttons for waypoint fourteen. The machine blinked, then ordered a course of 089 to reach a point 12.4 nautical miles away.

I went back to the cockpit. If I went more than a half-mile on a heading of 089 I'd pile *Marianne* on to the rocks of Herm, but I turned nevertheless. I let out the main sheet and *Marianne* picked up her dowdy skirts and fairly flew in front of the wind. I watched the shore approach.

"Twenty-five," the girl's voice said a few minutes before I would have struck rock.

I rammed the tiller hard over to bring *Marianne* swivelling round into the wind. I left her hove-to while I went down to the cabin and asked the Decca where to go. Waypoint twenty-five was ten miles due north. I wondered whether to compensate for magnetic north. The Decca could have been giving me a true course, pointing me at the North Pole, or perhaps it had the magnetic correction programmed in so that its instructions would match my compass. I decided my enemies had thought of everything else, so why should I guess the compass correction for them. I'd trust their machinery and see where it took me.

I eased *Marianne*'s head round, and settled back on a reach. The tide was with me, sweeping us north towards the open sea. I looked up and saw my attendant plane circling high above. And where, I wondered, was the girl who was transmitting the waypoint numbers? She had to be within my view, for a VHF will only work within line of sight, but it was hopeless to look, for she could have been on any of the score of boats within view, or on Guernsey, or on the smaller islands of Herm and Sark that lie to the east of the Little Russel.

I sailed on. The radio had gone silent, and I guessed that I had passed the first test by following the first instructions. I cleared the Platte Fougere light at the northern end of the Little Russel and felt the western swell lifting *Marianne*'s frail hull. The wind was light but steady, the air was warm.

"Thirty-six," the voice said from the radio, and there was something oddly familiar and annoyingly complacent about that voice. I was feeling rebellious, so I didn't obey, and a moment later the number was repeated, and this time I noticed that the intonation of the repeated message was exactly the same as when the number had first been transmitted. I also recognised the voice; it belonged to a girl who read out the marine forecasts on Radio Four. My opponents had taped her, chopped the numbers from her forecasts, and were now playing me those numbers over the air.

Damn their cleverness.

Waypoint thirty-six took me on a course fine into the southwesterly wind. *Marianne* was too light to head up into wind so I started the engine and let the sails hang while the propeller plugged me into the sea's small chop. The new course would take me plumb through a score of boats which fished for bass off the island's northern reefs. Any one of those boats could contain my enemies, yet I was helpless to determine which, if any, it might be. I deliberately steered close to some of the boats, yet all looked innocent. A woman waved to me from one boat, while a man on another called out that it was a fine day.

"Twenty-five," the voice said.

I'd been given that waypoint before and knew it lay due north. I let *Marianne*'s head fall off the wind, hardened her into a reach, then stopped the engine. The waypoint number wasn't repeated which meant they must have been watching me, for they only repeated the transmissions when I failed to obey. And that annoyed me. They were training me, programming me. I had become a rat in a maze of invisible electronic commands that spanned the sea, and their game was to spin me round the maze till I was tired, hungry and ready to be slaughtered.

"Six," said the voice, which took me northwest.

"Eighteen." Which took me a few points north of east.

"Thirteen." An unlucky number, but which merely took me west.

"Eighty-four." A brief curtsey to the southeast, then they gave me twenty-five again to send me reaching northwards once more.

They played with me for two hours. At first I could divine no pattern in the commands. I sailed towards every point of the compass, but was never given enough time to reach the invisible waypoint which lay at the end of the required course. Always, and usually within a mile of the last command, I would be made to change my heading. Gradually, though, I was being pushed northwards, zigzagging away from the fading coast. I was being sent into the empty sea, far from any help. My mouth was dry, but at least the humid air was warm on my naked skin.

"Forty-four." The voice broke into my thoughts.

Well practised now, I pressed the Decca buttons. Waypoint forty-four lay fifty miles off on a bearing of 100, virtually due east, which would place it somewhere on the Cherbourg Peninsula, so clearly waypoint forty-four was not my rendezvous. Yet, for the first time since I had cleared the Little Russel, my controllers let me sail on undisturbed. By now they must have been confident that I presented no danger to their careful plans. They had made me sail in a random pattern, and they must have watched till they were satisfied that no ships followed my intricate manoeuvres, so now the real business of the day could begin. They must, I thought, be unaware of my shepherding plane which was far off to the west.

The radio stayed silent as *Marianne* held her eastwards course. To the north I could see the sails of two yachts running away from me towards the Alderney Race, while to the south the islands of Sark and Guernsey were a dark blur on a hazed horizon. Behind me, in the west, a plane droned aimlessly about the sky, while to the east was nothing but the game's ending, death or revenge, and the waiting night.

I lost track of time, except for a rough estimate gained from the sun's decline. I was thirsty as hell.

The tide was ebbing from the east. There had been a time when these waters had been a playground for Charlie and me, and, in those happy days, we'd learned the vagaries of the notorious Channel Island tides. *Marianne* and I were fighting a neap tide, the weakest, but it was still like trying to run up a down escalator. I knew I'd have a couple more hours of contrary tide before a period of slack, after which the set would come strong from the north.

So we just plugged on. *Marianne* wasn't quick, and she wasn't elegant, but I was beginning to feel fond of her. She was, after all, my boat, if only for this one day. We received no more waypoints, but just stemmed the tide, always heading east. By low water, when the tidal force subsided, we were quite alone. We had crossed the passage line for boats coming from Cherbourg down to Guernsey. We were also well out of sight of land, which suggested there would be no more radio transmissions for a while.

The wind was light, but the long western swell was carrying the spiteful remnants of an Atlantic storm. *Sunflower* would not have noticed such small waves, but *Marianne* was light and short enough to suffer. She slapped her way across the crests and plunged hard down into shallow troughs. I had lifted her centreboard to add a half-knot to her speed, but the higher centre of gravity also made her roll like a blue-water yacht running before the trade winds. After living on *Sunflower* so long it seemed odd to be in such a cramped and low cockpit. I'd never thought of *Sunflower* as a big yacht, but compared to *Marianne* she had been a leviathan.

My aerial escort stayed in fitful touch. The pilot did not stay close to me, but rather he would fly a course which crossed mine, disappear, then come back a few minutes later. It wasn't always the same plane. Sometimes it was a single-engined high-winged model, and at other times it was a sleek machine with an engine nacelle on each wing. I imagined Harry Abbott plotting my course in the police station, the map-pins creeping east towards the French coast.

East and south, for the Decca betrayed the first twitch of the new tidal surge. From now until deep into the night the water would pour round the Cap de la Hague to fill the Channel Islands basin. I put our head to the north to compensate for the new drift, and knew that from now on I would be steering more and more northerly just to keep my easterly progress constant. *Marianne*'s speed over the sea bed slowed and, because we were now showing some beam to the ragged swell, we began to roll uncomfortably, so I sacrificed yet more speed by dropping the centreboard. The board damped the rolling a little, but *Marianne* was still tender, and every few minutes we would slam down into a trough and the water would come shattering back over the deck. If the game didn't end soon, I thought, then I'd be in for a cold wet night.

But it wasn't my game, it belonged to someone else, and they'd planned it well. Sometime in the early evening I saw the southern and eastern horizons misting. At first I dared to hope it was just a distant bank of cloud, but I soon knew the truth; that it was a rolling wall of fog. My enemies must have chosen today because the weather forecast had warned against fog, and it was somewhere inside that thick, shrouding, sea-hugging cloud that the game's ending would be played out. I knew that once I was inside the fog my shepherding aircraft would be useless, and even the Navy's radar would be fortunate to find such a tiny boat as *Marianne*.

Harry must have shared my fear for, when I was scarcely a mile from the fog bank, the twin-engined plane dropped out of the sky like a dive-bomber, levelled above the sea, and raced towards me. The pilot flashed bright landing lights as if I hadn't already seen him. The machine roared so close above me that its backwash of air set *Marianne*'s sails aback. She was so light and tender that she threatened to heel right over, but somehow steadied herself.

He came back again, but this time he flew slower and well

270

to one side of me. I looked up to catch a glimpse of Harry's ugly face. He was gesturing westwards, indicating that he wanted me to turn back. The plane roared on, banked and turned again towards me. Once more Harry pointed westwards.

I looked back. A tiny grey smear broke the horizon, and I guessed that the Royal Navy patrol boat was, after all, keeping me company. The Navy must have been shadowing me from below the horizon, kept in touch by the aircraft reports, but now the fast patrol boat was accelerating towards me to make sure I obeyed Harry's orders. He feared for my safety in that clinging, hiding fog, or perhaps, and this struck me as a more likely explanation, Sir Leon feared I'd use the fog to sail away with four million pounds' worth of unregistered bonds.

I waved reassuringly to Harry, shoved *Marianne*'s tiller hard over, brought her into wind, and started the motor. The plane flew over me, waggled its wings in approval of my obedience in turning back, then climbed away. *Marianne*'s outboard pushed us west. The patrol boat seemed to come no closer. So far as Harry was concerned the day's excitement was over and all we could do was lick our wounds and hope our enemies tried again.

Only I wasn't buying that safe course. I had a girl to revenge and a curiosity to assuage, so I waited till I could hardly see the plane, then I turned *Marianne* again. I let the sails out to catch the faltering wind, and throttled the motor hard up. Now it was a race between me and the patrol boat, but I'd gained some precious time by my pretended compliance, and it would be some minutes before the Naval boat was certain that I really had turned back to the east. I pulled the centreboard up to add that precious ounce of speed and raced for the fog which was much closer now, scarcely a halfmile away, and rolling fast towards me from the south. It looked white and pretty, but I knew what waited inside.

I watched westwards rather than east. Sure enough, after a few minutes, I saw a bow wave flash beneath the distant grey dot. The race was on now: one crummy little French yacht made of plywood and glue against the turbines of a fast patrol boat. Except the crummy little yacht was already so close to the concealing fog.

The first tendrils of the fog wisped past me and I felt the instant drop in temperature. The fog had been formed by warm air over cold sea, but the vapour stole all the day's warmth and it felt as if I had gone from summer into instant winter. I kept the motor at full throttle, banging *Marianne*'s light bows across the choppy waves. I looked behind to see the fog wrapping about me. I kept on my course, but, after a minute or so, I looked up and saw my mast-tip hidden in the vapour so I turned hard to port so that I was travelling behind the moving face of the fog bank and into the tide. I was hoping that my pursuers would presume that I had turned downtide to add the water's speed to my own. The outboard motor suddenly seemed very loud. I counted the seconds. One minute passed, two, then I turned off the engine and let *Marianne* drift.

Silence.

Already my sails, boom and sheets were beaded with moisture. It was a grandfather of fogs, this one, a thick grey horror that restricted visibility to less than thirty yards. The temperature must have dropped twenty degrees.

Marianne rocked in the waves. There was wind in the fog, enough to slap her wet sails about, so I sheeted her in and turned her bows northeast. I let most of the power slip from the sails so I could listen for the Naval vessel.

Silence again.

Then, apparently not far off my starboard bow, I heard the sound of engines idling. I knew the apparent closeness of the sound could be deceiving for noise does strange things in fog. The Naval crew might be a hundred yards to port or a mile to starboard. The only certainty was that they would be concentrating on their radar, but, without a reflector in *Marianne*'s rigging, my sails and wooden mast offered them lousy echoes that would be further confused by the water-soaked air. The wavetops were probably reflecting as much as *Marianne*.

It was dark, cold and dank in the fog. If it had not been for the compass I would have been lost in minutes, but I crept onwards. I was steering northeast, but the tide's effect was to drive me almost due east. I imagined the patrol boat would be idling along on scarce-turning engines, making a box-search in the whiteness. My hope was that I'd decoyed them into going too far south, then I dared to hope that I might have escaped them altogether by crossing the invisible line which separated British waters from French. That was a happy thought which I celebrated by rubbing my hand along the underside of the boom, then licking the condensation off my palm. I was parched, and the fresh water tasted good.

The patrol boat's engines suddenly roared, faded, roared again. I swivelled in alarm, but saw nothing. A moment later I thought I saw the patrol boat's lean dark shape in the fog, but the dark shape was just a phantom of the fog which roiled and faded. A ship's bell clanged, apparently from the port side. I heard a distant voice shouting and I wondered whether the game was over. Had they found Garrard and Peel? Was that it? Had Harry been cleverer than my opponents and already made his arrests? Was Elizabeth sitting in a police interview room, protesting her nobility? That thought almost tempted me to shout a reply, but there was only one way to be sure of this game's ending, and that was to see it through, and so I kept silent and let my little boat sail on.

After a half hour or so I hauled in the sheets to power the sails, and *Marianne* began to slam her hollow bows. This was a fog such as Charlie had described that morning; a fog that did not blanket a wind, but was carried by it. The fogs on this coast could come with gale force; ship-killing winds cloaked in invisibility, and this light southwesterly air would never clear such a fog, but merely stir it. I judged from our wake that we were making close to three knots and knew *Marianne* would go no faster without her engine.

I heard nothing more of the patrol boat. Maybe an hour passed, maybe more. The only hint of time was the slow darkening of the fog as it went from pearl grey to dirty smoke. My evasive action had taken me too far to port and the Decca was telling me to steer a good fifteen points further south. I obeyed it. I still didn't use the engine in case the patrol boat had not given up the chase. Another hour passed and the dirty grey turned into wet gloom. I didn't see the patrol boat again, nor hear him. I was alone. There was neither radar nor human eye, neither boat nor aircraft to watch me, there was only the dumb instructions of the Decca beckoning me on into the darkening fog.

It was a lonely place. Lonely and cold and frightening. The sea had lost all colour to become a dull grey and black broken by a few feeble whitecaps. Sometimes I would sail into a less dense patch of fog, but always the wraith-like clouds wrapped around us again, and sometimes so thickly that I completely lost sight of *Marianne*'s stemhead. Once night came it was as if we sailed in a thick, black and silent limbo. There was no light in the compass, no moon could penetrate this fog, and the stars were hidden. It was dark, but not quite silent; waves slapped against my thin hull, the frayed ropes rasped in their blocks and the mast creaked, but there was none of the sea's great noise because the fog absorbed it all. It also dampened my matches, but I managed to light a pipeful of tobacco with the last useful match.

I was cold, and beginning to think I was wasting my time. Perhaps Harry had won, and all I now did was sail blindly towards the treacherous coast north of Carteret. Surely by now, I reasoned, my enemies would have revealed themselves, but nothing untoward disturbed the thick, blank night. The pipe went out. I tried to light another match, but they were useless. For supper I scraped moisture off the boom, trickled it into my cupped palm, and lapped like a dog. I slapped my arms about my chest to keep warm, but still shivered.

"Fifteen," said a voice on the radio, and the sudden word made me cry aloud in scared astonishment. It had been so long since I had been disturbed by a command, now suddenly the radio had sounded and I twitched on the thwart then stared about the darkness as though I might see my enemy. Nothing stirred in the night. It was so dark that I could not even see the fog. I was in an absolute darkness, the blackness of the blind. I could feel the fog cold on my skin, but I could see nothing.

"Fifteen," the voice repeated again, only this command wasn't being transmitted in the voice of the radio announcer, but was being given in a man's voice. "Fifteen," he said yet again, as though he did not trust the electronic wizardry at his command, and this time I recognised the clipped, savage tones of Garrard.

I slid into the cabin and pressed the Decca buttons. The small illuminated numerals instructed me to head southeast towards a waypoint that was just 6.4 miles distant. That was a mere two hours' sailing away, less with the tide's help, and I knew I was close to the game's end, for my enemies had been forced to abandon their first radio, the one with the tape-cassette attached, and must be using a radio aboard a boat. My killers waited there, but they lacked the assurance of my first controller for they had repeated the number three times in quick succession. They didn't trust their machinery, and that lack of trust told me they were nervous. Garrard was a confident and able man, but perhaps he was no seaman. And perhaps he was frightened by this utter blackness above a colourless sea, and that thought gave me a pulse of hope in the cold darkness.

Marianne's motion was easier after we turned. Now, instead of fighting the tide set, we travelled with the water. The wind had edged southerly, so we were tight hauled, but I could hear the purposeful slap and hiss of the water at her bows that betrayed a quicker progress.

"Fifteen," Garrard said again, and I felt a fierce joy. He was nervous. He'd been told what to do, and he didn't really trust the instructions. He was making sure by repetition, and that repetition betrayed his uncertainty to me. He was not at home out here, but I had spent years of my life on the ocean. It was not much of an advantage, but it was all I had; that and two lengths of rope.

He did not transmit again. I had stopped noticing the cold because I was thinking hard, and the results of that thinking were helping my confidence. Till now, they had played with me. They had sent me on a variety of courses, but they had never once let me sail so far that I reached the waypoint to which they pointed me. They had used the courses alone and, when I had travelled far enough along any particular line, they had turned me in a new direction.

Yet this new waypoint was close, suggesting that I was being guided to the rendezvous itself. My enemies, I reasoned, would not trust the conjunction of two courses to define the rendezvous, for the crossing of two invisible lines drawn across the sea left too much room for error. Either of the boats could overshoot the mark, and the Decca would never betray that overshoot. Instead the careful, clever mind that had prepared this meeting would have made the rendezvous the waypoint itself, for the silicon chips inside the Decca were designed to take a boat to that exact spot. If I passed the waypoint the Decca would tell me, if I went too far to port or starboard, the Decca would tell me. The Decca was taking the four million pounds home, but the Decca was also telling me exactly where my enemies waited. They had set an ambush, but, to make their ambush foolproof, they had been forced to tell the victim just where it was placed. I knew where they were, and they did not know where I was. All they knew was that by some electronic trickery I should sail docilely into their grip.

So God damn their cleverness, because it might yet let me win.

I watched the Decca like a hawk. The tide was quickening, helping me. My speed over the ground inched up. Three knots, 3.1, 3.5. The distance decreased fast. I went too far to port and the Decca told me, so I took *Marianne* back until the little box said I was aiming true. Three point eight knots, then four, and I began looking about *Marianne* for a weapon. There was the Decca aerial itself, a whiplike thing, but it would be clumsy to carry, and I needed to keep it in place till the very last minute. I wondered if I could wrench the drive shaft from the outboard motor, but knew it would be a hopeless task without tools. So I had nothing but the two mooring ropes.

I also had cleverness, except that I wasn't being very clever, for Garrard must have known roughly what time I should reach the waypoint. Thanks to the tide I had little choice but to approach from the north, but I could control the time of my arrival, yet now I was doing exactly what he had been told to expect. He was waiting for me, and I needed to stretch his nerves in this cold dark, so I turned *Marianne* on to a broad reach that took her eastwards. I knew Garrard wouldn't give up; I was carrying four million good reasons why he wouldn't give up.

And why, I wondered, was Garrard trusted to collect the money? I could understand why Elizabeth would not get close to the transaction herself, but why trust a crook? I would not have trusted Garrard with four pence, let alone four million pounds in bonds. The only answer I could devise was that Elizabeth was relying on Garrard's lack of seamanship. He had a boat and, doubtless, a Decca like mine. If he followed the Decca's pre-programmed instructions, he would be safe, but if he struck out on his own he would be lost in some of the world's most dangerous waters. To the east lay a lee shore, to the west and south were the rocks about the islands and the savage rocks of the Minkies, while to the north lay the fearsome tidal races of Alderney and the Swinge. That thought gave me a new confidence; I was the seaman out here, and that had to be worth something.

"Fifteen," Garrard said again, perhaps an hour after he transmitted the instruction. "Fifteen."

So he was nervous, and he was wondering why the lamb hadn't turned up at the slaughterhouse on time. He'd be fidgeting at the waypoint, staring northwest into the black void, and wondering if everything had gone wrong. I sailed on eastwards. Let the bastard worry.

The Decca continually updated the waypoint's bearing. I went on sailing east long after the waypoint was due south from me. I sailed on for what I guessed was a further hour, and only then did I let *Marianne* run south and west. The Decca gave me the course, pointing an invisible line to my revenge.

Now, once more, the distance to the waypoint began shortening. The tide was helping me, and *Marianne* was making 4.5 knots over the ground. Two miles to go, 1.9. The wind had picked up. It was blowing against the tide with just enough force to make small bad-tempered waves over which *Marianne*'s light hull bounced sickeningly.

At one mile to go I dropped the mainsail. I let it fall

roughly over the boom. My speed dropped. I let the jib sheet fly and waited till I was sure we were dead in the water, then, as the boat wallowed drunkenly, I crouched by the Decca. I wanted to know exactly how the tide was flowing. *Marianne* herself was not moving in relation to the water, but the sea itself was sweeping us south at half a knot. The drift was not exactly south. The Decca said our present course was 144, which was east of south. I needed to know that tidal direction if the half-plan in my head stood any chance of working. That half-plan also needed the luck of the devil.

I hauled in the jib so that we ghosted onwards. The Decca told me *Marianne* had one mile to sail, then her job was done. I stared into the black fog seeking a hint of shadow, a sharper edge of darkness amid the night, a light; anything that would betray my enemies.

I was looking, but I heard them first.

Classical music. Vivaldi, I thought.

I rammed the tiller hard to port so that *Marianne* came slowly round. I tied off the tiller. *Marianne* was sailing a point north of west now, and I crouched by the Decca again, waiting till the machine told me that the waypoint was bearing exactly 144 degrees from me. Once it did, I went topsides, unlashed the tiller, and let the jib fall on to the foredeck. I was a quarter-mile from my enemies, drifting towards their soft, betraying noise. *Marianne* rocked to the waves as the sweet sound came intermittently across the water. Now I was drifting to the ambush, carried there by the weakening tide. And still I stared southwards.

And saw the light, and knew where I was.

The light flashed fast, nothing but a pearled flicker in the fog. The flicker was so hazed by the vapour that the quick flashes were reduced to mere dissipated blinks, but I could see it was a white light flashing nine times in quick succession.

A cardinal buoy. A buoy marking a hazard, and there was only one such buoy I could think of in this part of the sea. If I was right, we were four or five miles off the French coast, hard by the shoaling rocks called Les Trois Grunes which were marked by a single cardinal buoy which lay to the west of the dangerous bank. I was relying on my memory of the old days when Charlie and I had made these waters our hunting territory.

That the buoy was the rendezvous made absolute sense. Garrard, I suspected, was no seaman. For him to jockey a boat against wind and tide to hold it motionless at an exact point in the sea would be an impossible job, even with the Decca's help. Instead he had been guided to this lonely buoy to which, doubtless, he had made his boat fast.

The light flickered again, and this time I saw the boat which was indeed moored illegally to the buoy. She was a low-sterned working boat with a wheelhouse behind a raised foredeck. She must have been close to thirty feet long; a substantial boat, well-engined, sturdy, and solid enough to give its unfamiliar crew a sense of safety. I blinked as another light showed, this one a searchlight that flickered out into the fog. So Garrard was risking his night vision as well as his hearing. Put not your trust in killers, I thought, unless they're good seamen. I wouldn't want to meet Garrard on land, but out here he was in my cold world, not his.

I closed *Marianne*'s companionway, leaving the money below. I took the coiled rope from the cockpit sole and wrapped it round my waist. We were drifting towards the workboat and even the night-blinded Garrard must see us soon, so it was time to go. I took a breath, then lowered myself over *Marianne*'s port side.

The water was very cold. It might have been late summer, but the Channel waters can still strike to the heart like an icepick. I shivered and shuddered, but I had to depend on unsettling my ambushers. I'd frayed their nerves by coming late, now I must fray them further by a vanishing act.

I breaststroked away from *Marianne*. The tide was carrying us both southwards, but perhaps a little to the east of the buoy. I couldn't see the light now, not from the water, but I breaststroked southwards and hoped to God that I hadn't misjudged the tides. I was trying to keep pace with the drifting *Marianne*, but staying far enough away from her so that I would not be seen when she was discovered. The rope about my waist was absorbing the water and threatening to drag me down.

A bank of fog closed round me, hiding even *Marianne* from me. I trod water. The rope was getting heavy and I felt a moment of panic that I had already been swept past the cardinal buoy, but then I saw the nine flashes hazing in the fog and heard the small waves slapping at the hull of the big waiting boat. The searchlight stabbed out again, its beam swallowed and scattered by the fog, but this time *Marianne*'s red hull reflected dimly and I heard a shout. The music was abruptly switched off. "Get up front!" The voice was Garrard's, clear as a bell. I could see two men on board the workboat; clearly the old firm of Garrard and Peel had come to finish their work.

I swam southwards. I could hear Garrard shouting. He had assumed I was on board Marianne and now ordered me to steer for his boat. I was shivering. A drift of fog hid their boat from me, then I heard its motor choke into life and I feared being left in the cold water and turned desperately towards the noise and the now blinding flash of the cardinal buoy.

Garrard must have cast off from the buoy and was now edging his big boat towards the wallowing *Marianne*. My estimate of the tidal drift had been good, but not so accurate that the small yacht would have drifted directly on to the buoy, and thus Garrard had been forced to go to her. He only needed to travel about fifteen yards. The two boats were east of me and I swam hard, going close by the tall yellow-and-black buoy that heaved up on the short choppy seas. Its intermittent light strobed on the workboat's stern that was now just a few yards ahead of me. I heard a splintering thump as Garrard misjudged his approach and laid his boat's bows into *Marianne*'s hull, then his engine subsided into a soft thumping growl. A man – from his size and weight I guessed him to be Peel – was on the workboat's foredeck with a boathook. Then, when he brought it to his shoulder, I saw it wasn't a boathook, but a shotgun or rifle.

I swam a little closer. My teeth were chattering.

"Can't see the bugger." That was Peel.

"He's inside." Garrard was sheltering from the night's cold in the workboat's brightly lit wheelhouse. I saw him light a cigarette, then I swam under the workboat's counter and lost sight of him. The cardinal buoy flashed behind and, in its quick light, I saw the workboat's name painted above my head: *Mist-Spinner* of Poole.

Christ, but it was cold. The cold was slowing me. My wounded ankles were numb. I'd planned to climb aboard their boat somehow when they were busy with *Marianne*, but I doubted I would have the strength to make that climb. It sounds easy, climbing aboard a boat, but in a choppy sea it can take an immense effort without a helping hand or a boarding ladder. The workboat's platform was long and low, an easy enough gunwale to climb, but not when you're cold and weak.

"Get on board!" Garrard shouted. I guessed Peel was somehow clinging to *Marianne*'s shrouds, holding her alongside *Mist-Spinner* and fearful of making the jump between the unevenly moving hulls. "Tie her up first, for Christ's sake!" Garrard's temper was clearly at snapping point, but he must have turned on the searchlight to help his companion for I saw its reflection hazed in the fog all around me. "Drop the bloody gun, you fool! Tie her up, then get on board!"

They couldn't see me. They were blinded by their searchlight, and too intent on trying to lash the two bumping boats together. "Now jump!" I heard Garrard shout from his warm wheelhouse.

I was under *Mist-Spinner*'s stern. She was bucking up and down and I feared that her transom might crush down on my head. A foot above her waterline was an empty outboard bracket which I tried to hold on to for support. I missed the first time and the hull grazed agonisingly down my left arm. I grabbed again, held it, and gasped for breath.

I had to work fast, but it was hard. *Mist-Spinner*'s pitching threatened to pull my left arm out of its socket, but I held on while, with my right hand, I untwisted the rope from my waist. It was a heavy piece of old-fashioned manila; really nothing but a discarded piece of junk, but perfect for my purposes. Except my fingers were now so numb that I did not know if I could do what I had planned. I fumbled the rope, almost dropped it once, but finally managed to drape the rope over the outboard bracket. I took a deep breath, kept hold of the rope's end with my left hand, then ducked under the heaving stern.

I struggled forward, found nothing, took a numbing blow from the dropping hull on my left shoulder, and had to come back up for air. I took another deep breath, ducked again, and kicked my way forward under *Mist-Spinner*'s stern. The metal rudder scraped against my bruised and bleeding shoulder. It was black here, black and freezing and airless and frightening. Tons of thumping boat were rising and falling above me. I felt forward with my right hand and found what I wanted. A three-bladed propeller mounted amidships. Which meant just a single engine driving just this single prop. The engine was still in neutral and its throbbing seemed to fill the claustrophobic darkness with menace.

I dragged the rope behind me. I was holding on to the propeller which was vibrating with the rhythm of the idling motor. If Garrard put the boat into gear now I'd lose my hand.

I forced the rope into the narrow space between the propeller and the rudder. I was desperate for air, but I needed to fasten the rope first. I looped it over the upright blade, hitched it round once more, then dragged myself back and bobbed up to the surface where I gulped air into my lungs.

"He's not here." That was Peel's voice. I was gasping for breath, sure I would be heard, but they were too intent on their own concerns.

"Of course he's there!" Garrard snarled.

"He's bloody not."

"Then look for the damned money!"

I ducked down again, went forward, and this time, because I knew where the propeller was, I had more time to work. I had time, but fear and cold were making me clumsy. I remembered some old rules for bad moments at sea; don't hurry and do one thing at a time. I might be freezing and terrified, but all I had to do was work the thick rope round and round *Mist-Spinner*'s propeller blades. Barnacles on her hull scraped my back bloody as I stuffed handfuls of the heavy manila into the blade gaps. I finished the job by putting two turns of the rope about the rudder's stock, then, my lungs bursting with pain, I pushed myself back and upwards. Christ, I thought as I broke water, I must give up smoking.

"The money's here, but he must have fallen off and drowned," Peel shouted from *Marianne*.

"I don't give a damn where he is," Garrard said. "Just get back here!"

I was gripping the outboard bracket at *Mist-Spinner*'s stern. My lungs hurt, my back was stinging, and I was cold, but I knew I must push myself away from the hull before Garrard put his engine into gear. I knew he would probably use reverse gear to back away from *Marianne* and, if I had done a proper job, *Mist-Spinner* wouldn't move, but I still didn't want to risk the rope shredding, the propeller biting, and me being driven under her hull.

"Put it down and shut up," Garrard shouted from above me, "and untie that boat! Hurry!"

I had already paddled three or four yards clear of *Mist-Spinner*'s stern. I heard Peel shout that the yacht was free and I saw Garrard glance behind, as if he was reversing a truck, then he pulled the gear lever back and I heard the motor roar.

Then stop dead.

It just stopped. The gearing had transferred the engine's power to the shaft, but the propeller was held fast by the rope I had jammed about the blades, and the sudden resistance stopped the motor with a brutal abruptness. There was a second's silence, then Garrard swore, put the gear lever into neutral, and turned the starting key. The engine backfired, then settled into life. A billow of black smoke drifted over me. Garrard pulled the lever back and again the motor was jarred dead.

"Fucking thing's broke!" Peel offered helpfully.

Garrard cursed the engine and started it again. He left it in neutral while it settled into a steady rhythm. I had swum back to the stern and was once again holding on to the outboard bracket. I could see *Marianne* drifting away as

Garrard raced the *Mist-Spinner*'s engine, achieving nothing except a cloud of burnt oil that added to the fog. Then, when the engine was racing, he shoved it into gear.

It stopped dead.

"Christ Al-bloody-mighty," Garrard swore viciously.

I was praying he would not try to jar the motor into gear again, for, each time he did so, he put a killing strain on the engine. If he persisted, time and again, in forcing its brute power against the jammed propeller then he could shear the crankshaft. Then all of us would be stranded on this foggy lee shore. I glanced behind to see we had drifted a good two hundred yards from the cardinal buoy. Its light was again hazed by fog. I knew we could not be far from the rocks of Les Trois Grunes. I also knew the tide set was swinging and weakening, and, though the tide should take us south of the hazard, the wind was a counterforce that might just be driving us on to the danger. A seaman would have realised the danger, but Garrard and Peel were no seamen.

I heard the engine cover being lifted.

"All right, Mr Garrard!" Peel shouted.

The engine started. In neutral, without the obstructed propeller, it ran sweetly.

"Sounds all right," Peel said hopefully.

Garrard rammed it into gear.

The engine stopped dead.

Garrard let loose a string of curses. They were amateurs, their engine was broken, and they didn't know what to do. A seaman would have realised there was an outboard bracket on *Mist-Spinner*'s stern for just such emergencies and swum to retrieve *Marianne* so that her engine could be utilised, but Garrard and Peel didn't think of that. They were already in the spiral of self-feeding panic that causes most disasters at sea: one apparently small thing goes wrong, then another, and slowly, inexorably, the tragedies mount up. On land neither man would have been so prey to fear, but out here the unfamiliar cold and dark and sea-danger had unbalanced their susceptibilities.

They were drifting in the night. They didn't know it, but they were drifting towards Les Trois Grunes. I'd only seen those rocks once in my life, and then from a safe distance, but I well remembered the broken and turbulent water surrounding them.

I clung on to *Mist-Spinner*, shivering and weakening, waiting to add to their panic.

"It's the shaft," Garrard's voice sounded very close above me, and I guessed he must have been leaning over the engine. "Go and take a look," he said at last.

"I don't know about engines."

"I'm not talking about the engine, you fool! The engine works, doesn't it? I'm talking about the bloody propeller." Garrard had at last worked out what might be wrong. "Lean over the back, and tell me what you can see."

"He might be there!" Peel, at least, had not forgotten the mystery of my absence.

Garrard swore. I pulled myself round *Mist-Spinner*'s counter so that I would be hidden when Peel leaned over the stern. I held on to a rubbing strake and prayed that the cold would not sap my last reserves of strength.

Then, despite the cold, I almost screamed in fear.

A gun fired. The flash of it was blinding and the sound of it deafening. Garrard had gone to the stern and blasted a shotgun into the water. If I had not moved round the counter, I would have taken that cartridge clean in the skull. Garrard fired again. "He's not there now, Peel." I heard the heavy gun drop on to the deck. "So bloody look while I try again."

I was shivering with fear and cold, but made myself edge to the very corner of the stern. Peel was very close to me, but he wouldn't have seen me if I'd been waving at him; his eyes were so light-blinded. "Give it a go!" he shouted.

Garrard started the engine, put it in gear, and it stopped. I shivered and said a small prayer of thanks that the crankshaft had not broken. "Well?" Garrard asked. I don't know what they expected to see; they were just groping in the frightening dark searching for any straw to clutch.

"I can't see nothing!" Peel shouted.

"Then lean over properly, you bastard!"

Peel leaned over. There was a single lifting derrick at *Mist-*

Spinner's stern, put there for hauling pots, and he held on to it as he craned far out over the transom. "Go on, then!"

Garrard started the engine again, Peel leaned out to look down into the blackness, and I pulled myself up on the outboard bracket. As I pulled, *Mist-Spinner*'s hull dropped on a wave so that I shot up from the black sea, shedding water, like a drowned man coming to life. Peel could not even call out before my cold hands had gripped the collar of his coat. I fell back, pulling. He was a huge man, far heavier than I, but terror and shock were on my side. He was already leaning outwards, and now I dragged him down. He lost his grip on the derrick, opened his mouth to shout, then hit the water. The motor roared, surrounding us with noise and smoke, then abruptly died as Garrard pushed it into gear. I let go of Peel and twisted desperately away so that he could not grab hold of me.

Garrard, looking from the lit wheelhouse into the foggy darkness, did not know what had happened. He shouted for Peel, who was splashing and spluttering two yards from *Mist-Spinner*'s stern. "Help!" Peel finally shouted, then spluttered as he went under again. I was working my way forward along the hull. I was cold and weak, but desperation was giving me a last surge of warming adrenalin.

"You fucking idiot!" Garrard twisted off the helmsman's chair and ran aft.

"It was him!" Peel shouted; then, more urgently and pathetically, "I can't swim!"

Garrard seized a lifebelt and hurled it towards his partner. I grabbed the gunwale, said a prayer, and pulled.

I had worked my way forward so that I was close to the open after-end of the wheelhouse. The freeboard was low here to give men room to work crab pots or long-lines. I grabbed and heaved, trusting that Garrard would still be confused by the panic.

He saw me as I rolled my right leg up to the gunwale. For a second he didn't quite believe what he saw, then he ran towards me to kick me off the gunwale. He would have finished me there and then, but Les Trois Grunes saved me. We had been taken to where the sea bed rose to undercut the waves. The swell was breaking and lurching and *Mist-Spinner* suddenly heaved up to one such broken sea. Garrard staggered desperately away and almost went overboard, only steadying himself at the last moment with a despairing lunge for the derrick. The delay let me roll over the gunwale on to the deck. I needed a weapon, any weapon, and I saw an old rope fender by my hand so I picked it up and threw it blindly towards him.

Garrard ducked out of its way. The searchlight mounted on the wheelhouse roof was still pointing forward and I could see, in the pearly fog, where *Marianne* was rolling in water broken white about the shoals. I hadn't been looking for that danger, but for another weapon. The only thing I could find was an empty plastic fish-box, the kind that are packed with ice and newly caught fish. I snatched it up, turned back, and saw that Garrard had drawn his long-bladed knife. He ignored the discarded shotgun; clearly it was empty and he had no cartridges in the pockets of his tweed jacket.

"Very clever, my lord." He smiled at me. His confidence, so abraded by the night and the sea, was returning, for now he was in a situation he could master: one man against one man, with death as the finale.

"Very clever," he said again, then he let go of the derrick and came towards me. I raised the heavy fish-box as a shield. *Mist-Spinner* heaved up, then thumped down. Garrard lost his balance, and I charged him. I was still cold and weak, but I was used to a pitching deck and he was not. I whirled the heavy box like a club, hoping to slam him overboard, but he dropped to one knee, under my wild swing, and lunged the knife like a poniard. I stepped back just in time, tried to crush him with the box, but a heave of the sea threw him back from my blow. I could hear Peel splashing at the stern. He had the lifebelt now, and it could only be a matter of time before he was back on board. All around us the sea was fretting white, while beneath us the sea bed was rising to shatter the waves into churning chaos.

"Now!" Garrard shouted, at the same time glancing over my shoulder towards the companionway that led to the forward cuddy. I fell for the trick, because I had still not convinced myself that Elizabeth would trust Garrard, and that she might therefore have been sheltering in the tiny cabin. I glanced back for a half-second, realised I'd been fooled, but by the time I looked back Garrard was already moving. He threw himself forward, knife reaching. I swung the fish-box, but he was past my defence and I felt a dull punch on my right side. The boat rocked to port, Garrard staggered, and I hit him hard in the face with the plastic box. The blow jarred him sideways so that he fell on to the open engine hatch. I was hurt. Blood was streaming down my wet shorts and dripping on to the deck. Garrard had fallen heavily across the engine. It was the moment for me to finish him off, but I was too weakened by the cold. All I could do was clumsily swing the plastic box at him. The blow achieved nothing. Garrard rolled off the engine towards the stern and picked himself up. *Mist-Spinner* was broaching to the waves, jerking and rolling.

Garrard braced himself against the stern gunwale, waiting for a wave to pass. When it did, and *Mist-Spinner* was momentarily stable, he came forward with short dancing steps, like a boxer approaching cautiously for a final attack. I was only just realising how much the cold sea had weakened me. I was shivering, bleeding, gasping for breath, and I think Garrard knew I was finished. He smiled. "Had enough?"

"Fuck off." It was a feeble defiance.

He was still braced against the stern, one hand on the derrick, the other holding the knife. He gave the sea rapid glances, waiting for a calm trough of the waves to give himself a moment's peace during which he could kill me. Peel was clinging to the stern, unable to haul his huge weight over the transom.

"You didn't kill me before," I tried to goad Garrard, "and you won't now."

He laughed. "We weren't meant to kill you the first time, just scare the shit out of you." He edged forward, but a surge of sea water made him stagger back to the derrick's security.

I wondered if he'd been telling the truth, and that the

attempt on my life in Cullen's yard had been nothing but a scare tactic. "So why kill me now?"

"Why ever not?" He was amusing himself.

"Whatever Elizabeth's paying you," I said, "I'll double." I was not planning to make any deals, just to kill him, but I wanted to distract him for a few seconds.

Instead I had amused him. "Your sister's paying me nothing. We're partners!" He was mocking my ignorance, but behind the mockery I detected an odd tenderness.

"You're lovers!" I said in astonishment, and understood at last why she trusted him with the money.

"And partners. It was I, after all, who discovered the picture, and it was I who graciously allowed your sister to invest in that discovery." He glanced astern and I saw a smooth trough approaching behind a steep crest, and I knew that when that smooth water settled the pitching hull he would come for me.

"What do you mean," I asked, "discovered it? Elizabeth and you stole it!"

He laughed. "Proclaim your innocence to the end, my lord, and much good may it do you." He looked behind again, judging the wave's approach, and, while he was looking away from me, I charged. He must have sensed the attack for he looked back quickly, saw me stagger as the wave heaved *Mist-Spinner* high, then, as her bows dropped, he let go of the derrick and came at me.

He lunged with the knife. I swung the fish-box, but his lunge had been a feint. He danced away, but I had released the box so that it hit him a glancing blow on the hip. *Mist-Spinner* tilted backwards on the wave's crest and the violent motion together with my small blow gave me just enough time to twist away and scramble on to the narrow walkway beside the wheelhouse. Garrard followed me, but he wasn't so nimble about a boat, and his desperate slash at my right thigh missed.

I was defeated and fleeing. I wanted to reach the foredeck from where I would dive overboard and swim after the drifting *Marianne* which I'd last seen off *Mist-Spinner*'s bows. I was too cold and weak to defeat Garrard, but I could leave him here, stranded and helpless, while I sailed away to fetch reinforcements. It wasn't brave, but it was sensible.

Garrard clambered desperately after me. I limped forward. The searchlight was still switched on, aimed blindly forward to where the waves shattered about Les Trois Grunes. *Marianne* was thirty yards off the port bow and rolling violently in the shoal water. It would be a tough swim, perhaps a killing swim, but better to die in the sea's cold cleanness than from Garrard's knife. I took a breath, then, in the fogged beam of the searchlight, I saw the second shotgun. It was Peel's shotgun; the weapon he must have discarded on the foredeck when he had first boarded *Marianne*. The gun now lay in *Mist-Spinner*'s bow scuppers, trapped there by the pulpit bars.

I threw myself at the weapon. A lurch of the sea made me trip on the forehatch rim; I fell, but the boat's motion slid me on my blood-slicked belly to where the gun waited. A steel cleat ripped at my thigh. Garrard saw the weapon and jumped desperately from the small platform beside the wheelhouse. His knife was raised. *Mist-Spinner* corkscrewed in a sudden upsurge of the sea, then thumped down into a trough. My cold hands could not grip the weapon and, when the boat lurched to starboard, I almost let the gun fall into the water. I half slid off the deck after it, only saving myself by grabbing the pulpit rail with my left hand. White water seethed and broke under me. Garrard shouted as the deck heaved back up and I imagined his voice was shouting in triumph and I almost screamed because my imagination felt his blade's deep slash. The gun was precarious in my nerveless right hand. The knife still didn't strike. The shout had been Garrard's protest as a roll of the deck jarred him back against the wheelhouse.

I twisted on to my back. Life was counted in fractions of seconds now. If Garrard could reach me, then I would be dead, but if the boat's violence in the shoals made him clumsy and gave me time, then I would live. I turned to face him and could see nothing except the blinding white brilliance of the searchlight beam. I was still half overboard, clinging to the pulpit with my left hand. I tried to sit up, but an upward surge of the bows drove me down. I could not see Garrard. I was blinded by light, paralysed by weakness, and terrified. *Mist-Spinner* hammered off the wave crest and a spout of breaking water exploded up beside me.

I was tempted to let myself fall and to strike out for the drifting *Marianne*. I did not even know if this gun was loaded, let alone cocked, but then a slice of silver light dazzled from the great white blinding flood of the searchlight. It was the knife blade, raised to strike, and beside it was a ghost of a face, mouth open, teeth showing, shouting, then the light was blotted out by Garrard's body as he hurled himself towards me.

My thumb groped for the gun's hammers. No time. I was screaming defiance and fear. I barely had time to pull the triggers. My right hand was round the narrow part of the stock, the gun's butt was against my ribs, and the barrels were pointing somewhere at the shadow above me.

I pulled both triggers. I was still screaming, now in anticipation of the knife's strike.

The gun had been cocked. The butt drove into my ribs like a kicking horse. Noise filled the chaotic air.

Garrard's head simply disappeared. Blood fountained in a halo about the searchlight beam. I watched, appalled, the first strong colour of this black night. His knife clattered down to the deck and lodged against my right ankle while his body twitched back as if plucked by strings. It slammed against the sloping wheelhouse windows, then slid down on to the foredeck.

I closed my eyes. I was still half overboard. My ribs hurt. I was cold and shaking. I pulled with my left hand and, slowly, very slowly, I inched myself aboard. White water broke at *Mist-Spinner*'s stem and drenched the foredeck and, when I opened my eyes, I saw Garrard's diluted blood flooding the shallow scuppers. I rolled on to my side, safe now inside the pulpit rails and slowly, very slowly, knelt upright. I still clutched the gun.

Garrard's expensive tweed jacket was soaked in blood. The cloth of the jacket had snagged on a cleat and the motion of the boat was twitching him from side to side in a sick parody of life, but he was dead. I'd blown away his knowing, confident face. All that was left of his head was a butcher's mess of blood, brains and bone.

I just stared at him as if I expected the headless corpse somehow to stand and come back to the attack. I was shaking. I'd never killed a man before. I'd promised Jennifer to kill this one, but making the promise was one thing, fulfilling it was quite another. Blood gurgled in the scuppers and drained overboard.

"Help!" Peel shouted from the stern.

Very slowly, very stiffly, I picked myself up. I felt weak and sick and cold. *Mist-Spinner* heaved and fell. I took a huge breath, realised I wasn't going to vomit, so picked a careful path through the offal on the deck. I edged past the wheelhouse to see Peel clinging to the stern. He'd used the lifebelt's rope to reach the transom but he was too cold to pull himself aboard. I swivelled the searchlight to dazzle him.

His eyes became huge as I walked down the aft deck. I put the double barrels close to his left eye. "What was the signal you were supposed to send when you'd got the money?"

"Don't shoot! For Christ's sake, don't shoot!" His teeth were chattering.

"What was the signal you were supposed to send when you'd got the money?" My voice was toneless. There had to be such a signal, I knew.

"Fingers," he said.

I stared at him. Such a banal word. "Fingers?" I said incredulously.

"Honest! Don't shoot, please!"

"And where were you taking the money?"

"I don't know."

I jerked the barrels to cut one of his eyebrows. "Where, Peel, where?"

"It's on the little box. I can't work it. I don't know, mate." He was sobbing with terror and cold now. "I don't know. Mr Garrard worked the box, not me."

The Decca, of course. I pulled the gun's triggers, and the hammers fell on to the dead chambers. "Get in the boat if you can," I said, "and if you can't, drown."

The boat slammed down into white water. So far as I could remember the rocks at Les Trois Grunes only dried out at the lowest tides, yet that was small consolation. A dip in the long swell could easily drop us on to one of the rock pinnacles and rip the bottom out of *Mist-Spinner*, so my first task was to clear *Mist-Spinner* away from the hazard, and only then look for the clever mind that had spun me through this electronic maze. The night wasn't over yet, and maybe the killing wasn't done, but at least I had evened the game.

If Garrard had known boats, he would still have been alive and I would have been dead, for *Mist-Spinner* had a prop plate. Most working boats have such a plate, put there against the eventuality of drifting across their towed lines. Because no fisherman wants to go overboard to clear a fouled prop, just aft of the stern-box they put a bolted plate which, lifted, gives access to the propeller.

I found some tools in the wheelhouse. It needed all my strength on the big wrench to shift the bolts. One of the old rusted bolts sheared, but the others came free and I swung the plate aside to reveal the small black well of cold water. I could have fetched Garrard's knife from the foredeck, but I didn't fancy the sight of his corpse, so instead I rummaged through the wheelhouse cave-lockers and found an old gutting knife. I reached down into the cold water and cut the rope free from the propeller blades. It took less than five minutes.

Peel whimpered at the stern, alternately calling for help and cursing. Once or twice he tried to climb aboard, but the cold had sapped his huge strength. I ignored him as I bolted the prop plate home and laid the deck planks back into place. Then I picked up Garrard's discarded shotgun and tossed it overboard.

"Help. Please!" Peel whimpered.

I unshackled the pulley from the lifting derrick. "Hold on to that," I told him.

He grasped the pulley's hook with his right hand. I took the tackle's strain, inching him up the transom. *Mist-Spinner* was thumping and lurching in the broken water. I couldn't see any of the hidden rocks, but I knew where they were because their presence was betrayed by a swirling turmoil of water not far from the port bow. The water seemed to be sucked down towards the rock pinnacles, then to shatter upwards in a white misting spray. "Come on, you bastard!" I shouted at Peel, urging him to use some of his great strength to help himself. He must have sensed the danger, for he gave a great heave just as a surge of the swell tipped up the stern so that he fell, gasping and exhausted, into the boat.

I could hear the suck and rebound of the water about the

rocks. We were close to the rock pinnacles, too close, and the suction of the white water was drawing us closer. I staggered forward, started the engine, and pushed the gear lever forward. For a second the engine faltered and I thought for a terrible second that I hadn't cleared the propeller blades properly and that we would be drawn crashingly down into the rocks. I rammed the throttle forward, prayed, and somehow the engine recovered. The rocks were perilously close now, just off the port beam. We tipped towards them and I thought we were doomed to slide sideways down the smooth face of the indrawn water to hammer our gunwales on the black rock. I gave *Mist-Spinner* full rudder and raced the engine. A wave shattered to port, spewing water high over *Mist-Spinner*'s aerials. The propeller seemed to be spinning uselessly in the broken water, I felt a sideways lurch, then the blades bit the sea and the boat began to fight her way free. A rebound of water shoved us on our way. I spun the wheel amidships to lessen the resistance to the propeller's thrust and, inch by inch, then foot by foot, *Mist-Spinner* gained speed. I turned her to starboard again, and this time there was no resistance and she went sweetly away towards safety. I said a prayer of thanks, pulled back the throttle, then turned to watch the broken sea recede.

Peel had not moved. Perhaps he had been too scared to move, or perhaps he had been too weakened by his long immersion. He just watched me. Beyond him was the rock-shattered swell, and beyond that, somehow safe in the turmoil, was *Marianne*. She had drifted north of the rising pinnacle. She was pitching and rolling, and I supposed she would drift onwards to be tumbled ashore on a French beach. Then the fog and the night hid her from me and I turned *Mist-Spinner* westwards.

I'd found four spare shotgun cartridges when I'd searched for the knife to free *Mist-Spinner*'s propellers. Now I took them from the cave-locker and let Peel watch me as I loaded the shotgun. He didn't move, not even when I put the gun down while I checked the fuel. She had two extra tanks in side-lockers, plenty enough for whatever else this night might bring.

Peel watched me go back to the wheelhouse. "Where's Mr Garrard?" he asked nervously.

"On the foredeck. He hasn't got a head any more. If you move, you won't have one either." I lifted the shotgun on to my lap as I accelerated *Mist-Spinner* into the shredding fog. I saw the flash of the cardinal buoy, went past it, and only then did I let *Mist-Spinner* drift.

Because it was time to find my way out of the electronic maze. The Decca had two waypoints only. We were already at the first so the mystery's end must lie at the second. I summoned that second waypoint to the screen. It lay at fifty degrees, twelve minutes and forty seconds of arc north, by zero three degrees, forty-six minutes and sixty seconds of arc west. It was 87.2 miles away at a course of 311. So very precise, I thought, so very well planned.

"How were you supposed to kill me, Peel?" I didn't turn round to ask the question. That wasn't insouciance or bravery because I could see his reflection in the windscreen and he wasn't moving.

He did not answer.

"How were you supposed to kill me, Peel?" I asked again.

He still did not answer so I whipped round on the helmsman's chair and fired the right barrel two feet above his head. The pellets probably grazed his bald head, for he whimpered.

"How were you supposed to kill me, Peel?"

"We was just supposed to drown you," he almost whispered in reply, "then sink the little boat. To make it look like you'd drowned and the money had sunk."

"To make it look as if I'd stolen the money? As well as the painting?"

"Yes, guv."

"Thank you, Peel," I said very politely, then turned away from him. I found some old stained charts in a drawer, but I didn't really need them. I knew where fifty twelve zero three forty-six was. I could probably have got there blindfold, but I spread a passage chart out all the same, then reloaded the gun's right barrel. "Did you turn the gas on in my boat, Peel?" I asked it very casually.

"No, guv, honest."

"Did Mr Garrard?"

"No." In the glass I could see he was shivering. A big shivering musclebound man. "Honest," he added pathetically. He was trying to help me now.

I turned again and fired. The gun hammered at the night and Peel cowered and shivered.

I lowered the gun so that it was pointing into his face. "Did you or Mr Garrard turn the gas on in my boat, Peel?"

"No, guv, we didn't. As God is my witness, we didn't. I don't know nothing about any gas! We've been in France, Mr Garrard and me, we ain't been anywhere near your boat! Not since that night he tipped it over, and he wasn't even supposed to do that! We weren't even supposed to kill you that time, guv. We was only scaring you!" He was staring at me with doggish devotion now; I was his master and he would please me. "We was just supposed to scare you! And that first time, Mr Garrard was only going to talk to you, but he found the girl on your boat and he thought you was double-crossing us!" He was staring into the twin black holes of the gun barrels. "Honest, guv." He paused, evidently remembering who I was. "Honest, my lord."

I turned away from him. I reloaded the gun with the last cartridge, then laid the weapon down. The VHF was screwed to the wheelhouse roof and tuned to Channel 37; the private marina channel. That was the channel on which my instructions had been relayed, and presumably the channel on which my enemies were even now listening. They had to be close, within thirty or forty miles, which meant France or the islands. I thought France the likeliest answer. Perhaps it was Elizabeth keeping a radio watch, wondering what was happening out in the fog-shrouded waters, and it was time to put my sister out of her apprehensive misery. I unhooked the microphone, held it a little too far from my mouth, and said the single word. "Fingers." I paused, then repeated the word before hanging up the microphone. There was no acknowledgement, but I'd expected none. This night's trickery had been designed to keep the radio traffic to a minimum to avoid detection. It had all been so very clever.

And nothing, I thought, was cleverer than the way Elizabeth had used the Decca navigation system, for only a Decca set could have sent two landlubbers safely across the Channel. I doubted whether Garrard could have navigated his way through the shoals, tides and rocks of the Channel Islands, but any fool could read the little arrows on the Decca which told him to go left or right, forwards or backwards. Cleverest of all, I thought, was the selection of Les Trois Grunes; the only cardinal buoy in the islands which offered a straight course back to the second waypoint; a course that went arrow straight between the rocks of the Casquets and the northern reefs of Guernsey. No need to dog-leg, no need to read a chart, all that was required was to follow the little arrows. They had been clever, so very clever. Had Peter, in one of his soberer moments, told Elizabeth about the Decca? Or about the gas bottle she would find on any deep-sea yacht?

I turned. "Right, Peel!" I said enthusiastically. "On your feet and into the cuddy."

"The what?"

"The cabin. There." I pointed under the foredeck where a tiny space afforded two bunks and a galley. "Dry yourself off and make us some tea or coffee. No sugar for me, just milk. And hurry!"

He hurried. He saw his partner's blood smeared across the windscreen as he passed me, but he didn't react. I must have looked fearsome, half-naked and bloody, so he just ducked down and scuttled gratefully into the cuddy. "Throw me up a towel!" I shouted after him. "And any spare clothes down there."

I pushed the throttle forward and felt the stern dig down into the water. Eighty-seven miles to go, then the last confrontation. And all for one picture.

Peel made tea. *Mist-Spinner* thumped happily through the waves. I had dried myself, wrapped the towel about the cut at my waist, then pulled on a thick sweater which Peel had brought up from the cuddy. He was eager for my approval now. "Good cup of tea?" he asked me.

"What you're going to do now" – I ignored his friendliness – "is clear up the boat. You see that boxlike thing on the front?"

"Yes, guv. My lord."

"It's called a forehatch. Open it, then tip Garrard inside."

"Tip . . ."

"Do it!"

He did it. Once I'd heard Garrard's corpse thump down into the cuddy, I gave Peel a bucket and mop. "Now clean off the blood."

He started work. I pulled the case of bearer bonds on to the chart table and left it there. The engine ran happily. I was making ten knots, a good enough speed.

The fog cleared when we were north of the Casquets. I turned off all the wheelhouse lights so I could see better. We were about to cross the traffic separation zones where the big tankers thumped oblivious in and out of the Atlantic. *Mist-Spinner* left a clean clear wake on the dark swell. Peel, his job done, crouched at the far side of the wheelhouse and stared in awe at the giant ships.

"What's your name?" I asked him.

"Peel."

"Your first name, you idiot."

"Ronny."

I rewarded him with a smile. "Got any cigarettes, Ronny?"

"Don't smoke, guv."

"Garrard did, didn't he?"

"He did, yes."

"Any in his pockets, do you think?"

He stared in horror at me. "You want me to . . ." Then he realised that was precisely what I wanted him to do, so he opened the cuddy door, took a breath, and climbed down. I could hear his noises of disgust, but after a few minutes he reappeared with a half-empty packet and a lighter.

"Thank you, Ronny."

He was pathetically grateful for a kind word. I lit a cigarette and dragged the smoke into my lungs.

"Am I in trouble?" Peel asked after a while.

"A lot." I throttled back to let a bulk carrier slide a half-mile ahead of me. The beam from the Channel Light Vessel was reflected from the long waves to starboard.

"I only did what Mr Garrard told me to do," Peel pleaded.

"And what else did Mr Garrard tell you, Ronny? Did he tell you about my sister?"

He nodded. "She was going to get the painting when you was dead, see? And then she was going to sell it, and she was going to give Mr Garrard his share of the money. Because he bought it, you see."

"I don't see, no."

"Right back at the beginning. When he met your sister at the races. She asked him to help her find it, and she gave him money for the expenses, like, and he did find it, and he bought a third share off the bloke, because the bloke was short of readies and couldn't find a proper buyer. It's too hot, you see. Mr Garrard said you couldn't sell really famous paintings, only the rubbish."

I was staring ahead at the empty sea. Peel was worried by my silence, but for a long time I just steered the compass course and ignored him.

"A third share?" I asked him at last.

"That's right. One for Mr Garrard, one for your sister, though of course she didn't have to pay anything 'cos she was going to sell it, like, and the other third —"

"Shut up, Ronny."

"But . . ."

"I said shut up!" Because I think I'd known ever since I'd keyed *Mist-Spinner*'s Decca. Only I didn't believe it.

Dear God, I thought, but let me be wrong. I unhooked the microphone. I knew my enemies would be listening to Channel 37 and they would probably be monitoring Channel 16 as well, but unless they had two radios, each with a dual-watch capability, they could only monitor the two VHF channels. So I switched to 67, the coastguard's working channel. I broke all the rules: I didn't identify myself, I just broadcast a cryptic message to the whole English Channel. "This is a message for Inspector Abbott," I said, "of the Devon and Cornwall Police. Fifty Twelve Forty North, Zero Three Forty-six Sixty West. I say again. For Harry Abbott,

Devon and Cornwall Police, Fifty Twelve Forty North, Zero Three Forty-six Sixty West."

The coastguards were on to me like a ton of bricks. Who was transmitting? Why? Would I identify myself? I told them to get off the air and pass on the message and to do it fast. "But listen for further transmissions on this channel," I added before switching the radio off.

The first light was gilding the wavetops. "Fancy another cup of tea, Ronny?"

"Not really, guv." He didn't want to go below with the corpse.

"I do." I really wanted to be alone for a few minutes. "So get it."

An hour later I saw the English coast. I switched off the Decca because I didn't need it any longer. I hadn't really needed it at all, not once I'd known the final rendezvous, because these were my home waters, and here, in the dawn, was my last waypoint.

We came home in a lovely sunrise. It was all so ordinary, all so very ordinary.

The waypoint was outside the harbour, but even a helmsman as inexperienced as Garrard would have been able to negotiate the entrance: just keep well to the left-hand side of the channel, steer due north, and don't try it in southern gales.

There was a slight swell on the bar, then *Mist-Spinner* moved smoothly into the outer channel. We turned northeast and I let her idle through the moored yachts. It promised to be a warm day. Some yachts had already left the moorings while others were shaking out their sails. There had been a mist earlier, but it was gone, all but from the deepest creeks where the trees grew so close above the water. Gulls screamed and wheeled, while far to the north a helicopter chopped the air.

I had found some rusting binoculars in a cave-locker and I used them to search the anchorages. I knew what I was looking for, but somehow hoped not to see it.

Then I did. A man and a woman standing together on the flying bridge of a big motor cruiser. They were waving. Behind them, far off beyond the fields, I could see Charlie's house. The kids would be going off to nursery school and Yvonne would be wondering where Charlie was.

The man and woman waved again. They looked so happy together, like lovers at dream's fulfilment. Their boat gleamed white in the rising sun; the same sun that was reflecting off *Mist-Spinner*'s windscreen, so the couple could not see me behind the gold-glossed glass. They only saw their fortune coming, their damned great fortune, brought from the Channel Islands to Salcombe by the magic of a Decca set.

"That's them," Peel said helpfully, but I didn't respond. There was nothing to say.

I waited till we were fifty yards from the waiting boat then turned on the VHF and unhooked the microphone. "Harry Abbott?"

He answered immediately. "Is that you, Johnny?"

"I'm off Frogmore Creek, Harry. My boat's called *Mist-Spinner*, and the bastards you want are on a gin-palace called *Barratry*. Come and get them."

I killed *Mist-Spinner*'s engine and I ran her gently down the side of my best friend's boat. Charlie waited on *Barratry*'s afterdeck, boathook in hand. He hooked our pulpit rail. "Well done!" he called, "I told you it would be easy . . ." then his voice faded away as I stepped out from under the wheelhouse roof. I carried the shotgun and the attaché case.

"Hello, Charlie," I said.

Elizabeth screamed. She was still on *Barratry*'s flying bridge. I looked up at her; then, with the shotgun in my right hand and the money in my left, I stepped over on to *Barratry*'s stern.

"Johnny!" Charlie was staring in shock, but still trying to smile as if this was a fortuitous meeting of friends.

"Shut up, Charlie," I said; then, with a foul anger, "for Christ's sake, shut up!" I looked up at Elizabeth. "Come down!" She climbed slowly down the chrome ladder. She was dressed in a silk bathrobe as though she had only just got up from the big bed in *Barratry*'s stateroom. I wondered how long they had been lovers. "You bastards," I said.

Mist-Spinner and Peel drifted slowly away. Charlie and Elizabeth looked at the blood on my legs and at the gun in my hand and said nothing.

"Why?" I asked Charlie.

He didn't answer, but I suddenly saw how it must seem to him to be the lover of Lordy's daughter. That was the ultimate revenge, the sweetest revenge of all: when the despised labourer's son makes the Earl's daughter moan in his bed.

"And it was you," I said to Charlie, "who nicked the bloody picture."

He hesitated, then smiled. "It was just a joke, Johnny." He waited, but for what, I couldn't tell. For me to smile? To laugh? "It was only a joke!" he protested. "I did it for you!"

"For me, Charlie?"

"I did it for you! I thought that if your mother sold the painting then you'd never go back to sea! You'd become like your father! You'd have hated that, Johnny, because you never belonged in the big house. You belonged at sea,

303

Johnny, at sea!" He paused again, but I said nothing, and Charlie made an expansive gesture as if to suggest that, with a little humour and understanding, the whole mess could be resolved. "It was only a joke," he said again, but weakly.

And I wasn't laughing.

I looked at Elizabeth. It's hard to see your own sister as beautiful, but she looked beautiful that morning; beautiful and hurt. I think she was ashamed, not about the painting, but because I had found her with Charlie. That was a game she had played in secret, and now I had discovered her. "You knew," I accused her. "You knew I didn't steal it! You must have known that as soon as Garrard found Charlie!"

She shrugged, as if to suggest that my innocence was irrelevant.

"So why didn't you go to the police when Garrard found Charlie?" I asked her.

"Because the money would still have been yours when Mother died, and she didn't want you to have it. She hated you! You destroyed our family, and I was going to save it!" Elizabeth spat the words at me, and I saw that she, like my mother, hated me, and I saw, too, how much Elizabeth must have enjoyed betraying my closest friendship. She would win it all and leave me nothing, not even a friend.

I looked back to Charlie. It seemed so obvious now, and it must have seemed obvious to Garrard who, seeking the painting and still believing in my guilt, had gone straight to my oldest friend. "Why didn't you just ransom the painting?" I asked Charlie. "Was it really worth a death?"

"It wasn't like that, Johnny!" Charlie spoke energetically. He was still hoping that charm and friendship could ease him off this hook. "No one was supposed to die!"

"Garrard died," I said brutally. "I blew his head away. What's left of him is in that boat." I jerked my head towards the drifting *Mist-Spinner*, but I had been looking at Elizabeth as I spoke and I saw that her face had shown no reaction to my news. "Don't you care?" I asked her. "You were bedding him, just as you're bedding Charlie. Did you know that, Charlie, that she was screwing Garrard as well?"

He didn't reply, but all the charm and energy went from

his face as if he'd been struck. He hadn't known and he was hurt. He thought he had been using Elizabeth, and now, at last, he sensed that she had been using him.

Elizabeth's face still did not show any emotion. My God, I thought, but how she had used her men. She'd used Garrard to kill, and Charlie to set up the clever rendezvous with the Decca sets. And Charlie, clever Charlie, had coolly gone to Guernsey and sent me off to my death, then spun me through the electronic maze before flying home for this rendezvous. Clever Charlie. I raised the muzzles of the gun.

Charlie shook his head desperately. "I tried to warn you, Johnny! How many times did I warn you? How many times did I tell you to bugger off!" Charlie saw no softening in my face. "For God's sake, I even tried to stop you yesterday! I didn't want you to die! That was her and Garrard! I just wanted to scare you back to sea, out of the way! Good God, Johnny, I even repaired your boat! I only wanted the ransom, it was Garrard who said we should kill you to get the price as well! It was all Garrard's idea, not mine!"

It was a version of the truth, spoken passionately to carry conviction, and perhaps, at the beginning, he alone of the three had not wanted my death. And I thought how scared Elizabeth and Garrard must have been when I returned, when they found Jennifer on *Sunflower*, and how they must have believed that Charlie was betraying them, and how Charlie must have argued for my life, agreeing only that I should be scared away from England. And perhaps, I thought, he had only wanted the ransom, reckoning that I would share my good fortune with him if the painting was recovered and I sold it. But then I had given the painting away, and Charlie's friendship for me had been corroded by the acid of lust and greed, and so he had gone aboard *Sunflower* and filled her bilges with gas. I looked into his eyes, trying to understand. "Tell me about the gas, Charlie."

He found nothing to say. What was there to say? That he regretted it? I was sure he did, but he regretted the loss of all the money more. I looked past Charlie, far beyond *Barratry*'s bows, and saw two launches heading towards us. I looked back to my best friend, still trying to understand how he could try to kill me one day and smother me with his generosity the next. I'd slept in his house, but of course I had been safe there for he would never have wanted my death to seem like murder, but rather to have looked like an accident. That way he would have been safe. "My God, Charlie," I said sadly, "but you are a bastard." I remembered Jennifer and aimed the barrels at his eyes.

But I couldn't kill him. He'd saved my life once, singing his way through a ship-killing storm in the Tasman Sea. I stared at him over the gun's crude sights. "So where's the painting, Charlie?"

He didn't answer till I twitched the gun, then he shrugged. "In the cellar, Johnny. Wrapped up and safe."

"And it's mine!" Elizabeth almost screamed at me. "Mother left it to me! It's mine!"

"Damn you," I said, "damn you both." Then the first launch bumped alongside, and big efficient men climbed aboard *Barratry*. I dropped gun and money on the deck, then turned away to face the rising sun.

Friendship. Was anything worth the betrayal of friendship? Except lovers take precedence over friendship, and Charlie had found his Lady and he would kill his friend to make her rich, and himself rich with her. I closed my eyes. Not because I was staring at the sun, but because I had come home, and was crying.

EPILOGUE

Epilogue

Lazy water lapped at *Sunflower*'s hull. The sun was brilliant, remorseless, high, but the white awning which was stretched from *Sunflower*'s mizzen to her mainmast sheltered me. The ketch was properly called *Sunflower II*, but I'd left off the Roman numerals when I'd painted her name on the stern. I had wanted to call the boat *Jennifer*, but Jennifer Pallavicini wouldn't let me. She had dictated a letter from her hospital in Switzerland saying she didn't want the boat named after her. I hadn't understood her reasoning, but she had been adamant, and so I had called the boat *Sunflower II* instead. The new *Sunflower* was a good yacht; steel-hulled, eight feet longer than the original *Sunflower* and with two gas alarms in her bilges.

She had been launched five months ago, and now she was berthed in the Leeward Islands. It was midday, hot as hell, but I was shadowed by the awning and had a cold beer I'd taken from the galley fridge. I'd never had a fridge on a boat before, but nor had I ever been given a millionaire's cheque book to build a boat before. And, given that cheque book, I'd made a good sea boat. She'd rolled incessantly on the long crossing from Madeira to the West Indies, but every boat rolls in the trade route. She'd proved fast, despite her long keel and heavy hull. None of her gear had gone disastrously wrong; nothing but the usual small crop of problems: a chafing halliard, a lifting sail seam, a leaking deck fitting; nothing I couldn't mend with my own two hands, and nothing that would stop this long lovely boat from going around the world. She was, in truth, a proper job. The odious Ulf would probably find something wrong with her, but the odious Ulf wasn't here.

There was just me, *Sunflower II* and, at the landward end of the rickety wharf that jutted out into this impossibly blue water, a girl.

I'd watched the girl step down from the island bus. Once

the bus had growled away she had looked towards *Sunflower*, but then hesitated. She had been carrying four string shopping bags and perhaps they had been too heavy for her, because she had left two of the bags under a palm tree, adjusted the handles of the others, then walked slowly down the wharf towards my berth. Good legs, I thought appreciatively, very good legs. I could tell, for she was wearing shorts. A lovely body, really. I thought how wonderful that body would look in a bikini. The girl had short black hair and a suntanned skin and, as she came closer, a very nice smile.

"You might have helped me, you bastard," she said in greeting.

I nonchalantly waved the beer can. "I was watching you, and thinking what a very satisfactory crewperson you are."

"And one day you'll make a satisfactory galley slave." She tossed the string bags into my lap. "They actually had American lettuce at that nice little shop. It was horribly expensive, but I couldn't resist it, so that means we can have a proper salad at last. And I bought a very weird vegetable, I haven't a clue what it is, but that lovely lady who laughs every time she sees you says that you cut it in half, scoop out the pulp, and eat it raw. Oh, and you peel it as well." Jennifer, Countess of Stowey, stepped down into the cockpit and gratefully collapsed into the shade under the awning. "I left the two heavy bags at the end of the wharf," she added, "and you can go and fetch them."

"Did you buy my tobacco?"

"Of course I bought your tobacco, you horrible man. Oh, and there was a letter at the General Delivery. Mummy and Daddy are going to Antigua and would love to see us. They've taken a house there and we can have a proper bath." She closed her eyes in pretended ecstasy. "A proper bath!"

"Unfortunately," I said, "the winds are entirely wrong for going to Antigua."

"The winds," Jennifer said firmly, "could not be better. And Mummy's bringing Georgina." Sister Felicity had died, but somehow Helen, Lady Buzzacott, had gained Georgina's confidence. Georgina was hugely improved. She had her own

310

horse at Lovelace House and that therapy, together with Helen's friendship, had given her great happiness.

The cause of my own immediate happiness took the beer can from my hand and drank what was left of it. "Now go and get the groceries," she ordered me.

"Yes, ma'am."

Jenny still has some scars, but, except for those on her hands, you have to know her very well to find them, and I don't have any intention of anyone but me knowing my wife that well. Sir Leon would like her to go back to Switzerland for more cosmetic surgery on her hands, but I've said no, not till our year's cruise is over, and Sir Leon is learning that an earl outranks a mere knight. Not that he minds, because he has his picture. The Stowey Sunflowers hang in his gallery and one day I'll go and see them again, but not yet. I have a wife, and a boat, and a great happiness, though sometimes, when I look up to find a star among the million points of light, I remember a friend and his laughter, and I wonder just how it all went so wrong.

But things go right, too. It's called love, and even if it does mean eating salad sometimes, it works. And *Sunflower*'s a proper boat, and Jennifer's happy again, and the oceans are huge, and love seems to touch even the mundane with gladness; in short, it's a proper job.

He just wanted a decent book to read ...

Not too much to ask, is it? It was in 1935 when Allen Lane, Managing Director of Bodley Head Publishers, stood on a platform at Exeter railway station looking for something good to read on his journey back to London. His choice was limited to popular magazines and poor-quality paperbacks – the same choice faced every day by the vast majority of readers, few of whom could afford hardbacks. Lane's disappointment and subsequent anger at the range of books generally available led him to found a company – and change the world.

'We believed in the existence in this country of a vast reading public for intelligent books at a low price, and staked everything on it'
Sir Allen Lane, 1902–1970, founder of Penguin Books

The quality paperback had arrived – and not just in bookshops. Lane was adamant that his Penguins should appear in chain stores and tobacconists, and should cost no more than a packet of cigarettes.

Reading habits (and cigarette prices) have changed since 1935, but Penguin still believes in publishing the best books for everybody to enjoy. We still believe that good design costs no more than bad design, and we still believe that quality books published passionately and responsibly make the world a better place.

So wherever you see the little bird – whether it's on a piece of prize-winning literary fiction or a celebrity autobiography, political tour de force or historical masterpiece, a serial-killer thriller, reference book, world classic or a piece of pure escapism – you can bet that it represents the very best that the genre has to offer.

Whatever you like to read – trust Penguin.